COMMUNION
BLOOD

By Chelsea Quinn Yarbro from Tom Doherty Associates

Ariosto
Better in the Dark
Blood Games
Blood Roses
A Candle for D'Artagnan
Communion Blood
Crusader's Torch
Darker Jewels
A Flame in Byzantium
Hotel Transylvania
Mansions of Darkness
Out of the House of Life
The Palace
Path of the Eclipse
Writ in Blood

COMMUNION
BLOOD

A NOVEL OF SAINT-GERMAIN

Chelsea Quinn Yarbro

TOR ®

A TOM DOHERTY ASSOCIATES BOOK
NEW YORK

This book is printed on acid-free paper.

A Tor Book
Published by Tom Doherty Associates, LLC
175 Fifth Avenue
New York, NY 10010

www.tor.com

Tor® is a registered trademark of Tom Doherty Associates, LLC.

Library of Congress Cataloging-in-Publication Data

Yarbro, Chelsea Quinn.
    Communion blood : a novel of Saint-Germain / Chelsea Quinn Yarbro.
    —1st ed.
        p.   cm.
    "A Tom Doherty Associates book. "
    ISBN 0-312-86793-X (acid-free paper)
    1. Saint-Germain, comte de, d. 1784 Fiction.   I. Title.
        PS3575.A7C66   1999
        813'.54—dc21   99-38760
                                                                    CIP

First Edition: October 1999

Printed in the United States of America

0 9 8 7 6 5 4 3 2 1

for

Philip Quast

if only
you were
5'6"

Author's Notes

For most of its long history, the Roman Catholic Church and its Vatican have been as much political institutions as religious ones; this was never more the case than in the latter part of the seventeenth century when the combined forces of on-going war with the Ottoman Empire and colonialization of the New World, Africa, and Asia, made the Church a crucial center for diplomatic negotiations on the expanded world scale that was the fruit of exploration and conquest of the previous two centuries, as well as an arbiter among various European factions where hostilities often gave rise to war. This position of power was central to the authority the Church exercised, and complicated the stand-off between Catholics and Protestants from Scandinavia to Croatia, and from the New World to the borders of Russia, where Orthodox Christianity prevailed.

Long disputes between the Church and the Holy Roman Emperor (who was German, and therefore at the center of the Protestant movement) had left the German States in disorder and the Papacy a nest of political machinations that was as much or more embroiled in diplomatic intrigue as in any spiritual agenda, although within the Church various Orders struggled to establish superior spiritual claims. The long rivalry between the Franciscans (founded in Italy by Saint

Francis of Assisi, a man of middle-class background, in 1209) and the Dominicans (founded in Spain by Saint Dominic, a nobleman, in 1215, the same year the Magna Carta was signed) had been mitigated by the rise of Protestantism but was by no means at an end. Significantly, the Dominican influence in Spain—and hence the New World—continued almost without challenge until the founding of the Society of Jesus (Jesuits) by Ignatius Loyola in 1534, the same year that Henry VIII of England broke with the Roman Church to establish the Church of England.

At the time of the novel, the Papal States were controlled, religiously and politically, by the Pope, whose authority was absolute. The Vatican and Saint Peter's were the center of the Roman See, but the Pope at that time resided at the Lateran Palace, for the Vatican was not then the separate city-state that it is today. Therefore the business of the Church was centered in the Vatican and the business of the Pope was centered in the Lateran; references to both places occur in this story in accord with the usage of the time. The Guardia Laterana was more an honorary organization than an actual military force by the time of this story, but it continued to serve as the personal courier service for the Pope and the Curia. Some of the Church organizations had not lost any of their ancient power: the Roman headquarters of the Inquisition were in the Via Sacra and were called The Pope's Little House; agents for the Inquisition were known as familiars. The Inquisition had extra-legal jurisdiction and operated outside the rules governing the criminal and civil courts of law. This had far-reaching implications for the people of Roma, for there were no appeals possible to the Inquisition except through the direct intervention and order of the Pope which was a rare event.

There was a significant shift taking place in the power-structure of Europe at the time: the economics were no longer based entirely on protectionist policies and force of arms driven by the central or regional rulers, but by money as the great trading city-states began to dominate the flow of goods through the West and to sponsor trade with the East, which made many of the heads of state at least partially dependent on the success of the country's merchants instead of the other way around. Those nations which centralized their power, such as France and, until Cromwell, England, achieved absolutist rulers based as much or more on monetary success as military prowess, in which the Church could be put on equal footing with the State instead of superior, and in which the cooperation of subjects was more desirable—and profitable—than their capitulation, either to the monarch or to God. The rise of commercial centers supported centralized and uniform governments, and had the wherewithal to make an impact in the nature of government. France was especially canny in using material might; until the expenses of war demanded they be melted down for the wealth they represented, there were tables and desks of solid silver at Versailles and other royal residences, for it was understood by then that financial strength was the source of military potency, the first modern example of a military-industrial complex.

This change in economic balances had far-reaching implications that at the time of this story were just beginning to be felt throughout the Church; those countries committed to maintaining the old structure, such as Spain, declined, while those at the forefront of the change, such as the mercantile cities of Amsterdam and Venice, still an independent republic, flourished. The elevation of diplomats on merit rather than on family position was part of the shifts in government, as was a social eclecticism not seen since the height of the Roman Empire. Appropriately enough, Rome's solution to these adjustments at the end of the seventeenth century was as pragmatic as it was spiritual—Rome as a city became a center for tolerance and began to welcome tourists as well as pilgrims while Rome as the center of Catholicism became more entrenched in a structure based on Medieval monarchies, shoring up the Church with an expansion of dogma and an enhanced role in international politics. Challenged by the French, the Church and the Papacy were compelled to respond authoritatively.

Many of the figures around the Papal court are composites and inventions of my own; I have made every effort to make them representative of those men who were in the court of Popes Innocent XI (Italian, reigned 1676–1689), Alexander VIII (Venetian, reigned 1689–1691), and Innocent XII (Italian, reigned 1691–1700). Those who are actual historical figures are depicted from sources of the period, and in the light in which they were seen at the time of the story, including the occasional juggling of alliances and positions that the swift changes of Pope necessitated in those working through or at the Vatican. The shifts in Papal rulers brought about a scramble for influence and position that shook the complicated structure around the Papacy and sent ripples out through the Church that were felt for more than two decades after the hectic and unstable three-year period was over.

Thanks in large part to Pope Urban VIII (reigned 1623–1644) Rome had a fine new architectural face on it, although sections of the city still had expanses of ruins left from the glory days of Imperial Rome; these new buildings changed the appearance of the city and brought a grandeur Rome had lacked for centuries. The long period of general decay was at an end, and the city blossomed once more, and in a style grand enough to stand up to the ancient monuments of the Caesars. The outward expression of prosperity in turn spurred the middle- and upper-classes to restore or create private buildings of their own so that in the space of thirty years Rome was virtually transformed. The increased flow of pilgrims and tourists made the city prosperous. But all was not as well as the outward appearances would have seemed to suggest. The cultural and artistic climate of Rome was not what it had been a century before; the great flowering of the Renaissance had restored Rome to some of its former magnificence, but over time many of the artists, musicians, architects, and men of letters had been wooed away from the complicated, religio-diplomatic world of Rome, to the more congenial and affluent courts of France and Naples; Rome had become a place to make a reputation, not to maintain it.

In this sense, although the great composer Alessandro Scarlatti and his family had, by the time of this novel, left Rome and become part of the Neopolitan and then the Tuscan court, I have taken the liberty of extending his occasional month-long return visits to Rome to a two-year sojourn in the city. The other musicians are either composites of men and women of the period or, as in the case of Giorgianna Ferrugia, wholly fictional but drawn on contemporary Baroque artists. Composers and performers mentioned in passing are historical and are included for verisimilitude to complete the picture of the times.

The family of Martin Maria Valentin Esteban, Cardinal Calaveria y Vacamonte, is fictional, but is drawn from four illustrious Spanish families who over a period of three centuries, sent influential, high-ranking Churchmen to Rome. Spanish stakes were particularly high at this time, for the continuing support of the Church insured their hegemony in Latin America as well as a large portion of North America; with fewer colonies up for grabs after the vigorous expansion of the previous century, competition for what remained was hard-fought. Spain was determined to preserve its position in the world, and relied on the Church to maintain its endorsement of Spanish claims.

In the turbulent regions of the Balkans and Carpathians, where the Ottoman Empire had made such striking advances, Austro-Hungarian forces had established a presence that was precariously maintained, and that maintenance often took strange forms. Men of historical rank in these disputed regions often resorted to positions within the Church in order to continue to oversee those areas to which they had traditional claim. Many of them preferred the somewhat ambiguous position of Abbe, since it did not include the stringent vows that went with ordination, allowing them a flexibility they would not have had otherwise. It also meant that their lands could be passed to family heirs instead of becoming the property of the Church, a significant loop-hole for the aristocracy. This last proviso eased the strained relationship that existed between the Catholic and Orthodox Churches, which had been pressed to the breaking point by the Ottoman expansion and the fall of the tattered Byzantine Empire in 1453, by putting men of hereditarily legitimate power into the positions of protecting Christian claims—all Christian claims—against the Ottoman usurpers. The Turkish campaign into eastern Europe had brought about an uneasy tolerance among the two Christian Churches, but neither Catholic nor Orthodox forces were willing to make many concessions to the other in such fiercely disputed regions as what are now Croatia, Bosnia, Serbia, Romania, and Hungary.

The lavish, ornamented style known as the Baroque was originally a term used to describe irregular pearls, an application that survives to this day. In architecture, fashion, and art, the Baroque period is distinguished by elaborate accessories and embellishments, from Corinthian capitols on pillars to ribbons and laces on clothing to the grand display of tromp d'oeil murals to the grand statues of Bernini. Social forms were equally extravagant: lapses of taste brought serious consequences, and anyone failing to observe the complicated rituals of class would quickly become ostracized for such negligence. In the Baroque period, style *was* substance: clothing was as much political as social, revealing more than status and fortune, and those who observed the various strictures associated with all aspects of fashion had more than taste motivating their display. Competition in dress, housing, and entertainment was an accepted means of social advancement, and many families were forced into financial ruin in the pursuit of presenting a grander appearance than social peers. Formal to the point of artificiality, the proper conduct of middle- and upper-class persons of the Baroque period looks stilted and a bit absurd to late-twentieth-century eyes, but at the time these minutiae of manners and dress were significant and important, conveying status and affiliation as well as displaying wealth, which was, in itself, significant. The plays of the English Restoration—a court far less constrained than the one in Rome—the works of the brilliant French satirist Molière, and the operas of Jean-Baptiste Lully (born Gianbaptista Lulli in Florence, but resident in France, with royal patronage) are among the fruits of this period, revealing the complexities of a society that expressed itself through nuances of opulence. In contrast there were strict moralists, some Catholic, some Protestant, who railed at the excesses of the mainstream of middle- and upper-class society, and made as much a cult of austerity as the mainstream of society did with nimiety.

The Artei, or Guilds, were fairly powerful organizations at the time, being essential to the ongoing reconstruction of the city. Their ability to demand substantial deposits on contracted work is a clear demonstration of their strength. And for the record, the amounts demanded of Saint-Germain are roughly double what was required of Romans. A scudo of the period had an equivalent buying power—

as compared to actual value—of about fifty dollars in modern terms. Silver Emperors had a modern buying power of about sixty cents. Gold Apostles had the equivalent buying power of seventy-five to eighty dollars.

Those of you familiar with the three Atta Olivia Clemens novels (*A Flame in Byzantium, Crusader's Torch*, and *A Candle for D'Artagnan*) will recognize her ghoul-manservant Niklos Aulirios, as well as the now-aged Gennaro Colonna from *A Candle for D'Artagnan* and *Mansions of Darkness*. Although Gennaro and Ettore Domenico Agnolo Colonna are fictional, the Colonna family is very real and was an imposing presence in Roman politics for centuries.

Thanks this time around are due to (in no particular order) Jordan Scharf for his expertise on the long rivalry of the Papacy and the Holy Roman Empire; to Jeff Montgomery for laying out the terms of the Peace of Westphalia; to Laura Peligrino for allowing me to read her Master's thesis on Alessandro Scarlatti; to Jenna Cole for providing information on textiles and tailoring of the period; to Hugo Conners for information on the trading centers of Europe in the second half of the seventeenth century; to Christian Patterson for providing me with research materials on colonialism and the Papacy; to Mark Patterson for giving me access to his material on the musical and artistic world of Rome at the period of this story; and to Derek Tate for straightening out the tangle of eastern European politics of the period—as much as that is possible. On the other end of the process, thanks to Jim Taylor, Lois Davis, and Alicia Grant, who read the manuscript for clarity; to Ted Harrison, who read it for accuracy; and to Maureen Kelly, Stephanie Moss, and Sharon Russell, who read it out of habit. Thanks are also due to my agent, Donald Maass; to the good people at Tor, who keep Saint-Germain going; to Wiley Saichek, who keeps them on their toes; to the many independent bookstore owners who continue to carry the series; to my attorney, Robin A. Dubner, who preserves Saint-Germain's legal interests; to Lou Puopolo, whose long dedication to Saint-Germain is most gratifying; to Lindig Hall, whose newsletter *Yclept Yarbro* (Lin Digs the Book, P.O. Box 8905, Asheville, NC 28814 or lindig@mindspring.com) keeps my readers up-to-date on Saint-Germain's doings, as well as my own; to Rick Trykall of Trykall's Tees for the Saint-Germain shirts; to Ellen Holte and Carol Jenrette of Stone & Wing for the eclipse jewelry; to Stephen Charnas for securing trademark status on Saint-Germain's eclipse; to my sister Ann Erickson, who prepared the style sheet; to Tyrrell Morris, who understands computers and Web pages far better than I; to Alice Horst for those hours in the saddle; to Alison Scott and the Popular Culture library at Bowling Green University in Ohio; and ultimately, to my readers, for without you, none of the above would be much use.

Chelsea Quinn Yarbro
September, 1998
Berkeley, California

PART I

NIKLOS AULIRIOS

T ext of a letter from Niklos Aulirios in Roma, written in Latin to Ragoczy Sanct' Germain Franciscus at the Abby of Sanct' Parasceva above Brasso, or Kronstadt, in the Transylvanian region of the Kingdom of Hungary.

To the Abbe of Sanct' Parasceva, in Transylvania, the greetings of Niklos Aulirios in Roma, in the hope that the worst of the fighting now going on in the Carpathians that we hear reported here in Roma has passed you by;

It was my intention never to trespass on the friendship you have extended to me on behalf of my late domita, Atta Olivia Clemens, but I find I must do so, and I apologize for this urgent summons, and assure you that were not my situation dire, I would not have asked your help. I have done my utmost to resolve the matter without resorting to this appeal, and I have failed in every attempt. No other can aid me; if there were another, I would not approach you, for I know Roma is not wholly safe for you at this time. I would not ask your support had I any other recourse: could I avail myself of other counsel, I would not have to entreat you to expose yourself as you must do in this city.

Regretfully, I must add to the burden I impose, for I tell you there

*is no time for delay: my circumstances are grave and without your
intervention must have an outcome none of us would like. Here is
what has transpired that has led me to seek your help: as I know you
must be aware, Domita Clemens left the whole of her vast estates to
me, releasing me from all bondsman obligations, and giving me full
rights over her properties, her goods, stock, and movables. I, in turn,
have done all that I might to preserve her holdings as she kept them,
in accordance with her wishes. It is my sad duty to inform you I may
not be able to continue this any longer, for a suit has been filed against
my legacy, and the inclination of the court is against me.*

*How can this come about? Well may you ask. There is here in
Roma a man who claims to be the grandson of the legitimized son of
Olivia's late husband's father, and therefore a proper heir, entitled to
his widow's property as she had no legitimate children to leave it to,
or near relations such as a niece or nephew or cousin who might have
a claim upon it. At first this would seem easily addressed as the deliberate fraud it is, but I fear there are reasons that cannot be done.
The assertion is a precarious mendacity, and under ordinary circumstances there would be no difficulty in exposing the claimant as the
opportunist he is, but, as you know, mine are not ordinary circumstances. Of course Olivia's late husband was a convenient fiction, of
the sort she created for herself many times over the centuries, as you
yourself taught her; this is the heart of the issue, for to reveal her
deceit brings many more aspects of her life into question, including
that of her true nature. Her position as a widow was as well-
established in the years before her true death as it had ever been. She
had arranged for a number of well-forged testaments that set the place
of her husband's death many leagues away from Roma, so that it
should not be considered strange that no one remembered her spouse.
You know how well she kept up this benign deception, and how much
would be forfeit if that deception were brought to light. Should the
courts ever suspect she was a vampire, all her estates would be
claimed by the Church and I would have to flee or face eternity in
an Inquisition cell.*

*The courts have long preferred the claims of relatives over that of
servants, and I cannot yet imagine how to preserve Olivia's good*

name without sacrificing my claim to all she left me, and which I promised her centuries ago to maintain as she would maintain her holdings herself. Also, I am disinclined to surrender what is legitimately mine to a clever charlatan. I am also aware that if I capitulate, ceding my claim without contesting the other claim, I will raise the very suspicions I am seeking to obviate.

　Therefore I appeal to you, Sanct' Germain, for I can think of no other who can help me in this coil. If not for myself, then for the memory of Domita Clemens, come to Roma and help me. Her bond with you was that of blood, which is a claim I do not possess, but I beseech you to consider what she would do were she still alive to supplicate. I will do all that is in my power to ensure your protection while you are here, and to keep you from those who may have had reports on you while you were in Church prisons in the Americas, though their number is few and decreasing with every passing year. Your discovery would be as catastrophic for me as it would be for you, and I will make every effort to ensure that you will be in no more danger than I am. I reiterate, I am fully aware of the hazards that await you in this city, and I am reluctant to put you in a position that might expose you to unacceptable repercussions on my behalf; had I any viable alternative, I would not ask this of you, and I will understand fully if you decide the risks are too great. But for the sake of Olivia, tell me you will come.

Niklos Aulirios
former bondsman to Atta Olivia Clemens

By my own hand at Senza Pari in Roma, the 11th day of September, 1688; entrusted to Laszlo Czerny, laybrother of the Cistercian Order, for delivery.

1

"Actually," Ferenc Ragoczy, Abbe of Sanct' Parasceva and Count Saint-Germain, went on as he strolled down the length of the old-fashioned atrium at Senza Pari on the outskirts of Roma, "Olivia would probably have issued stern orders rather than have pleaded with me." The pain of speaking her name had faded but was not yet gone, and it showed in a slight tightening of his attractive, irregular features, and the momentary hesitation in his speech. "Of course I had to come, for her, as well as you. And she would have not accepted any delay; storms would have been no excuse." His ankle-length Hungarian dolman and mente of black silk made him an emphatic shadow in the rich Roman winter sunshine; the white chaconne at his neck identified him as an Abbe, his sole indication of his position; instead of a crucifix, he wore a pectoral of his eclipse device on a heavy silver chain.

Beside him, Niklos Aulirios was able to chuckle. "Yes, that would be more like her." His handsome face grew somber. "I could not make such demands, nor would I."

"No. You have too high a regard for her memory to do that," Ragoczy said. "But I apologize for taking so long to get to Roma. Had the messenger reached me sooner, I would have been here in November. The weather slowed my journey, unfortunately. I had hoped to be here before the Nativity, but Evangelista Giovan's Feast will have to do. At least it is only late December and we have a few days to make a response to the claim before the end of the year; the magistrates will expect that." They stopped by the fountain. It was larger than Ragoczy remembered, with a fine marble faun holding up his pipes, from which the water flowed. "This is new." They had been speaking Greek but now changed to Italian.

"It was installed just before she died," said Niklos, his brown eyes growing distant. "There was a fashion in statues and fountains, and she commissioned this. She was going to have more statues made, but—"

"Yes," Ragoczy said thoughtfully. "But." He had feared seeing Roma again would exacerbate the grief he had felt since Olivia's death; he was relieved when that did not happen, although he had a kind of indefinable soreness within him that twinged from time to time, reminding him of his loss.

"The man who has made the claim must sense that there is some reason that her estate may be attacked in this way," Niklos went on, determined to keep their conversation on the business at hand. His neat justaucorps was the color of wild honey, and his breeches, of the same cloth, were not quite as full as fashion required, but this conservatism in his dress was considered appropriately modest for a man in his ambiguous position. His jabot was edged in lace, but the ruffles at his wrists were moderate and unembellished. "I cannot think he would make the attempt if he had not some hope of gaining the prize he seeks."

"Possibly; or he may believe he can prevail against a servant, if you will pardon my saying so," Ragoczy observed. "He may be counting on the habits of the court, to favor heirs, legitimate or not, over servants, thinking that he will not have to do much to gain his ends."

Niklos shrugged. "Perhaps," he allowed. The two walked on to the nearest door that led into the house, entering the dining room where the steward, Alfredo Cervetti, was preparing an inventory of the silver. "The court has required it. We must inventory everything at her estates."

"It would be expected in a case of this sort," said Ragoczy. He glanced at the frescoes along the far wall that showed significant episodes in the history of the city, beginning with the building of the Flavian Circus, now called the Colosseum, for the huge statue of the Emperor Nero in front of it. The other events represented were the bribing of Attila, Pope Celestine III crowning the son of the Holy Roman Emperor, the death of Cola Rienzi, the elevation of Oddone Colonna as Pope Martino V, and the raising of the dome of San Pietro.

Niklos watched Ragoczy's perusal, saying, "She decided to depict events that the Church would approve."

"She was always a sensible woman," Ragoczy responded steadily; his grief was banked now, like a slow-burning fire. "After so long, she knew how to protect herself." He looked away.

"Not at the end," said Niklos in an emotionless tone.

"No," Ragoczy agreed. "Not at the end." He turned his back on the mural. "So you must tell me how you have fared since this . . . ambitious fraud began."

Niklos shrugged. "I have tried to find an advocate to support me." He stared toward the door into the corridor. "One has agreed to act for me: Marcaurelio dal Prato."

"And is he doing his work properly?" asked Ragoczy. He suited his pace to Niklos', ambling toward the reception hall. "Are you satisfied?"

"I don't know; I have paid his fee and I hope he will prove capable of his task," said Niklos. "I have never had to present a claim in court before, not on my own behalf. The man is not Catholic, which is both a strength and a disadvantage."

"He's not a Protestant, is he?" Ragoczy knew that Protestants were severely limited in access to court procedures.

"No. He's a Jew." He made a gesture to show he felt he had had no choice. "No Catholic would maintain an action against a member of an Archbishop's retinue, and no Protestant could act against him."

"Then you have chosen well, given what you must deal with," said Ragoczy.

"Unless the Church decides I am deliberately acting to insult the court, which is possible," Niklos cautioned him. "He has already told me this could happen. At which point I shall have no one to speak for me, unless you decide to."

"If I had not decided to do so, I would not be here," said Ragoczy quietly.

Niklos stared away, his brow contracted with emotion. "I did not mean to—"

"Yes; I know," said Ragoczy, his voice gentle.

"It is because I find myself without allies that I sometimes forget that I am not alone in my fight anymore." He stopped at the entrance to the reception hall. "It has been almost thirty years to the day since she died, but I still expect to see her come into the villa, or hear her voice."

Ragoczy's dark eyes were sad. "I know," he repeated.

"I served her for thirteen hundred years. It does not seem right that she should be gone." He stared into the distance. "I cannot forget her."

"Nor would I expect you to. I will never do so," said Ragoczy with such encompassing sympathy that Niklos blinked in surprise. "You did not think I would not share your sorrow, did you?"

"You were gone—" Niklos stopped himself.

"You had my letter when I returned; I would have sent it sooner had I been able to," Ragoczy said. "From the hour she died, I felt the loss of her."

"So you told me." Niklos gave a single shake to his head. "I still do not comprehend how."

"The bond of blood knows no distance," said Ragoczy slowly, his slight, unidentifiable accent becoming stronger.

Alfredo Cervetti appeared in the doorway, a tablet in his hand. "I have finished with the silver in the dining room. I will now begin on silver vessels in the kitchen and pantry, if it will suit you."

"Go ahead," said Niklos in an abstracted way. "You do not need my permission to do what the court has ordered."

"Very good," said Alfredo, bowing before he left Niklos alone with his newly arrived guest.

There was a short, uncomfortable silence between Ragoczy and

Niklos; then Ragoczy spoke. "How long have you been at this inventory?"

"Here at Senza Pari? For three weeks. I have sent word to the estates the court demands inventories of, ordering the staffs there to prepare them and bring them to Roma, but I doubt much work has been done yet, or if the orders have been delivered, for the passes may be closed." He placed the tips of his fingers together. "They know about six estates. One is in England, and the Pope has no authority there, and so the inventory cannot be decreed without the endorsement of the Crown, which will not be granted."

"That is something, at least. I will assume her other holdings are safe," Ragoczy said. "This is not a complete rout." He sighed once and sat down in a high-backed chair of rosewood. From this place he had an angled view of the corridor. "Who is this claimant, and how does he defend his claim?"

"Ahrent Julius Rothofen," said Niklos said flatly. "He is part of the entourage of Archbishop Siegfried Walmund."

"Graff von Oldenburg's tool, I believe," Ragoczy remarked. "Or do we call him Conte in Roma, and not Graff? Whichever title is used, the man is in a difficult position, being so much surrounded by Protestants. The old law that the faith of the ruler will be the faith of his people no longer holds true everywhere. He will want to demonstrate his dedication to the Church. The Pope cannot like to see so much of Germany lost to Protestants, and no doubt he occasionally vents his displeasure on the clerics from those regions where Protestants flourish, which would include Archbishop Walmund. To advance so far and be thwarted by the Protestants. He must feel his lack of promotion keenly; had he not been from Protestant territories, he should have had his red hat long since—he is doubtless aware of his foiled melioration, as is the whole of the Papal Court. He has much to prove, and he will do his utmost to do so, for himself as well as for his master: Oldenburg has need of men to do his bidding, and nowhere more than in Roma."

"He has stated he supports Rothofen's claim. I know the magistrate has been sent an official statement from the Archbishop," Niklos said, looking uneasily toward the doorway to the corridor.

"That is not convenient," said Ragoczy in a very unconcerned way, but with a warning flick of his fingers. "We will have to find some manner to address it."

"Do you think it wise to try?" Niklos asked, taking the hint from Ragoczy's signal. "I do not want to compromise my claim."

"Then we will have to make the effort. It is a question of finding the means to present the facts appropriately." He leaned forward. "How soon must the magistrate hear this case?"

"It is supposed to be argued in the spring." Niklos stood facing Ragoczy, resisting the urge to glance toward the door.

"Tell me how you intend to counter his—Rothofen's—claims." Ragoczy smiled encouragement. "I trust you are prepared. You will want to be able to present strong arguments in order to prevail."

"I have Olivia's Will," said Niklos. "It is very specific in its terms."

"I would expect no less." Ragoczy paused. "But it is the Will of a woman, a widow without sons or brothers to support her, and that is a disadvantage in these days." In Olivia's youth, when Claudius and Nero ruled, women had been able to bequeath their estates without male intervention. "It will take more than her Will to ensure your legacy."

"It is true," Niklos agreed. In response to a gesture from Ragoczy, he went on. "She was a widow and the executor appointed by her husband was dead. She filed a declaration to that effect. It was left to her to prepare her own Will."

"That makes your case more difficult, beyond question," said Ragoczy. "I am sure your advocate has told you as much."

"He has said it may," Niklos conceded. "But I must persevere. I would not only lose my inheritance, I would fail in my duty to Olivia, which is unacceptable to me."

"Then we must find some means to preserve her legacy," said Ragoczy, and stopped as footsteps sounded in the corridor, accompanied by a scurrying.

A moment later a lean, sandy-haired man of middle years in Hungarian servant's livery came into the room. "My master," he said to Ragoczy. "I have prepared your quarters."

"Rugerius," said Ragoczy. "Very good." He waited a moment, one hand raised for silence. "Who was listening?"

"A young man, ruddy-haired, with a cast in his right eye," said Rugerius without any change in his demeanor.

"Bonifaccio," said Niklos, as resigned as he could persuade himself to be. "I thought he would have to be the one. His father is dead and he has a sister in need of a dowry."

"He is not the only one, you may be sure," Ragoczy warned. "The Church has its familiars everywhere."

"I am aware of three others," said Niklos. "It is worse than Constantinople, for there we knew we were in a nest of spies; here I would have expected loyalty from Olivia's servants."

"But most of them were not her servants, for they never knew her—they are yours, and you are a servant made master by a dead woman," said Ragoczy steadily.

"That is true enough," said Niklos, his handsome features made somber by his concerns. "I have thought about it for many months now, and I know any number of them resent me as much as they envy me."

"That is, sadly, to be expected," said Ragoczy as he got to his feet. "You must have foreseen something of the sort."

"Oh, yes. I knew I would face some disapproval and estrangement because of my inheritance." Niklos indicated the marvels of the reception hall. "They see all this and it makes them long for what they know is out of reach, and that leads to more rancor. Once that path is chosen, I am no longer fortunate, I am a usurper, and as such, must be made to answer for my temerity."

Ragoczy's expression softened. "I am sorry, Niklos."

"I know," said Niklos, adding brusquely, "but it doesn't help."

"No," Ragoczy agreed. He was silent a moment, then went on briskly. "Which is why I am here to defend your inheritance. I can do nothing about your servants, but perhaps I can persuade the court that you are entitled to all Olivia left to you."

Niklos looked abashed and began to stammer an apology. "That wasn't . . . didn't mean . . . you shouldn't . . . I am grateful. Truly I am."

"You have no reason to be; I have done nothing to deserve gratitude," said Ragoczy. "And I would be surprised if you did not feel at a disadvantage." He pointed toward the doorway. "Incidents like this must be discouraging; they have certainly been so for me, in the past."

"I have encountered some of the same spitefulness," Rugerius added. "When my master and I have been separated for long periods of time, and it has been left to me to maintain his holdings, my position was not welcomed by other servants." There had been times he had been unable to keep Ragoczy's properties safe from the rapacity of others, but he did not mention any of these to Niklos.

"I will do all that I may to bring about a good resolution to your case," Ragoczy said, intending to reassure Niklos. "I only regret that the storms kept me from arriving sooner; I have much to do between now and February. Aside from offering my testimony and bona fides to the court on your behalf, I will need time to establish a presence here, or I will make myself as apt a target of spite as you are now, which will serve no one." He smiled, his dark eyes showing an emotion that was not quite affection but had a depth of empathy Niklos had rarely encountered, except from Olivia.

Rugerius glanced in the direction of the door. "I think it would be wise if we plan to talk where we cannot be easily overheard. These corridors might as well be whispering galleries." He looked toward Niklos, as much compassion as courtesy in his dark eyes. "The weather is good today. Perhaps you would like to take advantage of it and ride with us to the Villa Vecchia?"

Niklos winced at the name. "I go there rarely," he said.

"Because Olivia died there," Ragoczy said for him. "I understand your desire to avoid it; were it not my property, I would probably not visit it. But I will have to institute my claim to it if I am to restore it."

"Are you going to restore it?" Niklos asked in astonishment. He tried not to disapprove of the notion and failed.

"Or build something new," said Ragoczy. "I think I must. If I show no inclination to maintain my Roman property, it will not help your cause, Niklos, and it could bring about more unwanted speculation."

Niklos nodded, his expression severe. "I dislike going there. It is a dreadful place for me. I know it is your villa and has been for sixteen centuries or more, but all I can see there is Olivia's tomb."

Ragoczy shook his head once. "No. Her tomb is on the Via Appia and she left it when Vespasianus was Caesar. The villa may be her mausoleum, but it is not her tomb." His eyes had the distant look that told Rugerius that his thoughts were far in the past.

"It is where she died," said Niklos bluntly and with a trace of anger. "Her bones are under the fallen stones. Call it what you will."

"Niklos," Ragoczy said as he turned toward the bondsman, "pardon me. I did not intend to cause you any dismay. I have been maladroit; I should not have spoken as I did."

"I am not offended," said Niklos stiffly.

"No; you are hurt," said Ragoczy. He waited a long, awkward moment. "I will speak with you when I return. I should be back before sunset."

"They say the weather is turning again. We will have rain by midnight," said Niklos, to avoid mentioning the Villa Vecchia another time.

"Very likely," agreed Ragoczy. "I will be back long before then." He signaled to Rugerius. "If you will be good enough to put the crates of my native earth where they will attract no attention?"

"Of course," said Rugerius. He had already planned where the crates were to go but took no umbrage at the reminder, which he knew was intended as much for Niklos as for him.

"If you will tell me what is appropriate dress for visiting the Vatican, I will plan to present myself to the Curia immediately after the New Year," Ragoczy said. "I do not want to offend the very men whose good opinion will be needed for your claims to prevail."

"You are from the Carpathians," Niklos said, half-shrugging. "What you wear now should do."

"Ah, but it will not," said Ragoczy. "Not when I mean to live in Roma until this matter is settled. Were I asking for Papal support of my Hungarian troops, it would be different, but as I am to be an exile"—the light in his dark eyes grew more intense—"I must show my willingness to live as my new city lives."

"I have the court clothes you wore in Vienna," Rugerius remarked. "They were suitable for Emperor Leopold, it should serve the Curia well enough."

"Initially, perhaps," Ragoczy allowed. "But it will do once only, and then I must conform to Roman fashions or give offense to Vatican society. This is not a minor matter, as it would have been two hundred years ago."

Rugerius nodded. "That is apparent."

"And so," Ragoczy went on to Niklos, "if you can recommend a tailor for me? It is well enough to wear the dolman and mente for a few more days, as I am newly arrived, but if I am to remain here, then the dictates are plain, and I will have to present a Roman appearance." His smile was swift and wry. "The Magistrates' Court will not accept me in anything but correct Roman dress."

"I know of two or three who may meet your standards," said Niklos. "Their work is superior and their prices, while high, are appropriate for what they do."

"Thank you; I realize that foreigners are usually charged higher prices than Romans, and I am prepared to pay," said Ragoczy, starting toward the corridor. "I thank you for receiving me and Rugerius."

"There is no need," said Niklos, somewhat surprised at this courtesy.

"Of course there is," said Ragoczy. "You have undertaken a difficult task that will require your full attention. My visit, no matter how welcome, is also an intrusion. I will do my utmost to upset your work as little as possible." He stepped back and offered a short bow to Niklos. "My horses should be housed in the old stable, and put out into paddocks when the weather is good." He raised his hand as he saw Niklos preparing to protest. "No. I have fifteen horses with me. Your stalls are full in the new building, and the old is sound. Have your stable-boys give the stalls a good sweeping and bed them with new straw, and we will do well enough. My tack will be kept there, and my two carriages."

This concession from so honored a guest took Niklos aback. "You need not," he said, trying to determine why Ragoczy had made such a decision.

"It would lead to speculation about my motive for helping you if I did otherwise." Ragoczy continued to walk toward the door leading to the stable. "Roma is full of hangers-on who batten on the good-will of their more prosperous relatives or ambitious friends. I do not wish to appear to be one such, for it would compromise any efforts I may make on your behalf." The heels of his tooled black boots rang on the flagstones as he went out into the stable yard, Niklos half a stride behind him.

"No one would think that of you," said Niklos, moving up beside him.

"You think not?" Ragoczy challenged, and nodded when he received no answer. "We must be very careful to establish the separation of our interests. This is a beginning, and a necessary one." He raised a hand, calling out in Hungarian, "Matyas! The six-year-old. Saddle him for me."

Matyas appeared from one of the stalls, bowed hastily, and hurried off to do his bidding.

"The damage is severe," Niklos warned, referring to the Villa Vecchia that a thousand years before was still known as Villa Ragoczy.

"I supposed it would be," said Ragoczy, pausing while drawing on his black Florentine gloves. "It is good of you to try to soften the blow, Niklos."

"I think you should take a servant with you. There may be beggars and worse living in the ruins," Niklos said, as if this were somehow his fault.

Ragoczy laughed once. "I am not afraid of a fight, although I would prefer to avoid one." He put his hand on Niklos' shoulder. "It is kind of you to worry for me, but it is also unnecessary: believe this."

Niklos did his best to smile. "We fought well against the Huns, didn't we?"

"Yes. We did," said Ragoczy. He squinted up at the sky, the brightness hurting his eyes. "I will not be any longer than necessary. I know the way well enough. And I have my sword with me." He patted the side of his long clothing. "It is best if an Abbe wears his weapons out of sight."

"I should have thought you would not want to wear one at all," said Niklos. "The Pope has spoken against the clergy going armed. He says it shows a lack of faith."

Ragoczy laughed. "I assume his rule is more honored in the breach. Half the priests I have seen carry knives openly, and many of them have swords. As I am not known in this place, I believe caution would be my wisest course."

"Then I suppose I have little more I can say." Niklos stepped back, bowed, and was about to turn when he stopped himself. "I am grateful to you."

"Niklos, all I have done is arrive with horses, carriages, and servants, upsetting your life here, hardly an event to inspire indebtedness except on behalf of my entourage," Ragoczy said, his amusement faintly sardonic. "I remind you: worry about gratitude when I have done something deserving it."

"Very well," Niklos said. "But I will not be fobbed off forever. I know what you are doing is dangerous."

Ragoczy bowed elegantly. "Here, in Roma, everything I am is dangerous."

"For which you shall be recompensed," Niklos promised.

"As you wish," said Ragoczy, and went off in the same direction Matyas had taken.

Watching him go, Niklos felt both relief and chagrin—relief that he finally had a chance in prevailing in his suit, and chagrin that it had been necessary to ask for such help. After a short while, he turned and went back into the villa to finish accommodating his newly arrived guests.

Text of a letter from Bonaldo Fiumara to Ferenc Ragoczy at Senza Pari.

To the revered Abbe, Ferenc Ragoczy, the most heartfelt greetings of the builder Bonaldo Fiumara, with the hope that what follows will be acceptable to you.

For removal of damaged buildings at the site known as the Villa Vecchia, the sum of one hundred golden scudi, with twenty apiece for each workman participating, along with a grant of fifty golden scudi for every serious injury sustained by the workmen. The workmen are to be paid in accordance with the terms agreed upon: delay in payment will be held just cause for stopping work. Should any workman injured require a surgeon or a physician, it will be the responsibility of the Abbe to provide it promptly. Any additional funds for injuries will be determined by the Console Artei.

For the preparation of plans for a new villa on the site, one hundred fifty golden scudi.

The price of the building will be determined by the materials you may choose, Abbe, and cannot be presented with these figures.

The time to finish removal of the old buildings as well as preparing the site for new ones, three months, four if the spring is wet. All materials removed from the ruins, with the exception of human remains, shall become the property of the builders, and no claim of any kind may be made upon those materials without the approval of the Console Artei. Any delay occasioned by weather shall require a good-faith payment to cover half the wages paid for actual work to be done. Should weather cause further damage to the buildings being pulled down, or damage the preparations for new construction, a suitable adjustment in payment shall be determined by the Console Artei, the decision of which shall be final.

The number of mule-teams needed for the removal, five, of eight mules apiece. The cost of each team, twenty golden scudi per week, plus food and stalls for the mules. Wages for the muleteers, fifteen golden scudi per week. If weather prevents work being done, the teams and muleteers will receive half their established wage for the days when they cannot work.

In accordance with your stated wishes, I have ordered my men to restore the one undamaged wing of the main building for your occupancy. Your drawings are sufficient to make it possible for the work to be done without consultation with an architect, or an additional charge. I must tell you that accommodations that will result there will not be very modern, but as it is your wish, my men will strive to have the rooms liveable in six weeks, their pay to be set at fifteen golden scudi for each man.

I will attend the work every day, and keep a record of progress of work, along with a full description of materials removed from the site. These will be available for your review as described in this agreement. I will supply my men with such tools as they will need and do not already possess. I will also see to the feeding of the men, which cost will be borne by me and cannot be added to those required of Abbe Ragoczy. Any construction of specific tools such as scaffolding shall be shared between Abbe Ragoczy and me in equal portions at the time such expenses arise.

As soon as I am in receipt of your initial payment of seventy golden scudi, we will commence our tasks, and will keep you informed each Friday before the Angelus, of our progress, and to answer any reasonable questions you may have. A second payment of seventy golden scudi must be in my hands before the first day of February, so that work may continue unimpeded by lack of funds. Should the reserve monies drop below thirty golden scudi at any time, work will cease on the project until the balance is paid. Any complaints you may have may be addressed to me at that time, along with any orders of modification in your plans. Should any mishap befall the men or the buildings, you will be notified by a messenger before sunset on the day of the accident, and arrangements for compensation will be discussed within one full day of the incident.

A servant of Abbe Ragoczy is to be at the service of the workers, to carry any messages that may require prompt response. To that end, you will appoint a second authority to act in your stead if you are not available on short notice. That second authority is to have full power to order payments, summon any assistants needed, or fulfill any other obligation that would fall to you. The servant given the task of waiting on the workers is to be informed of all these matters before he takes up his post.

Any disputes between you and me or my men will be resolved by the Console Artei, in accordance with law and custom.

I thank you for this fine opportunity to serve you, and the chance to demonstrate the skills of the men in my work crew. Your name will be in our prayers for all the days we labor on your behalf. May God and the Saints favor this project and aid us in its completion.

> Most respectfully submitted, and trusting the amounts quoted will meet with your approval,
> I remain
>
> Your most obedient servant to command

Bonaldo Fiumara,
Masterbuilder
On the 30th of January, 1689, at Roma
True copy on file with the Console Artei Romana

2

As he elevated the Chalice, Martin Maria Valentin Esteban, Cardinal Calaveria y Vacamonte, did his best to convince himself that the wine was now the holy blood of Christ that would cleanse his soul and save all mankind. Now, when he knew his faith should be strongest he had the most doubts, and feared he damned himself with them. Devout as his habits were, they were rote, not pious. He celebrated Mass twice a day in his palazzo's private chapel: in the morning for his family and household, in the evening for his family only. His hands trembled as he lowered the Chalice to have the ritual sip. It still tasted like wine, he thought as he turned to Padre Alonzo Ricco, who always assisted him. He had to make an effort not to laugh—what would he do if someday the red wine actually did become blood? Would he be able to swallow it? He had to bite the insides of his cheeks to keep from smiling at the thought.

He glanced at his brother on the second bench in the chapel. Of four legitimate brothers, only this one had survived, and occasionally the Cardinal wished that God had chosen another to be left behind. Ursellos Gofredo Ponce Calaveria y Vacamonte was already half-drunk and would be out of their palazzo for another night of carousing before the Cardinal had finished removing his vestments. Young still, handsome, and dissolute, Ursellos had already made a reputation for himself among the wild bloods of Roma's rich aristocrats; at twenty-six his dissipation was already leaving its mark upon him in a certain slackness about the eyes and a hint of contemptuousness about his mouth. He glowered at his older brother, making no attempt to disguise his boredom as he played with the heavy double-

tiered ruffles at his wrist. His berry-red justaucorps—too gaudy for
Spanish tastes—was negligently laced, revealing his full-cut fine white
linen camisa beneath that hung without artistry. Although they were
beginning to be passé, he still wore petticoat-breeches, since they
showed off the curve of his leg from his knee to his shoe-buckle for
admiration. His under-hose were pale ivory silk, and his shoes had
red heels, after the fashion of Roi Louis of France, a snide insult to
Papal authority.

Three benches back their twenty-two-year-old half-brother Jose
Bruno sat, a puzzled expression on his youthful face. He was dressed
marginally better than the household servants, a slight which did not
bother him. Jose Bruno was good-hearted and loyal, which almost
made up for his apparent simplicity and bastardy. He had lived with
the Cardinal since the family had come to Roma, his favored-but-
ambiguous position in the household isolating him from his half-
siblings and servants alike, a situation he might not have been aware
of, for he never complained of it. He listened to the Mass with rapt
attention, reciting the tolling Latin phrases with his half-brother, but
with no sign of recognition in his large brown eyes.

At the rear of the chapel sat their only surviving sister, Leocadia
Perpetua Dulce Calaveria y Vacamonte. At nineteen she was a tur-
bulently attractive woman, with soft brown hair and startling black
eyes in a pale, heart-shaped face. Tall and youthfully slim, she attracted attention whenever she left the palazzo with her maid and
Jose Bruno to escort her. Just now her admirable looks were marred
by two bruises, one on her jaw, one on her right cheek; her stiff
movements were due as much to more extensive bruising as to the
whalebone corset she wore under her gold-and-black brocade gown.
A large jeweled crucifix hung at the center of her gown's corsage on
a swagged chain. She muttered the prayers with an intensity that
revealed her determination to placate her brother in some way.

The palazzo was new, built only fifteen years earlier on the foundations of an ancient Roman emporium. The Cardinal had purchased
it eight years ago and in the intervening years had added to its magnificence. Here in the chapel, the marble columns flanking the altar
in the chapel were twisted like the baldacchino supports of the altar

at San Pietro, and the floor was patterned in red and green marble which the servants washed and polished twice a week. Over the entrance the Calaveria y Vacamonte arms were emblazoned in inlaid marbles and semiprecious stone: on a sky-blue field, two kites beaked and taloned in gold, one above the other facing opposite sides of the shield to imply circling in the air; all the details were exactingly depicted, as it was in the mosaic medallion on the floor of the loggia. All of the palazzo was equally splendid, with a polished red granite staircase leading from the loggia to the reception hall and dining hall above, and murals in every public room. The furniture was the most modern, the most elegant that could be had in Roma. There were framed paintings in the corridors and the family's rooms; only in the servants' quarters was there any stinting of grandeur, and even these accommodations were considered better than could be had in most of the palazzi in Roma.

At the conclusion of the Mass the Cardinal asked his sister to wait for him, a request that she answered with an obliging nod of her head. Satisfied that she would not defy him, Martin Calaveria y Vacamonte withdrew to his vestry; he hurried through his prayers and left Padre Ricco to tend to his vestments. He was gratified to discover his sister still waiting at the rear of the chapel, for he had half-expected she might have gone to her apartments, forcing him to go to her in order to speak to her.

"You obeyed," the Cardinal approved, acknowledging her curtsy with a flick of his hand. "I will pray God has touched your obdurate heart at last."

"Pray all you want if it pleases you," she said sweetly but intractably.

Cardinal Calaveria y Vacamonte realized that Leocadia was not going to be as compliant as he had hoped she would be. He proceeded in the manner of one being forced to act against his inclinations. "Have you reconsidered your answer?"

"If you mean will I marry Hubert Walmund, my answer is no, and it will always be no." Her body began to shake. "It won't matter if you beat me again or not. I will not marry a man who has lost his nose to the pox. I will not do it. By Madre Maria, he wears a silk mask on the street so that no one will see how much his face is damaged! I don't care that his brother is Archbishop Walmund, or that Spain must establish new ties to the German Princes and the Emperor. I *don't care!*"

"You compel me to act in a way that distresses us both; you bring pain upon yourself by your obstinacy," said her eldest brother, putting his hands together as if in prayer. "I cannot accept your answer, and you must know it."

"And I cannot accept such a husband." Her voice rose. "My brother, think! You cannot want me to marry a man so far gone in pox. I would rather not have a husband at all," she said, forcibly calming herself by clenching her hands on the heavy brocade of her voluminous skirts. "If you would grant me permission to take my vows as a nun—I would choose any Order that suited you. Mendicants, teachers, nurses, cloistered penitents, they are all welcome to me. I wouldn't mind living a chaste life." She saw his face darken. "I cannot marry Hubert Walmund, and nothing will make me do it."

"You will change your mind," said the Cardinal with cool certainty. "It need not be forever," he went on soothingly. "I have said you will not have to continue to live with him when you have given him two sons. He will agree to let you live apart from him once his family line is assured. He may even prefer that he not be encumbered with a wife." His mouth turned up at the corners but there was no sign of warmth or amusement in his countenance. "The longer you delay the wedding, the farther off is the day when you may live independently."

Leocadia's eyes shone with fear and welling anger. "I cannot do it. I will not do it."

"But you will. I have given el Rey my promise that you will help Spain to continue her ties to the Holy Roman Emperor; this marriage will suit his purpose as well as mine. It will also suit the Church. For the honor of our House, you must not refuse." He reached out and sunk his long, blunt fingers into her shoulder, pleased when she winced. "I had never thought you would be ungrateful, Leocadia."

"I am not ungrateful. I know what is due to my family." She willed herself to stop trembling; for a few breaths her shaking ceased, then began again. "It is not my intention to stand against you, Eminenza."

She used his title deliberately. "I am prepared to marry any healthy man you wish me to. I do not have to know him. I do not have to like him. He may be old or young, rich or poor, Spanish or foreign, and I will not refuse, so long as he is not sick."

Her brother struck her abruptly, then took hold of her shoulder again. "You are a defiant, unruly trollop. I am ashamed to call you my sister. You disgrace the three Spanish women you are named for. They are saints because of their obedience."

"Let me be a nun and I will show you how obedient I can be," she pleaded, shamed by the tears that stood in her eyes.

"Six of our cousins are nuns. The devotion of our women to God is clear. You alone are putting your will above the family and Spain." He released her and struck her again, leaning into the blow this time so that she stumbled with the impact. "Go beg God to change your sin to virtue."

She took another step back from him. "God does not demand this sacrifice of me. You, and el Rey, want it."

"And you, had you any goodness in your heart, would acquiesce in what is asked of you. Madre Maria did not show Gabriel such unbecoming refusal." He saw one of his servants coming, so cut short his intended castigation. "I do not want to see you until morning Mass. You may go to your rooms."

"May I have anything to eat?" she asked, anticipating the answer.

"Since you wish to show me how apt you are at the discipline of nuns, you will have bread and water when I have finished dining." He gestured to his servant. "See my sister to her apartment and be sure the door is locked."

The footman bowed deeply, then started toward Leocadia. "You have heard the Cardinal's orders: my duty is clear. Do not make it necessary for me to summon aid."

"Why should I?" asked Leocadia. "My brother is granting me an opportunity I welcome." She stood as straight as she could and set out ahead of the footman, walking with her head up as if the places he struck her did not hurt, nor any of the many other places on her body where he had left impressions of his disfavor.

Cardinal Calaveria y Vacamonte clicked his tongue as he watched

Leocadia depart. "She will do my bidding." He was mildly surprised he had spoken aloud, but hearing his conviction gave him confidence; he knew women and believed they would not refuse anything a man demanded for long—particularly if that man were her brother, now the head of his family since the death of their father some five years ago. There was no authority other than the Pope to whom she could appeal, and without doubt the Pope would require her submission to the Cardinal's wishes. He strode along the gallery that curved away from the red granite staircase, descending the steps quickly, calling out for his coachman as he went. "I have an urgent task for you. I want you to go to the house of Ahrent Rothofen and bring him here to me. Tell him I bid him to dine with me." This grand concession would bring the ambitious Rothofen running, the Cardinal had no doubt. "I will sit down in an hour. I will expect you here by that time."

The coachman, a stalwart young man from Calabria, flourished as much of a bow as his caped cloak would allow; he knew the testiness of Cardinal Calaveria y Vacamonte's temper, and he had no wish to displease his employer. "I will have the horses put to immediately. I will depart as soon as they are harnessed." He understood the Cardinal's intent sufficiently to plan to use the second-best carriage.

"Very good." This settled, he was about to depart. "Oh, and Giuliano," Cardinal Calaveria y Vacamonte added, as if it had just occurred to him, "did you happen to notice if my younger brother went out?"

Giuliano Buonfratello hesitated, trying to decide how best to answer. "His red horse is not in its stall. I did not see him leave. If you wish, I will ask the grooms."

The Cardinal sighed. "You needn't bother. No doubt he will return before dawn." It was more of a hope than a certainty, but he spoke with no trace of apprehension.

"Then I will be about my task, Eminenza," he said, and strode quickly along the corridor through the ground floor of the palazzo to the stable at the rear.

Cardinal Calaveria y Vacamonte waited a short while, looking out into the street beyond his loggia, his eyes far away. Then he shook himself and called out to a footman for a glass of Sangre del Torro wine. He had crates of it shipped to him from Spain and it was his wine of choice for all occasions but Mass.

The footman scurried off to obey, returning promptly with the glass on a silver tray, a small fruit pastry accompanying it. He bowed without speaking and waited while the Cardinal took the glass and the pastry, then withdrew at once.

The Cardinal strolled along the gallery, sipping his wine and occasionally nibbling his pastry: his thoughts were preoccupied. He was a Prince of the Church, yet he was prey to many checks and humiliations, unacceptable to a man of his rank. That his position was the result of simony did not make it any less genuine in Cardinal Calaveria y Vacamonte's eyes; almost all high Churchmen paid for their advances. He occasionally wondered if he had the support to become Pope, for it was whispered that Innocenzo XI would not last many years longer, and when he died there would be many men vying to fill the vacancy. Carlos el Rey had discouraged Cardinal Calaveria y Vacamonte from setting his sights so high—the Spanish crown could not afford it. But Carlos was no longer young himself, and would die without legitimate issue. The Cardinal could not banish his sense of injury at this, for when Spain passed from Hapsburg hands, he—the Cardinal, and the other Spanish Cardinals—would no longer be assured of royal support.

At the end of the gallery was his smaller dining room, suited for groups of up to twelve. It was as elegant as any chamber in the palazzo, with a tall marble fireplace at the far end, the mantel supported by life-sized statues of Saints Hippolytus of Porto and Frutuosos of Tarragona, two significant bishops, one Italian, one Spanish. Today it was chilly enough to require a blazing log to make the place comfortable, making it appear that the Saints were presiding over the flames in Hell. The Spanish theme was continued throughout the room, with paintings by Spanish artists, including a recently completed portrait of Cardinal Calaveria y Vacamonte by Velasquez. The table had been made in Barcelona ten years ago when the Cardinal had first come to Roma as an ambitious bishop of twenty-five. It was rubbed with oil-and-beeswax twice a month and was nearly as glossy as the red silk soutane the Cardinal wore daily. The chairs, more Spanish than French, were high-backed and straight, upholstered in specially woven tapestries showing various martyrdoms of Spanish Saints.

Cardinal Calaveria y Vacamonte sat down at the head of the table and finished his wine and pastry. He did not want to ask Rothofen to delay the negotiations with Archbishop Walmund any longer, but unless Leocadia relented, he would have to do so. He clapped loudly, knowing a footman was never far away.

The youngster who answered the summons had just begun shaving a few months ago, and he was still awed by the Cardinal. He bowed deeply. "What am I to have the honor of doing for you, Eminenza?"

"Which one are you?" the Cardinal inquired.

"Ernani, Eminenza. I have been in your service more than a year." He did not dare to look his employer in the face, but stood still, his eyes on a spot a stride in front of his feet.

Gratified, Cardinal Calaveria y Vacamonte smiled. "I will want supper served here within the hour. While I wait you may bring me another glass of wine. The service will be for two, but lay three places."

"Of course," said the footman, bowing and withdrawing hastily, only to return a short while later with a goblet of wine and two other footmen to set the table.

By the time the Cardinal's carriage returned, the dining room was in readiness; silverware, settings of crockery with the Calaveria y Vacamonte arms painted on the faces, and three crystal goblets were ready, snowy napery waiting. As the steward escorted Rothofen to the dining room, the first of the waiters arrived bearing the first course of a lavish meal.

Ahrent Julius Rothofen aspired to dandyism but had neither the figure nor the style for it: he was angular and graceless, with a bit too much jaw and nose to be handsome, and a bit too little flair to be amusing. Tonight he had dressed in a long, dark-turquoise justaucorps with forty-eight covered buttons down the front. His doubletiered ruffles fell over large, big-jointed hands. He carried a walking stick as tall as his shoulder and minced along on high-heeled shoes with elaborate, enormous silver-and-tortoiseshell buckles. He had given his cloak to the servant at the door, or the Cardinal would have seen a dark-green garment lined in fawn-colored satin. Rothofen should have been elegant, but he failed to carry off the air that would make his clothes seem appropriate; instead he gave the impression of a man in borrowed finery. At the sight of his host he doffed his wide-brimmed hat and made a leg. "How very magnanimous of you, Eminenza, to bring me to dine with you. I confess I am overwhelmed by your unexpected courtesy," he enthused in his German-flavored Italian.

Cardinal Calaveria y Vacamonte achieved a frosty smile, and answered in Spanish, "You and I have much to discuss. I thought it would be advisable to do that where I am certain the servants spy for me, not for those who pay for whispers."

Rothofen made a leg again, saying in Spanish, which he spoke marginally better than Italian, "You are a wise man, Cardinal Calaveria y Vacamonte. I bow to your superior understanding." When he donned his hat again, his chestnut-brown wig shifted a little, giving him a rakish air.

Cardinal Calaveria y Vacamonte liked flattery as much as any man of high position, but only when it sounded convincingly sincere; this had not persuaded him. He made a moue of distaste at Rothofen's inept technique. "Let us say I have lived in Roma long enough to know how the city works."

The laughter with which Rothofen greeted this was as overdone as his compliments had been. "Very true, Eminenza."

"Shall we sit down?" the Cardinal suggested, nodding in the direction of the table. "I will send word to my sister to join us, and then the waiters will serve us." The offer was sham—he had no intention of allowing Leocadia to speak to this man—but his strategy for the evening required it. He clapped for a waiter to hold a chair for his guest. "And summon my sister."

The waiter bowed as his superior held out the chair for the Cardinal. As soon as the two men were settled and wine poured for them, the younger waiter hurried away on his errand.

"She can be headstrong," said Cardinal Calaveria y Vacamonte as he lifted his goblet.

"What woman cannot?" Rothofen asked, chuckling. "Vain, willful creatures, all. Yet where would the sons of Adam be without them?"

"The sooner in Heaven, Señor, the sooner in Heaven," said Cardinal Calaveria y Vacamonte piously. As he drank, he watched his guest over the rim of his goblet.

"Ah. Ah, yes," said Rothofen, laughing immoderately once more. "I can see why you, Eminenza, have a reputation for wit." He drank thirstily, using his drinking to make a covert adjustment to his wig. "Fine vintage. Excellent savor."

"There is none better in Spain," said Cardinal Calaveria y Vacamonte proudly.

"I should think not," said Rothofen, "for surely a man in your position should have nothing less than the best to be had."

This fulsome praise was beginning to wear on the Cardinal. "The world, as we know, does not always reward merit fittingly."

"True, Eminenza, sadly true," said Rothofen, and had another large sip of wine. As he put his goblet down, the waiter at the sideboard refilled it from the fine decanter of Venetian glass. "This invitation was an honor I did not anticipate," he said suddenly but with caution.

"I have a few matters to discuss. I thought this would be an appropriate setting." Those familiar with the Cardinal would have known that the news was not good, but Rothofen did not have the close acquaintance he claimed, and so he smiled as the Cardinal went on. "There is some concern about Hubert Walmund's . . . health?"

Rothofen's smile vanished. "We've discussed the matter, Eminenza," he reminded the Cardinal cautiously.

"Yes, we have. Unfortunately something of his condition has become known to my sister. She is reluctant to pledge herself to one who is so . . . so clearly afflicted." He paused delicately. "I told you of my own reservations in this regard, and you answered my inquiries most frankly."

"As well I should," Rothofen could not resist saying. "I have done all that I can in order to ensure a good marriage contract between your sister and the Archbishop's brother. Anything that will hasten the happy day I must make it my obligation to accomplish." He drank again, a bit less than before.

"I am aware of that," said Cardinal Calaveria y Vacamonte soothingly. "But when a girl is pretty, she thinks she can dictate to the
whole world."

"So she does." Rothofen wagged his finger sagely. "They are not
easily instructed, pretty girls."

"No, they are not," the Cardinal agreed. He paused as if what he
was about to say had just occurred to him. "And yet, if Hubert Walmund is as far gone as they say, it might be fitting to make provision
for his illness in the contract. Oh, I know it is agreed she can live on
her own when she has provided him with two sons, and the settle-
ments will specify an annual pension for her. What troubles me," he
said, choosing his words, "is that the pox sometimes brings . . . well,
madness can be the only word for it. If that should happen, my sister
must have assurance of protection from her husband. It should not
have to fall to her to provide for him in his . . . decline."

The waiter appeared in the door, standing respectfully just inside
the dining room. As the Cardinal paused, he coughed discreetly.
"Eminenza?"

"Yes?" Cardinal Calaveria y Vacamonte inquired politely.

"She says she will not come." He repeated the message he had
been told to give, and the shame of the lie made his lie more convincing.

"Will she not?" the Cardinal mused. "Well, perhaps she will
change her mind. Leave the setting, in case she does."

The waiter blinked, for good manners required that the place setting be removed; if Leocadia escaped from her locked room, a place
would be laid for her then. Still, he was unwilling to challenge this
breach in manners. He bowed and prepared to bring in the tureen
of oxtail soup.

Rothofen was aware of this lapse as well as the waiters. "You expect her to relent?"

"Eventually," said the Cardinal with studied indifference.

"Then so be it," said Rothofen, and drank in salute. "Capricious,
is she?"

"She is young, the youngest in the family, and the only girl to
survive—my mother indulged her because of that." He realized he

may have gone too far, and added, "Not that she is irresponsible, like those flighty women one sees everywhere. Not she. She has mettle, and wants careful handling."

"Like a high-bred mare?" Rothofen suggested, and sniggered.

"High-bred and very valuable; of impeccable breeding, in fact," said the Cardinal haughtily. "I will not permit the Archbishop to have a free hand with her where his brother is concerned. She must be protected from his ailment."

"That is clear," said Rothofen, stopping to sniff the aroma of the soup as the tureen was put before the Cardinal. "Most savory," he approved.

The Cardinal nodded to his servants, leaning back in his chair as much as the high, straight back would let him. "I know certain concessions have already been made, but I am certain it is wiser to make provision in the marriage contracts before the question arises."

"*If* it arises," Rothofen dared to correct his host. He stared at the vacant place setting across the table, and bit his lower lip. "There are those the pox abandons. It is not unknown. The Archbishop's brother has been in the care of a Greek physician, and it is said he is improving."

"That must please all his friends; I will pray for the success of his physician," said Cardinal Calaveria y Vacamonte. "Yet I am certain it would be appropriate to include allowances for that . . . unhappy turn."

Now Rothofen frowned, for such a concession would mean the Archbishop would have to pay more money than he wanted to. "I will mention it, and I will inform you of the Archbishop's decision as soon as he has reached one," he said, watching for the Cardinal to pick up his spoon.

"I would be most thankful if you would," said Cardinal Calaveria y Vacamonte, his silverware untouched. "And a few other minor matters, as well, if you can see your way to? For I think we are agreed that this union is an ineluctable necessity." He finally picked up his spoon and took his first taste of soup. He paid no apparent attention to the fervor with which Rothofen fell to.

Only when he had finished his plate of soup did Rothofen say, "Yes, Eminenza, we are agreed on that."

"Very good," said the Cardinal and signaled to the waiter to remove their plates in preparation for the scallops in saffron sauce that was the next course.

Text of a letter from Marcaurelio dal Prato to Niklos Aulirios, delivered by private courier on February 10th, 1689.

To the most worthy Niklos Aulirios, the greetings of Marcaurelio dal Prato,

It is my sad duty to inform you, Signore, that the magistrate Benedetto Silviano has ruled that I may not represent you in his Court. Word has come from the Lateran that in a case where the Church may be involved, the magistrate must be persuaded my presence in the process would not be acceptable to those in authority. I have asked if there is any appeal I may tender, but I have been informed this is impossible. Magistrate Silviano has agreed to take into evidence all the material you have vouchsafed me, and for which I include a receipt. The materials provided by the Abbe Ragoczy will have to be submitted again, for only my direct dealings with you have been allowed as acceptable to the magistrate.

I must also tell you that it is the intention of the magistrate to put the hearing into his calendar for March. I apologize that so little time is granted to you to find other representation and to appear before him, but such is his will, and the Pope, as Bishop of Roma is the only one who may change this if the magistrate will not reconsider his decision.

Please accept my apology for being unable to fulfill your commission in this case. If there is any way by which I might assist you in your case as it continues, it would be my honor to put myself at your service. Should it be your decision not to do this, I will comprehend your decision fully.

You will find enclosed forty-four Venetian ducats, the unused balance of the fifty Venetian ducats you advanced me for the trying of this suit. Again, I regret I was unable to do more for you.

                                    With sincerest regards,
                                    I remain,
                                    Marcaurelio dal Prato

On the 9th day of February, by my own hand, at Roma

3

By the time the tailor departed, Ragoczy was as tired as he was well-dressed; the fruits of the visit were strewn about the room, resting on tables and flung over the backs of chairs—new clothes sufficient to half a dozen occasions, and two riding ensembles as well, the very minimum of what was regarded as respectable. During the five-hour fitting the tailor had passed on every rumor circulating in Roma, while Ragoczy had been treated to the significance of every nuance of current fashion and was by now prepared to go out into the world in his new finery, happily confident that his appearance was as faultless as money could make it.

Rugerius, who had watched most of the procedure, sighed. "It's endless. Ribbons and bands and justaucorps and cloaks and jabots and breeches and hose and boots and gloves and wigs and hats . . ." He flung up his hands in mock surrender, then began to pick up the various articles of clothing with the purpose of taking them to Ragoczy's private apartments to pack them away. "What can I do about it? There is so much to remember."

Outside the sound of builders at work provided a steady level of noise that was constant enough to be unnoticeable; there was a sudden emphatic bang, but as no shouts or screams followed it, both Ragoczy and Rugerius ignored it.

"You will do as you have done so well in the past: managed expertly." Ragoczy glanced down at his thick-soled, broad-heeled boots from Antwerp that were decades out of fashion. "I don't like to think about finding a new bootmaker."

"No," Rugerius agreed. "Explanations will be needed in regard to the construction."

Now it was Ragoczy's turn to sigh. "I suppose you will know what to tell him."

The smile that greeted this was rare. "All servants complain of eccentric masters."

"And you as well," Ragoczy said. "How wise of you." He did not bother to look for a mirror, knowing he would have no reflection in it.

Rugerius noticed his careful omission and said, "The tailor was curious about the lack of mirrors, and your claim that you had none to avoid the sin of vanity might not be as readily accepted by him as by others living far from Roma." He indicated Ragoczy's finery. "You have given him ample cause to wonder."

"True enough," said Ragoczy. "But fortunately I am still an eccentric foreigner." He lowered his head. "Wigs again, with curls this time."

"And hats atop them," said Rugerius. He shrugged and summed up his thoughts in a single word. "Fashion." He looked about the room. "To think this was once your laboratory. This is the place where you restored me."

"Sixteen hundred years ago, more or less," said Ragoczy. "Yes. But it is laboratory no more. The baths are gone, too, which is unfortunate. I should like to spend an hour or so in the calidarium. Perhaps I will have baths built in the new villa."

"The men will talk about it," Rugerius warned.

"There is nothing in Roma that men do not talk about, from what I can tell; the worst they can think of me is that I am self-indulgent," said Ragoczy as he slipped his heavy silver collar over his head, placing his eclipse device pectoral in the center of his chest. "Too foreign."

"If you must go to court, certainly it is too foreign. To convince them you are a true Abbe it must be crucifixes and rosaries." Rugerius hesitated. His arms were now full to overflowing with the clothes Ragoczy had just purchased. "On that head, what do you plan to do now that Niklos has lost his advocate?"

"Apply to the Court to fill that position. They cannot refuse me on grounds of religion—not this century. So unless they decide my foreignness disqualifies me, no doubt I will be permitted to address the Court, which is better than what faces Niklos at present. We are fortunate that the man making the claim is German: if he were Roman, I doubt we would encounter such leniency. To hear Rothofen, they will have to allow me to speak as well." He went to the window and looked out on the work going on under grey skies. "We will lose a few days to rain, I fear."

"It is February. What else would you expect?" Rugerius remarked. When Ragoczy volunteered nothing more, he assumed an expression of kindly exasperation. "You have said nothing about Olivia since our last conversation with Niklos."

"No; I have not." He paused. "You have been very patient. All right. I will tell you what has been in my thoughts since we arrived here: I mourn her." He said it simply, stating what was obvious. "The grief never goes away, not entirely. The severity diminishes over time, but the loss continues, for the person is still gone. You have seen me after Xenya and Ranegonda and Demetrice and—" He gestured an end to his unhappy catalogue. "But I learned millennia ago that no one can be called back again, nor their time. The True Death cannot be circumvented. If I should cling to their memories, I would lose every one as much as if I thrust them away." He turned his back to the window and looked directly at his manservant. "You fear I am trying to hide my loss, to escape from it, but that would be folly for one of my blood. As their blood and life is part of me, so is their death. There are soldiers without arms whose loss is as keen and constant as mine. And like the maimed soldiers, I live with what is gone. I do not want to turn away from it, I want to know it so that I can continue to know Olivia, and the rest. If I grasp her memory too closely I will strangle it as surely as if I put my hands around her throat; I must hold it lightly. She is a part of me, and her death—" He stopped, holding up his hand. "Someone is at the door."

Rugerius heard the knock repeated. "Is anyone expected?" When Ragoczy shook his head, Rugerius told him, "I will go admit him. And I will bestow these garments in the wardrobe on the way," he said as he left the room that had been turned into a reception hall for Ragoczy and his occasional visitors. A few minutes later there was the sound of the door opening, and Rugerius' courteous greeting.

Ragoczy sat down in the chair near the small hearth where a fire blazed against the cutting chill of the afternoon. He looked up as Rugerius brought a stranger dressed in fine riding clothes to him; Ragoczy nodded but he did not rise. "God give you good day, Signore."

The stranger made a graceful leg. "I trust I address Abbe Ferenc Ragoczy, Count of San-Germain?"

"You do," said Ragoczy. "And you, Signore?"

"I am Celestino Bruschi, my father is Barone di Rilievoduro. I have the happy duty to be among those attending on Ettore Domenico Agnolo Colonna." He obviously expected Ragoczy to know who this was, for he did not bother with titles or family connections. "He has been managing those Italian parts of the estates of his late great-uncle, Giulio Mazarini, which, as they include the holdings of Olivia Clemens, have been entrusted to his custody." He smiled winningly, his handsome features slightly flushed.

"You mean Cardinal Mazarin," said Ragoczy, a hint of a question in his tone.

"To the Colonnas he is always Giulio Mazarini, their most cherished cousin. The French may call him what they will." His supercilious expression bordered on comic.

"Sit down, Signore Bruschi," said Ragoczy, indicating the chair opposite his own. "Permit me to offer you some refreshment. I am sure we have much to discuss." His courteous demeanor concealed his lively curiosity.

Bruschi remained standing. "Alas, I fear I must return; perhaps another time you will be good enough to extend your hospitality to me. I have come only to give you these." He reached into the tooled leather satchel he carried on a wide strap over his shoulder and across his chest.

Ragoczy rose. "What on earth?"

"The account books and maintenance records for your property.

You will want to review them." Bruschi handed them over with a flourish.

"You ask for no bona fides?" Ragoczy was suspicious of this ready acceptance.

Bruschi laughed. "As to that, Signor' Conte, you have provided them to the Curia and the magistrates' court. If you are accepted there, who is Ettore Colonna to cavil?"

"Who indeed?" asked Ragoczy, amused, as he took the proffered articles. "Thank you and Ettore Colonna for bringing these."

"No thanks are necessary," said Bruschi, more for form's sake than for his actual feelings. "Ettore Colonna has asked me to extend an invitation to you so that you and he may discuss any questions you may have regarding what has been done to your property. He would call himself, but it is more—"

"Fitting," Ragoczy supplied. "Truly." He made a leg. "Tell Ettore Colonna I will make it my business to call upon him next week. All he need do is inform me what days are more convenient, and what hours he receives visitors and I will suit my time to his."

"I shall be pleased to tell him," said Bruschi. With another sweeping leg, he stepped back and left the room, Rugerius accompanying him.

"What do you make of that?" Rugerius asked when he returned from seeing Bruschi off into the gathering mists of evening.

"I will know when I have examined these books. I am relieved to have them." He held them up. "It was good of him to send them to me. I admit I am surprised he waited until now to do it."

"Perhaps he was waiting on the approval of the Curia?" Rugerius suggested. He was speaking Hungarian, as much to foil any eavesdroppers as to enforce their position as coming from Hungarian territories. "Your status as Abbe may be in some doubt."

"If it is, so must a hundred others be," Ragoczy replied, a faint line deepening between his fine brows. "The Curia must know that men of hereditary rank in the Carpathians have found their way into the fringes of the clergy to preserve their estates from Ottoman claims. I am no different than they are, and the Curia undoubtedly is aware of it, for they encourage the practice." He looked down at the books again. "Perhaps the Curia wanted to review these before I saw them. That could explain the delay."

The sound of work had stopped, leaving the air eerily silent. It took both Ragoczy and Rugerius a moment to realize what the change was.

"The worker have left for the night," said Rugerius. "The question of your position in the Church is going to have to be settled."

"So long as I defend my native earth against the forces of the Ottomites, the Church will not mind if my vocation is less than pristine, or if she does mind, it will be for other reasons than that." He held up his hand. "Even here in Roma, the Church knows she needs every ally she can find if she is to sustain any of her claims on Balkan or Carpathian lands. I have been considering the matter for several days and I believe I may have hit upon a solution. My vocation or lack of it will be overlooked if I do not claim too much by its right. As an Abbe, the Church may find me unacceptable, so I will begin to style myself Conte da San-Germain and that should forestall any but the most zealous of critics. I will try to make my representation of Niklos on grounds of noble obligation, and use my position of Abbe only if it is utterly necessary. In regard to San-Germain, make sure it is understood that it is *da*, not *di*. I have no wish to find myself disputing an Italian over his hereditary rights."

"*From* and not *of*," Rugerius approved. "Splitting hairs, but it provides you some leeway."

"And by retaining the Frankish style, it removes my claim beyond the Papal States—even beyond Italy." Ragoczy went back to his chair near the fire. "*From* worked before, in Fiorenza." He used the older form of the name of the Tuscan city now called Firenze.

"I hope you may be right," said Rugerius. "There are no Medicis here to protect you, and no easy escape, if that is required. Roma is the lion's mouth of the Church. The Pope is monarch here, and his armies are everywhere. If any of your claims fall under suspicion—" He held up his hands to remind them both of how powerless they would be.

"I do not dispute you, old friend," Ragoczy said, settling himself comfortably, his dark eyes fixed on the middle-distance. "Olivia was right to build fireplaces in this room as she did in so many of the others. It would be very cold without it." He did not feel the cold himself, but had long ago made a point of keeping warm enough to avoid questions. "The old heating channels under the floor must be filled with debris by now. Even if the holocaust had not"—he faltered—"not been blown up, it would not be safe to try to use it after so many centuries."

"The fireplace is pleasant," said Rugerius. He brought a standing candelabrum up next to Ragoczy's chair. "I will light the candles, if you like."

"It is light enough," Ragoczy said, who was rarely troubled by darkness.

"It is customary to use candles or lamps after sunset," Rugerius reminded him.

"So it is," Ragoczy responded, no longer in a reverie. "And you are quite right to light them. We are in Roma and we must assume we are being watched."

"So we must," said Rugerius. He bent and took a long, narrow kindling spike from the iron basket beside the fireplace. Lighting this from the fire, he used it to set the candles burning. "There. You are going to read the account books?"

"I am," said Ragoczy.

"And you are preparing to ask questions of Signore Colonna?" He was fairly certain this must be the case.

"I am," Ragoczy repeated.

"Will you be staying in tonight?" Rugerius pursued. He was looking a trifle impatient, his faded-blue eyes fixed on Ragoczy.

"I should think so. If I venture out at all, it will be well after midnight," Ragoczy said with unruffled calm.

"I suspect this house is being observed, even late at night," Rugerius warned. "If you travel any distance from this villa, someone is apt to notice it."

"Rugerius, old friend, I am not so hungry that I must raven about the countryside. If I leave, I will be careful, and I will . . . dine wisely," he promised with a faint, wry smile.

"I do not question your circumspection, my master, I only mention the dedication of those you may encounter in your search." Rugerius showed his concern in a gentling of his austere features.

"No doubt you are right. Yet long hours in the cold and rain can make any man less attentive than he ought to be. By the time I prepare to leave, any observer is likely to be groggy; he will pay no attention to me if I take reasonable precautions. I have eluded spies before; I have not forgot how to do it." His smile was ironic. "If the Turks did not succeed in catching me these last six years, why should I fear the Romans? Particularly *these* Romans."

"If you mean that Nero or Vespasianus no longer reigns here, I will allow that. Nevertheless, I would prefer the Praetorian to the Swiss Guard," Rugerius said. "For the city is not benign simply because what was Caesar's is now the Pope's."

Ragoczy nodded to show he understood. "Let me get to my reading. I will call you if I decide to go out."

"As you say," Rugerius conceded and was about to depart when something struck him. "Will you build another laboratory in the new villa?"

"Oh, yes, I think so," said Ragoczy with such lack of concern that Rugerius was instantly alerted.

"Is that entirely prudent?" he asked, trying to conceal the sudden alarm that seized him at this apparent recklessness. "You are aware of the spies. Is it wise to give them something so irrefutable as a laboratory to watch?"

"I would rather they watch my laboratory than many other of my activities," said Ragoczy in a pointed way. "I know there is reason to be uneasy; do not think I am unaware of it. But if the worst the spies can find is experimentation, then I will be safe. It will be assumed that my eccentricities are part of my researches." He chuckled. "Even a Cardinal or two dabbles in scientific experiments these days. So long as I provide medicaments and astrolabes and chronometers, I think I will be safe. The Romans have always liked toys. I may even say I am trying to invent an automaton. That would be fitting enough, for there are all those clockwork figures in church belltowers."

"Not in Roma," Rugerius pointed out sternly.

Ragoczy made a gesture of acknowledgment. "But I am from Hungarian territories, and this would be a harmless reminder. An occasional eccentricity is expected of foreigners. This will be mine, I think. It's harmless enough, particularly if I do not do anything too well. They will ignore my other . . . eccentricities if they can attribute them to this. Besides," he added, a bit more briskly, "I am not about to publish anything, no matter how trivial, under my own name, and certainly not in the Papal States. If I want to put my thoughts into print, I will use my press in Amsterdam and find a wholly changed name—no trace of Ragoczy or San-Germain in it. The censors will have nothing to attach to me other than Hungarian caprice."

"I hope you are right, my master," said Rugerius. "The Pope's Little House would not be an easy residence to leave."

"I do not intend to run afoul of the Inquisition, I promise you," Ragoczy said levelly; he had spent nineteen of the last forty years in Church prisons in the Americas. He closed his eyes briefly, as if shutting out a memory.

"Who does have such intentions?" Rugerius countered. "And yet the Little House is never without guests." He turned away and left Ragoczy to his reading.

By noon the following day, Ragoczy had finished perusing the two books Celestino Bruschi had given him; he had made two closely written pages of notes of entries to clarify with Colonna. He dressed at leisure in his Hungarian clothes, his sword worn in plain sight this time, his pectoral device on his chest, and went down to his makeshift library to speak with Rugerius. The sound of rain had replaced the constant noise of the builders, and the four servants Rugerius had hired went about the duties in near-silence.

"How long do you expect the rain to last?" Rugerius asked in Italian when Ragoczy requested he put a stop to his sorting of books.

"Three days—at most. The wind is too high for it to last. I do not know how long we will have to wait for the next rain. We may not dry out enough for work to be resumed." Ragoczy glanced over the stacked crates and the partially built shelves. "Do you want to wait until the new villa is built to do all that?"

"It is pleasant work, and the servants talk of the quantity of books instead of wondering about their contents; at least they do while I am by," said Rugerius. "The servants are not entirely trustworthy."

"Why should they be? I am a foreigner to them. They have no duty to me other than to perform the tasks they are hired to perform. The Church is everywhere and her power exceeds mine no matter how honorably they labor." He set down the two books on a tall stool. "Ettore Colonna is a very precise man. Or his steward is."

"You are satisfied?" Rugerius asked, his face revealing nothing of his thoughts.

"I am not *dis*satisfied," Ragoczy replied. "When I have spoken to Signore Colonna I will know more." He strode down the room. "I should help you with this. Two of us working would speed the task."

Rugerius shook his head. "The servants might think that you and I are concealing something among the books. Just as well to leave it to me."

"Perhaps I should call on Niklos. He will be kept in by the rain," Ragoczy said.

"Will this present the separation of interests you wish to maintain if you do?" Rugerius asked with such formality that Ragoczy knew they were being listened to.

"If I am to represent him, I must occasionally consult him," Ragoczy said. "I should discover how things stand now with Niklos so that I may make the most of my forthcoming discussion with Signore Colonna: I will need to be informed on all points. If you will be good enough to continue on here as you've begun?" He bowed without making a leg. "I shall not be long, old friend."

"Will you take the smaller carriage?" Rugerius asked, anticipating the answer.

"Why should four men and four horses get wet when only one must? No; I shall ride. I think the eight-year-old mare, the one from Vienna, will serve. She's probably eager for a chance to sport a little." He cocked his head toward the blowing rain against the windows. "I see no purpose in taking an escort, either. I will not be entering Roma, and have no need of showing my consequence." He swept the dull-red riding cloak he had been carrying around his shoulders and fastened the elaborate frogging at his neck.

"Very good, my master," said Rugerius, lowering his eyes. "I will send word to the stable."

"Never mind. I will do it myself." He swung about on the thick heel of his boot, and walked away toward the corridor that would take him out to the stable beyond. When Nero was Caesar, there had been stalls for nearly four hundred horses here, and was thought a smallish enterprise. Now there were stall for twenty, and many of the neighbors had fewer. He stepped into the aisle between the stalls, which was wide as the deepest box-stalls, brushing the damp from the cape of his cloak as he made his way to where his riding horses were kept.

Two were recent purchases from Senza Pari, for he trusted Olivia's horses above all others; though he elected not to ride one today, preferring the mare he had trained himself.

The grey mare was glad for the attention he gave her as he brushed down her coat and combed out her mane and tail. As he picked out her hooves, he realized she would need new shoes in a fortnight at the very latest; he would have to refit the smithy before then. He patted her flank, haltered her, and led her out of her stall, looping her lead to a large ring secured in the pillar in the center of the aisle. Then he went to fetch his tack, choosing a wide fleece saddle pad to help keep her warm. He politely declined the stablehand's offer to tend to the chore, enjoying what was usually grooms' work, talking to the mare as he buckled on her breastplate and tightened her girths. The current fashion in double-bitted military bridles he disdained, using, as he had done for two thousand years, a simple snaffle. He brought the reins back over her head and swung up into the saddle, spreading out his cloak to cover her rump and securing his broad-brimmed hat with its braided cords in a knot under his chin. Then he nodded to the stable-hand. "Open the end door, Lotario. Grazie."

The young man hurried to obey, holding the door against the insistence of the wind as Ragoczy passed out of the stable and into the storm.

Responding to the wind, the mare frisked her way up the drive, dancing around mud-puddles all the way to the main gate, minced through it, then steadied down to a well-disciplined trot for the three-league journey to Senza Pari. As he rode around the northeastern flank of Roma, Ragoczy kept a careful eye on the countryside around him, wary of any danger that might be present. After a quarter of an hour the mare slowed to a walk, and continued on at that pace all the way to Senza Pari.

As he dismounted at the door of Olivia's villa, Ragoczy handed his mare to the groom who hurried forward. "Wipe her down, if you would; loosen her girths, keep her warm, give her water when she is cooled—not before."

The groom bowed as he led the mare into the shelter of the stable, leaving Ragoczy to find his way into the villa, searching for Niklos and finding him eventually on the second floor, in the guest room over the kitchen. "Good afternoon," he said, making a leg in case any of the servants were watching.

"Good afternoon," said Niklos grimly. "I am glad you have come. We must talk."

"Dear me, what can have happened?" Ragoczy asked with the air of one much astonished. He surveyed the room without changing his stance, and satisfied himself that they were not observed. Abandoning his grand manner, he began to speak, this time in the Greek of Byzantium. "I take it there has been some trouble."

"Yes," said Niklos bluntly. "Two of my servants are gone, and no one knows where—or if they know, they are not willing to tell me. Whether the Inquisitors came for them in the night—which is what the cook thinks—or they have fled for fear of what may come of this suit, I don't know."

"But you are rightly troubled that there could be a Process against you. Very wise. Once Inquisitors start asking questions, no one is safe," said Ragoczy.

"You know that better than I," said Niklos, and began to apologize for his impertinence. "I did not mean to make light of your imprisonment, Saint-Germain; I did not think—"

"No; you are right to say so, and these servants have every right to worry. Right now it would serve your opponent's purpose very well to have your servants under suspicion of heresy, since heresy can be committed in thoughts as well as deeds." Ragoczy shook his head. "If this is the ploy and it is intended to intimidate your supporters and allies, I must suppose it will be successful." He looked directly at

Niklos. "You will have to be very careful, or you could place yourself at even greater risk than you already have."

"How?" Niklos demanded, scowling. "Unless they already suspect me, and are trying to get confirmation through my servants."

"You realize this may have nothing to do with the Inquisition," Ragoczy said in the same unruffled calm. "The servants may be frightened and have run off for fear, or they may have been bribed to leave, in order to throw your household into disorder." He waited for Niklos to consider this. "If that is the case, and the servants are not in the hands of the Inquisition, then you will have to be particularly careful in how you deal with the development, so that your opponent, emboldened by his success, does not take it into his head to try something even more outrageous."

"What would that be?" The sarcasm in Niklos' voice caught Ragoczy's attention.

"Anything that would discredit you; he has already shown himself capable of perjury and fraud; I cannot think he would stop at suborning witnesses," he answered with a composure that was tinged with reserve. "And that could prove more troublesome than the demands of this ludicrous suit. As you have pointed out, neither you nor I would befit from close scrutiny."

Niklos made himself smile, but it was a brittle effort. "I am stymied, it appears."

"That appearance is useful for you. I would advise you to maintain it as long as you can." Ragoczy saw the disgruntled expression in Niklos' handsome features. "There are times, and this is one of them, when you will find a patina of confusion or ignorance will serve you very well, for as long as your opponent is certain he has flummoxed you, he will not be as attentive to your actions as he would be if you appeared clear of purpose, and he may do something foolhardy and overstep himself; he might expose his mendacity through such foolishness. Let him underestimate you—and me—so that he will not prepare as he should." He gave a bleak smile.

"Yes. Yes, I know it is a wise thing to do," Niklos said in weary resignation. "Many times in the past I gave Olivia just such advice. I did not understand why she found it so galling. Now I do."

Ragoczy nodded. "I agree it is a blow to pride to do this. But rather a blow to pride than a disaster, which is what Rothofen is seeking."

"I know," said Niklos shortly. He paced a short distance from Ragoczy, then shrugged and came back. "All right. You are protecting me, I am aware of it. But it is most vexing to be saved from myself in this manner."

"I am familiar with the problem, as Rugerius would tell you." Ragoczy laid his small, gloved hand on Niklos' shoulder. "I must add one more unwelcome recommendation to my irksome list—that you be patient while I undertake to discover how great a fabrication Rothofen has achieved. I realize I have tried to impress the need for patience before, but I must reiterate it, for both our sakes. We must tread very carefully, but not so carefully that we attract unwanted scrutiny, for that would redound to your discredit. Patience is essential if we are not to expose ourselves to God's Hounds"—just using this unflattering nickname of the Dominican Order could be risky— "for their questions are more stringent than any magistrate's. When we have a better notion of what he proposes to use to establish his claim, we will be able to decide how to deal with him."

Niklos folded his arms, his jaw tight. "I will promise to make an effort. I may not succeed."

"Do your utmost," Ragoczy advised, his dark eyes stern. "Or you and I could lose far more than six of Olivia's estates."

This severe reminder brought Niklos up short. "Of course," he said; his single nod was pledge of his compliance.

Text of a letter from Alessandro Scarlatti to Ferenc Ragoczy, Conte da San-Germain; delivered to the Villa Vecchia by Celestino Bruschi.

To Su Eccellenza il Conte da San-Germain, Ferenc Ragoczy, the greetings from Napoli of Alessandro Scarlatti, with his gratitude for the kindness il Conte has shown in approaching me for the purposes of engaging my services.

If it pleases Su Eccellenza, I will make it my pleasure to wait upon you when next I visit Roma, which should be in March. I confess I am anticipating that sojourn with the liveliest relish: I have a stunning new soprano to delight my gracious patron, Ettore Colonna. As it was he who provided you with my address, you will no doubt want to attend her recital at Gran Segretto. I have already arranged for at least one performance at that splendid estate; if the occasion is not suitable, I will be honored to arrange a private concert for Su Eccellenza to hear her. I predict she will take the world by storm, for her voice is enhanced by artistry of such refinement that no one can listen to her without knowing she is a treasure from God.

My family will not accompany me, but I will bring my consort of ten musicians, all of whom will need to be housed and kept where we perform. I mention this for my most valued patron Ettore Colonna informs me that you are rebuilding a villa and you may not have sufficient room to house my men. If that is the case, I must rely upon you to find suitable accommodations for my musicians, and, of course, for my soprano.

When you have heard Giorgianna Ferrugia, you will be transported. Everyone in the Court here in Napoli has been enchanted by her. I am certain that you will find her a most remarkable singer, as well as being of a pious and humble character. I mention this only to ensure that she will not have to endure assaults on her virtue while she is in Roma; there are those who believe that any woman who stands before an audience to perform must be wholly lacking in modesty, but in cases of such musical gifts as this woman possesses, you will understand that her conduct is of the highest order.

I am imposing on the good offices of Ettore Colonna to see this safely into your hands, for I believe a message to one of so distinguished a Roman family will be afforded more respect on the road than one to a man of distinguished title but few known connections. I pray you will take no umbrage at my action, or think unkindly of Signore Colonna for acting in the capacity of secretary, for it is meant to be mutually beneficial.

I look forward to offering you my bow in person, and I pray that God will look upon all your endeavors with favor.

Until we meet,
I commend myself to Su Eccellenza, and to your good opinion,
Alessandro Scarlatti

By my own hand at Napoli on the 18th day of February, 1689

4

Palazzo Colonna was magnificent even by Roman standards; designed to impress, it had a broad front of three-story columns, trading on the family name in a glorious architectural pun. Six of the columns framed a vast loggia with grand staircases at either end leading up to a tall gallery above, with many gorgeous rooms beyond which could be glimpsed through great doors now open for the many guests. Murals glowed on the walls and ceiling, and at the top of the two staircases, enormous mirrors of the finest Venetian glass served to make the whole elaborate display appear more grand than it already was. In a family newer to Roma, such a palazzo would be considered ostentatious, but as it belonged to the Colonnas, it was recognized as a fitting tribute to an admirable family history that could be traced back more than a thousand years. In contrast to the other Palazzo Colonna in Roma, this one was called II Meglio—The Best. Built more to lessen the stifling heat of the long Roman summer, the palazzo was draughty as a tree in winter, so that the guests—most of them experienced in the climate—wore not only their most sumptuous ensembles, but their warmest as well, and the footmen who waited upon them were rigged out in woollen livery.

Ferenc Ragoczy arrived in his fine new carriage in the midst of the first wave of guests. His new clothes attracted the notice of several of the other new arrivals, for he had achieved an elegant balance of finery and restraint that was rarely seen in Roma: his justaucorps was of black brocaded silk shot with silver and piped in a deep-red silken twist, all setting off his ruby-studded collar of silver from which depended his eclipse device with silver wings raised and displayed above a black sapphire disk. On his left breast he wore the diamond Order of Saint Stephen of Hungary. His camisa was white silk edged in point lace that made a double collar at the neck; the sleeves were triple-tiered with ruffles at the wrist. His breeches were more fitted than the usual fashion and were closed just below the knee with ruby studs instead of the usual knot of ribbons. His underhose were black silk, his thick-soled shoes had buckles of diamond-ornamented silver. He had acquired a lustrous black wig that leant his whole appearance the final tasteful coup. Unlike most of the guests not in religious garb, he did not carry a tall walking cane.

Ettore Colonna and his cousin Giancarlo, Cardinal Colonna, stood at the center of the gallery to receive their guests, Ettore in clothes as exuberant as his cousin's were constrained. The azure of his satin justaucorps did not wholly complement the Cardinal's glowing red silken soutane, nor did the elaborate curls of his auburn wig look entirely appropriate beside his cousin's tasseled hat. Nevertheless the two welcomed the new arrivals in perfect amity, occasionally poking good-natured fun at each other, using their diversity to entertain as much as the more usual signs of hospitality.

"Eminenza," said Ragoczy, dropping to his knee to kiss the Cardinal's ring. He then rose and made a graceful leg to Ettore Colonna. "A good evening to you, Signore. I am filled with deep appreciation for the honor you have done me this evening."

"Conte," said Ettore Colonna. "A pleasure to meet you at last. Welcome to Il Meglio. I hope you will make the most of the evening. You will discover a great many of our guests are looking forward to knowing you better." He had something of the dark handsomeness of his late second cousin, Giulio Mazarini, but his eyes were more cynical and his mouth more sensual; he was one of the tallest men in the room, a height he accentuated with jewel-encrusted heels on his shoes. He realized that his advantage in inches did not impress his guest, whose presence made up for his moderate height.

"What can I be but gratified?" Ragoczy said, with a glint of enig-matic amusement in his dark eyes. He passed into the reception hall where most of the guests were gathered at the eastern end of the room to be as near the fireplace as possible. Approaching the glittering assembly, Ragoczy made a sweeping leg as a general courtesy before he advanced on an elderly man in fine garments twenty years out of fashion. "Do I address Signore Ennio Lampone, the mathematician?"

The man did not attempt to make a leg for fear of setting off his gout; he nodded instead. "I am Lampone," he confirmed. "You, Signore, are unknown to me."

"I am Ferenc Ragoczy, Conte da San-Germain," he said, bowing without making a leg so as not to make Lampone's lack of one a discourtesy.

"Ah." Lampone's rheumy old eyes lit up. "The *Hungarian* everyone is talking about. You have the appearance of your rank," he approved. "The Order of Saint Stephen. Very commendable. You make a most creditable presentation of yourself, Signore Conte. It is a pleasure to know you."

Ragoczy's heritage was far older than any Hungarian claims in his native region of the Carpathians would be, but he said nothing beyond, "Thank you. When one is a foreigner, one must be meticulous in such things as presentation, and be at pains to observe all codes of conduct. I am pleased to know I have offered no inadvertent offense to anyone at this grand event." He paused, and went on in an amiable way, "One of the many delights I have been looking forward to since my arrival in Roma is learning more about your theories on large and small attractions. I have read your writings with considerable admiration. Perhaps you might appoint a time when you would be willing to undertake such a discussion."

Lampone shook his head. "I do not make it a habit to discuss my work, Signore Conte." His politeness was turning frosty.

"No, no, Signore Lampone, you misunderstand me." His cordial urbanity did not waver. "I have done some studies in a related field and I hoped to benefit from an exchange of information. It is not often I find someone with the interests and skills I myself have pursued for many years. When I do, I am eager to engage in such exchange as will—I hope—stimulate both of our endeavors."

"Is it so?" Lampone asked, his hauteur fading a bit. "I might be kinder to refuse you. Well, let me give it some consideration. There may be some advantage to speaking with you after all." He motioned to indicate Ragoczy could come a bit nearer. "In a place like this, it is wise to guard one's tongue. There are those who hear heresy in every word."

"That is the case throughout Roma; I too, rejoice when I discover a colleague who knows truth is always acceptable to God," Ragoczy agreed, and encouraged Lampone to talk, all the while keeping a close yet covert watch on the parade of guests. In the next half hour he learned the old scholar was a widower with three grown sons, two in holy Orders, one in self-exile in London; Lampone had considered joining him in England but could not bring himself to leave his native language behind. "Rufio is young: learning another tongue is not a burden for him. But for me—?" He shrugged to show impossibility.

"But having your son gone must make the Church more wary of you," said Ragoczy.

"Possibly," said Lampone, "though a man in my position is generally regarded with some suspicion, no matter what his sons might do." He glanced toward some of the new arrivals, his expression unguarded enough to show dislike for an instant. "There are those who do the Church more honor than others," he muttered, distaste curling his lips.

Ragoczy understood this was critical of the guests who had just entered the reception hall—a Cardinal with a handsome young woman in striking apparel on his arm and a sulky exquisite behind him. "Who is that?"

"Martin, Cardinal Calaveria y Vacamonte. The woman is his sister, Leocadia, and the dandy is his brother," said Lampone, his eyes bright with contempt. "He is a great believer in stringent adherence to dogma, except where his family is concerned."

"So many of the Spanish are dogmaticians," Ragoczy said, his words neutral enough in case they were overheard. His years in Spanish prisons in the New World had left a powerful impression upon him; his reserve returned. "Perhaps we should select another time to converse? There are so many people here—"

"My notion precisely," said Lampone, clearly relieved. "I am at

home to callers every morning after Mass. The Villa Santa Lucia. Go
to II Gesu and turn east."

"I shall find you; thank you for your most gracious invitation," said
Ragoczy, and moved away from the old mathematician.

There were more than two hundred guests at II Meglio now, all
of them turned out in their grandest style to show their high social
standing and their regard for the Colonnas. The reception room rang
with conversation and the footmen and waiters passed busily through
the glorious throng.

Ragoczy moved to the side of the fireplace, out of the heat and
away from the drops of wax falling from the candles in the chandelier
above. From this vantage-point he could look over the crowd without
appearing to do so. He noticed that among the fifteen Cardinals attending the festivities there was an ill-concealed rancor just beneath
their veneer of politeness. The most acrimonious of all was Martin,
Cardinal Calaveria y Vacamonte, who openly rebuked one of his
fellow-Princes of the Church, making no apology for his conduct. The
startled guests waited for an escalation of their dispute, but the offended Cardinal chose to walk away, disappointing those hoping for
scandal. Deprived of sport, the guests moved away from the Spaniards. Ragoczy continued to watch as an angular young man in unflattering German finery approached Cardinal Calaveria y Vacamonte.
The Cardinal greeted the German with an affable display that was in
sharp contrast to his sister's response.

"That is the man you should be wary of," said Ettore Colonna in
Ragoczy's ear.

Ragoczy gave no sign of being startled. "Why do you say so?"

"That is Ahrent Rothofen," said Colonna. "He is the man you will
have to prevail against in your petition. Be wary of him, for he is a
hungry cur." He smiled with genuine amusement. "He is trying to
arrange a betrothal between the Cardinal's sister—you see her there
with him—and the brother of his patron, Archbishop Siegfried Walmund. The Cardinal and the Archbishop are for the match, but the
woman refuses, which is wise of her."

Ragoczy turned to his host. "Why do you say that?"

"Because Hubert Walmund is poxy," said Ettore Colonna with unusual bluntness.

"Ah." Ragoczy watched the Spanish family more closely. "And the gaudy young buck? What of him?"

"The Cardinal's brother? Ursellos is a wastrel, without any means but what his brother provides. You need not fear him unless he takes you in dislike. He is one of the wild set." Colonna gave a languid sigh. "What he would do without his brother to vouch for him, I cannot think."

"With so high an opinion of the family, I am surprised you have numbered them among your guests," said Ragoczy, more interested in Colonna's answer than he revealed.

"Men like Calaveria y Vacamonte are best kept under watch. I would rather have them here, where I can see them, than let them go unchecked and be forced to speculate on their dealings." He smoothed the front of his justaucorps, sensual as a cat. "It is foolish to think that they cannot be our implacable enemies simply because they exchange compliments with us. Calaveria y Vacamonte has thwarted Giancarlo at every turn. The Pope has spoken sharply to them both about it."

"One day you must tell me the cause of their dispute," Ragoczy said carefully. He suspected that his host was testing him so he chose his words carefully.

"True enough; this is no time to gossip of such matters when there is so much more to talk about. We have many rumors flying tonight. If you listen, you will hear them like themes in a concerto. The Pope has been ill, and at his age, all the Church is abuzz with tattling whenever he sneezes. When the weather is cold, half the Cardinals rush to the Lateran to keep vigil, and to promote their own chances." He pointed to an Austrian Cardinal. "He has been hard at work, trying to convince the other Cardinals that he can preserve the Church in the east, reclaiming lands from the Turks and the Orthodox."

"Will he succeed?" Ragoczy asked, knowing it was expected of him as one who had lost his holdings to Ottoman encroachment.

Colonna shrugged. "I doubt it."

"Too much opposition?" Ragoczy ventured.

"Too many Italians," said Colonna, chuckling. "We are in the Papal States and our allies are Italian. If the Church wants help in the east, she will elevate a Venezian, not someone who is surrounded by Protestants."

"If not the Austrian, what of Cardinal Calaveria y Vacamonte?" Ragoczy inquired. "Is the Spanish influence still strong enough to elect a Pope?"

Ettore Colonna nodded. "Very astute, Conte. Yes. He seeks to achieve for himself what Rodrigo Borja y Lara did."

"Would that be impossible?—if he became Italian by name?" Ragoczy recalled the powerful Spanish Pope Alessandro VI, who had Italicized his name to Borgia in order to make his way in Roman politics; corrupt as the man had been, Ragoczy still could not despise him, for it was Alessandro VI who had put an end to Savonarola's pillaging Fiorenza in the name of Christ almost two centuries ago.

"Not in these times," said Ettore Colonna. "It would be too blatant an indication of intent."

"What about your cousin, then?" Now that he understood his host's game, Ragoczy was truly curious.

"Too young. Giancarlo will have to wait awhile before he is considered." The scented, azure handkerchief Ettore Colonna dangled between his long fingers gave emphasis to the wave of his hand. "Innocenzo has been strong in his Poping, therefore most of the Cardinals have had firm alliances during his reign, to advance or hinder Innocenzo's work. Once he dies, those alliances will falter and dissolve. If the next Pope is equally forceful, then we might have a level of steadiness. But if the Cardinals elevate one of their number who is capricious or a poor leader, then everything will be thrown into disorder." He raised his thick, well-shaped brow. "It has happened before."

"So I understand," said Ragoczy, who had avoided Roma for centuries for just such reasons.

"There is also the question of the Protestants," added Ettore Colonna with a frankness that startled Ragoczy. "Little as the Cardinals say they are influenced by the Protestants, of course they are. They have much to consider in that regard, for it is hard enough to hold the Turk at bay—as I need not tell a Transylvanian—without having to contend with half of the German states as well." He sighed again. "When Innocenzo dies, there will be a scramble, and the rest of us will have to weather the storms the Cardinals, in their inspired wisdom, make."

Ragoczy studied Ettore Colonna for a moment. "Tell me," he began lightly, "do you not worry about what might be reported of you? You must be aware of those listening to you—do you make it a practice of saying provoking things?"

"Provoking things," Ettore Colonna repeated, savoring the words. "I have been saying such things since I was a boy and the despair of my tutors." He laughed, this time with underlying sadness. "I have seen for myself how the Papacy runs; perhaps I saw it too clearly, too young, before the pomp and glory overwhelmed me. There was a time that I feared the Church, but no longer." He studied the rings on his fingers. "Now I look upon the pageant without awe."

"Do you like playing with the . . . hosts at the Pope's Little House?" Ragoczy challenged, though he spoke genially enough.

"No. And I do not like to see anyone be invited there. It happened too often when I was younger and did not comprehend the purpose of the Inquisitors. I have learned my limits, and theirs. I am aware of as much as they are." He smiled with vulpine satisfaction. "You may mention what I have said to your Confessor. The Church is riddled with Colonnas: it will not harm me."

"If I do not, it could harm *me*," said Ragoczy, far more bluntly than good manners allowed.

"I doubt it, but speak of it if you will." Ettore Colonna bowed slightly, no indication of annoyance in his polished conduct. "Come, Ragoczy. You have heard far worse, I am certain of it. Defending the Carpathians from the Ottomites must have revealed heresy and apostasy and tergiversation at every turn, as you must have told your Confessor by now. A few worldly slights such as mine must be seem more amusing than dangerous."

"Pray God my Confessor will find it so," said Ragoczy, adding, "Those who listen report who hears as well as who has spoken."

"True enough," Ettore Colonna said, conceding the point. "And I should be a most egregious host to expose my guests to the tender mercies of the servants in the Pope's Little House. Your point is well-taken." He gestured gracefully. "Then perhaps you should come with me and spend a little time with Alessandro Scarlatti before his consort begins to play. Once the music begins, there will be no opportunity for conversation for perhaps two hours." He nodded to the cavernous door leading into a brightly lit hall beyond. "He is looking forward to knowing you."

"So he said in the letter your Signore Bruschi was good enough to bring to me," said Ragoczy, falling into step beside the tall Italian.

"He is an energetic man, Celestino Bruschi," said Ettore Colonna, then changed the subject. "I have asked Scarlatti to perform an aria by Monteverdi. It will come toward the end of the concert, so as not to offend him by putting Monteverdi before him. I know Monteverdi's work has gone out of fashion since he died, but I find it most appealing."

"An aria? He has brought a singer with him?" Ragoczy asked, recalling Scarlatti's boast about his new soprano.

"Yes. She will scandalize some of my guests, who still believe all soprano roles should be reserved for castrati. I, for one, can accept a castrato as a man, but not as a woman." He held up a cautioning finger, his handkerchief emphasizing the implied admonition. "Yes, Signore Conte, it pleases me to scandalize them. And they expect it of me. Half my guests would be vastly disappointed if I did not do something outrageous."

They had passed into the music hall, a high, vaulted room with a gallery along one side and tall windows along the other. At the far end of the room was a low platform where chairs and music stands were being set up for the musicians. Overhead five massive candelabra glowed, their shine echoed by tall mirrors set at regular intervals between sconces along the walls; small puddles of wax were already forming beneath the sconces and candelabra. The room lacked a fireplace and was uncomfortably cool, but neither Ettore Colonna nor Ragoczy mentioned this.

One of the musicians, properly dressed in black-and-white livery, emerged from a side room, part scores in his hands, and began to put them in place on the stands. When he finished, he took a long, thin strip of wood and lit it from one of the candle-sconces, then lit the music-stand candles. He turned and bowed to Ettore Colonna, reciting a few polite phrases before he withdrew.

"You are planning to have them begin shortly?" Ragoczy asked, and drew out his Dutch pocket-watch; it was nearly seven.

"In half an hour or so. While the musicians are playing my servants will lay out the buffet for supper." Ettore Colonna fingered his neat little beard.

Ragoczy looked about the music hall. "Will you bring chairs for your guests?"

"My servants will be putting them in place shortly. I do not like to leave them here to be smirched by wax any longer than necessary." He indicated the candelabra. "As you can see, they are something of a hazard."

"Truly." Ragoczy peered upward. "You have no cups to hold the wax under the candles?"

"I do, but they are not large enough." Colonna slapped his thigh through his justaucorps. "If they were large enough to hold all the wax, they would also block the light, so I must make do as best I can."

Another musician came from the side room; he was better dressed than the previous man, his dark, fashionably conservative clothes set off by the pristine white silk of his camisa. He was of moderate height, about thirty years of age, with regular features and kindly brown eyes. His neatly curled wig was powdered white, making his straight black brows more prominent. Catching sight of Ettore Colonna, he made a leg and smiled. "Signore Colonna. A great pleasure to see you."

"And you, Maestro," answered Ettore Colonna. "I cannot thank you enough for agreeing to play for my guests tonight."

"Che piacer'," he said. "But then, you are paying us very well." He glanced in Ragoczy's direction. "I do not believe I have the honor . . . ?"

"Signore Conte, may I present Maestro Scarlatti?" said Ettore Colonna. "Maestro, il Conte da San-Germain, Ferenc Ragoczy."

Scarlatti smiled broadly and made a profound leg. "A *very* great pleasure, Signore Conte. I have looked forward to meeting you since I first received your letter."

"Grazie," said Ragoczy, although it was not necessary that he thank the composer, nor that he return the leg, he did. "I, too, have anticipated this moment." In response to the inquisitive look Scarlatti shot him, he went on, "I have heard your music, Maestro, and I am most impressed by it."

Scarlatti made no effort to hide his gratification. "You are most kind, Signore Conte. I hope to deserve it."

"Certainly the Queen of Sweden is happy with your service to her Court," said Ragoczy. "Napoli fairly rings with your praises, thanks to her."

"I would not go so far as that," Ettore Colonna said, cutting off Ragoczy's appreciation.

"Nor would I," said Scarlatti promptly, taking his tone from Ettore Colonna. "For if you anticipate too much, what can I do but disappoint you?" He did not wait for an answer but addressed his patron. "Signore Colonna, I have taken the liberty of bringing the new violinist I mentioned in my letters with me! He shows talent and promises great things to come. He must play in public to improve. I trust you will not refuse him this chance."

"You mean you want him to play tonight?" Ettore Colonna asked, startled.

"Yes. He will not bring shame upon you, I promise you," Scarlatti said. "He may even cause a sensation."

Ragoczy saw the pleasure in Ettore Colonna's brown eyes and realized this was exactly what Scarlatti had intended. "Who is this marvel, if you will permit me to ask?"

"Ah, Signore Conte," Scarlatti declared. "You will be enchanted. He is a wizard on the violin. You cannot imagine how well Maurizio Reietto plays."

"An interesting name," said Ragoczy.

"The Sisters who raised him gave him the name. His mother was—" He stopped, looking directly at Ettore Colonna as he began again. "His mother was in a brothel. She entrusted her child to the Sisters. They gave him his surname because his father was a Moor, and his Christian name because he has woolly hair and a broad nose."

"Is it so obvious?" Colonna asked sharply. "That he is mulatto?"

"Yes," said Scarlatti. "But he plays like an angel."

"The violin is a demanding instrument," said Ragoczy, who played it, viola, lute, guitar, and keyboard instruments with the expertise of long, long practice.

"True. He has the gift of it," Scarlatti declared. "Once you hear him—" made a gesture implying capitulation.

Ettore Colonna grinned. "A half-Moorish lad from a Napoli brothel. Wonderful." He clapped Scarlatti on the shoulder. "By all means have your protégé play. I look forward to his performance more than you can possibly imagine."

"I thank you profoundly, Signore Colonna," said Scarlatti sincerely. "I did not think anyone but you would be willing to give the boy a chance. And I know that Maurizio will be grateful to you for all of his life."

"How old is this Maurizio?" Colonna asked. "You make it sound as if he is barely out of leading-strings."

"Sixteen, he believes. He has been playing since he was old enough to hold the instrument. The Sisters maintain their orphanage with concerts by their charges. He showed great talent very early." Scarlatti dared to smile a bit. "I first heard him four years ago, and I was astonished. I have purchased an Amati violin for him, to show his ability to the fullest."

"You purchased it?" Ragoczy asked, who owned two Amatis himself and knew them to be superior instruments. "For a sixteen-year-old musician?"

"He needed an instrument worthy of him. What else was I to do?" He looked from Ettore Colonna to Ragoczy and back again. "When you hear him you will understand."

"I am all agog," exclaimed Ettore Colonna, half in jest, half in earnest. "If he is a quarter of what you claim, his fortune is made."

Scarlatti inclined his head. "You will hear for yourselves: I have pledged it."

"So," Ettore Colonna said with relish, "we will have Signora Ferrugia *and* this Maurizio Reietto to perform tonight?" As Scarlatti nodded, Colonna beamed and clapped his hands for servants. "Wine! Bring us wine! We must celebrate this extraordinary evening. A toast to Maestro Scarlatti and his musicians!"

Two footman appeared almost before the echoes of Ettore Colonna's clapping died away. Both bore a tray with four goblets upon it, and both hurried up to Colonna to proffer their wine. One of the two frowned at the other, but the other stood his ground.

"An embarrassment of riches," Ettore Colonna cried as he reached for two goblets, holding one out to Ragoczy.

Ragoczy held up his hand as Scarlatti took a goblet for himself, "I thank you for your kindness, and I most assuredly wish every success to Maestro Scarlatti and you. But I do not drink wine."

Text of a declaration by Niklos Aulirios, submitted to the Magisterial Court of Roma.

Under pain of perjury, and with an oath before God for the salvation of my soul, I declare that the following items are true.

Item One: That I am Niklos Aulirios, native of Greece.

Item Two: That I was personal bondsman to the Roman noblewoman Atta Olivia Clemens, a widow, from the day she acquired my bond until the hour of her death in December of 1658, when the holocaust at Villa Vecchia exploded, collapsing one wing of the building upon her.

Item Three: That in her Will, she named me as her sole heir, as she lacked sons or nephews or cousins to whom she could bequeath her properties; no other blood relative was named in her Will for any purpose whatsoever.

Item Four: That, in accordance with her stated wishes recorded in her Will, I have striven to maintain her properties in the manner she wished.

Item Five: That I have not profited from the sale or other disposition of any of her lands or other goods, livestock, or chattel that would diminish the sum of her estates.

Item Six: That I have not sought to defraud any man of any inheritance legitimately made, nor do I do so now.

Item Seven: That I have authorized my late employer's blood relation, Ferenc Ragoczy, Conte da San-Germain, to represent my position in this test.

Item Eight: That Ferenc Ragoczy, Conte da San-Germain, although a blood relation of Atta Olivia Clemens, has made no claim and will make no claim on her estate, as testified to in the declaration appended to this one.

Item Nine: That I uphold my claim to the estate which was legally left to me; it is my contention that any claim upon this estate is the result of fraud and unworthy of consideration by the Magisterial Court, or any other legal body.

Item Ten: That I proclaim my rectitude in this, and I pray before Almighty God that the truth of my claim prevail.

Duly submitted
Niklos Aulirios
Witnessed by Padre Orlando Rastrello
Notary, Gesuita

Sworn to on the 2nd day of March, 1689, at Senza Pari, provincia di Roma, in the presence of Ferenc Ragoczy, Conte da San-Germain.

5

It was a perfect note: a pianissimo B-flat, pure and high, floating over the soft pizzicato of the strings. Giorgianna Ferrugia spun the note out, then cleanly dropped an octave-and-a-third, ending the song as the orchestra sobbed out a G-minor chord. There was a moment of silence and then applause filled the Santa Cecilia hall; she acknowledged it with a curtsy and a slight smile, then she walked off the stage, into the wings and Ragoczy's arms.

"They adore you," he whispered as he kissed her, her brocaded taffeta skirts rustling against the silk of his justaucorps; the brim of his hat cast their faces into shadow.

She lingered in their kiss, making the most of it, then stepped back as the applause grew more insistent. "They will want an encore," she said, tweaking the lace of her corsage, taking care not to shift her jeweled necklace.

"Then you must give them one," he said, relinquishing her to the demands of the crowd. "Or more, if it seems wise."

"I suppose so; Maestro Scarlatti and I have prepared three. I imagine we will do two at least," she sighed. She looked at him longingly, then turned back onto the stage, returning to the center where the light was brightest. She smiled at the audience in their finery, noticing two Cardinals among the attendees. "I will sing 'Gli Occhi Brilliant e Cari'," she announced, and nodded to Alessandro Scarlatti, who lifted his cane to give the downbeat to his musicians.

This was a livelier and showier piece, with runs and fioriature throughout its intricate melody. Giorgianna sang with verve, showing off the agility of her voice in leaps and roulades that delighted the audience. When it was finished, the ninety people were enthusiastic in their response. Under the shining candelabra that filled the hall with their brightness, Giorgianna could see that almost all were applauding. She glanced down at Scarlatti, saw his signal, and began, Scarlatti's own setting of the Milanese folk-tune, "La Civetta," which most of the audience knew, and with which one or two hummed along. Her flourishes in the third chorus silenced those the hall in rapt admiration. It was an easy finish to a triumphant evening, she thought as she again sallied toward the wings.

Ragoczy made her a profound leg as if she were nobly born and not the daughter of a sausage-maker from Assisi. "Brava, carina," he said to her.

Flattered as she was, she held out her arms to him, preferring passion to courtesy. "You need not. How gracious of you, when I have you to thank for this. If you had not hired the hall and paid Maestro Scarlatti and his musicians, there would be no—" She waved her hand in the direction of the stage where the sound of the applause was just beginning to die down.

"You discovered that?" he asked in mild surprise. "I wonder how."

"Maestro Scarlatti told me last night. He thought I knew." She wanted to sound accusing and failed utterly. "Why did you say nothing to me?"

"For such a trifle? It was hardly worth mentioning: a favor, carina, nothing more," he said as he went to embrace her, holding her tenderly as the treasure she was. He finally told her the one thing he had hoped he would not have to admit. "I did not want you to feel beholden to me."

"But can I not be grateful?" she asked, her head on his shoulder. She had a bewitching smile and knew how to use it.

"I would rather you not be," he said ruefully, "since it is unnecessary." He could sense her emotions: jubilation vied with desire, and satisfaction was tinged with burgeoning greed; it saddened him to realize their affaire would be even briefer than he had first anticipated. When he kissed her this time, his pleasure was no longer unalloyed.

She clung to him now, her hands on the heavy silver links of his jeweled collar where it lay on his shoulders. When she broke her hold on him, she was breathless and her color was heightened in her cheeks. "You are so good to me, Conte," she said, ducking her head as if this admission embarrassed her. "I do not know what I have done to deserve your many kindnesses."

"You needn't concern yourself," he said gently. "Do you want to take another bow?"

She listened to the applause, evaluating it. "No. They are beginning to leave, and they are now more interested in one another than in my singing."

"More fools they," said Ragoczy, touching the artlessly curling tendril of hair at her ear. "They can compare clothes and jewels at any time; you are a unique marvel."

"And you the most elegant of them all," she said, smiling her satisfaction. "Diamonds in your rings and rubies on the links of your collar with a pectoral of silver and black sapphire: silken clothing of a quality to equal the Pope's. No one can compare with you." She was only half a head shorter than he so she did not need to look up at him. "I know that when I am seen with you, no one can doubt I have arrived." She kissed him again, this time playfully. "Between you and Maestro Scarlatti, my future is made."

"If this is what you want, what can I be but delighted?" Ragoczy was not troubled by her directly voiced ambitions—such candor was usually impossible for Roman women since the time of the Caesars— and he admired her for it, as he had admired her deliberate pursuit of him since they met, three weeks ago. He had been amused at first, and then, when Scarlatti had told him that Giorgianna's pursuit was in earnest, he had allowed himself to succumb to her determined lures. A week ago he had sent her a diamond pin and asked if she would spend an evening with him, an offer she had accepted with alacrity.

"And I am thankful to you for offering to write songs for me, Conte," she went on, as if mindful of her lucky happenstance; just using his title made her exhilarated. "Maestro Scarlatti spoke well of you and your music. If he had not, I might not have realized your worth for months."

"Again, what can I be but delighted?" He had offered to compose a cycle of songs for her, based upon Carissimi's Cantata *Sciolto havean dall'alte Sponde*, a project that would serve his purposes as well as hers. He held out his arm to her so she could lay hers upon his, saying, "The musicians are leaving. We should probably do the same."

"No doubt; it is time for our tryst," she said, mimicking his tone. His slightly old-fashioned courtesy charmed her as much as his generosity did, and she strove to suit her tone to it. "Il Maestro will not expect me to linger?"

"Not tonight. It is late." Ragoczy understood her hesitation. "Whatever he wishes to discuss with you about your performance will wait until tomorrow."

"He should be happy," she said with naive certainty. Then she caught herself, as if she had overstepped. She touched the necklace of topazes set in gold which he had given her shortly before the evening's performance began. "These brought me luck, I think."

"Then continue to wear them, by all means. You honor them." His smile was brief but satisfied her; too often men did not want their gifts displayed publicly for fear of damaging their reputations.

"You are too good to me, Conte," she murmured provocatively, making a promise of things to come by the caressing tone she used.

He glanced at her as he swung his triple-caped cloak around his shoulders and then opened the door. "Do you think so." They went out the side-door of the Santa Cecilia hall where Ragoczy's coach was waiting, the four matched greys fretting in harness. The footman at the side of the carriage opened the door and let down the steps, assisting Giorgianna to climb inside. He moved back a pace as Ragoczy entered the coach, then put up the steps and closed the door with Ragoczy's eclipse device emblazoned upon it, before climbing onto the back of the vehicle. It was a cold night and Ragoczy had permitted him to wear a woollen cloak over his livery, a concession that earned him the footman's whispered blessing, for it was not often men of high birth were willing to acquiesce in such matters.

"It will take some time to get beyond these streets with so many other carriages; fortunately we are in no hurry," said Ragoczy as he settled back against the tooled-leather squabs, facing backward in order to look directly at Giorgianna; the light from the small candle-lamps shone on her face. He rapped sharply on the ceiling of the coach; the horses were given the office and they began to move slowly into the tangle of coaches, sedan chairs, mounted riders, and a few dandies on foot with lackeys carrying lanthorns, all gathered in the Piazza Santa Cecilia in le Rovine where the new hall stood at right angles to the old church.

They had got just beyond the piazza when Giorgianna yawned suddenly. Blinking in surprise, she said, "I am sorry, Conte. I did not mean to. I don't know why I did." Her cheeks reddened at this lapse.

"Never mind," said Ragoczy. "You have worked very hard this evening. Now that you need no longer perform, you are weary, though you have not yet released the excitement of your performance." He leaned forward and laid his small hand on hers. "Do not be distressed on my account, I pray you."

She summoned up a smile. "I am not tired at all," she declared, and had to bite the insides of her cheeks to keep from yawning again. As it was her eyes watered and she shivered a bit.

He brought her hand to his lips and kissed it. "You need not dissemble, carina. All performers know the exhaustion good work brings." He had known it many times himself in the past. "You have no reason to be ashamed. Rest. There will be time enough to wake you later."

"You indulge me, Conte," she said contentedly. "I am—"

"—grateful; so you have told me," he finished for her.

"I have known so few men who would not demand from me now as much and more than I gave in performance," she persisted, determined to say awake.

"Carina Giorgianna, I thought we had settled that I am not like other men." His reminder was given lightly but there was purpose in his dark eyes. He released her hand and leaned back, then astonished her by reaching up and removing his hat and wig in one easy motion. Laying them on the seat beside him, he said, "I am going to be comfortable; you need not hesitate—"

"If you think I am going to unlace in a moving coach, you are mistaken," she said sharply. "What if we should have an accident or were forced to alight? What then?"

He held up his hand to indicate he was convinced. "I want you to be comfortable, carina. If remaining laced makes you so, then, va bene."

Giorgianna was not mollified. "You are capricious, Conte, too capricious. I do not know where your whims may end." She took hold of her skirts and gave them a shake to spread them over the whole of her seat. "There. That is better," she announced.

"And it makes it impossible for me to sit beside you," he pointed out, a sardonic inflection to his remark. "It is a most attractive barrier, but you do not need it. I will not impose myself on you; I have promised you from the first."

She shot him a frown of disbelief. "Men always tell women that, and we, poor creatures that we are, we believe you out of our hopes, not out of anything we have seen."

"I will not argue that point with you," he said, calm as she was agitated.

"You will one day tire of me," she told him defiantly.

"I rather think it is *you* who may tire of *me*," he said gently.

"And when you do, I will be alone in a harsh world again." She folded her arms, the ruched silk of her inner sleeves falling back to reveal her forearms; she was being deliberately provoking, and she sensed he was aware of it, a perception that confused her, for it kept her from feeling as sorry for herself as she intended to feel.

"I have settled one hundred golden sceptres on you against that day. Soon or late, when it comes, that day will be of your choosing. The order has no limitations on you. You saw me sign the order." He did not raise his voice or make any gesture that could be thought threatening, but something inexplicable in his demeanor impressed her and she abandoned her posture at once. "No doubt you have been ill-used in the past, and may be so again, but, Giorgianna, it will not be by me."

She considered him, wishing she had more light than the single candle to see him by, and troubled that he continued to be such an enigma to her. He had given her a promise of settlement when he had first sought to make her his mistress, only a week ago. "You could rescind your order; the Magistrates' Court would not enforce it if you abjured it," she said, beginning to sound more frightened than defiant.

"You will have to take me at my Word that I will not," he said.

She half expected him to chide her for foolishness or to demand that she cease to accuse him. When he did neither, she hesitated before going on. "What if I should have your child? You do not make provisions for any child in your order."

His smile was quick and disconcerting. "Have I done anything that would get you with child?"

She thought a moment and shook her head. "No." That still bothered her—his insistence that his fulfillment came only through hers. That he had not been as other men had pleased her at first: now it was beginning to alarm her.

"I told you that I would not. But"—he held up his hand to keep her from interrupting—"if I ever do use you in any way that could allow you to conceive, I will settle ample funds on you for your maintenance."

"Will you? Or do you say so just to quiet me?" She was trembling, afraid she would forget herself, frightened that she would let slip some word about the daughter she had borne nearly seven years ago, who was now being raised by nuns in Umbria to whom Giorgianna sent money every year; her daughter's father had washed his hands of them when their child was born. It was the most stringent, painful secret Giorgianna had ever had to keep in her twenty-two years.

"I shall give you another order, if you like, one that would grant support to any child you have by me. When we reach the Villa Vecchia I will summon the notary if you want it tonight. If morning is time enough, I will attend to it immediately after dawn." Darkness did not hinder his vision as it did hers; he saw the tears in her eyes. "I have no wish to distress you, carina."

"I know," she said. Her tears spilled over but she would not let herself sob.

"But you are not willing to trust me," he said sadly. He was quiet while she composed herself. "Would you rather I give you gold instead of an order? Would that suit you?"

She tried to make out his features once again, and could not. "Would you be willing to do that?" Involuntarily she touched the necklace he had given her for it seemed suddenly heavier.

"Yes, of course." He could sense her relief. "It's settled, then. When we reach my villa, I will prepare a strongbox for you which you may take with you in the morning. We will not bother with orders." He had more than enough gold to give her triple the sum he had promised without having to make more.

"You will not change your mind? Or denounce me as a thief?" she asked, her voice rising.

"No." He sighed. "I wish you could believe me."

"And I," she admitted in a small voice.

The coach slowed as they neared the city gates where a sleepy watchman asked the coachman where they had been and where they were bound.

"Villa Vecchia, out to the north-east," said the coachman. "This is the coach of il Conte da San-Germain." He used the long handle of his whip to indicate the heraldic device on the door. "From Hungarian territories."

"You are not known to me," said the watchman, peering up at the coachman.

"I was engaged two days ago," said the coachman. "Amerigo Scarto."

"I will record your name in our register, and the coach," said the watchman as he accepted the toll required of all vehicles leaving Roma between sunset and midnight, then raised the barrier to permit the carriage to go on its way; inside, the passengers said nothing as this ritual was completed. The coachman whistled his team to a trot and set them on the broad road home.

"You see," Giorgianna said several minutes later as if they had been conversing all along, "I know it is easy for a man to promise anything if he wants a woman; when the need is on him, he will pledge the moon if it will achieve his ends. And it is easy for us to agree, with such sweet promises in accord with our desires. But when passion is spent, then the promises are forgot and the pleasure is gone."

"That is why I am offering to give you the gold you want tonight," he said, no trace of irritation in his words, "before we go to my apartments, so that you may be sure that I will not refuse you. You will not have to worry if I am going to keep my Word, for the money will be in your hands."

She bit her lower lip. "I appreciate this, of course. And I thank you. But it is not seemly, speaking so candidly about . . . payment." The chagrin in her voice was eloquent.

"Ah," said Ragoczy. "You do not want to be thought mercenary." He reached out and took her hand. "Carina, I think none the less of you for your apprehension."

She started to pull her hand away. "You are too fastidious to want to talk about this, surely. A man of your position must not—" she objected, not wanting him to feel how much her hand was shaking.

He would not release her. "Listen to me, Giorgianna. Please." He waited as the carriage swung off the main road to the one looping to the north-east. The horses were pulled into a walk, for the ruts here were deeper and the coach swayed as it went. "You have few reasons to have faith in anything I say to you, but let me say it anyway. I am willing to pay you in gold now, against the time we are no longer lovers. I have no objection to this. I am not displeased that you make such a request of me, carina. I do not think the less of you for seeking to secure what I have promised now. I do not think the less of you because you tell me other men have not honored their promises to you. Those of my blood are not jealous."

She was determined not to cry again; she swallowed hard twice before she was sure she would not. "I . . . I have not . . . I do not . . ."

"Since marriage is not likely to be offered to you, as you told me when you first accepted my invitation, you must ask for what wives receive in the course of contracts, upheld by the Magistrates' Court and the Church. Very sensible." He had not intended to be so blunt, but he now thought it was necessary. "If you were nobly born, I would discuss these matters with your father or brother or uncle, and you could pretend no money changed hands, as many women do. In your circumstances you cannot put such matters aside simply because you must negotiate on your own."

Scarto began shouting to his team, trying to avoid the muddiest part of the road. The carriage rocked on its leather springs like a ship in a high swell.

As much to steady herself as to show affection, Giorgianna reached out and took hold of Ragoczy's shoulder. "You don't have to . . ." The movement of the carriage impelled her forward, into his embrace. For an instant their knees were tangled, then he shifted and he could put his arms around her without impediment. She waited for him to use kisses to silence her, to fumble with the lacings of her clothes.

He held her tenderly but without urgency. "Once this is settled we may be at ease." He did not kiss her.

She shook her head. "I do not understand you, Conte."

He nodded, saying nothing for a short while. "You will want supper when we arrive?"

She was pleased he did not mention gold again. "Oh, yes. I am famished." Not only was it what he wanted to hear, it was true—she was very hungry.

"Then you shall have the best my cook can supply." He smiled at her and eased her back in her seat before leaning back in his. "Duck with plums and rice with pine nuts? Would that suit you? And some sweet cheese?"

Just the thought of it made her mouth water. "Wonderful. I look forward to it." Her spirits were no longer dejected. "How much longer until we arrive?"

"Not more than an hour, very likely less," said Ragoczy. "There is also some wine from Chianti. You may find it to your liking."

"There are many good wines from that region," she said, pleased that she had found something safe to discuss. "Although Maestro Scarlatti would not agree. He is fond of Lachrymi Christi nel Vesuvio."

"So I understand," said Ragoczy, knowing that she was deliberately trying to keep from mentioning the gold he had promised her. "You shall choose which you like."

"It is strange that a man who does not drink would keep so fine a cellar," Giorgianna observed as if this had only now come to her attention.

"I do not expect all my guests to share my tastes," Ragoczy said smoothly. "A good cellar is one of the marks of a gentleman, whether he indulges or not."

"So I have heard," she said, reassured by this safe discussion. If only Ragoczy would devote the rest of the evening to small-talk, she would finally be comfortable. She felt herself shivering again. "It is cold tonight."

"Winter is making its last assault. In a month or so, it will be spring." He smiled at her, genuine warmth in his dark eyes. "If you are cold, I can pull a fur lap-rug out of this seat."

She shook her head. "No, I don't think so. We will arrive shortly; you will just get the lap-rug out and the footman will be asking us to descend." The offer was another sign of his very excellent manners; few men were so gallant as to treat her well in private. "You are most hospitable, Conte. I am fully aware of it. I have not known many men who were as well-disposed to others as you are."

"You need not say so, carina," he replied. "I am pleased to serve you." He heard the coachman curse. "Best hold the hand-strap," he recommended. "We are about to go down the dip by the back of the Cameldolese monastery." That meant it was just a quarter of an hour to his villa.

She reached out for the strap and not a moment too soon, for the carriage lurched and the brakes shuddered as Scarto did his best to ease the vehicle down the incline. Shouting encouragement to his team, and trying to keep the coach from tipping over demanded all the coachman's concentration and strength, and he paid no attention to the peasant boy driving half a dozen goats toward the monastery until he was nearly on top of them. Then he pulled on the brake so that the wood howled, the carriage tossed, nearly righted itself, then fell heavily, leaving the horses to strain and whinny in panic as the weight of the carriage bore down on them. The coachman was bruised and his face bloody as he scrambled out of the driver's box and reached to open the door on the side of the coach that faced upward. "Eccellenza!" he shouted as he tugged on the door.

Ragoczy's response was calm. "We are all right. Perhaps a bit bruised. What of the team? Is the footman safe?" He looked over at Giorgianna, who lay tumbled against the window of the carriage. "Are you all right?" He blew out the lamp-candle, to prevent any possibility of fire.

She nodded. "Nothing to speak of. For God's sake, get us out of this, Conte." She looked about her in dismay. "What if we should be found like this?"

"I'll have to climb out," he told her. "Will that trouble you?"

"Lying here on the road is more troubling than—" She managed to bite back the recriminations that came too readily to her tongue.

Ragoczy gave her a swift glance of approval. "I will be as quick as I can."

"Put the carriage upright and you may take until morning," she said, an edge in her voice.

Ragoczy reached up and slapped the door. "Coachman. I'm coming out."

Scarto mustered his thoughts. "I'll help you directly—"

"Tend to the horses, man," Ragoczy told him. "I will get out on my own, and my companion can remain safely here for the moment. The footman?"

"I'll have a look," said Scarto, and stumped around to the rear of the coach where he found the footman sitting on the ground nursing a wrenched shoulder. He shouted to Ragoczy that the footman was hurt but not badly. Then he went to deal with the horses. By the time Ragoczy emerged from the coach, the team was no longer plunging in harness; the coachman had managed to call them to order and was contemplating the carriage. "I think one of the wheels is broken." If he thought it odd that Ragoczy no longer wore his wig and hat, he attributed their absence to the accident.

"The brake certainly is," said Ragoczy, showing no sign of ire. The cold wind had wisps of fog riding on it and lending the air a keenness that cut to the bone. "Well. We will have to leave the coach here for the night. I fear I must ask you to unhitch the team and ride to my villa to bring back the lighter carriage. You might also alert the household that we will be coming, but a bit later than expected." He regarded the coachman steadily. "We are depending on your good offices. Speak to my manservant, Rugerius. He'll know what to do." He laid his hand on the underside of the carriage, now facing to the west. "Are you willing to do this?"

"Of course," said Scarto. "But do you want me to take the whole team with me, or leave two of the horses with you?"

"Leave one, in case we have need of it," said Ragoczy. "The footman?"

"Behind there," the coachman said, waving in the direction of where he had left the footman. He began to unharness the horses, piling up the tack he would not need against the driver's box.

"I may try to right the coach while you're gone," Ragoczy called to the coachman. "I may be able work some leverage." He was deliberately vague as to how he would do this.

"It's hard work, Eccellenza," warned the coachman. He had the lead pair free and was working on the pair of wheelers. "If we had postilions, we might not have tipped over."

"Or we might have had more injuries," said Ragoczy as he went to the footman. "Your shoulder is pulled."

The man was white and his face shiny with sweat. "I fear so."

Ragoczy bent down. "If you will permit me—?" He began to feel the footman's shoulder, his small, strong fingers seeking out the damage. Superficial though his examination was, he could feel the bones at the top of the footman's shoulder were farther apart than they should have been. "You are in a great deal of pain."

The footman grunted, ashamed to make such an admission to his employer. If only he could keep his teeth from chattering.

Ragoczy removed his cloak and bent to wrap it around the footman, paying no heed to the man's whispered protestations as he eased him back against the sloping ground. "You are cold and the garment will only interfere with my working." He was more concerned for the abiding cold that had seized the footman; he knew from millennia of experience that such gripping gelidity was more dangerous than many injuries.

"Eccellenza, you mustn't—" the footman protested.

"But of course I must," said Ragoczy kindly. "Lie still and stay as warm as you can." As he straightened up, he saw Scarto vault up onto the off-leader's back, gather up and cut the reins to the mare's bridle, then tugged on the gathered reins of the other two to pony the horses with him; the remaining wheeler neighed and pulled against his harness, trying to follow his departing fellows. Ragoczy went to the horse and calmed it, freeing it from the tangles of harness before tying it to the coachman's box with the reins. "You can help me," he said as he made his way around to roof of the coach. "Giorgianna," he called, "I am going to try to right the carriage."

"By yourself?" She sounded so incredulous that Ragoczy almost laughed.

"I have a horse to help me," he answered as he bent to secure his hold on the side of the coach. "Take hold of the straps again, carina, if you would."

She said something pithy he did not quite hear, then said, "Very well. I'm ready."

Ragoczy signaled the horse to back up, knowing it would not do much more than drag the coach on its side unless he could use the impetus to raise it. Fortunately his compact body was much stronger than it looked, and in one emphatic effort the coach swung upward, coming to rest listing at a distinct angle.

From within the carriage Giorgianna squealed in relief and began to heap thanks on God, His Saints, and Ragoczy for sparing her any more embarrassment.

"I will help you down," he offered to Giorgianna, his tone remote as he stared at the broad leather spring nearest his hand.

"I think I prefer to remain inside," she said in sudden primness.

"No doubt," he said sympathetically. "But I fear I must insist. You see," he went on, his voice level, "the spring is about to break." He studied the clean, deep incision in the leather. "Someone has cut it more than halfway through."

Text of a letter from il Podesta Narcisso Lepidio della Rovere, Magistrate, to Ahrent Julius Rothofen. Presented under official seal by Magisterial courier.

To the most distinguished German gentleman of Archbishop Walmund's suite, Ahrent Julius Rothofen, the greetings of the Magisterial Court.

Loath as I am to mention such a problem as this one, I feel it is my duty to your master, Archbishop Walmund, to inform you of an unpleasant circumstance that has arisen in your petition: it has been brought to the attention of this Court that you have, among your bona fides, a Will imparting rights of inheritance to an illegitimate son that was apparently never recorded in the church where your records say it was. While I have no doubt as to your integrity in this affair, I feel you should be made aware of the questions that have arisen. This discrepancy provides your opponents with the means to call all your proofs into question, which is not what you would wish to have happen. If you are aware of some good reason why this Will is not recorded as you have declared it is, then I urge you to present this to the Court before the case is heard. You will need to produce sworn and notarized statements in regard to the lack of records, these from men—preferably Churchmen—whose testimony is beyond all reproof. These must be witnessed by well-reputed men, men of utter probity, and true copies put among the archives of the church where the records were said to be kept. Natural disasters often account for the loss of such records, as do wars. In either case, the sworn testimony of worthy men will suffice for my purposes.

I pray you will remind the Archbishop of my many sentiments of regard in which I hold him, and to what a high degree I esteem his calling. It is ever my wish to be of use to the Church, for what man of faith cannot be sincere without such aspiration?

To permit you to gather the testimony I have mentioned, I am postponing the presentation of the case until the second week of May. This should allow your factors to journey north and secure the testaments you will have to produce in order to be granted your inheritance. Let me impress upon you the urgency of this matter: should you be unable to do this, then I will be constrained to endorse the original Will of the late Atta Olivia Clemens, and permit her bondsman to retain her estates as stipulated in her Will. Should you require more time to secure such sworn statements, then I will be compelled to inform your opponents the reason for the second delay, and that might well work against your claim. Speed is of the utmost importance just now. Do not dally in your efforts, I implore you. Let me further urge you to keep the contents of this to yourself, for should others learn of it, some would claim I have given you an advantage to which you are not entitled in such an action as the one you have before my Court. Such misconstruction could prove adverse to your cause, and might impede my efforts to do right in your cause.

Extend my highest affirmations of respect to Archbishop Walmund, and inform him I am always ready to serve him in any way I can.

Believe me, Signore, your most devoted
Narcisso Lepidio della Rovere
Podesta
The Magisterial Court of Roma

By my own hand on the 29th day of March, 1689

6

When the light from the lanthorn struck her eyes, Leocadia winced. She lifted her hand as a shield. "Please," she said. "Turn it away."

Instead Martin, Cardinal Calaveria y Vacamonte, raised the lanthorn as he came into the open door. "Have you been praying?"

"And thinking," said Leocadia, sounding more defiant than cowed. "Alone in the dark there isn't much more to do, but wait for bread and water." She calculated she had been in this improvised cell for ten days, but was not entirely certain. "I am a penitent. In this place I can be nothing else."

He shook his head regretfully. "And you claim you want to be a nun. You complain of the dark and the simple fare after so little time, and still have the audacity to pretend you have a vocation?" He shoved himself a bit farther into the confines of the little room, his very presence seeming to rob it of air. "If this is beyond you, how can you profess a desire for the cloister? If your claim to a calling were true, you would welcome all that you endure, and you would seek more stringent means to show your humility." Drawing himself up, he said in an affronted way, "Surely you know your life would be more austere in a convent than anything I have required of you."

"If I were in the cloister, I would be beyond your reach," she said contumaciously, trying to match his manner. She was not as certain of this as she hoped; a Cardinal had powers second only to the Pope, and the Church was his fiefdom.

"Not in Roma, dear sister, not in Roma," said the Cardinal, watching Leocadia move away from him, trying to escape his presence. "No convent will accept you, should you try to join a Sisterhood. If any should dare to take you in, all the Sisters will be tried as heretics. I have put the convents on notice."

Leocadia did not want to believe him, but could not summon up the courage to say so; it was exactly the sort of thing Martin would do, she thought bitterly. The cell was so dark and so cold. Her clothes, she knew by touch, were filthy, and her hair was in complete disorder. She was chilled through and her whole body ached from the last beating her brother had administered three days ago. "You cannot want me to marry anyone with the pox," she said, trying not to weep.

"I do not want you to marry a man with the pox—I want you to marry the brother of the Archbishop of Oldenburg. It is lamentable that he should have the pox, but that is not the reason the match is a good one." He held up his lanthorn and moved a step nearer. "You will do my bidding, Leocadia."

"I can't," she protested, dreading what was coming. "You can keep me in the dark until I am blind, you can starve me to death, you can beat me until you kill me, but you cannot force me to marry a man with the pox. Even the Pope would support my refusal." She made herself face him though the light stung and dazzled her.

"If you were brazen enough to speak of such a thing to Sua Santita, he might." There was menace in every aspect of him, from the way he held his head to the abrupt way he thrust the lanthorn toward her. "But no sister of mine will be allowed to mention such disgusting things to him. You should know nothing of such things, and neither should the Pope. If you should try anything of the sort, I will be forced to reveal the witchery you work on me, and that will put you beyond all redemption. We Spaniards have not yet forgotten that working magic on virtuous men is still a crime in the Church. We are not afraid to burn those who are servants of evil." His wrath increased as his attack escalated.

This threat shook her to her heels. "My brother. You must not. You cannot." She crossed herself, her hands visibly shaking. "I swear it is not my doing. I would do nothing, nothing, nothing to cause you to—It must be some infernal spirit that claims us both—" She was unable to finish as his open hand slammed against her cheek.

"You are vile," he whispered. "You are the get of Satan Himself." He was breathing faster as the back of his hand struck the other side of her face; his rings left ruddy marks on her jaw. "Are you so lost to all your sins that you do not know when you are guilty?" His hand struck again twice with increasing force. "How can you suggest so appalling a thing? It is you—*you*—who brings depravity to me. You are spawn of devils!"

She could back up no farther, so she hunched down, trying to escape the blows. His hand bunched into a fist and slammed into her chest. With a single howl, she dropped to her knees, the air seeming to burn in her lungs as she strove for breath. As she steadied herself, she felt her skirts flung up and suddenly the weight of her brother was on her back and hips, so intrusive that she nearly fell.

"See how you degrade me!" he shouted in her ear as he plunged into her dry, resisting flesh three agonizing times before shuddering and collapsing upon her.

The burden bore her down and she lay under him, still struggling for air, crying from outrage and shame. She knew what was coming next, what always came next when he sated himself on her. "Martin. For the love of God—" She held up her hand imploring him to spare her any greater humiliation.

He shoved himself to his feet fumbling with his clothing and trying to steady his breath. Before she could persuade him not to, he lashed out, his foot thudding into her ribs. "Whore! Pernicious woman!" He kicked her again, then stepped back, smoothing his soutane and running his hands through his hair; his voice had gone up half an octave in pitch, and he wheezed as he went on, "You have tempted me again, haven't you? I come to admonish you to righteousness and you pervert my duty. You think I do not know your purpose? Leocadia? You suppose I am ignorant? All these years you have preyed upon me, and you think I do not know? You want to drag me down to your depths. But I will not be ruined by you. No." A third kick sent her sprawling onto her side. "You have disgraced me. I will not permit it."

"Then send me to a convent, where I may spend my days in repentance," she begged, pulling her knees toward her chest and crying miserably. Was it possible? she asked herself in a distant, numbed part of her mind. Had she, all unknowingly, caused him to attack her?

"No, No. You will marry as Eve married. You will be the handmaid of your husband." He loomed over her, disgust and odium making his features look like a mask from a play.

"No," she whispered. She could not look at him, for she had no doubt he was right: she lured him in some way so native to her that she did not comprehend it. "You must not punish me with such a husband. Isn't it enough that I bring shame to you?" So much sin had to be bred in the bone; she should despise herself for how she had brought her brother to the brink of damnation. "I never meant . . . I have no desire to . . ." Suddenly she vomited, and curled more tightly into herself out of abasement.

"You will marry who and when I say," her brother told her in a cold voice. "And you will remain here in the basement until you are contrite enough to make you receive your bridegroom with true submissiveness, not this cozening modesty." He gathered his clothes about him and swept out of the cell, pulling the door closed behind him.

The return of darkness was oddly welcome to Leocadia, who huddled on the floor, her arms wrapped around her body, an enormous ache blooming in her, a terrible flower that sent its odor through every particle of her being. "I can't," she whispered as she would pray, "I can't, I can't, I can't, I can't."

Much later—she supposed it must be well into the night, for the noise in the kitchens above her had subsided to nothing more than the occasional sound of a scullion making the rounds to be sure all the fires were banked—there was a sound outside her cell door, a soft sound, between a murmur and a purr. She ignored it at first, as if she thought it must be rats or more disgusting vermin. But when it became more persistent and audible, she recognized her name. This sent a new frisson of terror through her and she managed to struggle to her feet and shuffle to the door. "Go away," she said, quietly and distinctly.

"Are you all right?" came the soft voice on the other side of the door.

Ordinarily Leocadia paid little attention to her half-brother, for he was not only a bastard, he was known to be simple. But tonight was different. Just his voice jolted her and she had to steady herself against the door. "Jose Bruno," she whispered, hardly daring to hope for an answer.

"Leocadia," he said, as if overjoyed to listen to her speak. "You are cold?"

"Yes," she admitted, though she feared her brother Martin could hear every word and would punish her for talking to their unfortunate relative. She could not summon the courage to tell him to go away.

"And hungry, too?" He did not seem to be upset about this, and so she did not hesitate to answer.

"Yes." In a sudden rush of embarrassment, she remembered she had vomited earlier. What sort of disgusting creature was she that she would consider eating now, no matter how famished she was? She had been living on bread and water for as long as she had been confined to this basement cell, and the dreariness of her fare was offset by its infrequent appearance. "I am very hungry."

"Do you have shoes?" The question was so wholly unexpected that Jose Bruno had to repeat it before Leocadia could gather her thoughts.

"I have no proper shoes, only felt slippers," she replied, wondering what the young man meant by asking her such things.

"Then I will bring some," he said, not quite merrily, but with a jauntiness that alarmed Leocadia, who was beginning to think this was a very clever trap her brother had set for her.

"Thank you," she said sincerely, but remotely, as if she were an orphan promised a feast at the Mass of Christ.

"I'll be back when the house is asleep," said Jose Bruno.

"That's good of you," said Leocadia, who realized she would be grateful for his company. "But don't put yourself in danger for my sake."

"I am not in danger—you are," said Jose Bruno, his voice so low she had to strain to hear him. "Martin has been in a rage since he came to pray with you. Everyone is in uproar. In the third hour after midnight the whole house should be asleep. I'll come back then and get you out. If you stay here, he will kill you."

"At least it would be over," she whispered.

"I could not bear that to happen," he said, slightly louder. "If I do not do something to stop him, I will be as guilty as he. When he beats you to death." He managed to drop his voice again. "So I must get you out of here."

She could not believe this was possible, especially not for this dull-witted young man, but she was grateful that he would care. "I thank you for your efforts, Jose Bruno," she said quietly. "But you should not."

"If you stay, he'll beat you again, and again," Jose Bruno warned her. "Do you want that to happen?"

She shuddered at the thought, feeling sick. "No."

"Then be ready." There was a rush of excitement in his admonition. "I'll try to find some clothes for you, as well as food and shoes."

"All right," she said, beginning to be angry at him for giving her false hopes. "This is good of you."

"You aren't out yet. It will be good of me when you are," he said, the ghost of a chuckle in his voice. "Don't fall asleep, will you?"

"No. No, I won't," she promised, doubting he would return. She could not abandon all hope, though she knew it would be wise to do so, for another disappointment would further crush her spirit and make it increasingly difficult to resist Martin's demands; he already had cause enough to despise her, and would be grateful for any excuse to be rid of her in order to preserve himself from the sin she brought upon him. The enormity of what she had done to him bore in on her, filling her with self-loathing so intense that it sickened her. How could she commit such unspeakable sin and not know it? Had the Devil made her so blind to her own faults? She heard Jose Bruno's soft steps fade, and the blackness of her cell seemed vaster once he was gone. Feeling her way back to her heap of musty straw that served as her bed, she was nearly overcome with despair. Despite all her efforts, it had happened again. What was wrong with her? How did she behave, that Martin should be moved to use her so? Her long hours of prayer and meditation had brought her no revelation. Perhaps Martin was right and she was truly lost to grace. How could anyone as corrupt as she dare to plead for intercession? Jose Bruno was as good-hearted as he was simple, so his kindness was nothing more than the friendliness of a child. Yet no one else had shown any compassion for her, for detestable as she was, she could not deserve any. She was so alone! In her prayers even God refused to comfort her. Doubtless He, like her brother, found her despicable, beyond salvation and unworthy of the sacrifice of His Son. No wonder her prayers were ignored. She squatted down in the corner, rocking in misery, her whole being consumed with wretchedness.

The night deepened. Household sounds, rarely loud enough to penetrate Leocadia's cell, grew infrequent, then ceased. Slowly her rocking ceased and she fell onto her side, her knees drawn up to her chest, her arms around her legs in a belated effort at protection. She was in too much pain to sleep, but a kind of stupor claimed her. Now she was adrift in a dark, dream-like sea, with only her pain for company: and because it was all she had, she clung to it with a passion, making a consolation of anguish.

"Leocadia?" The voice was soft, so distant from her thoughts that she paid no attention until Jose Bruno declared, "Wake up. We haven't much time." He tapped on the door. "Leocadia."

She sat up, all her attention on the door. "Jose Bruno?"

"Yes," he said impatiently. "Hurry."

For a moment she was frozen with indecision. What if this was a trap and she was being tested? Might not her punishment be more severe than any she had known? But the very thought of release was too tantalizing for her to resist. "I'm coming," she whispered, and crawled to the door, no longer caring that her ribs ached and her jaw was bruised. She gathered her grimy skirts so she could get to her feet without difficulty.

The key grated in the lock as the wards opened. The hinges moaned softly, and a faint sliver of light shone in. "Hurry. I want to lock this and put the key back."

"But how will we get out?" Leocadia asked, remembering that the household doors were locked, making her escape only an arrival in a larger prison. Still, she squeezed out the door and stepped into the crate-and-casque-filled basement and at once was nearly overcome by terror at being out of her cell.

"There is a passage. It's part of the old foundations," said Jose Bruno. He held a candle in one hand and a heavy packet in the other and he was smiling. "I stumbled upon it months ago. It leads out past the old columns."

"A passage?" she repeated, making an effort not to raise her voice.

"It is a bit overgrown, but you can get through it," he said, so casually that she was astonished all over again.

"But . . . how did you . . ." She had an instant when she wondered if this were really Jose Bruno. Might he not be some devil come to claim her and lead her off to Hell for her many sins? How could Jose Bruno know of these things? Had she perhaps died and was now going to Judgment?

"The trouble is that I see most things skewed but I can see well enough to manage when I come close to them. Martin does not mind me going about the palazzo so long as I disturb no one." He chuckled, and it was a sound Leocadia had never heard from him—sarcastic and sad at once.

She stared at him, her eyes watering in the faint candlelight. "What are you saying?"

He shook his head. "There isn't time. We must go now, while everyone but the night porter is asleep." With that, he started away toward a stack of wine-barrels lying on their sides and piled almost to the ceiling. "Come with me."

Leocadia hung back. "Why are you doing this?"

"Because I can and because Martin does not know I can. When they find you gone, I will claim ignorance and no one will doubt me." His expression was almost as cynical as the one Ursellos wore, and it unnerved Leocadia to see Jose Bruno look so. "Hurry."

As if she had been struck, Leocadia nodded in obedience and prepared to follow her half-brother into the darkness that no longer frightened her. "We can hide here," she muttered as they made their way, crouched under the low ceiling.

"No. Come along," said Jose Bruno. He kept the candle raised so that they could see their way. Their shadows accompanied them, huge and bobbing, like monsters out of the Vision of San Antonio; chitterings and scuttlings in the gloom ahead made the association all the more certain. "You will have to duck down. The roots of trees have grown through."

Leocadia did as he ordered, feeling that she must be an automaton, moving by clockwork and not by will. Her feet were sore from stepping on pebbles and ancient, broken masonry, and she recalled his promise of shoes. "My slippers are wearing through." She said it timidly, half expecting Jose Bruno to beat her for complaining, or to return her to her cell as punishment for ingratitude.

"When we reach the other end, you may have shoes," said Jose Bruno. "It isn't much farther."

"But where are they?" To her disgust, tears rolled down her cheeks. To weep for shoes! She chided herself for such a want of purpose.

"In the sack I carry. And your penitent's gown. No one will notice you in that, and we are in Lent. Penitents are everywhere in Roma." He kept moving, forcing her to follow him to keep up with the light.

"That is clever," she said, thinking she had never understood anything about Jose Bruno until this night.

"The north-east gate opens before dawn for the farmers," Jose Bruno went on. "You can get out of the city there."

"But where will I go?" Now that she was getting out of the Cardinal's palazzo, the problems facing her seemed enormous, far worse than anything her brother had ever done to her. "What will become of me?"

"You had better leave Roma," said Jose Bruno. "The convents in the city will not take you in—Martin has seen to that; it was not an idle threat. But if you go north, toward Toscana, you will probably find an Order that will receive you. If you remain here, you will be forced into whoredom." He stopped and looked back at her. "Say you are on a pilgrimage, and don't admit you're Spanish, and you should do well enough."

"But—" She was once again filled with desolation.

"In penitent's clothes, you will be able to ask for food anywhere. Mendicants are not left to starve. Whores are." He held up an admonitory finger. "Stay away from the big churches. They will look for you in such places first."

"Do you mean they will hunt for me?" Leocadia demanded, nausea coursing through her. From a cell to the fate of a rabbit in the field. What did God want of her, that she was made to suffer so?

"You know Martin. He wants you to marry. Do you think he will allow you to slip through his fingers without complaint?" Jose Bruno resumed walking. "Think of how he has been behaved."

Leocadia trailed after him. "He is not . . ." She lost the sense of what she was saying; she was trying to imagine what her life would be like now, and for a hideous few heartbeats wondered if she should go back.

"Come. It is only a dozen steps more. Then you can change and I will go back and do what I can to delay the discovery of your disappearance." He relished the prospect. "How angry Martin will be."

"Yes," Leocadia whispered. "He will be furious."

"Furious," said Jose Bruno with abiding satisfaction. "And he will be embarrassed. Better still, Archbishop Walmund will be dissatisfied."

"Why does this make you so happy?" she asked, summoning up all the courage she could.

"It makes me happy. That is all you need to know." He pointed ahead to a slight lessening in the darkness. "See? You are nearly out."

"You aren't close to that," she said, growing apprehensive again. "Yet you see it."

"Light and dark are not the same as the shapes and details of things," he said patiently. "At half an arm's-length, the things become hopelessly skewed. Right now you appear to me very tall and long-faced, with a twist in your stance. I know this is not how you really look, but that is . . . not important." He motioned her to come a step closer. "You will have to change here. Do not worry. I will take your old clothes. Martin will never find them." He felt along the wall and found a small ledge where he set his candle. Then he reached into the packet he carried and lifted out the penitent's dress he had brought for her. "Here. Put this on. There are underhose in the sleeves. I will give you the shoes when you have gone halfway across the field here, so that no one can track you. Go on. I will step outside. Make haste. Leave the candle. I will fetch it on the way back. We do not have much time."

She made a gesture of consent, and watched him move out of the small glow of the candle. He might well watch her from the dark, the way Martin had done since she was a child. But this held no terrors for her. She skinned out of her old clothes, touching them with a distaste that surprised her. When they lay at her feet, she took a little time to inspect her bruises, the new ones purple, the old ones yellow and green, that mottled her body. Then, with a sigh, she leaned against the wall of the tunnel and slipped off her felt slippers so she could draw on her underhose, fixing each just below the knee with simple garters before she donned the slippers once again. That done, she pulled on her rusty-black penitent's gown; it hung shapeless as a miller's sack on her, the pleating at the shoulder making the body and sleeves voluminous, the high neck had a small, neat ruff— the only indication that she was a person of means and not a poor widow or orphan. She tugged the garment into place, then made her way out into the small field where fallen columns of long-vanished times lay amid the weeds and brambles. A pile of brush lay near the entrance to the tunnel, providing cover for its entrance. Some distance away a grand palazzo, still being built, loomed up against the fading night sky.

"You see?" Jose Bruno said, looking up. "Dawn is coming. You must be out the gate while the night-guard is still on duty." He took her by the elbow. "When we have crossed the field, I will give you your shoes and some food."

For Leocadia, her freedom still seemed wholly unreal. She felt light-headed and almost foolish, as if she were trusting a dream. "I am very hungry," she said, and yelped as she stubbed her toe on a broken capital. At once she hunkered down, her arm raised to protect her head from the blow she expected.

"Hush!" he ordered in an undervoice. "If we are discovered now, it will the worse for both of us."

This was certainly true; she did not need a second reminder. Ducking her head in mute apology, she hobbled after him. Only when they reached the limit of the field did she dare to speak again, in a whisper. "I don't want you to get into any trouble."

"I won't. I'm simple, remember?" Making a face that was pleasantly vacant, he held out the packet. "Your shoes are on top. The food is wrapped in a cloth. I couldn't get you much. And you will have to make it last until you are beyond the city walls; do not eat it all at once, or you will be hungry at mid-day. Try not to speak to anyone until you have covered seven leagues at least."

"Seven leagues?" she protested. "That will take most of the day."

He shrugged. "No doubt. But if you walk steadily, you should be able to go as many as nine, I daresay. You have little to carry, and the shoes I brought you are stout." His face was near enough for her to see the determination in his features. "You will need to find a place for the night. Try a barn or a stable. You do not want anyone seeing you if you can avoid it, not for a day and a night at least."

"But . . . I am tired," she said, afraid to tell him she was in pain.

"If you want to elude Martin, you will manage to do these things," said Jose Bruno, so purposefully that he reminded Leocadia of her oldest brother. The resemblance troubled her and she shook her head to rid herself of the image. "Leocadia," he went on, "I can help you only this far. From now on your fate is in your hands. I will pray for your safety and deliverance from our brother-Cardinal."

It was a feeble joke, but Leocadia obliged him by smiling. "And I will thank you in my prayers every morning and every night," she said, opening the packet and taking out her shoes. Now that she had them in her hands, she sensed the finality of the moment. "Jose Bruno," she said as she bent over to remove her tattered slippers and put on the shoes, "if I never see you again in this life, I will still hold you my dearest friend in all the world." It was difficult to say this, the words coming slowly.

"Find yourself a powerful husband and send for me," he recommended with a chuckle that convinced neither of them. Then he turned away and started back toward the tunnel entrance.

"Jose Bruno," she called after him, afraid now to be parted from him. "Don't go yet. Please."

But he continued walking, steadfastly refusing to answer her call. As he reached the tunnel entrance, he pulled the pile of brush up to the entrance, blocking it as he made his way back into the darkness.

Leocadia found she was weeping; she reminded herself her bruises were sore, and taking what consolation she could from this, she began her journey to the north-eastern gate and the road beyond the walls of Roma. The streets were nearly empty but for occasional servants and mendicants out on pre-dawn duties, and she made her way through the streets without attracting any attention. For the first time it struck her that she might never see the Eternal City again once she left it this morning. She was still trying to comprehend the significance of this when she informed the sleepy watchman that she was bound for the convent of San Chrysogonus at Aquileia, in the north.

Behind her, the first of the churchbells began to ring, heralding the brightening sky.

The watchman waved her through, muttering, *"Pax vobiscum,"* to her, because she was on a religious journey and the law required that all such pilgrims leave Roma with a blessing.

Text of a letter from Alessandro Scarlatti to Ferenc Ragoczy, Conte da San-Germain.

My greetings, Eccellenza, with the assurances that your scores have arrived in Napoli intact. I will bring them with me on my return in two weeks, when I trust I will have the pleasure of seeing you at the entertainment at Ettore Colonna's country villa.

I am particularly struck with the violin pieces you have been kind enough to compose for Maurizio; I have wanted him to play music other than mine, to hone his skills. Your work shows your understanding of the instrument, which is rare in a man of your position, if you will pardon my making such an observation. You do not compose like one of the dilettanti. I might almost suppose you have been a practicing musician, for your work is that of depth and artistry.

You cannot imagine how pleased I was to receive your commission for a little opera. I must suppose that Giorgianna is delighted. Not only is the money most welcome, to me, and to her, the text is a good one for Roma: Nero's Fire. *I look forward to your text, and I ask you to remember that Nerone's role must reflect the degeneracy that everyone associates with him. Monteverdi portrayed Nerone in other light in* L'Incoranazione di Poppea. *I do not think it would be suitable in these times to cast him in such an heroic mold. The Pope is inclined to view that time with a more critical eye than was the case when Monteverdi created his splendid work. With that caveat, I turn myself and my talents over to your services, and anticipate the day we may perform the opera.*

Since your villa is still being rebuilt, I wonder if it might be possible to arrange with your friend Aulirios to rehearse the opera at his villa? I have seen Senza Pari, and I know there is a reception hall of good size where the musicians can play and the singers may learn their movements for the stage. If you agree with me in this regard, will you add to your kindness by making such arrangements with Aulirios as may be appropriate for such usage? I imagine we shall have the beginning of our work ready for the first rehearsals at the end of summer. If the heat is not too oppressive, we may tentatively plan for the first days in September. With rehearsals and revisions of the work, we may present it in November. If you have some preference in regard to where you would like it to be premiered, you may want to consider that in how you prepare your text, for the stage often dictates the action as much as the reverse is true.

I look forward to seeing you once again, and until that happy day, I commend myself to your good opinion, and pray that God will look upon all your endeavors with favor.

Your most obedient to command,
Alessandro Scarlatti

At Napoli, the 7th day of April, 1689

7

A great rope of pearls hung over Ettore Colonna's open camisa, and he had rouged his cheeks; his perfume smelled strongly of roses, and his wig was a cascade of girlish ringlets. He lifted his wine-glass in an ironic toast. "To the Pope, who has done so much for us." Glancing over his shoulder at the gathering in the villa's grand salon, he said to the man standing beside him, "Not that I would be so cocksure in Roma. Here in the country, I can protect myself, and my friends."

Ferenc Ragoczy, dressed in subdued elegance, was conspicuously at odds with most of the guests; tonight he was in Hungarian clothing, his heavy black silken dolman and mente a reminder of his foreignness as much as his faint accent and his pectoral eclipse hanging from his ruby-studded silver collar. Although he was noticeably shorter than his host, he carried himself with the easy authority of one his equal in height. He regarded his host with concern as they stood walked a few steps out onto the terrace. Twilight glowed, anticipating the rising of the moon. "Do you think you are safe, even here, amico?"

"As long as my family does not disown me," said Ettore Colonna with a single, somber laugh. "The day they cast me out is the day I become a guest in the Pope's Little House."

"You say it without distress," Ragoczy pointed out, his expression revealing very little of his thoughts.

"Because I cannot bear to think it might happen," Ettore Colonna replied. "I know too well what becomes of those who venture into that place; I have had nightmares of it for most of my life. I am not so brave that I want to be of their number; I have no taste for martyrdom. And once accused, martyrdom is certain." He shook his head and swung around toward the villa. "There can be no release from that house, for that would mean a blunder has occurred. But how can that be? The Pope is incapable of error. Therefore once someone is denounced it follows that he is guilty, for otherwise the Pope has made a mistake, either in his judgment of a man or in his selection of his deputies, and neither is possible, so . . ." His heavy, arched brows rose and he drank the last of his wine.

"I do not fault you, Ettore, I only express concern. The Church has a very long arm, and many fingers to grasp with." Ragoczy indicated a fair young man in gorgeous women's clothes, his face white with paint and his elaborate wig perfectly combed, crimped, and curled who flirted with a courtier in a flowered blue justaucorps near the terrace doors. More than half the guests were masked, some in fanciful creations that were as beautiful as they were capricious; some were simple white masks covering the upper face such as the Venezians wore at Carnival. "You see how many seek anonymity, even here. If one of your guests should be taken, might not the rest of you suffer?"

"Because of the Church's three greatest sins?" Ettore Colonna asked cynically. "Simony, sodomy, and heresy. No matter what they say, little else matters. And my family has profited from all three."

"Succinct," said Ragoczy, "and the more dangerous for being accurate."

"Are you disagreeing with me?" Colonna challenged, expressing his indignation with a wink. He looked toward the far wall, lined with costly mirrors, and said, "You would think half of Roma were here."

Three young men, two in women's dress, all in elaborate masks and luxurious clothes, careened by them, laughing as they went.

"Not at all; I have nothing to disagree with," responded Ragoczy. "But you are at double risks with such a gathering as this, and with such sentiments."

"So might you be," Ettore Colonna pointed out. "You are here, and we are talking. Many would think that grounds for suspicion."

"True enough," Ragoczy agreed, with hard-won self-possession; his years in the prisons of the Inquisition in the New World were still fresh in his mind.

"Of course," he went on, "you are keeping that soprano—everyone knows it. That should gain you some protection, for with such a mistress, the worst you can be accused of is tolerance. Not that tolerance isn't a sign of heresy, according to Sua Santita." He clapped his hands for a waiter. "More wine. More for everyone." Then he cocked his head to Ragoczy. "Except for my friend, who does not drink wine."

"Grazie," said Ragoczy.

"You have nothing to thank me for," said his host, turning once again to look out into the balmy spring night. "It is a rare thing to find a man unlike us who is not revulsed by what we are." He laid his free hand on Ragoczy's shoulder. "You surprise me, and I am not often surprised."

Ragoczy studied Ettore Colonna's face for a brief moment. "I don't know why that should be," he said, though he knew well enough what Colonna meant. "We must, all of us, be true to our natures, or live a sham."

"Very true," said Ettore Colonna as his servant brought him another glass of wine. "Alas; if only my Confessor could see it that way." He smiled lopsidedly as he drank deeply. "Perhaps I should embrace the Ottomite faith and have all the youths I could desire."

"Others have," Ragoczy reminded him. "The Sultan would be proud of such a convert as you would be."

Ettore Colonna sighed. "It would come to that, wouldn't it?"

"That you would be displayed? Oh, yes; I think so. The Sultan would not be able to resist such a triumph. Of course you would not be able to drink wine or spirits, for your conversion would have to be exemplary." He had seen it happen when he was in the Carpathians, often for someone no more important than an army officer. To have the cousin of a Cardinal convert to the faith of the Prophet would result in fanfares and celebrations that would be as sumptuous as they were oppressive.

"Because I am a prize?" He laughed. "How my family would boggle at that."

"Perhaps. Some of them would be shocked, but most, I think, would be saddened. They have protected you thus far, haven't they." Ragoczy knew enough about the Colonnas to realize that such a defection would be a terrible blow to them. As much as they might deplore Ettore's tastes, they would never recover from his loss.

"Yes. I depend upon them to continue," he said archly. "As long as we Colonnas stand in good stead with the Lateran and the Curia, I am proof against the whispers. For which I am heartily grateful."

"They would be shamed to have you taken to the Pope's Little House," Ragoczy said, and watched Ettore Colonna flinch at this home truth.

"As would I," Ettore Colonna admitted. "So I must worry for my friends and pray my cousins do not run afoul of the Pope." He chuckled. "It may be foolhardy of me, but I cannot see myself anywhere but here, not when I think about it."

"I doubt it would please you to have to leave Roma," said Ragoczy lightly but with intentional severity.

"You're right about that. I've smelled camels. Vile creatures." He drank as if to clear his thoughts of the remembered odor. "And I cannot see myself in sand, but in the fancies of an idle hour, nor can I live without art or the stage. To have to exist as the Ottomites do, I think I would perish."

"It is a hard life for many of them. But then, it is a hard life for many Romans," Ragoczy observed, thinking of the beggars who daily huddled in the streets.

"Perhaps I should consider the New World. Though if it is as wild as my ancient cousin Gennaro says, then I doubt it would be to my taste, either. I have become very spoiled, I confess: if I cannot have pheasant and truffles and sweet wine and the paintings of Raphael, oh, and Scarlatti's music, I cannot bear to live." Ettore Colonna sighed in self-mockery. "So it would appear I am condemned to Roma."

The mention of Gennaro Colonna's name caught Ragoczy's attention, alarming him. "Regarding the New World, you should listen to your cousin, I suspect." This said, Ragoczy changed the subject. "When is your little ball going to begin? I know Scarlatti has his musicians in place."

"Shortly, very shortly, although why a man who does not dance would want to know, I can't imagine," said Ettore Colonna, and ambled back into the grand salon, motioning to Ragoczy to follow him. From the way he presented himself now he might not have a care in the world. "He tells me you have composed some airs for that new violinist. You are a man of many talents, it would appear."

"I am an exile. An exile has need of talents," Ragoczy replied.

"Like that alchemical workshop you have?" He did not wait for an answer but went on, "I know about that, and your efforts to build an automaton. Be careful you do not succeed, for no doubt someone in the Curia would find it heretical."

Ragoczy smiled wryly. "I am a long way from success. The clockwork alone is more complex than you can envision." He was relieved that the automaton was uppermost in the rumors about his alchemy; his real work—the making of jewels and medicaments—was disguised by this diversion.

"Just as well." Ettore Colonna had almost reached the platform where a consort of ten musicians sat. Maurizio Reietto was in the first chair of violins, his kinky auburn hair powdered white, in accordance with proper appearance for the consort. The other musicians followed the same fashion but for the one whose hair was already turning white. Ettore Colonna motioned to Alessandro Scarlatti, who sat in the alcove near the platform, a sheaf of scores in his hands. "We're about ready. You may begin as soon as I announce our start."

Scarlatti looked up. "Very good." He caught sight of Ragoczy. "Eccellenza. A great pleasure to see you at last."

"And you, Maestro," said Ragoczy, making a leg to the musician, a compliment that caught the attention of the musicians as well as Ettore Colonna.

"Oho!" he exclaimed. "You *do* have a high opinion of il Maestro."

"Only what is deserved," said Ragoczy steadily.

"No, no, Eccellenza. You do me *more* honor than I deserve," said Scarlatti, answering this courtesy with a formal bow.

"Nonsense," said Ragoczy, and stepped aside so that Ettore Colonna could proclaim the beginning of the dancing.

It was nearly an hour later that Scarlatti called a short halt to the music, sending his musicians off for refreshment, and went to fetch a glass of wine for himself. That done, he searched out Ferenc Ragoczy, who was seated in the gallery above the salon, where there were no mirrors. He began to bow only to have Ragoczy wave him to stop. "You had my letter?"

"In very good time," said Ragoczy, indicating the chair across from his own. "Prego. Sit down." He waited until Scarlatti was seated before continuing. "I appreciate your suggesting we work at Senza Pari. Signore Aulirios has consented to the arrangement you recommended. I thank you; we must all be very well-pleased." It had not been difficult to gain Niklos' permission, for such a project was welcome to him. Ragoczy regarded Scarlatti steadily. "Tell me, how long should this little opera be? I had thought no more than two hours, but that may be too short."

"Two hours is short," said Scarlatti. "The current fashion is closer to three, with two or three intervals, so that the audience may relieve themselves in whatever manner they like." He paused and went on as if the idea were new to him, "But if you would permit me to include a ballet within it, as the French do, then it could be a respectable length."

A sudden eruption of laughter from below caught their attention for a moment. A single voice rose above the hilarity, declaiming in exaggerated accents that he had just had a vision of God surrounded by the Saints in a celebration exactly like this one. "In Heaven, God's love is felt by all, and all glory in it according to how they are given to show grace."

"Would not a French form offend the Pope?" Ragoczy asked, anticipating the answer.

"Not if the Queen of Sweden sees it first," said Scarlatti with a quick smile. "I could have the ballet performed at Napoli for her, before your opera is premiered; she would not withhold her approval, I am confident of it. That would forestall any suggestion of offense to the Pope."

Ragoczy nodded. "I assume you have a ballet already composed and that you have been looking for an opportunity to present it." He saw the hesitation in Scarlatti's eyes and went on. "Oh, do not deny it. I am not slighted by such a ploy; in fact, I am inclined to think it is a very good strategy."

Scarlatti relaxed. "Very kind of you, Eccellenza."

"And prudent, too," said Ragoczy, a touch of irony in his dark eyes.

The noise from below abated as the dramatic visionary finished his outrageous recitation; a smattering of applause followed.

"I suppose you expect la Ferrugia to sing the Vestal Virgin you mentioned in the notes you sent me?" Scarlatti asked, doing his best to show his concern.

"If she is interested, I should think it would be a triumph for her." Ragoczy smiled at the composer. "You have the gift to make the role one that displays her strengths."

With a nod, Scarlatti said, "It is always a pleasure to compose for so talented a singer." He slapped his hand on his knee. "Very well. I will do that role for Giorgianna and you may supply the poetry for her. We are both devoted to her, in our own ways. She knows it and she will not take too much advantage of us. Between us we should create a showcase for her talents."

"And Nerone? What of that role?" Ragoczy had heard Nero sing on more than one occasion, and recalled that the young Emperor had not been without ability; his bass voice was well-trained but hollow in character, more booming than melodic. Ragoczy knew better than to suggest that the role be written for bass. "I suppose it must be a castrato?"

"What have you in mind?" Scarlatti asked, intrigued by the question. "What other voice will do?"

"Why not a tenor?" He said it nonchalantly in the hope that Scarlatti might consider the possibility.

"A tenor!" Scarlatti repeated, at first shocked and then less so as he weighed the notion in his mind. "It would create a sensation, wouldn't it?"

"Is that unwise?" Ragoczy asked. "Sensation could be an advantage. If it serves the work, why not a tenor?"

"That is a most . . . unconventional notion," said Scarlatti, his eye narrowing as he mentally tested the vocal potentials in the tenor voice. "It would be a startling idea. The sound is less heroic than the heights castrati achieve, but who knows? Nerone isn't supposed to be much of a hero, so that might be in our favor. Some of the Churchmen would like it—they do not like to see the Emperors of Rome portrayed unless they are shown to be ambitious and untrustworthy. Tenors will do for that. It may also be of dramatic value, the octave contrast in the voices." He looked into the middle distance. "Let me think about it, Eccellenza, and when next we meet, we may discuss this in greater depth."

"Sta bene," said Ragoczy. He rose to his feet, motioning to Scarlatti to remain seated. "You have been on your feet for some time and will be again. Take advantage of this respite for as long as you can." He went to the low railing of the gallery and looked down on the gaudy assembly. "How very startling they are."

"They intend to be," said Scarlatti, fidgeting in his chair. Gracious as Ragoczy was to allow him to remain seated he could not be comfortable going so much against convention. He stood up, saying, "I should go down to my consort. They will drink far too much if I do not keep them from it. Signore Colonna is always generous with his wine, even in the servants' rooms."

"As he himself has said, he has the grand manner, and the wealth to support it." Ragoczy gestured his permission for Scarlatti's leaving, but said, "Maurizio is a very good violinist when he is given a difficult piece, isn't he?"

Scarlatti stopped where he was. "You have hit upon it precisely, Eccellenza. When the work is demanding he puts his heart to it, but when it is not as engaging, he becomes sloppy. That Sarabande we performed—he was so lax that I wanted to take my stick and cuff him with it." He indicated the tall, thin cane which he used to sound the down-beats.

"Poor youngster," said Ragoczy, surprising Scarlatti. "He has so much to prove that he tries to make every piece a display of his skills."

"That may be so, but he has much to learn," said Scarlatti severely.

"As have we all." Ragoczy held up his hand. "In our little opera, write him some long legato passages, the kind that must be done on a single down-bow, and long enough that he must ration his bowing carefully. That should give him something to think about."

Scarlatti laughed once. "Yes, indeed. You are a canny one, Eccellenza, and no doubt about it."

"I would not have said so," Ragoczy remarked urbanely.

"Of course not," said Scarlatti. "The canny ones never do." He bowed shortly, retrieved his cane, and made his way to the stairs leading down into the grand salon.

From his vantage-place in the gallery, Ragoczy watched the musicians reassembling on the platform, shuffling with their music and tuning their instruments. He could see that the oboe d'amore player was bleary-eyed and slightly flushed with wine, and that the traverso flautist, who was older than the other musicians, was looking tired. The violinist seated behind Maurizio had attracted the attention of one of Ettore Colonna's guests and the musician was enjoying the flirtation. The second part of the evening promised to be more troublesome than the first.

And so it was: the guests were rowdier and the music more hectic, the playing becoming strident to cut through the din of conversation and laughter. Dancing quickly became a scramble, more for mock pursuits than Terpsichorean art. The candles in the chandeliers burned down so that the floor was soon slippery with wax, a development approved with hilarity even by those who slid upon it. The grand salon was uncomfortably warm except near the terrace doors where a chilly breeze drove the rollicking guests back into the center of the huge room. Ragoczy remained in the gallery for the greater part of an hour, descending only when the music stopped again and most of the guests hastened off to the supper room for a late-night buffet.

"Conte!" Ettore Colonna called out as he caught sight of his black-clad guest. "You gave me a start. I thought for a moment a priest had arrived." He was leaning on the arm of Celestino Bruschi, smiling at his own mistake.

"I apologize for alarming you," said Ragoczy drily. "From what I can see, your evening may be counted a success." He heard a clock sound the six chimes of midnight. "You will none of you be asleep before dawn."

"Yes—I think so, too," said Ettore Colonna with a kind of innocent pride. "At least no one is bored."

Celestino Bruschi laughed aloud at such an absurd notion.

"I should think not," said Ragoczy with a lift of one brow. "How could anyone be at such an entertainment." His compliment was sincere enough but it was tinged with an element of the isolation which overcame him from time to time.

"And yet," said Ettore Colonna, "I sense you are about to desert me and all these guests."

"You cannot go, Signor' Conte: it is too late," Bruschi seconded.

Ragoczy nodded. "It is as I told you when I came. I regret that I must return to my villa tonight. The workmen will be arriving before dawn and they will need my instructions for laying the foundation in the new wing." That this would mean putting down a cushion of his native earth he kept to himself.

"I suppose I need not remind you that you have a two-hour ride ahead of you? And that the roads are not wholly safe? Are you determined to go?" Unlike Bruschi, Ettore Colonna made no effort to dissuade his foreign guest from leaving. "If you decide to remain, you will be welcome."

"The road was as long coming here," Ragoczy reminded him, "and I have my sword and a pistol."

"Well, under the circumstances, I do perceive that you might prefer la Ferrugia to any bed partner you could find here tonight. I will resign myself." He disengaged from Bruschi and made a leg. "Then I must thank you for accepting my hospitality and for being good enough to make your way here for so short a stay."

Ragoczy made an answering leg. "What can I be but grateful for your invitation and the splendid evening you have provided?" He knew more fulsome praises were required of him if he were not to offend Ettore Colonna. "Your villa is beautiful; it is a pleasure to see it at last. The service your staff offers is above any fault. And the quality of the music exactly suits the most exquisite taste."

Ettore Colonna held up his hands in mock surrender. "Basta. Basta." He began to laugh. "All right. We must agree you have had a pleasant time and you admire Gran Segretto. I appreciate your courtesy, Signor' Conte. Many a Roman could learn politesse from you." He clapped his hands, and when a servant appeared, he said, "Send word to the stable to saddle Signore Ragoczy's horse and bring it round to the carriage-door." Then, as he dismissed the servant, he said, "Why did you ride? Surely it wasn't necessary. You have two fine carriages, don't you?"

"Yes. And had I come in one, I would have to contend with a coachman, a footman, and four horses late at night on the road. I might as well hire a herald to announce my presence and be done with it. I've already come to grief through such recklessness." He made no mention of the nearly severed spring, or his apprehension that another similar misfortune could befall him; he saw Ettore Colonna look mildly surprised. "I can make better time riding alone, don't you think? and be safer doing it."

"I'll concede that," said Ettore Colonna, and then glanced about to be certain they were not overheard, his long saturnine face becoming earnest. "The suit you'll present to the Magistrate?—it's Narcisso della Rovere, isn't it?"

"Yes," said Ragoczy, suddenly guarded in his manner. He paused in buckling on his sword, putting all his attention on Ettore Colonna.

"Celestino, give us a moment, will you?" Ettore Colonna waited until his companion had withdrawn, then he said, "You want to be careful of him. Narcisso della Rovere is known to favor Churchmen in all causes." He lifted his long, well-shaped hands to show how philosophical he was about it.

"There are no Churchmen to be helped in this case," Ragoczy pointed out, finishing with the belt-buckle and fingering the hilt of the sword to make sure it hung properly. He patted his deep pocket where he had already placed his pistol.

"The man making the claim is in Archbishop Walmund's suite," said Ettore Colonna. "The Magistrate surely knows this; you cannot think it will have no bearing upon him. He is a creature of the Church more than an enforcer of the law." He held up his index finger in warning. "Be careful. That is all I can say."

Ragoczy considered this. "I thank you for your concern, Signore Colonna. I had not factored that possibility into my plans." This was not entirely accurate, for he was well-aware that the Magisterial Courts were biased in the Church's favor, but he was grateful to have his apprehension confirmed.

"The della Roveres are as thick with the Church as we Colonnas are," Ettore Colonna declared. "And they have as much to protect as we have."

"I will bear this all in mind." He studied Ettore Colonna for a moment, scrutinizing him without apology. "Do you ever worry about how this could end?"

"For me? No. I know I am safe. But for some of the others, yes, I do. When Rufio Lampone left to go to England, I knew he was being wise. He was in danger not only from his academic work, but from our—ah—association. The Church was going to use the latter to condemn him to the flames." His expression was emotionless but there was something in his eyes that was disquieting. "He is Rufus Berry now, and teaches in Cambridge in England. From time to time I receive a letter from him, carried by one of our mutual friends, and I feel my loss afresh. I am grateful for his deliverance even as I miss him as I would miss my own eyes."

"This cannot be an easy life for you, amico mio." Ragoczy regarded him steadily.

"It is not easy for any of us," Ettore Colonna said bluntly. "In our own land we are as much foreigners as you."

"A pity," said Ragoczy. He made a point of looking about, taking in the sumptuous surroundings. "Still, you have the advantage of living well."

"Yes, indeed," said Ettore Colonna with relish. "If one must be imprisoned, at least the cell is pleasant and the jailers nearly invisible." He coughed. "And Cousin Gennaro makes a most inconspicuous chaperon."

At the reminder of that name, Ragoczy felt twinge of anxiety. "We did not see your cousin tonight, I think." He did not want to appear too inquisitive for he was not eager to meet Gennaro Colonna again.

"No. He is not comfortable with strangers; he does not see well and that adds to his sense of confusion when strangers are about. He is quite ancient and so steeped in goodness that it is assumed he will have a beneficial effect upon me by virtue of his presence." He shook his head. "Not that he wasn't a wild youth. There are tales in the family that he debauched a young woman of good family, which made it necessary to send him away. From what I have been told, he was shipped off to the New World in disgrace, and found salvation instead of his fortune there." He chuckled. "Perhaps the family still hopes that I will repent and follow my cousin's example."

Trying to show nothing more than courteous interest, Ragoczy said, "Quite a tale." He recalled his first meeting with Gennaro Colonna, and could not help but be curious about the old man this young reprobate had become.

"And all the better for being true." Ettore Colonna grinned humorlessly. "If I am reminded one more time that he owes it all to—" He stopped himself. "—a foreigner," he went on in another tone. "A Conde de San Germanno."

"My uncle," said Ragoczy quickly. He had decided on this history some weeks before so that the mendacity now came readily to his tongue.

"Got tired of fighting the Turks, did he?" Colonna shrugged. "Well, why not the New World? Did your uncle prosper there?"

"For a while," Ragoczy answered truthfully.

"My cousin says he was in Church prisons." He shook his head gravely. "That must have been terrible. My cousin lost track of him for a time, but apparently was able to help gain his release, or so he tells me." There was enough doubt in his voice to show he was uncertain that such a deliverance was possible.

"I don't know," said Ragoczy, keeping to the story he had made for himself.

"So." Any further discussion was forestalled by the arrival of the groom saying that Signore Ragoczy's horse was saddled and waiting at the carriage-door. Relieved not to have to delve into matters that were probably painful, Ettore Colonna sighed and made a leg. "Well, another time, Signor' Conte."

"I anticipate it with pleasure," he replied with more courtesy than truth.

"My guest's cloak and hat," Ettore Colonna commanded, and a lackey hurried off to do his bidding. "If you cannot be persuaded to remain the night, all I can do is wish you a safe journey and a speedy return."

Ragoczy continued the ceremony of leave-taking. "I am most grateful to you for a—"

"—for a most stimulating and entertaining evening. Yes, I know," said Ettore Colonna, cutting short the ritual. "Come again when you like; you will always be welcome here, although whether that is a kindness to you, I do not know."

"I will consider it an honor," said Ragoczy, standing still while the lackey draped his cloak around his shoulders and handed him his hat.

"Then I can only appreciate your kindness and pray you will never have cause to regret it." Ettore Colonna stepped back and waved, about to return to his guests when something else struck him, and he said, "Be careful what you tell your Confessor. He reports to the Curia."

"So I supposed," said Ragoczy, with a half-salute in acknowledgment. He turned on his heel and stepped out into the night where a groom was holding his mare's bridle. Ragoczy lifted the stirrup and checked the girth, tightening it one notch as he said, "She holds her breath." He had also been able to ascertain that no mischief had been done to the saddle.

"Many do," the groom said with the patience of long experience with horses.

Ragoczy vaulted into the saddle, fixed his feet in the stirrups, gathered up the reins, flipped a silver coin to the groom, then touched the mare's flank with his heel; she moved forward at a fast walk which turned to a trot on the broad, well-kept road that led up to Gran Segretto.

Soon the private drive reached the main road, still rutted from the mud of winter; Ragoczy was forced to pull the mare into a walk and let her pick her way over the uneven ground. She fretted at first, then settled down to a steady pace that covered the distance twice as swiftly as a man could walk. Ragoczy kept his seat and let the night fill him, restoring him and bringing ease to his complicated thoughts: the dangers around him seemed to multiply as he let his mind drift. How strange it felt to be riding to Roma with no Olivia to meet him. From the days of Nero she had been as bound to Roman earth as he was to Carpathian. He could not keep from missing her though he knew he was indulging himself, a luxury that vampires could not afford—memory was one thing, nostalgia was another. He had long ago learned the futility of yearning for what was past. Keeping his attention on his horse, he let the apprehensions that had risen during the evening fade as he made his way home.

Now Giorgianna claimed the center of his reverie; their affaire was going well, but he knew it would not last; neither of them wanted that, as Giorgianna had told him more than a week before. She was as delighted with his generosity as she was puzzled by his lovemaking, which she assumed was intended to keep her from becoming pregnant, a gallantry that pleased her only because he gave her such intense pleasure when they lay together. Currently she regarded his expression of passion as a courtesy, but the day would come when she would not be so understanding. When that happened, the small villa he had hired for her in Roma, and the jewels he lavished on her, and the lyrics he wrote for her, would not be sufficient to keep her from finding a more usual lover. "Probably just as well," he said aloud, and the mare angled her head to listen. He had tasted her blood three times, one more time would be safe still, but if he should do so a fifth or sixth time, Giorgianna would be at risk, which he was well-aware was no kindness.

Finally he reached the turning for the Villa Vecchia; the monks at the monastery were chanting, the sound spiraling on the air like an audible fragrance. Ragoczy checked his mare as she began to trot again, murmuring, "One accident on this road is enough, my girl." The mare whickered at the sound of his voice, and obeyed his hands.

The stable was largely complete, and Ragoczy turned his mare toward it, sensing her eagerness for her stall and a late meal. He passed under the hayloft and halted the mare in the wide aisle between the ranks of box-stalls. As he dismounted, he looked about in the vain hope that he might find a groom still awake. Unperturbed to discover he was alone, Ragoczy began to remove the mare's tack, starting with her breastplate and crupper, which he hung on a bracket for the groom to clean in the morning. He had stowed the saddle and its pad, brushed the mare down, cleaned her hooves, given her mane and tail a cursory brush, and had brought a halter to replace her bridle when he heard someone weeping. It was a plaintive, forlorn sound, hardly louder than a whisper. He stood very still, listening, and watching the mare's ears swivel to catch the sound. "Steady, girl; don't fidget," he breathed in his native tongue as he patted her neck. Carefully he removed the mare's bridle and put the halter on, then, with the bridle hung over his arm, he led the mare toward her stall— it was the only stall with an open door. As they neared it, the mare balked abruptly, stopping and bringing her head up.

"Yes, I thought so, too," said Ragoczy quietly but clearly.

The weeping stopped.

"Whoever you are in the stall, come out," Ragoczy said, his voice still low but with an undeniable authority in his tone. "I will not harm you." There was a rustling in the straw; the mare tried to back up but was held in place by Ragoczy's firm grip on the lead. "Pray don't make me come in and get you."

"Have pity," came the soft response. "Signore. Have pity." A hand took hold of the edge of the stall door and then a bedraggled figure tottered into sight, a rail-thin figure in an engulfing, smirched penitent's habit.

The mare stamped in alarm; Ragoczy tied her lead to a metal bracket next to the stall before he went to the woman in dusty penitent's garb who was clinging to the stall door. "What on earth?"

"Help me, Signore. I am so hungry," whispered the penitent.

"Please." Her grip began to fail her and she nearly slid down the wall.

Ragoczy went to hold her up. "Here." He swung her into his arms with an ease that would have astounded the woman had she been more alert. As it was she gave a little shriek and began to struggle. "No, no," Ragoczy soothed. "Be calm."

"Let me go!" she exclaimed in Spanish, trying to push away from him so frantically that he swung her down to her feet. As she did her best to stand upright her veil fell aside and Ragoczy saw her face.

"I know you," he said, looking past the bruises on her gaunt face. "I have seen you before."

This did not reassure her. "Alas no, Signore. I do not . . . You cannot know me. I am only a penitent, committed to expiating my sins before I answer to Christ." That had been enough to get bread at the monastery, and she did not want to reveal anything more.

"Nevertheless I know you," said Ragoczy, thinking back to the grand reception that Ettore and his Cardinal-cousin had given. "You are—"

"You do not know me." Leocadia put one hand up, pressing it to his mouth to silence him. "I am no one. I am nothing."

His curiosity ignited, Ragoczy studied her. "Very well, you are no one." He noticed the slight tremor in her hand, and the papery texture of her skin. "How long is it since you last ate, No One?" He knew now who she was and recalled he had heard rumors of her disappearance a few days since, rumors he had discounted at the time, for Cardinal Calaveria y Vacamonte had announced that Leocadia was visiting relatives in Barcelona.

"A day or two," she said evasively; in truth she had been to the monastery only twice since she fled the city and she could not summon the courage to return there, in case her brother had ordered a search made to find her. "Maybe three."

Ragoczy shook his head. "And perhaps four or five. You're weak with hunger." As she began to deny this, he interrupted her. "I know what it is to starve. You have the look of it."

She slumped, letting him support her for a short while. "If I may have some bread, I will be on my way."

"You need more than bread," Ragoczy informed her. "Here. Lean on the wall. As soon as I stall the mare, I will make sure you have a proper meal and a real bed to sleep in."

Much as she longed for these things, Leocadia stepped back. "I cannot . . . no. It would not be right to accept what you . . ."

Ragoczy went about tending to his mare, pleased that the stable-hand had left a measure of grain in the manger as Ragoczy had instructed him to do. "Good girl," he said to the mare as he removed the halter and checked her water barrel before closing her in for the night. Then he turned his attention to the Cardinal's sister who had been hiding in his stable. "Come. I will wake the cook."

"Oh, no. No, no. No one must know I am here," she whispered as if terrified of being overheard. "A little bread to eat, and I will be gone. Please, Signore. *Please.*"

Making up his mind, Ragoczy said, "We will discuss it when you have eaten."

She shrank back. "But—"

"I will prepare your food; do not worry. No one will see you," he said at his most compelling, all the while appreciating the irony that he, who had not eaten food in more than thirty-six centuries, was reckoned to be a tolerable cook.

She hung back. "No one will know," she insisted.

"If that is what you want," he told her, and led the way from the stable into the old kitchen of the Villa Vecchia.

Text of a letter from Archbishop Siegfried Walmund of Oldenburg to Podesta Narcisso della Rovere; delivered by personal messenger.

To the most respected Podesta Narcisso della Rovere, the blessings of God and the Archbishop Siegfried Walmund upon you;

My dear Magistrate, I approach you to ask a favor of you, one that I dare to hope you will be gracious enough to grant to me: if you would postpone the hearing of the suit of Ahrent Julius Rothofen and Niklos Aulirios until the middle of May, I would deem it a personal service, one that I will remember for as long as I am in Roma.

It has come to my attention that certain new proofs have been found that bear favorably on Rothofen's cause, but they are not yet in Roma, and it will be some time until they are. In these circum-

stances I ask you to consider granting a reasonable postponement. It is in your power to grant a respite, shall we call it, so that the papers may be brought to you for your consideration. If you wish to have the whole of Rothofen's claim before you, you will welcome this delay in the name of justice and the honor of the Magisterial Courts.

Do not suppose that I am unaware of the inconvenience this may impose upon you, for that is far from the case. Indeed, I have prayed long hours before charging my secretary with the task of writing to you, in the hope that such measures would not be necessary, for it is repugnant to me to intervene in matters not of the Church. Yet in spite of my reservations, I find it necessary to make this request so that you may, in all informed fairness, decide the matter. You must not want to err in your decision as it will have a far-reaching impact on many lives, therefore it will behoove you to authorize the delay in order to have the whole of the case before you.

I trust you will forgive my intrusion into the dealings of the Magisterial Court, and account my action that of one attempting to see justice done.

With the assurance of my continuing interest in this proceeding, and with the promise to remember your kindness to my associate, Ahrent Rothofen, I am

> *Your most devoted to command,*
> *Siegfried Walmund of Oldenburg*
> *Archbishop*

In Roma by the hand of Padre Giacomo Belorcio, on the 19th day of April, 1689

8

Another month!" Niklos Aulirios burst out as he flung down the notice from the Magisterial Courts. "I begin to think this will *never* be heard."

Ragoczy looked up from the score spread out on the trestle table at the far end of the reception hall at Senza Pari. "More delay?" He was preparing for the rehearsal scheduled to begin in an hour, and this outburst demanded an immediate response.

"Until the third week in May," Niklos said as he picked up the folded vellum and smoothed it out. "Podesta della Rovere has decided to wait for more evidence, or so his clerk tells me." He had switched from Italian to Byzantine Greek as a precaution against any eavesdroppers.

"Rothofen has been busy, it would seem," Ragoczy said quietly in the same language. He straightened up and stacked the score carefully. "What is the excuse this time?"

Niklos made an impatient gesture with his hand. "There is supposed to be a new proof of his claim in the north that will prove his case beyond all question. Podesta della Rovere has decided to grant him time enough to have it brought to Roma. For fairness' sake."

"A clever ruse, under the circumstances," Ragoczy said. "To claim that the father of Olivia's fictitious husband legitimized a bastard son and made him his heir is shaky enough, but to claim that takes precedence over the Will of her husband which left all to her beyond any reasonable claim."

"But, Conte, that so-called Will of Olivia's supposed husband is as false as any proof Rothofen may put forth," Niklos reminded him.

"No doubt. But that Will was accepted by the Roman Magisterial Courts decades ago," Ragoczy reminded him.

"That is one thing we may be thankful for," Niklos agreed. "There are many sitting Magistrates who would support that Will because it has been accepted. But della Rovere might not be such a one."

Ragoczy recalled Ettore Colonna's warning, that della Rovere was eager to please the Church, and so he said, "It may depend on where the request is originating. If Archbishop Walmund has interceded on Rothofen's behalf, it is probable that della Rovere will try to oblige him."

"That is what I feared," said Niklos, a frown setting into his handsome features. "Nothing I have can combat the favor of the Church, if it comes to that."

"And, sadly, it may," Ragoczy said, unable to console Niklos with half-truths. "We must prepare for that eventuality. I have a few schemes in mind that may suffice." He laid his small hand on the score and said, "If you are to prevail, we must be as conniving as Rothofen is, but without the appearance of it."

"So easily done," said Niklos without apology for his sarcasm.

"More easily than you might think." Ragoczy stood very still for a long moment, then strode energetically down the room, the heels of his soft-topped boots making a sharp report with each step. "You and I must not seem to be doing anything to counteract the work of Rothofen, for we might easily be dragged into conflict with the Archbishop, and that is something neither of us wants."

"I am listening," said Niklos, observing Ragoczy closely as he moved.

"I will need you to bring me some of the old parchments from Olivia's muniment room. Nothing essential, nothing that cannot be spared, but yet old enough that the age of the parchment is readily discerned." He switched back to Italian. "I want to examine some of the records, if they still exist, to show the manner in which this villa has been maintained over the years, and by whom."

"Of course," said Niklos, feeling baffled; he, too, spoke in Italian. "But for what reason?"

"Why, to establish that Olivia has kept the estates in accord with the traditions of their previous owners, and to show that you have honored their traditions." Ragoczy came back toward him. "After the rehearsal, give them to me and I will inspect them."

"Very good," said Niklos. He was about to leave the reception hall when Giorgianna Ferrugia appeared, her cheeks slightly flushed from the wine she had drunk at her mid-day meal. Her arrival startled him, and he bowed to her. "God give you good day, Signora." He used the more complimentary honorific, for although she was not married, she was accounted a woman of substance.

"And you, Signore," she said automatically; she was intent on Ragoczy, and she made no apology for her direct approach to him. "Conte, I have wanted to talk to you about the opera."

Ragoczy smiled at her. "What is it?" He came and kissed her hand, then lightly touched her lips with his own. "Does something bother you, carina?"

"Not *bothers* me, exactly," she said, wheedling charmingly. "But are you *sure* that Nerone should be a tenor?"

"Of course I am; and so is Maestro Scarlatti." He did not mention that it had taken several discussions to persuade the composer to write the role for a tenor. "Think how far above his voice your voice will soar. He will make declarations with fervor, but you will be beyond his reach."

She dimpled in elation, and with such open smugness that she made her ambition quite engaging. "Oh, yes. I hadn't thought of that. Yes, I will, won't I?"

"You will. And the tenor will sing close harmony with you in some passages and will support your melody line in others." It was a gross oversimplification, but it served its point. "You need not worry about being—"

"I am not worried now," she interrupted. "This will be exciting. A new work, and one you have given me." She beamed at him as if he were already her audience. "You are too good to me, Conte."

He made her a very gallant leg. "Impossible, carina."

She blushed prettily and achieved an adorable confusion. "I am left with nothing to say." This disarming admission over, she went on pragmatically, "I should warm up. Where is the clavichord?"

"In the antechamber. My servants will bring it in here shortly," said Niklos, nearly bowing to the statuesque young woman.

"I must practice my scales and intervals," Giorgianna said, and in a burst of grandeur sallied forth in search of the clavichord.

"She is . . . um . . . delightful," said Niklos. Then his expression sharpened. "Do you intend to remain with her for long?"

"My dear Niklos," said Ragoczy in the currently fashionable languorous drawl, "I would think that is for la Ferrugia to decide, not I."

Niklos shook his head. "You know what I mean. Do not bother with the pose." His tone was as near to acerbic as respect would permit.

In the antechamber there was a sound of an A-major chord, followed by an arpeggio up, scale down, played, then sung. Giorgianna's voice had not yet achieved the large, warm sound for which she was famous; that would require a quarter of an hour of exercise.

"How much you learned from Olivia," said Ragoczy.

"And what is your response?" Niklos pursued.

"Va bene. She is already searching for someone of higher rank and greater wealth than I possess," said Ragoczy calmly, with no trace of affectation. "This was understood between us from the beginning. In the meantime, I suit her purposes well enough, for I add to her consequence and her wealth, but she will soon accomplish her aspirations, I have no doubt."

"And no regret, either," said Niklos, his features shrewd as his thoughts.

"No. No regret."

The exercise was repeated a full step higher.

A commotion at the main door of the villa stopped their conversation, as Alfredo Cervetti appeared in the door, announcing that Maestro Scarlatti and his musicians had arrived.

"Good," said Niklos. "Show them in." He turned back to Ragoczy. "We will continue our talk later."

"Assuredly," Ragoczy said in the exaggerated manner of a dandy.

Giorgianna was now vocalizing the C-major scale, a little of her renowned vibrancy coming into her voice.

"All you lack is a lace handkerchief and a tall cane." Niklos flung up his hands in capitulation. "Tend to your music, then."

"As you wish," Ragoczy imperturbably; he made a leg and went back to the trestle table to examine the score again.

Alfredo Cervetti returned with Alessandro Scarlatti close behind him. "Maestro Scar—" he began, only to have the composer interrupt him.

"We are expected, man. Be good enough to stand aside." He indicated the fourteen men with him, including Maurizio Reietto, who looked about with open curiosity. All the musicians carried their stands as well as their instruments. "We are ready." He motioned to his consort to set up their stands in the center of the room. "Face the south. We will have better sound from that direction, I think."

He turned to Ragoczy. "It took four carriages to bring us all here. They have been sent to the stables. May we arrange for food for the coachmen and water for the horses?"

Niklos spoke up. "It will be my pleasure."

Ragoczy bowed to Niklos in perfect form. "Signore Aulirios, may I present Maestro Alessandro Scarlatti? Signore Aulirios is your host here, not I; in this villa, I am as much a guest as you, Maestro."

Scarlatti blinked, then recovered himself sufficiently to make a leg and say, "I am honored to meet you, Signore Aulirios, and I am grateful to you for allowing us to practice here."

"The pleasure is mine," said Niklos, as custom demanded. "I will order my servants to attend to your coachmen and see they have food and drink. I have ordered a buffet for your musicians to be served in two hours."

Giorgianna's vocal exercises had now reached F-major.

This magnanimous demonstration astonished Scarlatti, who took a long breath before he said, "Very good of you, Signore Aulirios. I know the consort will be grateful." He glanced at Ragoczy. "There are two more coming: Andrea Puntello and Tancredi Guisa will be here shortly."

The mention of these two famous singers made Niklos smile. "I will alert my staff. They will want to hear such splendid voices."

Scarlatti bowed to show an audience was fine with him. "This is only a first rehearsal; nothing polished about it."

"I will make sure they understand." Niklos used this as an excuse to leave his guests to their practice, only saying on the way out, "Alfredo, bring chairs for the musicians and have the clavichord brought into this room."

"At once," Alfredo Cervetti said, and hastened away to summon help.

"So, Maestro," said Ragoczy as he handed the score to Scarlatti, "what do you think? Will this place do?"

"Very well indeed," said Scarlatti with a short, approving nod.

Anything Ragoczy might have said was cut short by Giorgianna, who came sailing out of the antechamber, her lovely eyes brilliant with excitement. "Maestro! Isn't this wonderful?"

The musicians in her path moved aside for her, the viola da gamba player doing so with ill-grace. Maurizio shook his head in youthful incredulity that such excesses should be tolerated: women were troublesome, and no one knew this better than he.

"It is very fortunate that il Conte da San-Germain has such friends as Signore Aulirios," Scarlatti said, using Ragoczy's title for effect.

"Yes. Yes, it is," enthused Giorgianna. She was decked out in a grand jonquil taffeta battantes, with the outer skirt pulled back to reveal the deep flounces of her embroidered ivory petticoat; her loose, elbow-length sleeves revealed three tiers of lace-trimmed engageantes that reached her wrists. She wore a topaz lavalier and four gold rings with precious stones. The ensemble was more suited to a public performance than a first rehearsal, but no one mentioned it to Giorgianna. "I am beside myself, I am so happy."

"May you say the same in three hours," said Scarlatti. He motioned the servants bearing chairs to put them down where he wanted them. "We will begin shortly," he told Giorgianna. "When the clavichord is here, you may continue to practice."

Giorgianna nodded. "Who is to play the clavichord, Maestro? You?"

"No," said Ragoczy. "I will." He had arranged this with Scarlatti a few days before.

Maurizio, who had been shamelessly eavesdropping, exclaimed, "You?"

Ragoczy bowed to him. "Do not despair. I will strive to be a credit to the rest of you."

At this urbane response, Maurizio bristled. "I did not mean to insult you." He was about to say more, then thought better of it, seized a chair, and put it down at his music stand.

Scarlatti frowned at his musicians, some of whom were chuckling at this exchange. "We have other matters demanding our attention," he told them. "I will need a—" he began, addressing Alfredo Cervetti.

"You need a podium for your music. Yes. We have one that will do." He hurried off and returned quickly with another of the servants:

they carried between them an old lectern, one ornamented with carved eagles and the scales of justice.

"That is a very ancient piece," Scarlatti observed as it was set down in front of him.

Ragoczy recalled the last time he had seen it, on a day when German soldiers were rioting through the city, behaving more like pillaging conquerors than the saviors they claimed to be. That was more than a thousand years ago. "Rare work." He went into the next room to get a chair for the clavichord, and missed Scarlatti handing out the parts to his musicians. By the time he sat down at the keyboard, Scarlatti had opened his master score and was explaining about the opening bars.

"I want them largo, but not ponderous and not dragging," he said. "You strings, I do not want any scraping—just a clear attack, as if you were stops on an organ."

The five violinists exchanged uneasy glances. "Do you mean we are to begin—" Maurizio demonstrated a down-bow.

"Yes," Scarlatti approved. "Just like that. All of you." He next addressed the oboe da caccia. "When you begin the"—he sang out the melody, tapping the time on the lectern with his finger—"I want the same clean start."

The second viola da gamba player looked uneasily at his score. "How are we to be heard without the scraping?"

"Think of yourself as a chorus, blended voices," said Scarlatti. "Now, when we reach the andante, see that you play the pizzicato like whispers. It will let the flute warble like a nightingale. If you are too loud or too marcato, the effect will be ruined."

The second violinist held up his bow for attention. "For the repeat as well?"

"Yes," Scarlatti told them, an instruction that made the musicians glance among one another at this radical departure from style. "Think of yourselves as the wind in the trees; it will follow the sentiments of the text to come."

Maurizio's expression was eloquent of doubt, but he managed to say nothing; he flipped his part ahead and saw a twelve-measure stretch of double-bowing, the attack on the up-bow. He shook his head: more innovation.

Scarlatti continued to prepare the musicians for nearly a quarter of an hour by which time they were becoming restive. "All right. The Overture and the opening Cabaletta. Signora Ferrugia, if you please?" He indicated a place near the clavichord. "We will read it straight through without stopping; then we will discuss what you have done. We have no chorus, but that doesn't matter right now." He picked up his tall cane, lifted it and tapped it down four times to set the pace, then nodded to the consort to begin.

Ragoczy followed the parts provided for him, playing in strict accord with the down-beat Scarlatti sounded. The declamatory opening bars were startling, as Scarlatti intended them to be; the score read, *like the sounding of a lyre.* He was close enough to Giorgianna to see her readying herself to sing, concentrating with a dedication he knew was reserved only for music. The next passage began, the traverso flute plaintive above the plucked strings. Ragoczy provided an emphasis in bass, as the score intended. Then the Vestal Virgin began.

> *I, my soul given to Roma, fear for her*
> *Such things have I seen!*
> > *Such things have I seen!*
> *Great and mighty Giove, spare Roma*
> *From the horror of my dream!*
> > *From the horror of my dream!*

The plaint went on for another six lines of long legato suspensions followed by coloratura plunges. Then the pace picked up, and Giorgianna began to display the vocal ability which had gained her her glowing reputation. Ragoczy filled in the chorus notes on the clavichord as the Vestal Virgin described the fire that would bring fire and destruction upon them all.

"Very good," Scarlatti approved as he stopped the music. "For a first reading, I am very pleased." He turned the score back to the beginning. "Now, the pick-up in the third measure need not be so sharp. A bit more lento, if you will." He went on, measure by measure, discussing the manner in which he wanted the music played. He was nearly finished when Alfredo Cervetti came to announce the arrival of the last carriage.

"That would be Guisa and Puntello," said Scarlatti. "In buon punto. Bring them in."

The musicians made a pointed effort to show their annoyance at having to accommodate singers, but it was as much a ritual as any demonstration of real rivalry, for the tenor Guisa and the bass Puntello were both well-thought-of.

Niklos Aulirios himself escorted the two men to the reception hall, making a show of welcoming them to Senza Pari. "I am grateful to you for doing this villa the honor of hearing you sing."

Andrea Puntello, an ample-bodied man of about thirty-five dressed in the height of fashion including a magnificent wig of cascading russet curls, made a leg to his host. "On the contrary, Signore, it is you who honor us."

Although somewhat younger, leaner, and less extravagantly dressed, Tancredi Guisa had the same flamboyance of manner. Not to be outdone by his colleague, he also made a leg. "To permit us to practice this new work is a kindness indeed."

Scarlatti stopped this effusive flow with a calm observation: "Signori, it is not yet time for curtain-calls."

Guisa laughed and, after an instant, so did Puntello. "As you say, Maestro," Guisa responded for them both. "We must earn our keep." With that, he hastened over to Giorgianna, seized her hand and kissed it. "La Ferrugia!"

"Che bellezza!" Puntello exclaimed, and claimed her hand from Guisa. "What good fortune for us, to sing a new work with you."

Ragoczy watched this enthusiastic exchange with amusement; he had heard Giorgianna speak of these two colleagues in roundly condemning terms as well as affectionate ones, and that she was not impressed with their ebullient displays.

"Signori," said Scarlatti with exaggerated patience, "if it would not disturb you too much, may we resume?"

"Of a certainty," said Puntello, all magnanimity. "We will take out our parts and be prepared to sing."

"Tante grazie," said Scarlatti with mild sarcasm. He spoke to his consort next. "We will do it again, to the same point. And you, Puntello," he added, "you will sing next as the voice of Giove. Follow the music to learn your cues."

Puntello bowed in gracious acquiescence. "As you command, Maestro."

Again Scarlatti gave the four downbeats and the signal to begin. The playing was less tentative this time, and as Ragoczy filled in for the chorus, he earned a look of surprise from Tancredi Guisa.

When they had been working for just over two hours, Scarlatti called a break and sent his musicians off to the buffet Niklos had ordered laid out for them. He did not join them at once, preferring to have a word with Ragoczy before eating.

"The Overture is not long enough," he said to the foreigner. "It needs another sixteen measures at least."

"At least," Ragoczy agreed, "but in a less declamatory style."

"That would be wise," Scarlatti nodded. "Perhaps an arpeggio obligato in the bass would soften it, if I added a variation on the opening chords."

"You need not decide this instant," said Ragoczy.

"No; I will have time to think it through," said Scarlatti. "I should probably enlarge the duet between Giove and the Vestal Virgin. The Church would approve."

Ragoczy gestured his endorsement of the idea; he had considered the Church when he prepared the libretto, having the Vestal pray not to Vesta, as they had in Imperial Rome, but to Jupiter, whom the Church viewed as an acceptable pagan substitute for God in such entertainments. He asked, "Should I write another few lines for them?"

"Full of noble sentiments, if you will," Scarlatti said, smiling a little. "And if I may ask another favor of you?"

"Of course," said Ragoczy. "Tell me what you would like."

Scarlatti glanced toward the sound of conversation coming from the buffet. "Will you take Maurizio with you and make him practice? He has begun to realize how talented he is and has stopped being willing to practice. Nothing I can say to him convinces him that no matter what gifts God has bestowed on him, he still must practice." He shook his head. "I am about to despair of him."

"If he is willing to come, then certainly," said Ragoczy, wondering what Giorgianna would say to this plan; she was already displeased that he had provided separate quarters for the penitent woman—to have Maurizio in residence as well might aggravate her beyond her limits.

"Thank you, Signor' Conte. I am in your debt." Scarlatti put his hand over his heart to show his sincerity.

"I have done nothing yet," Ragoczy reminded him. "Speak to me when Maurizio has improved his habits, not before."

"Then I will thank you for being willing to undertake the task," said Scarlatti. "It would be a pity to see such ability fall short for lack of—" He broke off. "You have been very good to me and my musicians, Signor' Conte, and not only because of this opera."

"As you have been good to me," Ragoczy countered with genuine appreciation as well as social expectations. "You have allowed me to bring my libretto to you and you have set it to wonderful music."

Scarlatti held up his hand. "We have both made our contributions and now it is up to the consort and singers."

"Truly," Ragoczy agreed, glad to have the exchange of compliments at an end.

"And if you will excuse me, I will go and have a bite to eat before it is wolfed down," Scarlatti went on. "I will speak to Maurizio before we resume our practice."

"Excellent," said Ragoczy, and stepped back to show he was willing to relinquish his claim on Scarlatti's attention. Then he went back to the clavichord and sat down at it once again, his small hands stroking easy runs from the keys. Gradually he began to play, starting with fragments of melodies he had remembered from the past, and evolving them into a haunting suite. For a while he was held in thrall to the sounds, but then he abandoned his remembrances and turned his attention to what he would be playing that afternoon.

"It is a pleasure to hear those songs again," said Niklos from the anteroom door. "I had forgot that tune that Nicoris used to sing."

Ragoczy shook his head, banishing the image of that lovely, long-dead woman from his thoughts. "It was a captivating tune." He rose from the bench. "What is it? Has this rehearsal disrupted your household too much?"

"No; nothing of the sort," said Niklos. "For the first time in weeks they are in good humor. If I could have you here every day, I would be glad of it." He folded his arms. "These constant delays, and all to Rothofen's advantage, have weighed on all of us, I fear."

"That is hardly surprising," said Ragoczy.

Niklos sighed. "Truly. And it will give those who serve other masters something to report that does not cast me in an evil light."

Ragoczy's wry smile came and went swiftly. "It will have a similar benefit for me."

"Yes, of course," said Niklos; adding in Greek, "It will also give the appearance of unconcern, so that no one will believe that we are worried about the outcome of the suit."

"Precisely," said Ragoczy in the same language. "It will also make your opponent assume that we do not understand the gravity of the situation, which is also to our advantage. Let him underestimate us by all means."

Niklos frowned. "It is no pleasant thing to be thought a fool."

"Better a fool than an enemy," Ragoczy pointed out, and began playing again as the viola da gamba player wandered back into the reception hall; Ragoczy added in Italian, "So, my dear Aulirios, strange as Roman ways may be to Greeks, as you say, they have their uses."

"Surely a Transylvanian finds them strange from time to time?" Niklos took his tone from Ragoczy, punctuating his remark with an arch expression.

"Certainly, as I am to the Romans," Ragoczy replied, recalling his many visits to Roma over the centuries.

"So we are in accord," said Niklos, bowing. He turned to leave, but added as a parting shot, "I look forward to your rehearsals more than I can say."

By the time Scarlatti called his consort and singers to order again, most of the servants at Senza Pari were gathered around the reception hall in avid anticipation of a glorious afternoon. The composer took advantage of this impromptu audience, saying, "You have listeners. Do not give them cause to regret they are here." As he tapped out his first downbeats, he wondered why Ragoczy seemed to be silently laughing.

✵   ✵   ✵

Text of a letter from Bonaldo Fiumara to Ferenc Ragoczy at Villa Vecchia.

To the reverend Abbe, Ferenc Ragoczy, Conte da San-Germain, the greetings of your builder, Bonaldo Fiumara, with the assurance that what follows is a full and accurate account of our accomplishments to date, and the further certainty that the schedule proposed may be maintained if nothing untoward interrupts our efforts on your behalf.

The removal of the ruined portion of the Villa Vecchia has been completed, as you are no doubt aware. Such stones as we have been able to salvage have been put into use in the new structure, in accordance with your stated instructions. Those which were beyond restoration have been turned over to the Console Artei, as you provided for in our discussions. All payments agreed upon for this work have been made, and bonuses provided for all those engaged in readying the site for new construction.

For purposes of speeding up the new building, one mule-team and muleteer have been kept on at the same rate: fifteen golden scudi for the muleteer, twenty golden scudi plus food and stalls for the mules per week, with the same provision for half-pay in case of bad weather.

The new structure foundation has been laid and finished in accordance with your instructions, complete with the layer of earth you stipulated be spread; as you must be aware, the first skeleton of the villa is now standing. Your willingness to take on a half dozen more workers has enabled us to finish the work stipulated in less time than was our initial estimate of time needed, which prudent decision ensures the continuing efforts of all the workers. The payment for this clearing and preparation has been received, along with the thirty golden scudi for the next stage in construction, which will commence within the month. The bonuses provided to the workers in recognition of their efforts are much appreciated, and I relay to you their expressions of gratitude.

Payment for injury has been received in a timely fashion for Vitale Inizia and Mario Dritto; the care given to the latter by you, Eccellenza, must surely have saved his arm, and he is returning half of his injury pay in acknowledgment of your prompt action, which has doubtless preserved his arm and his livelihood; the Arte also expresses its appreciation for your timely efforts to minister to his injuries, in recognition of which they have sent an account of your care to the Console Artei for the purpose of giving official approval of your generous act.

New workers will be needed for this stage of the building, and with that eventuality in mind, I will outline the terms of employment their Artei require in order to ensure the work and the earnings be equitable for all: for skilled carpenters and joiners, fifteen golden scudi per month, with a deposit of ninety golden scudi in the Artei of each trade to be held against payment and credited to injury payment and extra work at the time of completion of the new buildings; for skilled glazers, twenty golden scudi with a similar deposit to their Arte and the same provision for injuries and extra work; for stone masons and finishers, fifteen golden scudi per month, and the same deposits stipulated to their Arte.

You must understand, Eccellenza, that many foreigners come to Roma and begin their projects well enough, but then run into debt and flee the city, leaving those of the Artei with no recompense for their labors. While your conduct has thus far been admirable, the time may come when you run out of gold, and therefore we cannot make an exception for you, as we might come to rue our magnanimity. The Console Artei is most specific because previous experience has shown that these requirements, as well as the high prices charged to foreigners, are necessary precautions against the losses we would all sustain were you to depart suddenly from Roma. Therefore I must request that you deposit another fifty golden scudi in the reserve account before we may go forward with the next stage of the project.

As to the accommodations you are providing for the penitent, we must have the full amount for the work immediately: forty golden scudi. For that amount, the quarters you have said you intend to provide may be readied to your specifications within six weeks. If the current state of the quarters is not wholly unacceptable to the penitent, then our task may not be so urgent, but that is something you must determine. Your request of an additional chamber suitable to housing a servant for the penitent may require another ten golden scudi be deposited to the carpenters' and joiners' Artei; the whole cost of such an addition should not exceed twenty-five golden scudi for supplies beyond the workers' pay.

I will continue to present myself to you on Friday to tender accounts of work accomplished during the week and to collect any monies due at that time. As you have said you find our work satisfactory, I will plan to remain with this project in a supervisory capacity until it is finished and you have moved into the new building.

Any disputes regarding this work are to be submitted to the Console Artei, and the decision of the Console will be final and binding on all parties to this agreement.

Submitted for your review with my utmost expression of regard

I am ever at your service,
Bonaldo Fiumara
Masterbuilder

At Roma on the 1st day of May, 1689
A true copy of this report is filed with the Console Artei.

Post Scriptum: I thank you for engaging my unmarried sister to serve as a maid to the penitent to whom you have given shelter. The sum of ten golden scudi for a month of service is acceptable to my sister and to me. If you continue to employ her for more than three months, an increase in her salary will be expected.

9

Long ago this piazza had been the site of a temple to Magna Mater, and Roman women had visited it as much for social display as for worship; Olivia had come here to seek consolation from the soft-spoken priests and the sweet odors of incense and flowers. Now the temple was gone and it was surrounded by small, elegant villas, none of which was more than a century old: after a millennium of neglect and decay, the Piazza della Buona Donna was once again a prized and discreet address.

"You will not take this from me, Conte?" Giorgianna asked, half-pleading, half-defiant as she addressed Ragoczy across the expanse of her bed, where she reclined on a mass of satin-covered pillows, her hair done in an artless knot, her lips rouged and her lashes darkened, as was the current fashion for privileged interviews. She was en dishabille in a charming confection of lawn-and-lace that made her appear caught in sea-foam.

The room smelled of flowers from two enormous bouquets set out in ornamental vases in front of her two tall mirrors which made the bouquets appear more abundant than they were; for Ragoczy they served a double purpose, for they obscured the view of the bed as they scented the air.

"Of course not, carina," he assured her: unlike Giorgianna, he was dressed with utter correctness in a glossy-black brocaded justaucorps and narrow breeches with neat white bands at his neck. If not for his ineffable sense of fashion and his manner, he might have been mistaken for a priest in such austere garments. He wore high boots for riding; his only fault was that he had donned no wig—his own dark hair was caught at the back of his neck and clubbed under the wide brim of his hat. "The deed is yours. I have no power to take it from you." This was not wholly truthful: the Magistrates Court would uphold his claim on this property against any woman, and they both knew it. He removed his hat, hanging it on the back of a gilt-finished chair, one of three in her boudoir, a gorgeous chamber that occupied a quarter of the second floor.

"But you . . ." She struggled to find the words. "If you are . . . I don't suppose . . . You will not change your mind? You will not abjure your gift?"

"No, I will not, Giorgianna," he said, leaning toward her and taking her hand in his. "I am not such a paltry fellow as that."

"You are not jealous?" She seemed shocked that she had put the question so bluntly, and she tried to pull her hand away.

He did not release her. "No, Giorgianna," he said gently. "I haven't been jealous since I was very young and absurdly hotheaded." While this was true, it did not begin to describe the ferocity of his emotions in the first two centuries after he had become a vampire, but that had been thirty-five centuries ago. "Do not think you are slighted because I am not."

She managed to smile at him. "You are always so *good* to me." With that, she leaned forward from her mound of pillows and kissed his hand. "If Ilirio had not offered me marriage, I would never part from you, but—" She shrugged.

"I understand completely," Ragoczy assured her, and it was true. "No matter. The villa is yours to do with as you wish; I will not interfere in anything you decide. But if you will permit me a word of advice?"

The delight vanished from her face. "What is it?"

"Keep it. Let it if you and Ilirio live elsewhere; put by the money it earns for yourself. I have prepared the deed so that it can only be sold by you, and that it remains your property during your marriage, and cannot be subsumed by your husband to his estates, or be attached through any claim of his family." He had included a provision for her heirs, but thought it would be tactless to mention that just now.

"How can you do this?" she asked, curious and indignant at once. "I am not your relative, to allow you to deed this place to me in such a fashion."

"It is done," Ragoczy said firmly; he had found an obscure law from the thirteenth century that allowed property to be willed to female heirs to establish a residence for any widowed or unmarried women who might otherwise be unable to obtain a residence and be cast destitute upon the world. "You may want something of your own one day."

She laughed delightedly. "Ilirio is very rich and his family name is ancient. How can I lack for anything now?"

Ragoczy smiled but there was sadness at the back of his dark eyes. "Old fortunes are not built on philanthropy. You do not know what constraints may be upon Ilirio to keep his wealth in his family's hands, to the detriment of his widow—his second wife—in favor of his children."

"That isn't a nice thing to say," she pouted.

"Perhaps not, but it is a concern," Ragoczy told her. "If your husband's family—which is powerful and ancient, as you have said—should lay claims against you, it would ease your situation to have something of your own in the world."

"I have many jewels, most of them are gifts from you," she reminded him. "I will not part with them lightly." Her charismatic smile faded completely. "I do not want it said I have taken advantage of you."

He studied her face, contemplating her mix of art and ambition. "If I do not say that, then who in Roma can make such a claim."

"You know how people talk," she said darkly. "They say women who accept such extravagant gifts do it to ruin their benefactors."

"They say that when men come to impoverishment; surely you don't suppose that will happen to me." He stroked her hand gently. "In indulging you, whom do I deprive? What disadvantage is there in providing this villa for you?"

"But, Conte, you are generosity itself, and you are still very rich. Aren't you?" There was a quaver in her voice as she asked the last.

"Oh, yes. I am exceedingly wealthy. And mine is a special case." He sat more comfortably on the bed. "I have very few . . . relations to provide for, and no children. I can afford to be eleemosynary on a large scale: Ilirio cannot."

"But I do not seek alms or charity, Conte. I will be his *wife*. Surely he will not leave me without means . . . when he . . . he dies." She held on to Ragoczy's hand very tightly. "And he is not *that* old—only fifty-eight."

"And no novice at marriage," Ragoczy agreed. "But it is not Ilirio who might deprive you of your inheritance. He has six surviving children, and they might make claims against your legacy."

"You only think that because of Signor' Aulirios; he makes you worry that everyone might be set upon in court," she said, as if relieved to be spared any more concern about her good fortune. "Still, if you wish it, I will keep this villa as a kind of remembrance of you, as I will keep the jewels you have given me."

"Grazie, Giorgianna," said Ragoczy, and was startled when she moved swiftly to wrap her arms around his neck.

"One last time, Conte, please," she said teasingly before she kissed him eagerly.

This might be dangerous to her after she died, and for that reason he faltered. "Ilirio might not like it," he said with a wry smile to account for his hesitation; he did not know how to explain the risk he now posed to her in a way that she would believe or accept, and yet her yearning tugged at him with all the force of her emotions.

She kissed him again. "He will not mind that I say farewell to one who has been so very kind to me."

He could feel her longing in her touch, and that alone weakened his resolve. If only he did not sense her so keenly! If only her craving were not so overwhelming! He reached out and touched her cheek. "You don't know what you are seeking."

"Oh, yes I do. You have lain with me four times, and each time was . . . bliss; better even than singing. I cannot hope to find the same in Ilirio, admirable though he may be in other ways. So." She locked her fingers behind his neck, under his clubbed hair, and drew him toward her. "One last time, Conte. Te prego."

He saw the passion in her eyes, a passion she usually reserved for her music, and he was caught by her fervor. "If you will not curse me, carina, what can I be but honored?"

"Why should I curse you?" she teased, pulling him with her as she lay back on the bounty of pillows. "I would be more likely to curse you if you were to refuse me this last favor." She melted into his embrace, all but purring with satisfaction. "It would be cruelty to deny me," she murmured as she opened her lips to his. The kiss was long, gradually growing in intensity, a poco a poco crescendo of exaltation that was as thrilling as any she had ever sung. Desire mounted within her as their kiss lengthened and deepened. When she finally drew back, her pulse was racing and her cheeks were flushed. "Ah, Conte; I am going to miss you."

He stretched out beside her, taking his pace from her burgeoning need. "And I you, carina." He had removed his gloves upon his arrival at the villa, so his small, beautiful hands were unencumbered as he unfastened the satin ribbon at the top of her corsage, gently caressing the swell of her breast, tracing its opulent curve with attentive care, feeling her appetence and his esurience increase together.

"How do you know where to touch?" she marveled, as her senses grew more acute. "Where did you learn such things?"

"From you, carina," he said, his tone soft and deep as he bent his head to tongue her nipple, taking pleasure from the shiver of satisfaction that went through her. He opened her corsage, fully revealing her flesh, sumptuous as a pagan goddess painted by Rubens.

"How sweet this is," Giorgianna whispered as a glorious frenzy continued to well in her blood and she moved to fill his hands with the whole of her as his adept arousal continued. She let her sheets slide away from her, as if removing the wrapper from a valuable gift. She felt as if her body were wax deliciously melting and molding through his ardor; her excitement increased with the realization that she could inspire such veneration in him that he sought to offer her this luxurious gratification. She closed her eyes so that she could experience his virtuosity more totally, how his small hands teased and coaxed delectation from every part of her, how his mouth awakened frissons of anticipation, how he found the hidden bud at the apex of her thighs that trembled and pulsed eagerly with every new caress he bestowed upon her. Slowly her breathing changed, and slowly she felt release gather deep within her. "No," she protested as she took hold of his shoulder, not wanting this glorious intimacy to end.

Ragoczy stopped at once. "This is not to your liking?" He was surprised, for he knew her response was genuine. "Have I done anything—"

She sighed her exasperation. "I wanted to have longer, that's all."

He understood his mistake at once. "Your pardon, carina. What may I do to restore your pleasure?" His hands again sought the petaled grotto at the core of her arousal.

"Do everything. Everything. Oh, go on; go on," she urged him, distantly vexed that he could have misunderstood. Sighing, she strove to recapture the excitation she had mistimed; gradually her desire rekindled and grew beyond what she had reached before. Every nuance of stimulation increased her rapture; her entire being trembled with the immensity of her need, as vibrant as a violin in the hands of a master. As her passion reached culmination and he nuzzled her neck, she began to laugh with a joy she had not known before, as all-encompassing as the rapture that rocked her. Far sooner than she had hoped, the jubilant delirium began to fade, leaving her replete but wistful as she basked in her happiness on her satin pillows and her gladsomely rumpled bed. "Ah, Conte," she sighed. "How do you know me so well?"

Her fulfillment had revealed her abiding craving, needs wrought in childhood that no gratification could fully alleviate. Her appetite, unlike his, could not be assuaged. He was also aware that she expected no answer and would have been distracted by anything he said, so he kissed the corner of her mouth as he rose on his elbow. There was still enough ecstasy in her that this made her heart leap.

"And you're not a bit disheveled," she went on, watching him languidly. She began to play with the ribbon-ties of her corsage. "You need hardly do more than straighten your neck-bands to walk outside in perfect form." She wanted to chide him, but all she managed to do was to sound slightly envious. "I must look a fright."

"Hardly that," Ragoczy said with a mix of affection and amusement. "To me you look tantalizing and magnificent."

"But you are supposed to—" she began, then stopped herself. "No. I will not wrangle with you, not this day." She reached out and touched his face. "You cannot imagine how much I am going to miss you."

"I know how much I will miss you: that will have to suffice." He kissed her again, this time in the center of her forehead.

"Oh, dear," she said as he did this. For a long moment she studied his attractive, irregular features; then she sighed. "You truly *are* leaving me, aren't you? Men only kiss me in that place to say farewell."

Ragoczy chose his words carefully. "This is not quite farewell. There are a few more things you and I must deal with before I say that." His voice was low and his dark eyes held hers. "For your sake."

"You're not going to be dreary, are you, Conte?" she challenged him. "You have already given me two warnings, and if this is another—Well, whatever it is, it can wait."

Ragoczy continued to direct his penetrating gaze at her. "There is something I must tell you: about what may become of you."

"You've already done that," she said. "And if there is anything more, perhaps we will discuss it when we meet again. But not now. I am not inclined to hear anything dreary just now, and from your expression, you want to tell me something ponderous." She ran her fingers down the fine brocade of his justaucorps. "For now I want to relish all you have given me. We will have time to be private with one another, never fear."

He caught her hand in his. "This is not something that can be put aside forever, and we will not have many opportunities to talk. Giorgianna, carina, I do not think your affianced husband would be pleased if I continued to pay court to you," Ragoczy said, his tone level but kindly. "It may be awkward enough that you will continue to sing the Vestal Virgin; I cannot think you would want to give him any grounds to doubt your fidelity."

She stared at him. "Are you mocking me?" she demanded suspiciously.

"Certainly not," he replied, soothing her. "I would never mock you, Giorgianna: believe this. I am trying to show you that I regard your marriage as highly as any, and that I wish to do nothing to diminish the esteem Ilirio has for you." Now he kissed her hand and rose from the bed. "But there is something you must know."

Her face became petulant. "Not now, Conte. I am too happy and too sad to discuss anything more with you today." She waved him away from her.

"It is important," he insisted.

"Then we will take a few minutes during tomorrow's rehearsal, when everyone else is at lunch, and you will explain it to me: tomorrow," she said, as if he had just imposed a burden upon her. "That will suffice, won't it?"

He realized she would not permit him to say anything more today; he made a leg. "If that is your wish, I would be ungracious to require anything else." He took his hat and went to the door. "Until tomorrow, carina."

She watched him, a trace of regret in her eyes. "Have Edmea bring me up some chocolate, will you?"

"It will be my pleasure," he said, and bowed himself out of her room. He stood in the corridor for a long moment, contemplating what he should say to her when she finally allowed him to speak. Giorgianna was not inclined to put much faith in anything men told her and that alone made his task doubly difficult, for she would not be apt to believe any counsel he might give her. He started for the staircase, his step brisk as if nothing weighed upon him. At the foot of the stairs he found Edmea waiting, her hair covered by a servant's cap, her simple housedress clean, her demeanor quiet.

"You are leaving, Eccellenza?" she asked.

"Yes, I am," he told her, adding, "Your mistress would like a cup of chocolate."

Edmea curtsied. "Very good, Eccellenza. Bortolo will see you out."

"Grazie," he said, as he handed her a silver coin before making his way to the front door where Bortolo was waiting for him. "Never mind bringing my horse around. I will attend to her myself."

Bortolo had been in service most of his life and had schooled himself to reveal little of his thoughts or feelings. "Very good, Signor' Conte," he said, bowing and opening the door.

Again Ragoczy handed over a silver coin. "You have done well by your mistress."

"She is a great lady, no matter what the world may think of singers," Bortolo said with as much determination as he was capable of expressing.

"You will get no dispute from me," Ragoczy assured the major-domo as he left the house and walked around the side to the stable, where he found his mare loose-girthed and watered. As he checked and tightened the girth, he heard a noise from the street and saw half a dozen ill-dressed young men gathering at the head of the alley. All of them carried wooden clubs, and they approached with the insolent swagger of men used to bullying others. Ragoczy betrayed no alarm, finishing his work without apparent haste. Then he loosed his horse from her rein-cleat, vaulted into the saddle, as he pulled the reins into his hand and reached for his long crop which had hung from a clip on the saddle. Abruptly he spun the mare around, and faced the young men who were making their way in his direction.

"That's the one, ragazzi," the leader called out, pointing to Ragoczy. "Bring him down. Don't let him get away."

Ragoczy took a firm hold and drove the mare forward at a bound, pulling her up short in the middle of the gang, setting her on her back legs, her hooves pawing at the air.

The young men had readied themselves to stop his flight, but were unprepared for this. They scattered as Ragoczy lashed out with his crop, laying open the cheek of the nearest who had tried to grab his off-side stirrup. The man screamed obscenities and swung his club wildly, striking Ragoczy's arm an indirect blow as he howled in fury.

Ragoczy backed his mare up a few steps, then clapped his heels to her sides and sent her hurtling forward.

The bullies ran, all but their leader who threw his club at the mare's front legs in a vain effort to bring her down. The club missed the horse and rolled harmlessly down the alley, well behind the grey mare and her rider.

Reaching the piazza, Ragoczy again pulled his horse in to a decorous trot, proceeding as if the young louts were no concern of his. A few of the people abroad in the piazza made a point of noticing him, and those who did he greeted with a slight bow from the saddle. His arm ached where the club had bludgeoned him, and he knew it would take a long time for his full use of the limb to return; the fingers in his right hand tingled unpleasantly and his elbow had a gnawing ache that suggested more than a bruise. Nothing in his posture or his demeanor revealed any of this; his seat was as admirable as ever and his features were calm as he rode out of the gates of Roma and continued on toward Villa Vecchia.

By the time he arrived at the Villa Vecchia, he found the workers sitting at a plank table for their mid-day meal which would be followed by an hour-long nap to avoid the heat of the day and to allow their food to settle before they undertook the strenuous labor they had been hired to do.

For once Ragoczy let his head groom take care of his horse. "She is a little warm. Walk her before you put her away," he ordered Matyas. "And have a look at her off-side hock."

"Is she having trouble?" Matyas asked, patting the mare's shoulder before he began to unfasten the girths.

"I think she is a little stiff. She may have pulled a muscle." A frown flicked between his brows and he studied the mare intently for an instant, then he thanked Matyas and turned on his heel, bound for the side entrance to the villa. The sound of Maurizio practicing his violin accompanied him, and he wondered vaguely why he should be playing his exercises outside. Then he entered the villa and called for Rugerius as he hastened along to his library.

One of the understewards was busy in the room, sorting out a stack of music manuscripts; he looked up as Ragoczy came in, and ducked his head out of respect for the foreigner who paid him so well. He saw that Ragoczy was surprised by his presence, and quickly put his work aside. "Shall I leave?"

"For the time being, if you please. If you have not had your prandio, now would be an excellent time. If you have already eaten, take your afternoon rest now," said Ragoczy, not wanting to send the servant away too abruptly.

"I am hungry, Signore," said the understeward, and bowed himself out of his master's presence just as Rugerius came into the library.

Rugerius watched him go. "What was he looking at?" he asked without preamble.

"Silvano? Music scores, or so it seemed," Ragoczy answered, gesturing to the manuscripts. "Why?"

"He has been very curious about your books; an odd thing in an understeward," said Rugerius with a note of apprehension in his voice.

"You think he is spying?" Ragoczy did not wait for an answer. "Half the servants here are spying. If I permit that consideration to bother me, I might as well leave now." He sat down in the old-fashioned high-backed chair near the window where the light came in through the shutters in brilliant bars.

Rugerius realized that something more than his servants was bothering Ragoczy. "What is the trouble, my master?" he asked in the Spanish of his youth.

Ragoczy frowned, and replied in the same language, "I wish I knew." He allowed himself to rub his arm where the cudgel had hit. "A half-dozen street-toughs were waiting for me outside Giorgianna's villa when I left."

"Waiting for you—to what purpose?" Rugerius' faded-blue eyes grew keen and icy. "They attacked you, is that it?"

"Yes," said Ragoczy slowly. "They came after me deliberately. I was not simply convenient." He began to unbutton his justaucorps with his left hand. "Youths of that sort do not haunt the Piazza della Buona Donna habitually."

"You are hurt," said Rugerius as he came nearer to Ragoczy.

Ragoczy nodded as he eased his shoulder free of the garment. "Struck just above the elbow. Nothing is broken. The bruise is. Damnably inconvenient." His abrupt tone implied more than his perfunctory curse revealed.

Much as he wanted to pepper Ragoczy with questions, Rugerius checked himself, asking only, "Does it have anything to do with the damage to the coach?"

"Not that I am aware of," said Ragoczy, as he unfastened the last button and tugged himself out of the black brocade garment, sitting still for a short while, regaining his composure. "And since Giorgianna was with me when the spring was cut, I must ask myself if I am the target, or Giorgianna is."

"But why should she be?" Rugerius pursued as he came to take the justaucorps from Ragoczy.

"I haven't the least notion," said Ragoczy. "She has no rivals I am aware of; it is possible that she may have someone jealous of her who is trying to do her an injury. Barring that, I can think of no reason why she should be the object of malice. But then, why should I be, either."

"There is the matter of you defending Aulirios," Rugerius pointed out.

"There is. And my opponents would be foolish to try to harm me. That would only serve to alert me to their designs. If they intend to warn me away from the case, I would expect them to be more specific in their threats. These incidents—if they are connected—are much too obtuse in their intention."

"Unless they simply want to be rid of you," Rugerius observed.

"If that is their design, they will find it harder to accomplish than they expect." He unfastened his camisa and slid it off, inspecting the place where the club had battered him. "No, nothing broken, thank all the forgotten gods. But this will not heal quickly; bruises on the bones are hard enough on the living. For those of my blood—" He began to fasten his camisa once again. "I will put hot compresses on it tonight, when the household is abed."

"Not now?" Rugerius made no attempt to conceal his concern.

Ragoczy shook his head. "I do not want anyone in this household reporting to anyone outside the villa that I have been injured. It might encourage others to try something similar, or worse." He went on in Italian, "How fortunate it was only a glancing blow. I might have been hurt had the rogue succeeded in his action."

Rugerius took his tone and language from Ragoczy. "Truly. It is a shameful thing that such criminals should walk the streets of Roma so boldly."

"Yes," said Ragoczy. "If you will bring me my dressing gown, old friend—the dark-red Transylvanian one with the satin-lined sleeves?—I will spend the afternoon reading more of the cases for which we have records. I want to be prepared when the Magistrate finally agrees to hear Signor' Aulirios' vindication."

"Very good," said Rugerius, preparing to go to fetch the dressing gown.

"Oh. One other thing: why is Maurizio serenading the coach-house?" He asked this lightly enough, but with an underlying purpose that required an answer.

"Not the coach-house, my master, the little casetta beyond it, where the warder used to live." He paused. "Our penitent guest has taken up residence in that place, and Maurizio has taken it upon himself to ease her hours of meditation." As Leocadia had not vouchsafed her identity to Ragoczy, she was called *our penitent guest* to ensure the anonymity she so clearly desired.

Ragoczy was startled to hear this. "When did this begin?"

"A few days since," Rugerius said. "They met by accident when our penitent guest came into the garden to pick herbs. Maurizio was taking an hour for himself, and had strolled about the grounds. I saw no harm in that. I was unaware of the meeting until Maurizio asked me about her when he came back in to resume practicing."

"Um," said Ragoczy, reserving his opinion for the time being. "At least he is playing, which is all to the good." He rubbed his arm again. "My bowing isn't going to be worth much for some months, I fear.

I don't know how well I can tutor him in this condition."

"Do you have to play to teach him?" Rugerius asked. "You have often avoided having to play while you taught."

"True enough; but not for such a talented student as Maurizio Reietto is. His gifts demand more attention than many others have, including that musician from Aragon Csimenae found so . . ." Ragoczy shook his head. "I don't know how much good I can do him now."

"Will you send Maurizio away?" Rugerius kept his voice level, without a trace of opinion in it.

"Probably not, at least not in the next several days. He would assume he was being punished for playing for our penitent guest, which would benefit no one. And I can see that he practices, which is what Scarlatti is most concerned about." Ragoczy gave a short sigh. "Still. This could be inconvenient."

"That is one view of it, certainly," said Rugerius.

"If only she would tell us who she is, we might handle all this more . . . diplomatically. Until she does, we can do nothing more than house her." He fell ruminatively silent for a short while, then said, "Has anyone inquired about her—other than Maurizio?"

"Not that I know of," said Rugerius carefully. "She keeps to herself, and her conduct would do a cloistered nun credit. With penitents of all sorts flocking to Roma, this one is not remarkable, or so I have heard. I have told the staff that you are providing for her out of Christian charity and your duty as a nobleman."

Ragoczy breathed a single, soft laugh. "And they accept it?" He did not expect an answer. "Well, nothing we do can change her situation just now. Perhaps this evening we might try to come up with a solution to this perplexing state of affairs."

"As you wish, my master," said Rugerius, again preparing to leave the room.

"Rugerius, you are a prince among men," said Ragoczy with a quick, wry smile.

"Certainly," said Rugerius as he at last closed the door.

Text of a letter from Delfinio Crecione to Martin, Cardinal Calaveria y Vacamonte, delivered by messenger instructed to wait for a response.

To Su Eminenza, Martin, Cardinal Calaveria y Vacamonte, the most respectful greeting of Definio Crecione, landlord of the Sorcio Buffone, with the sincerest apologies for this intrusion, but which, lamentably, cannot be helped.

All appeals to your brother have gone unanswered, and for that reason alone I am addressing this to you for your review as well as the prayer that you will provide the recompense that your brother has admitted is due to me, but which he has not yet discharged in any form that could be regarded as acceptable to me or those others who were involved in the incident I will now outline to Su Eminenza.

On the 14th day of last February your brother Ursellos arrived at my inn in the company of four young men. They stated they had been gambling and wished to celebrate their winnings by drinking their good fortune. To that end, they were admitted to the larger private parlor I maintain for visitors of quality. Two waiters were assigned the task of providing their wants, all of which was unremarkable.

After an hour or so, the young men grew rowdy, as young men will when they are drinking to celebrate a great occasion. This was not unexpected, and the waiters knew how to deal with youthful carousers. On my suggestion, a half a spit-roasted piglet and new bread was carried in to provide them with more than wine to lighten their hearts. This was received well, and the young men ordered roasted onions and baked pears as well, which was duly carried to their parlor.

Some time after midnight, a carriage arrived bearing Barone Larice and his niece. They had paid for rooms for the night and had been delayed due to inclement weather—as Su Eminenza will recall, it rained that week and the roads were unusually muddy—and so did not come until several hours after they were expected. The Barone was tired and a bit ill from his long travels, and his niece was quite exhausted, so when they arrived at my inn, they sought their private parlor without ado. The carriage bringing their baggage was delayed due to a broken wheel, and so neither Barone and niece had servants beyond two footmen; this led to what must have been confusion on the part of the young men, for when they discovered that these worthy people had reached their smaller parlor, just behind the larger one where the young men were, your brother decided he had discovered an assignation, and took it upon himself to investigate. Had there been more of the Barone's staff, your brother might not have been so foolish. As it was, his impetuosity and his misapprehension of the situation served to bring about this dreadful situation.

The Barone and his niece had ordered a small supper and hot wine to ameliorate the exigencies of travel, and had disposed themselves for their repast. Being weary, they did not require their servants to remain with them, but dismissed them to permit them to dine even while they—the Barone and his niece—did. Thus it happened that the Barone and his niece were unattended when your brother took it upon himself to break into the parlor to apprehend them in what he supposed would be the excesses of sin, or so he claimed. Whatever his intentions, he was the man who sinned in this encounter, and so grievously that some redress is required to make amends for the extent of the insult he has visited upon the Barone and his niece, to say nothing of the damage he has done to my inn, both in actual damage done to the property as well as the harm he has inflicted upon the reputation I have worked so long to maintain.

According to the servants who were roused in answer to the screams and imprecations of the Barone's niece, your brother, Eminenza, attacked the Barone with a chair, breaking his shoulder with the force of the blow, and causing him to lose consciousness for a quarter of an hour. Your brother then turned his attention to the niece, a virtuous girl of spotless character, and with the aid and encouragement of two of his companions, ravished her. My servants who tried to restrain these young men were beaten for their trouble, one of them so severely that his right eye has lost its sight; the other still has bruises to show for the drubbing he took at your brother's hands.

The Barone has informed me that he will seek no legal retribution for the sake of his niece, who has withdrawn to a convent in the wake of your brother's deplorable activities. Her family does not want to expose her to the vilification that must result if your brother's debauch of her becomes known. The Barone blames himself for this tragedy. His silence will insure his niece's continued good name. It therefore falls to me to pursue all remedies at my disposal. As your brother has admitted that he has gravely injured my inn and the persons of my servants and has stated that he will render compensation, I have not brought my complaint to the Magisterial Court. If, however, some portion of the amount promised is not put into my hands before the last day of this month, I will have to reconsider my position, for to fail to do so will not only cost me money, it will leave a terrible blot on the reputation of my establishment, which will inevitably lead to a loss of clientele

I have no wish to bring embarrassment upon you or your family, Eminenza, and I will not unless I am driven to it by the continued refusal of your brother to provide the monies he has promised to me. I most sincerely wish to accommodate you in any way I might, short of resigning my claims in this most egregious business. To that end, I reluctantly submit my claim to you, and hope that my messenger will bring your assurance that my petition will be honored promptly. I give you my word I have no desire to cause your family any humiliation, but I will be forced to do so if you decline this petition. I am willing to extend you the same courtesy I have shown your brother, and give you my word that if my very reasonable demands for recompense are met there will be an end to my actions against Ursellos or any other member of your family in regards to this instance. Should you be willing to provide me reasonable compensation, you may rely on my discretion in regard to the activities of your brother and his reprobate companions. If you cannot provide me with any certainty of remuneration then I must, with utmost regret, place my claim before the Magisterial Courts and permit the judgment of the worthy Podesta to determine how I shall have my losses compensated for. I beg you to think about the Barone and his niece as well as your brother as you ponder your decision, for their fates are as much in your hands as is that of your brother.

With every assurance of esteem and regard,
I am your servant,
Delfinio Crecione
Landlord, the Sorcio Buffone

By my own hand and under seal, at Roma, on the 11th day of May, 1689

10

In the study just off the courtroom Narcisso Lepidio della Rovere sat at his imposing writing table, a pen in his hand poised over a pristine sheet of paper, stacks of parchment and vellum spread out around him. His wig was in the highest fashion, with cascades of ordered rust-colored curls falling to his shoulders. His neck-bands, seen at the top of his official robe, were of layered lace, an affectation perilously close to dandyism for one holding a post of such dignity as he did. He signaled his clerk impatiently. "How much longer?"

"The parties are supposed to be here in an hour, Podesta," was the answer.

Della Rovere muttered something that might have been a curse; feeling uneasy for that lapse, he glanced at the crucifix hanging over the hearth on the far wall. "I may not have finished my reading," he said fretfully.

"They can be told to wait on your convenience," the clerk reminded him with a gesture of respect. "It is your right as Podesta to determine when the case will be heard."

"I know; I know," said della Rovere. "But Archbishop Walmund is pressing for a resolution in favor of Ahrent Rothofen, and I have assured him that I will render a decision quickly. If I do not, he will have reason to complain of me." He coughed. "Of course, the Archbishop will be pleased if I delay, should it seem I must uphold Aulirios' inheritance. Which," he added with a fatalistic sigh, "on the strength of what is here, I must do."

The clerk shook his head in commiseration. "If you have to disappoint the Archbishop, do you think your decision might be reviewed?" This was a development no Magistrate could face with equanimity.

"I would think it would be required." He slapped his free hand on the shiny tabletop. "I have never had a decision reviewed before."

"The Church would surely consider that; your record is known.

They would not fault you for deciding against the Archbishop's wishes this once," his clerk said, making an attempt to soothe him.

"But they will," said della Rovere with certainty. "The Archbishop is from the north, and the Pope is determined to ensure their support. If I cannot uphold Rothofen's claim, the Pope will regard it as an opposition to his authority."

"Are you definite that any action would be taken against you?" His clerk, who was only a few years younger than della Rovere, could not imagine a della Rovere being reprimanded by the Pope, even in such a case as this.

"I fear it would come to that," della Rovere said, as he thumbed the sheets in front of him. "But, Ruperto, my hands are tied. I must not accept false testimony, and I am convinced that one of these bona fides is counterfeit. If I say so, it will redound to the Archbishop's reputation, and the Church will have to make every effort to restore his good name or the smirching of his honor would be intolerable." He stared at the crucifix. "Rothofen may have accepted the bona fides in the belief they were legitimate, so that perhaps it is no fault of his that this suit has been presented to me. However, I cannot overlook something that is so clearly—" He lifted his hands to demonstrate his predicament.

"Are you satisfied that it is counterfeit?" The clerk, Ruperto Smeriglio, looked seriously alarmed now, for the submission of fallacious testimony was a very serious infraction of the law and carried stringent penalties. "Can the counterfeit be proved?"

"Yes. It is beyond cavil." Della Rovere pulled out the suspect parchment. "See here, where it says the contents are verified by the canon of the Church of Saint John the Evangelist in Oldenburg?" He pointed to the seal. "The name of the Bishop there? The man was not yet Bishop in 1638, not even in November; he was made Bishop early the next year. I have proof of this. Oh, he was *in* Oldenburg, but his . . . promotion did not arrive until after the New Year. There are many letters from 1638 that bear his name as well as his location in Oldenburg, so it was easily overlooked. Anyone might have done so, in understandable innocence. And the declaration says the testimony was sworn to at the church altar. But the church was then under repair from damage done during Protestant riots. No Mass was celebrated there that year, or for two years before. The records are scanty and not easily found, but Ragoczy has unearthed them and brought them officially to my attention: I cannot argue with the Church's own reports—Oldenburg's Saint John the Evangelist was finished being restored in the early spring of 1639; in February of that year it was rededicated and reconsecrated."

"An oversight, perhaps?" the clerk suggested. "A slip of the pen? An eight and a nine can look very much alike."

"That is what I have been trying to tell myself," della Rovere admitted. "But I cannot make myself believe it. The declaration cannot be admitted in the suit, not with its contents being so questionable." He shook his head. "If only the statement Rothofen presented were not so specific. Had they said winter, it might have been January or February as well as November or December that was meant, and so I would not have to disallow this statement, which is the key to the whole of Rothofen's claim, for it purports to legitimize Rothofen's grandfather."

"Do you think you could explain it any other way?" The clerk went to the sideboard and poured out a goblet of wine for the Magistrate which he carried back to the writing table. "Here, Podesta. Drink this. This will calm your nerves."

Della Rovere took the goblet eagerly. "You are very observant, Ruperto. I thank you." He lifted the goblet as if offering the wine to the crucifix. "I am worried that I might be forced to make a decision in the name of justice that the Church would not like."

As he watched the Magistrate drink, the clerk said thoughtfully, "What if you were to delay the matter again? Surely you can declare that you have insufficient material to make a judgment."

"I have already told the Archbishop that I will make my decision known," said della Rovere, his words muffled by the rim of the goblet.

"Then there must be another reason to postpone the presentation of the suit again." He paced as if movement fueled his thinking. "What about the mal aria? They said the bad air is killing people in the city again. If that is the case, haven't you a reasonable excuse to adjourn your Court for the summer? You would have to leave the city, of course, but that is not remarkable—so many others do."

For the first time Narcisso della Rovere did not sound glum. "Yes.

Yes, there is sense in that. I could declare a long recess for my Court in the name of prudence. It would not be wise of me to require these litigants remain in Roma if they stand in harm's way doing so." His face brightened, as he went on. "If the mal aria has come, it would not be sensible for any Magistrate to continue to hear cases; surely I cannot be faulted for my decision. Many another Magistrate has done so before. That way I could inform the Archbishop privately about the reservations I have in regard to Rothofen's evidence. If the Archbishop decides to act upon this, I am not responsible, am I?"

There came the sound of a churchbell from the nearby San Erasmo, a tiny, ancient building that could barely contain the windlass of the saint's martyrdom. The bell, as hoary as the church, doddered through its sounding of the hour.

"Certainly not," said Ruperto quickly. "You have very good reason to discuss your apprehensions with Walmund, since he has taken such an interest in the matter. You are known for your dependability in regard to your Church obligations."

Now della Rovere was beginning to smile. "Yes. I have striven to do what is right. It is the responsible thing to do, is it not?"

"Very responsible," Ruperto approved. "The parties in the suit need know nothing of it, for it does not deal directly with their causes, and the Archbishop cannot claim that you have not done your utmost to serve him as best you can."

"Yes." Della Rovere sighed, partly in relief, partly in dismay. "How difficult it is, Ruperto, to try to fulfill the law and keep the Church approving of one's decisions; few understand the burdens we Magistrates have to bear."

"Onerous, Podesta," said the clerk, as he brought the wine carafe to refill della Rovere's goblet.

Before he drank, della Rovere took hold of his clerk's arm. "You are certain about the mal aria? There truly have been deaths from it? I do not want to be called a coward for recessing the Court."

"There are four reported, which always means more; the poor do not usually report the mal aria," said Ruperto. "You cannot be criticized for your circumspection."

Della Rovere finished his wine. "Just as well. No doubt the Pope will want to remove from the city as well."

"If Sua Santita is up to traveling. It is rumored he is not in good health," Ruperto said in the manner of one used to communicating deferentially.

"You mean the College of Cardinals is already jockeying for San Pietro's," said the Magistrate. "It is all very sad."

Ruperto refilled the goblet again. "You may find it best to send word to the Lateran, informing the Pope's staff of your decision, so that it cannot be thought you are indifferent to Innocenzo's health."

"A wise recommendation." Della Rovere approved. "Yes, it would probably be best to make an effort to keep my bridges to the Pope in good repair. If he is ill, then it will be useful to have it known that I have not forgotten my obligation to the Church; I do not want to appear lax." He smiled suddenly at his clerk. "I am grateful to you, Ruperto. I do not know how I could go on without you."

"Nor do I," said Ruperto with such a self-effacing tone that it was impossible to think him insolent.

Della Rovere sat straighter in his high-backed chair. "I will make a decree postponing all suits scheduled for my Court. If I order that the parties reconvene before me in September, there should be enough time for the Archbishop to sort out the matter of the questionable bona fides. Don't you think?"

"Very likely. His man, Rothofen, will benefit from the additional time, which will suit the Archbishop's purposes. He will be grateful to you for your warning, in any case." Ruperto smiled his best obsequious smile and said, "The time, Podesta. You had best go into your courtroom. The litigants will be arriving shortly."

"Yes. They will not want to wait for me." He rose from his writing table. "Put those into a portfolio, if you will," he said, pointing to the parchment and vellum.

"That I will," said Ruperto, and stood aside so that della Rovere could kneel at his prie-dieu to recite his petitions to God before he went to consider those of men.

As della Rovere adjusted his judicial robe and placed his cap atop his wig, he cleared his throat. "I do not want to anger the Church."

"Or God," Ruperto said conscientiously. "It is fitting that you do your work in the world so that the Pope may better fulfill his duties to man and God."

This blatant flattery did not completely fool della Rovere, who shook his head. "You are too ready with your praise," he chided his clerk, which Ruperto accepted with the semblance of humility as he went to summon the bailiff to announce the Podesta.

The bailiff was a stout man of middle years, stiff with self-importance and pride of office. He stood waiting for Narcisso della Rovere in the attitude of a man accommodating an inferior. Only when the Magistrate approached him did he change his demeanor, bowing della Rovere through the door to the courtroom with dignity and respect.

Half a dozen men sat on the plain benches, ready to hear the proceedings. Four of them were priests and each carried a portable desk equipped with sheaves of notepaper, pens, quills, standishes, and sand. At the foot of the Magistrate's high bench was a long table where the bailiff and the clerk sat, the clerk with writing equipment laid out, the bailiff with his staff laid in front of his chair. The windows were open, cooling the room but letting in flies; the noise from the street was so common that no one paid any heed to it.

"Have the parties come in," said della Rovere, showing his authority grandly.

The bailiff went to open the door, and called in Rothofen, Aulirios, their advocates and their supporters, then stood aside to allow all these to enter; he directed the litigants to the long table in front of the Magistrate's bench, indicating that only those four men could be allowed a place at the table. Niklos Aulirios took his place with Ferenc Ragoczy, Ahrent Rothofen with Enzio Frantume; they remained standing while all the rest sat down.

When everyone was seated, Podesta della Rovere cleared his throat and began to speak. "I have reviewed all the material presented to me, and it is my opinion that your dispute is apt to be long. I cannot suppose that all the points may be disputed and resolved in less than a month." He paused to let either advocate speak up. When no one did, he went on, "I have decided that both parties need more time to make a full presentation of their bona fides, and for that reason, I have concluded that it would serve the Court to recess this hearing until the end of the mal aria. It will be dangerous to remain within the city while the fevers are abroad. I therefore decree that we shall commence this hearing in the third week of September at this place. I am going to retire to the country while the mal aria is in Roma; while I am there I will be at pains to make every effort to consider any and all pertinent material either disputant may see fit to present to me."

Enzio Frantume spoke up in the silence that greeted this announcement. "We are prepared to present our cause now, Podesta."

"Then you may spend your summer in salubrious retreat," said della Rovere. "Were I in your position, however, I would seek to use these weeks as advantageously as possible, as I have no doubt Signor' Aulirios will."

Ahrent Rothofen glowered at the Magistrate. "How can you do this?" he muttered. "I thought everything was in order."

Beside him, Enzio Frantume had the grace to look discomfited. He whispered something to his client, then addressed della Rovere. "I apologize for the outburst, Podesta. It is only that Signore Rothofen is eager to have his claim recognized which leads him to make inappropriate remarks."

"I can understand his disappointment," said della Rovere. "But I pray he will use the time between now and September to strengthen his presentation to me." He turned to the other litigants. "Signor' Conte, have you nothing to say?"

Ragoczy made a gesture of concession. "I have brought another bona fides for your examination, Podesta," he said. "Other than that, I can think of nothing that would be suitable, given your ruling."

This courtesy earned Ragoczy a favorable nod from della Rovere. "You may present it to me now," he informed Ragoczy, and motioned him to hand the material to the clerk. "What is it? And why have you not produced it before now?"

Ragoczy offered the rolled parchment to the clerk. "We have only just found it, among a stack of ancient records stored in the attic of Senza Pari," he explained. "At first we did not understand its importance, for it was among so many other records that until the parchment was cleaned, we did not know what it addressed. Fortunately most of the ink has neither faded nor flaked." He had spent nearly a week preparing the old parchment for its new use, and then another five days aging the writing. "If you will take the time to read it, I think you may find it will clarify Signor' Aulirios' position."

Della Rovere handled the parchment with care. "How old is this?"

"The seal is that of Pope Sergius IV, the date August 9, 1011, in Roma," said Ragoczy with a calm that suggested that such documents were commonplace. "The style of writing is antique, but it may, with patience, be read. The Papal seal is very fragile and brittle with age, so it must be handled carefully; one section of the edge is chipped already." He bowed slightly, continuing in the accepted form, "I commend it to your consideration."

"What does it assert?" della Rovere asked, as he ran his fingers over the parchment, feeling its age in its texture.

"I think it would be more suitable for you to determine that for yourself, Podesta," said Ragoczy. "It would not be fitting for any remark of mine to influence you in your assessment of its importance."

Della Rovere nodded his approval. "I applaud your respect of this Court, Signor' Conte, and I hope that you will provide an example that others may follow." He punctuated his remark with a glare in Rothofen's direction.

Enzio Frantume folded his arms. "How can you accept this . . . this blatant attempt to introduce false testament into this proceeding?"

The Magistrate glowered at Rothofen's advocate. "Were I you, Signore, I would not raise such questions, lest your own submissions come under scrutiny."

"I resent the implication of your remarks, Podesta," Frantume blustered, more for his client's benefit than with any hope of changing della Rovere's mind. "We have given you genuine proofs of our claims, which we fully expect to be upheld."

Leaning forward on his bench, della Rovere said, "If you are so confident, you have no reason to fret at delay."

"But we do," Enzio Frantume protested with a swift glance at the outraged Rothofen. "Every hour that Niklos Aulirios enjoys the bounty of the Clemens' estate is robbery from Signore Rothofen." His deliberate omission of *Signore* in reference to Niklos carried the sting he intended it should.

"Say nothing," Ragoczy warned Niklos in an undervoice.

"Unless the estates are legitimately Signore Aulirios'," said della Rovere at his most ponderous. "Then you may be certain that your client can have no reason to feel abused."

Ahrent Rothofen looked directly at Niklos. "You are contemptible. My claim is just, and you know it."

The bailiff took his staff of office in his hand and pointed its head in Rothofen's direction. "Silence," he ordered.

Frantume lifted his hands as if it were beyond his power to control his client's outburst. "You cannot blame him for his indignation, Podesta."

"There you are wrong," said della Rovere, suddenly genteel in his manner. "This is my Court, and you are the petitioner coming to redress the wrong you claim has been done. I will decide if your proofs of claim are genuine, and make an appropriate judgment. In the autumn." This last was more pointed.

"But Signore Rothofen fears his inheritance will be abused by the man holding the Clemens' estates now," Frantume asserted.

"He has not done so before," said Ragoczy mildly. "And since he has honored the Will of Atta Olivia Clemens, and will continue to honor it, how can Signore Rothofen assume that Signore Aulirios will forget what he owes to his legacy?"

"An excellent point, Signor' Conte," approved della Rovere; he paused and added, "If it will ease your worries, Signore Rothofen, I will enjoin Signore Aulirios to sell no portion of the estate and to maintain it at the standards he has maintained in the past decade. Will that do?"

Rothofen stared down at his hands, watching them gather into fists as if they had volition of their own. He did not speak for a short while, and then folded his arms, tucking his fists in. "If you will lay down penalties for failing to uphold your order, I suppose I must. But when you decide in my favor, I will demand recompense for all I have lost in the intervening months."

"Very well: if Signor' Aulirios fails to maintain the estates of Atta Olivia Clemens in the manner he has done so in the past, and if no act of God may account for his failure to do so, he will be fined three hundred florins. As to additional monies allocated to you, Signore

Rothofen, if I should uphold your claim, I will entertain such a petition." Della Rovere sat very straight, his imposing posture somewhat marred by the presence of a fly that persistently tried to find a place on the Magistrate's wig to alight.

Enzio Frantume laid his hand on Rothofen's shoulder—it was shrugged off, but the advocate spoke as if this slight meant nothing. "Podesta, your fairness is our surest hope. We will use the time to good advantage." With that, he sat down once more, indicating he had finished.

"And you, Signor' Conte—are you satisfied?" Della Rovere studied Ragoczy, making an effort to look unimpressed with the compelling foreigner.

"Certainly; why should I not be." Ragoczy inclined his head in a display of respect. "As to your instructions, Podesta, I give you my Word that, barring Heavenly or Hellish intervention, Signor' Aulirios will do nothing to diminish the quality or quantity of the estate in question—indeed, why should he? for they are his."

In spite of himself, della Rovere found himself warming to Ragoczy; the Magistrate recognized the authority in the distinguished stranger, and he responded to his elegance of manner, as well as his serene self-possession. "That remains to be seen. This suit addresses that question, does it not?" He smiled at his own witticism, then went on in more formal accents. "I will, of course, give this new . . . information my full attention, and when we resume this case, you will have my decision."

The bailiff gave the signal for the litigants to rise; he tapped his staff smartly on the floor and the litigants all made legs to show their respect to the Magistrate. "This case," the bailiff announced, "is recessed until the third week in September. God give wisdom to this Court and defend Sua Santita, Pope Innocenzo."

Everyone in the courtroom made the sign of the cross; della Rovere stood. "Do not fail me, you advocates," he admonished them before he returned to his study, trailed by his clerk.

"Well," said Niklos to Ragoczy, as soon as the Magistrate was gone.

"Possibly," said Ragoczy, nodding in the direction of the priests with their portable desks. "It might be advisable to discuss this later."

He picked up his leather portfolio and tucked it under his arm, using the broad straps to hold it securely.

Rothofen had overheard this, and spoke up. "Yes. Later. So you can scheme without fear of honest men apprehending you."

Niklos bristled but Ragoczy answered mildly. "We have nothing to fear from honest men, Signore Rothofen. Believe this."

Before Rothofen could become abusive, Enzio Frantume laid his hand on Rothofen's arm. "This is not the place, Signore." His voice was soft but his caution did little to mollify his bellicose client.

"What is the point!" Rothofen exclaimed, and flung out of the courtroom with no regard for ceremony.

Looking abashed, Enzio Frantume turned to Ragoczy and Niklos. "I ask you to pardon his . . . lapse, Signor' Conte, Signor' Aulirios. He has been distressed by the many delays we have encountered, and this one is—" He shrugged to demonstrate how he felt about the Magistrate's decision.

"Podesta della Rovere is a thorough official," said Ragoczy smoothly. "For which we must all be grateful."

Frantume was relieved to have this support. "Oh, most truly. When he finally reaches his conclusion, it will be unquestionably sound." He slapped absentmindedly at a mosquito that landed on his face.

"Perhaps that is why he declared such a long recess," Ragoczy mused aloud. "That, and the mal aria, of course." He faced the crucifix above the Magistrate's bench, crossed himself, and turned toward the door in the rear of the chamber; beside him, Niklos did the same.

As they left the room, they heard Enzio Frantume call after them, "Until September."

"What do you think—" Niklos began as he and Ragoczy started down the wide marble stairs to the loggia and the street.

Ragoczy held up his hand. "In the carriage, I think, would be wiser."

Niklos took this to heart, putting his head down as if in thought until they were in front of the building and Ragoczy had sent a footman to summon Amerigo to bring the coach around. "Why did Rothofen leave so . . ." He faltered, trying to find a tactful way to describe his opponent's departure.

"So impetuously?" Ragoczy suggested, at his most urbane; one of the priests with his portable desk now slung across his back was emerging from the building, and he paused near them, not obviously listening. "No doubt he was disappointed at the Magistrate's decision."

"That was clear," said Niklos with a tinge of sarcasm. "Did he hope to have a judgment in his favor? Today? How could that happen? You have just presented new information to the Magistrate— he could not possibly render a decision until he has assessed what you've provided?" His doubt turned this observation to a question.

"As Signore Rothofen did not linger to explain himself, I regret I can only guess at what his expectations might have been," said Ragoczy, glancing to the left as his black coach with its distinctive team of matched greys, came rattling up to the steps of the Magisterial Courts. "In buon punto, Amerigo," he called up to the coachman.

Amerigo bowed from his position on the box. "Buon pomeriggio, Signor' Conte," he replied, calling for one of the two liveried footmen on the back to step down and open the door for their employer.

Knowing that Niklos and he were under scrutiny, Ragoczy waited while this service was performed. As he climbed into the coach behind Niklos—a courtesy not lost on the curious—Ragoczy handed the footman a silver Apostle as a gratuity. Then he stowed his portfolio in a compartment in the back of his seat and sat down with his shoulders comfortably against the squabs as he studied Niklos' face. "You have no reason to worry," he said, as he tapped the ceiling twice, signaling Amerigo to set off.

"Not until September, certainly," said Niklos, his handsomeness marred by a scowl.

"Not at any time." Ragoczy spoke now in Byzantine Greek. "Podesta Narcisso della Rovere's hands are tied. If he awards the estates to Rothofen, he contravenes the orders of the Pope. Oh not Innocenzo XI—Sergius IV—not that that would make any difference."

"Do you think he will not challenge the order?" Niklos asked nervously, glad to use his native tongue again.

"How can he? The parchment, inks, and Papal seals are authentic. The writing is of the period, and there are half a dozen such orders of Sergius' in the Papal archives. Someone at the Lateran will surely vouch for its authenticity. No servant of mine—aside from Rugerius—saw me prepare it, and the materials I used are in the hidden room at Villa Vecchia."

"No one knows about that room?" Niklos could not keep from wondering. "How can you be certain?"

"I am certain," said Ragoczy quietly, but with such purpose that Niklos did not pursue the matter.

"What do you think about Podesta della Rovere?" It was an adroit turn of subject and both of them knew it.

"I think he is being pressured." Ragoczy studied Niklos a moment in silence.

"Oh, certainly, certainly," Niklos agreed, bracing himself as the coach swung around a crowded corner. "But is it the Church, the Archbishop, or Rothofen doing it?"

An outbreak of shouting from the street, with cries of *"Ladro!"* halted their carriage for a short while as market-vendors ran down the thief.

"All three, I surmise, given his capacity for endless delays." He sighed once. "He knows he will have to uphold your legacy in the end, and he knows this will cause hard feelings in the Church. The Pope needs the support of the German states if he is to keep Louis of France from establishing himself as the equal of the Pope."

Niklos said nothing for a short while. Then, as they reached the gates of the city, he said, "I may be Greek, but after so many centuries with Olivia, I feel part of my soul is Roman."

"Very likely," Ragoczy concurred. "At least as Roman as half the people who live here."

"Not if Rothofen gets his way," said Niklos glumly. He fingered the chain on his quizzing glass, and did his best not to look worried.

"Rothofen has given della Rovere false material, if what Ettore Colonna tells me can be believed." Ragoczy was not as edgy as his companion, but he spoke with care.

"And you rely on him to tell you the truth." Niklos let his sarcasm color his voice. "Why should he be any more candid than any other man in Roma?"

"Because he dislikes Rothofen and he has no reason to lie," Ragoczy replied.

"Except that he is a Colonna, and the Colonnas have been ambitious since Romulus and Remus suckled the She-Wolf," said Niklos testily.

"All the more reason to trust what he says; he knows the wheat from the chaff." Ragoczy contemplated Niklos' downcast appearance. "Remember you are a ghoul and you will outlive Rothofen; if you must, you can buy the estates again—Olivia did that more than once."

For the first time in several days Niklos chuckled. "You're probably right," he allowed ruefully. He leaned back against the upholstered supports. "At least we may arrive at Senza Pari before Scarlatti and his musicians are quite finished rehearsing for the day."

"Does that intrude?" Ragoczy asked with concern but no apprehension.

"No. Nothing of the sort," Niklos said quickly. "After even a short time in Court, I welcome harmony and sweet voices." He folded his arms comfortably. "What an exhausting day. And for so little result."

The coach swayed again as it rumbled over the broken paving at the edge of the old Roman paving; Amerigo cursed vigorously as he tugged the horses back onto the ancient, dust-covered surface.

Ragoczy said nothing; he could feel the annealing presence of his native earth that lined the floor and the seats of the carriage, begin to restore him. He noticed Niklos was sunk in thought, his broad-brimmed hat pulled down to shade his eyes. Ragoczy understood that Niklos did not want to talk any longer and so he gave himself up to assimilating the welcome succor of his native earth for the rest of the journey to Senza Pari.

Text of a letter from Giorgianna Ferrugia to Ferenc Ragoczy, Conte da San-Germain.

To the most generous of patrons, Ferenc Ragoczy, Conte da San-Germain, the most respectful greetings of the Marchesa di Scosces-erto:

*How can I thank you enough for the generous gifts you have lav-
ished on me on the occasion of my wedding? Many thought our haste
was inappropriate and their gifts reflected that, but not yours! and
not one gift inappropriate! The lovely pair of silver candle-sconces
are even now being mounted on the withdrawing-room wall, flanking
the mantel mirror, as you suggested. Such artistry, and so unusual. I
am agog to know where you found such unusual work. The bolts of
sculptured velvet will make magnificent draperies for the same room,
which I assume was your intention. Such a wonderful shade—not
blue, not grey, not green, but taking some of each color and making
it a shade that is so like silver that some might be excused for thinking
it was.*

*Ilirio is delighted with the four horses you sent to him as his gift.
Such splendid animals! Our head coachman says that they are a perfectly matched team. I confess, I do not usually like roan horses, but
these are such a color that their red manes and tails are almost as
red as cherries, and their coats are like new, pink copper. They have
none of that patchy look so many roans have.*

*We will return from our nuptial retreat in a month. We were going
to Livorno, but there have been such rumors about the French King
seeking to confront the Pope, now that Sua Santita is ill, that we have
decided to go to Venice, instead. The Turks seem less dangerous than
Louis of France just now. Ilirio is disappointed, but I confess I am
not. Venice delights me, even in summer. I promise I will continue to
practice the Vestal Virgin's music while we are gone so that little
ground will be lost when I return to rehearsal. Do, please, convince
Maestro Scarlatti that I have not so forgotten myself that I will shirk
my art. That will never happen, for not only do I know that my voice
is God's most sacred gift to me, I also know that Ilirio is most delighted in me when I am singing, and the admiration my voice inspires fills him with honorable pride.*

*I also apologize for not having that discussion you requested, but,
Conte, as you yourself reminded me, my conduct must be exemplary.
I can do nothing that smacks of the clandestine, not even for you. I
ask you to consider that as you weigh the advantages of speaking of
this urgent matter against the advantages of keeping silent. Perhaps
as we continue to work on the opera you will be able to have an*

opportunity to tell me those important things you mentioned when you were last at my villa. And perhaps you will decide they are not so important after all.

Your generosity and your kindnesses to me have brightened my life more than I can tell you, and your—I can only call it largess that you have shown my husband and me, is beyond anything I would ever have expected. There are those who have decided that married or not, I am little more than a courtesan because I have sung in public, and their spite is beyond anything I thought I would encounter. Your cautions were well-intentioned, I realize that now, and I thank you on that account, as well.

Know I remember you in my prayers, as I remember Maestro Scarlatti. Surely God will be gracious to you for your benignancy to me. And while you may not always be completely welcome in my husband's house, you will always have a home in a special corner of my heart.

> *Believe me, Conte, one who holds you in highest esteem,*
> *Giorgianna Ferrugia, Marchesa di Scoscerto*

at Ognissanti near Roma, on the 29th day of May, 1689

PART II

Leocadia Perpetua Dulce Calaveria y Vacamonte

Text of a letter from Archbishop Siegfried Walmund to Martin, Cardinal Calaveria y Vacamonte, delivered by Ahrent Rothofen.

To Sua Eminenza Martin, Cardinal Calaveria y Vacamonte, the most reverential greetings of Archbishop Walmund of Oldenburg, written by my own hand and with the prayers that God will preserve the Cardinal's family from any ill or evil:

It can come as no surprise to you, Eminenza, that my brother and I are disappointed to learn that your sister is not yet returned from her travels, for we both long for the day we may see her again, and resume the negotiations that were so abruptly discontinued when your sister left for Barcelona. Not that I do not enter into your feelings in regard to arranging marriages—truly, both parties should be aware of the agreements. I cannot think that the methods of our grandparents, when unions were negotiated without any consideration of the parties to be married, was preferable to our more tempered, modern approach. Therefore I beg you to inform me the moment you know that your sister is coming back to Roma, so that we may begin where we left off.

I pray that the family emergency that called her away has been successfully resolved, and that she will not be burdened with grief when she arrives, for a mourning bride is said to be a poor omen for a marriage. I trust, Eminenza, you will take no offense when I tell you that I would hope to see my brother and your sister united before Advent. We are agreed, are we not, that finding ways to continue the bonds between Spain and the German and Austrian states is a most desirable end, for the Hapsburgs will no longer occupy the Spanish throne when your King dies, and unless marriages of this sort are made, the unity that has served our countries and our faith so well, could suffer. You and I know what perilous times we live in, and how necessary it is to preserve the bonds holding Spain and the German states in alliance. The French have necessitated the Pope founding the Holy League, for Louis has issued challenges to the Church that cannot be tolerated, nor shall it be.

I recognize it is in Oldenburg's interest to have some link to the Spanish colonies in the New World; since few German states have colonies, the holdings of the Spanish have long been our link to the New World; it is a link we would not like to lose when the Spanish throne becomes vacant. Marriages like the one you and I contemplate for our families can establish the ties we all seek, and make it possible for the German states not to have too little influence in the affairs of the New World. You and I are agreed, I think, on the importance of German troops to support the Spanish presence in your colonies; without the musquets and pikes of our soldiers, the Spanish monks and priests might well have good reason to fear the ferocity of the natives, whose conversions are not always as certain as they profess. Think of what the Graff von Oldenburg may provide to aid your Spanish religious. For the sake of our countries and the True Faith, we must continue to support one another in our endeavor to bring the world to Christian order.

I realize your sister has reservations about my brother, Eminenza, and what woman would not have doubts about a man who wasted his youth in foolishness, and for which he is now suffering? God has brought him face-to-face with his sins and has marked him as one who must spend his life in penance for his failure to heed the loving admonitions of the Church. I do not seek to excuse his excesses, or to deny the burden this has placed on his health. But I am not convinced that these considerations are reason enough for a marriage to be refused, not with so much more than the lives of your sister and my brother in the balance. You were good enough to inform my courier, Ahrent Rothofen, that she—your sister—was uncertain about my brother, and, as I have said already, there is no fault in her for such cautions; few women wish to be joined to a man afflicted, no matter what sort of wretchedness he endures. Ordinarily I would not think a young woman ill-advised if she refused such a husband as my brother must be. If these two young people were peasants' or merchants' children, it might well be that their marriage would serve no purpose. But they are not from insignificant families, and these are not insignificant times, and their obligations extend beyond those of farm and market. You say your sister has long understood her duty to marry. It remains only to show her why her acceptance of my brother fulfills that duty.

The Graff von Oldenburg has informed me that upon the announcement of the nuptials of your sister and my brother, he will dispatch a company of pikemen to the American destination of your choosing, Eminenza, as a token of his appreciation of your efforts on behalf of Oldenburg and the Church. He would prefer to send the men before the worst of the winter storms make for a hard crossing, but that, of course, is in the hands of your sister.

I will be attending the Mass for the Pope's health tomorrow afternoon. Perhaps you and I will have a few moments we may discuss this further at its conclusion. If the heat is not too oppressive, perhaps we might have a stroll in the gardens? I will not, of course, press you for your answer then, but we may be able to reach a more comprehensive understanding after a little conversation. I hope you will spare me time then. If you cannot, then I ask you, Eminenza, to appoint another place and hour when we might conclude our negotiations. You have intimated to me that you are eager for this match, as you know I am. Should we not then, do all that we can to see our hopes come to fruition?

*With my prayers for your wisdom and well-being and the pledge
of my fidelity to our mutual cause, I sign myself,*

*Your most devoted and sincere
Siegfried Walmund
Archbishop of Oldenburg*

In Roma on the 17th day of June, 1689

1

Moonlight limned the rising walls of the new buildings at the Villa Vecchia, its limpid touch softening and concealing, like the veil over a bride's face. Summer filled the night air, warm and fecund, every breeze laden with the aromas of the burgeoning largesse of fields and orchards and vineyards. Making his way back to this place very late, Ragoczy could hear the distant call of night-birds and the gentle sloughing of the wind against the counterpoint of his horse's hooves on the flags of the courtyard; his ride had been contented, for the lovely dream he had provided the widow two villages away had not only assuaged his esurience, it had held some of the amelioration of loneliness that such encounters rarely provided, and for which he was deeply grateful. As he neared the stable, he became aware of another sound coming from beyond the coach-house: the sing-song repetition of the Rosary prayers, punctuated by the occasional slap of leather on flesh.

At the stable door he dismounted and led his grey inside; a single lamp left burning for his arrival provided illumination Ragoczy did not need as he began to unsaddle the grey gelding. He was stowing his saddle in the tack-room when the side-door opened and Matyas stepped in; the chief groom and occasional coachman made a gesture of welcome to his employer.

"I'll take care of the grey, Signore," he said, speaking softly in a mixture of Hungarian and Italian. "It is late and you have need of sleep, I do not doubt. Amerigo has been abed since the cook retired." There was a world of implication in this report, all of which Ragoczy ignored.

"The lamp is a kindness in you, Matyas," said Ragoczy, knowing that his ability to see easily in the dark would attract attention he did not want.

"Then perhaps you can see what the penitent is doing? I hear her with her scourge at night, and I fear for her." He pointed to the open side-door. "She has been praying for hours. I dare not think what she has done to herself."

"I'll see to her," Ragoczy told him. "Make sure the gelding has grain as well as hay. It may be summer now, but that does not excuse us from feeding animals."

"Of course," said Matyas, a bit impatiently for being reminded of his job. "And he'll have a brushing-down before I retire."

"Including the mane and tail," Ragoczy said. "The insects are plentiful: use the orange-peel oil on his coat."

"I will," said Matyas, and left to attend to the horse.

Ragoczy stood for a moment, gathering his thoughts in preparation, then he went out into the night again. He paused for a moment to listen to the sounds coming from beyond the old coach-house: there could be no doubt—Leocadia was beating herself with a scourge. Steeling himself against what he would see, he made his way to the small building she had made her cell. He hesitated once again, his senses keen. The odor of her sweat and blood, and the faint, acrid sweetness of infection filled him so intensely that he had to bank his feelings against them as he went to knock on the crude wooden door. When the prayers continued, he knocked again, more firmly.

"Is someone there?" Leocadia called out, fear making her voice hoarse.

"Yes. It is Signore Ragoczy," he replied gently, his voice low and pleasant. "I am . . . concerned for you, Penitent. It is very late and I am troubled by the rigors of your devotions."

The laughter that answered his words was strident. "They are not

rigorous enough for what I must expiate." As if to underscore her
words, the hiss and slap of the scourge sounded again. "I am as yet
unworthy of salvation. God let His Son suffer more anguish than
anything I have known." Her voice was sing-song and thready, both
worrisome signs.

Ragoczy knew better than to challenge this; instead he asked,
"Have you been feverish? The weather has been so warm and close
that I sense you might become so. That is more than chastisement,
Penitent, it is dangerous."

"God sends the weather as surely as He sends retribution," she
said. "I have not completed the Rosary yet. I beg you will permit me
to." Without waiting for anything more from him, she began to pray
again, punctuating the cadences with the whack of her scourge.

"Penitent," Ragoczy said a little louder to catch her attention, "you
are in my care and I will be held accountable if any ill should befall
you."

"God will absolve you of all responsibility," said Leocadia, before
beginning another Ave Maria, the scourge keeping cadence with the
salutation of the Angel Gabriel.

"Ah, but the earthly courts may not be so compassionate should
you ail while you stop here," said Ragoczy, and gave her time to think
of this before he went on. "If anything should happen to you, it will
fall to me to answer for it."

"But how can you? I am nothing to you." She spoke anxiously, her
prayer abandoned. "You do not know me as more than a penitent.
Who is to act against you if I should perish? How could you be held
to answer for an unknown?" The edge in her voice revealed the terror
that he had inspired.

"Unknown you may be to me, but you must be someone's daughter, or sister," he said persuasively.

"I have *no one*," she whispered fiercely; there was the sound of
her moving, and when she spoke again she was immediately on the
other side of the door. "I am *nobody*."

Ragoczy considered his next remark carefully. "That may be true,
but the Church values the least of her children as greatly as the
mightiest."

"Ha!" came the rejoinder. "No one believes that. The mighty are mighty and the rest are dust beneath their feet."

Aware that her sudden anger might work against him as readily as for him, he went on carefully. "If you accept that, why do you spend your days in prayer?"

"Because my *sin* is mighty." She began suddenly to weep in hard, desperate sobs. "God will not overlook my sins simply because I am not of any importance in the world."

"Penitent," Ragoczy said firmly, "please let me in. I want only to see that you are well, or, if you are not, to provide succor."

"*No!*" She retreated from the door, her crying becoming whimpering, as if she dared not raise her voice.

"Signorina," Ragoczy said, his voice gentle and urgent at once, "I mean you no harm. You have my Word that I will do nothing more than I have said I will do."

It required some effort for Leocadia to collect herself enough to speak. "I don't believe you."

The resentment in her voice shocked Ragoczy; he had expected many things of her, but this surprised him. "Why should I dissemble?" he asked at his most reasonable. "As you say, I know nothing of you, but I suspect you have taken some infection from your . . . exercises. I would like to be certain you are not ill, for your sake as well as mine."

She muttered something under her breath that Ragoczy could not hear, and then she raised her voice enough to be heard. "I will not be turned from my penance."

Ragoczy raised his hands in aggravation, although his voice did not change. "I have no wish to do so," he said mendaciously. "But I want to assure myself that you are not so ill that your penance is . . . tainted."

"Tainted." Leocadia fell silent: no prayers, no scourging came from the improvised cell. Finally her steps approached the door, and she drew back the bolt that secured it. "See for yourself." She was in her camisa, which had once been white but was now dirty and stained, the back nothing more than tatters, matted with old and new blood. Her face was gaunt and her color high, her lips cracked and dry, revealing the extent of the infection that possessed her. In her right hand she held her rosary, the amber beads clouded, in her left she held her scourge, the four lashes darkly glistening with wetness.

"You are ill," Ragoczy said calmly enough, though he was struck by the lack of concern she displayed.

"Not beyond God's cure," she said, preparing to close the door again. "I entrust myself to Him and the Virgin, and pray for mercy," She tried to swing the door closed, but could not; she clung to it, swaying slightly.

Ragoczy held the door open easily. He spoke kindly and simply. "Penitent, I ask you—I beseech you—let me tend to your injuries, so that you do not pray in delirium. Who knows what forces you might invoke in such a state."

She gazed at him, blinking frequently. "You shine." With that, she dropped to her knees, trying to steady herself as she began praying.

"Penitent," Ragoczy said gently and persistently, "listen to me. You have become fevered. This fever may be ended, if you will permit me to treat you. Do not refuse the healing I can offer, for I do it in the name of charity. Recover from your fever, *te prego*. Then you may continue your devotions without the distortions that such febrile infection brings."

"I pray, and offer up my burning," she said, her voice becoming fainter. "Like . . . the Saints . . ."

"It cannot be God's wish to see you die from illness," Ragoczy said, a wave of hideous memories coming over him, from his days at the Temple of Imhotep to the cholera-stricken streets of Athens to the devastation of Europe when the Black Plague first struck. "There is no piety in disease, Penitent, only suffering."

"God's Son suffered," Leocadia murmured. She crossed herself, lassitude making it difficult to complete.

"But not from disease," Ragoczy insisted as he swiftly bent and lifted her into his arms, saying, "You will need to get well if you wish to continue your devotions." Her sickness struck him with a force that was almost physical. He could feel the heat of her through her ruined camisa and his own riding clothes. "When did you last eat?" he asked, expecting no answer. "Or drink?"

Leocadia flailed at him silently, but her weakness quickly exhausted her and she lay limp and unprotesting as he carried her into his house; her head lolled over Ragoczy's arm as if she had completely lost consciousness.

"Rugerius," said Ragoczy, as he came down the hall toward his study; he knew his manservant would be waiting for him there, and would know how to explain his actions to the servants if they should gossip.

"My master," Rugerius exclaimed as he held the door wide for Ragoczy. "Our Penitent Guest? What is wrong?"

"She's flailed her shoulders to bits and is burning with fever. Those welts are infected." He cocked his head toward the trestle table. "Move the books and papers off that, will you? I need to have a proper look at her."

"No, no," she whispered. "No, brother, you must not . . ."

"Penitent, you are ill. I have a remedy for you," said Ragoczy as calmingly as he could; he moved to the table Rugerius was clearing. "God will not mind you being treated for your sickness." He spoke to Rugerius in a crisper tone. "At least we have trestle tables in plenty; without one this would be more difficult. We have something more to thank the builders for." Then he spoke to Leocadia again. "Do not worry; you will be better."

Her mumbled response was incoherent; she turned her head away from him.

"I think, old friend, she had better lie prone. Her back will need attention first." He nodded in the direction of a small settee. "Take one of the cushions, for her head."

Rugerius finished stacking the books he had cleared on a stool and put the papers on a tall lectern, then fetched the cushion, placing it at the end of the table nearest Ragoczy. "What more shall I do?"

"She needs a clean camisa; there is a linen night-rail in the clothespress as I recall: it will do. Bring that, and a vial of the sovereign remedy. I'll need a basin and a sponge to clean—" He indicated her back as he laid her very tenderly facedown on the table, her head resting on the brocade-covered cushion. "And a topical anodyne as well, I think," he said impassively as he looked at the ruin of her shoulders and back.

"What has she done to herself?" Rugerius asked after a single glance at the young woman's back. "Some of those—" He went to the far side of the room for a tree of candles which he brought back to the trestle table. "You may want more light. This calls for more than you can see in the dark."

"Yes. Thank you," said Ragoczy, bending over the young woman. "I will need the spirits of wine to clean this, I fear. A pity we have no housekeeper to whom we can entrust her, but—" He nodded toward the door. "Do not rouse the household if you can avoid it."

"Of course not," said Rugerius, and went off to do as Ragoczy had charged him.

Removing his gloves, Ragoczy made a careful study of Leocadia's back, taking care not to touch her, for he did not want to give her any more pain than she had inflicted upon herself. The flesh on her shoulders and her upper back was the most damaged; the sweet, metallic odor of it revealed its rottenness as much as the puffy, discolored tissue did. Her hands and feet were grimy, with dark stains from her blood as well as fine lines of dirt; one long, matted braid fell over her shoulder, the hair stiff with blood. Ragoczy wondered how long she had been beating herself, and how many blows she had inflicted.

On the table Leocadia stirred a little, suppressing a moan as she did; her eyes came open, but the stare with which she took in her surroundings was blank, and she closed them again.

As he watched her, Ragoczy could not rid himself of an uneasy worry: should he inform her brother of her condition? He knew that the Cardinal had announced his sister was away from Roma, saying she was visiting in Spain. The trouble was, as Ragoczy saw it, that if the Cardinal believed this to be true, he would regard any information from Ragoczy regarding his missing sister as an attempt at embarrassing him; if the Cardinal was aware that she had disappeared, he might decide that Ragoczy had kidnapped her, or taken her as a concubine. The punishment for such crimes was severe and deadly; there would be no mercy for so great an insult.

"Here are the items you requested," Rugerius said as he came back into the study and closed the door behind him. "All but the night-warder are asleep, and he is posted at the new house."

"Excellent," Ragoczy approved. His swift perusal of the items on the tray revealed that Rugerius had brought scissors and a small jar of ginger-willow-and-valerian tincture as well as the sovereign remedy, the spirits of wine, and the topical anodyne. "Very sensible. I should have thought of that," he said as Rugerius dragged a small bench nearer on which he could place his tray.

"The night-rail is much too large for her, but it will do for now," Rugerius remarked as he took the lawn garment from hanging over his arm and draped it over the chair with the highest back. "I will go get the basin of water now, if you do not need me."

"I do, but I need the water more," Ragoczy said with a trace of mild self-mockery in his tone. As soon as Rugerius left the study again, Ragoczy shrugged out of his riding-coat, took the anodyne tincture and using the long stopper, began to drop single droplets of the solution onto her shoulders. "This will numb your hurts," Ragoczy explained, although he was not sure she heard him, or paid him any attention. "You will not mind so much when I clean the pus from your wounds, which I must do if you are to fight off your infection. There is pus in the exposed tissues, and I want you to be rid of it. Your physicians may say what they will—I do not think any pus is laudable." In his black-brocaded waistcoat and white camisa, he looked severe as a priest, though the rubies securing his neck-bands were too ostentatious for the clergy, who saved their jewels for their reliquaries, monstrances, crucifixes, and ceremonial vestments.

As she stirred, he stopped his ministrations. "Where am I?" she asked in Spanish, her eyes again coming open.

Ragoczy answered in Italian, to keep from confusing her more than she already was. "In the study of the Villa Vecchia. You collapsed, Signorina. Fortunately one of my servants heard you, and summoned aid." He could see that this had little impact upon her; her gaze was unsteady and with little animation.

"Oh," she said, and closed her eyes again.

Very carefully Ragoczy resumed his treating of her back until he had covered most of the mangled flesh in the pale-green liquid. Then he waited, allowing the virtue of the tincture to work upon her, dulling the sensation in her wounds so that he would not make her agony worse as he treated her.

When Rugerius returned the second time, he said, "Matyas is cleaning her cell. He plans to wash down the whole building, inside and out. He wants no site for the fevers of summer to take hold at the Villa Vecchia."

"Not an entirely foolish notion." Ragoczy approved, as he took the basin from Rugerius. "It will help our guest, if she decides to remain with us."

"And do you think she will?" Rugerius asked, lifting the ewer he had brought with the basin to the bench next to the trestle table.

"I have no idea," Ragoczy said as he bent over Leocadia again. "I'll need the spirits of wine to wash my hands."

"Of course," Rugerius said, and selected the spirits of wine from the tray. Then he took one of the strips of linen and held it between his hands. "Go ahead."

Ragoczy took the spirits of wine and opened the container, pouring a palmful onto his open hand. Then he set the container down and rubbed his hands briskly together over the cloth Rugerius held. Only when he had taken care to lave every part of both his hands did he allow Rugerius to dry his hands. "Stow the cloth for washing," he said as he gave his entire attention to Leocadia again.

"And wash in boiling water," said Rugerius, repeating the rest of the instruction.

"Add the rest of the spirits of wine to the basin," Ragoczy went on as he touched the scoring on Leocadia's back. The anodyne tincture had done its work; she did not flinch, nor was she roused as he continued to study the extent of the damage she had done herself. "There are bits of cloth buried in the welts," he said. "I will have to clean them out or the infection will come again."

"Of course," said Rugerius, taking a boiled sponge and putting it into the basin along with rest of the spirits of wine. "You will need to soak them out, I suppose."

"I see no alternative." His voice was distant, his concentration so great that words seemed trivial. "Hold the basin near."

Rugerius did as he was told, watching while Ragoczy laid the sopping sponge on Leocadia's back. "How long will you wait?"

"It will depend on how swollen the tissues are. I will have to be very careful, however long it takes." His expression was oddly serene as he went about the task of soaking her injuries, and then cautiously drawing out the bits of thread and cloth that clung there. Only when all trace of fabric was gone did he sponge away the pus and caked blood. Finally he dropped the sponge back in the basin, saying, "Boil the lot. And burn those scraps of cloth. They are full of infection and cannot be saved."

"The cook will be in the kitchen soon, and the workmen will arrive soon after that." Rugerius indicated the window where the sky was beginning to lighten. The first rustle of the morning breeze plucked at the leaves of the cypress and peach trees growing near the villa, like the whispered hush before a concert or the anticipation of Mass.

"Yes. I will wrap her in clean linen, but it will have to be changed this evening." He frowned briefly. "She will have to be tended until the fever is past. You may need to find a maid to look after her."

"I will ask the cook to recommend someone," said Rugerius. "There must be someone in the village who will undertake to care for her."

"I have no doubt of that," said Ragoczy drily. "But she must remain incognito, and the curiosity of servants is legendary." He glanced toward the window, his attractive, irregular features made stark by the increasing light. "Choose someone who is discreet, for the sake of this young woman."

"I will do so," said Rugerius. He paused. "Do you want to notify her family?"

Ragoczy paused in cleaning his hands in the last of the spirits of wine. "If she admitted to having one, I would, but as she claims to be alone in the world, it would be the worst breach of trust I could—" He stopped as Leocadia sighed.

"Is she waking?" Rugerius came to the side of the table and looked down at her.

"She might be. Get me the bandages so I may finish my work," Ragoczy said crisply, and for the next little while he busied himself with putting clean linen strips over the torn flesh of her back. When he was through the sun was rising, and the first, pinkish rays of light were coming through the windows and the sounds of the builders arriving rivaled the birds for command of the morning.

"What about the room at the end of the back hall? Shall I carry her there? It is isolated enough for our penitent," suggested Rugerius.

"I suppose so," said Ragoczy, his tone distant. "Have the cook be her chaperone, if you think she will be agreeable to the idea, at least until you can find a maid for her."

"What troubles you, my master?" Rugerius asked as he went on with his task of cleaning up.

Ragoczy gave a single shake of his head. "She is so much . . . alone."

"And she is like Nicoris and Xenya," said Rugerius. "Oh, yes; I have seen that aspect in her, and I have hoped I was wrong. It may still be that I am."

"We cannot be certain," said Ragoczy, his voice quiet, his eyes like banked embers.

"No; yet I have seen it in you, too, that you sense her des—" He went silent as Leocadia moaned.

"She will be awake soon, and she should be stowed in her bed shortly," Ragoczy said, his expression keen again. "It will not do for her to discover me here, not after her travail. She will need some time to comprehend what has happened to her, and why. I will speak with her later." He gathered up his gloves and riding-coat on his way to the door. "I regret this will demand so much attention from you, old friend."

"You're being kind to a frightened young woman—why should I not assist you?" Rugerius shook his head. "If I have not become accustomed to this aspect of your character by now, my master, I deserve banishment." There was amusement in his faded-blue eyes that took any sting from his words.

"And she came here for protection," Ragoczy said. "What else could I do?"

"Nothing that you could bear to do," said Rugerius. "So she is a guest here, however strange she may be. It is my honor to care for her well-being. And yours." This last implied a warning that Ragoczy did not address.

"I hope you are repaid commensurately," said Ragoczy as he left Rugerius with Leocadia. By the time he came down from his private quarters shortly after the builders and the servants had had their mid-day meal and nap, the villa was thrumming with activity, from the builders working on the new structure to the servants bustling about their tasks, to Maurizio, who practiced out in the garden in spite of the heat of the day.

Rugerius met Ragoczy in the corridor outside the withdrawing room devoted to music. Ragoczy was neatly dressed in black brocade piped in red silk; he was expecting Alessandro Scarlatti to visit him a bit later in the day. "What of our Guest?"

Rugerius answered in a low voice, as if to quiet the sounds of construction from outside. "She is resting. I have found someone to watch over her, but she has not come yet. The cook's cousin will be here later in the afternoon. I promised her a gold sceptre for every day of service, provided she is loyal."

"Generous pay: do you think that might make her too curious?" Ragoczy asked, half-listening to Maurizio working at his exercises.

"It is a risk, but given that there is building going on, she will probably consider the amount a sign of your wealth. The builder are boasting about the outrageous amounts they are charging you, and she may think this is more of the same." Rugerius indicated the activity on the far side of the carriage drive. "The noise alone demands higher pay."

"Is that what you told her?" Ragoczy asked, a trace of mischief in his dark eyes.

"No; that is what the cook told her," Rugerius replied. "Do you plan to visit her?"

"After her maid arrives I will spend a short while with her, as I must, being her host," Ragoczy said at his most urbane. "She will expect that courtesy."

"And what about Maurizio?" asked Rugerius, falling into step beside Ragoczy as he made his way toward the garden and the sound of the violin.

"I doubt his playing will distress our guest," said Ragoczy, deliberately obtuse.

"That was not my meaning," Rugerius responded. "The lad is infatuated with the penitent. What are we to do about it?"

Ragoczy stopped and looked directly at his manservant. "As little as possible. Maurizio already has far too grand a notion of himself. Let him think he is thwarted in love and there will be no bearing him." His tone became more somber. "And I fear our Penitent Guest may not welcome his attentions beyond his music."

"He knows she is ill," Rugerius remarked.

"I would imagine everyone from here to the high-road knows that by now," said Ragoczy. "It is dread of the mal aria that makes everyone fear sickness."

Rugerius considered this. "Can Maurizio's ardor be dampened by his concern about illness? He is impetuous, but would he do anything . . ." He tried to find the right word.

"I think Maurizio would not let disease or war or religion lessen his affection; only time will do that." Ragoczy remembered how turbulent and difficult it had been for him, the first time he had grappled with passion: though it was nearly three thousand years ago, he could still wince at the recollection of his impulsivity. He had not comprehended its meaning at the time; his understand came only in retrospect, long after he had left the Temple of Imhotep, long after the sun-ravaged girl was dead.

"Do you think he would—" Rugerius did not go on, as if speaking his apprehension aloud would increase the chance of its becoming reality.

"I think he is a young man caught in the throes of his first real devotion, and I suspect he is not very prudent just now. There is such mystery in his inamorata, which helps to fuel his predilection. He is very likely confused by all that is happening; such attachments often take one by surprise." Ragoczy smiled swiftly. "Don't worry for the time being; Maestro Scarlatti will keep him busy as our opera rehearsals continue."

"A pity Maurizio does not have the benefit of your instruction," said Rugerius.

"I may not play for him, but I do instruct him," he reminded Rugerius. "There is no point in playing for him—it would only serve to make him more competitive than he already is, which would benefit no one." He paused at the door to the garden. "If only he will use a little sense in regard to our Penitent Guest this will be easier for him as well as for her."

"Do you think he will—use sense?" Rugerius had a hint of amusement in his question.

Ragoczy shook his head once. "No," he said evenly. "I do not."

Text of a letter from Niklos Aulirios to Podesta Narcisso della Rovere, accompanying two deeds of title.

To the most worthy Magistrate, Podesta Narcisso della Rovere, Niklos Aulirios sends his respectful greetings and begs that the Podesta will consider the attestations he is sending to you when making his final decisions regarding the egregious suit Ahrent Rothofen has seen fit to bring against him.

I have taken the liberty of sending these materials to your clerk, with the earnest supplication that he will bear them to you at your country villa, for although you have recessed the hearing of the suit, it cannot be possible that so meticulous a Magistrate as you are known to be would refuse to scrutinize all appropriate exhibits pertaining to this affair.

Good Magistrate, I appeal to your sense of justice in this difficult contest. I repose utmost confidence in your prudence and your rectitude, and now I lay the whole of my claim open to your perusal. You have already in hand the record made of Pope Sergius IV's gracious permission for the Clemens estates to be maintained through the female line and exempted from any claims of husbands or other male relatives. These two deeds show that the Clemens women have exercised their right of matrilineal inheritance from the time of Pope Sergius' dispensation until Atta Olivia Clemens, who was a widow, died without female issue to claim the estates of her inheritance.

Let me assure you, Podesta, that I do not want to cheat any legitimate heir of any valid legacy, but as Rothofen is claiming that his grandfather's legitimization is grounds for his inheriting, I believe it is incumbent upon me to bring you these deeds as a demonstration of the Clemens women's long history of exercising their prerogatives as granted to them so long ago. If you have any doubt as to their traditions in this regard, you may see for yourself that they have continued to manage their affairs in accordance with the privileges Pope Sergius granted them.

If, upon examination of these deeds you still cannot support my right to the estates left to me by Atta Olivia Clemens, then I will have to submit my records to the Pope for his judgment. I doubt Innocenzo will be inclined to countermand the rulings of his distant predecessor, particularly since the precedent he established has been so regularly maintained.

I thank you for the careful perusal you will give my case and I welcome the wisdom of your judgment. I am always at your disposal to answer any questions you may have, and to bring about a reasonable disposal of this suit. May God guide your meditations and may your Good Angel reward your impartiality in this matter, for I am confident that you will not seek to pervert the spirit and letter of the law in order to please the caprice of powerful men whose purpose is not justice but avarice.

Believe me, Podesta, to be one who holds you in highest esteem,

Your most unassuming petitioner,
Niklos Aulirios

At Senza Pari, on the 2nd day of July, 1689

2

Age had not been kind to Gennaro Colonna; his face had lost all its handsomeness in a fretwork of wrinkles, his nose had become beak-like, his eyes were clouded, his voice was reedy, and his joints were knotted. All that was left of his once-glorious dark curls was a wispy fringe of white, insubstantial as gossamer. He sat in a chair on the terrace of Ettore Colonna's villa, his head cocked so he might hear the sound of the birds more clearly, for he could no longer see them as more than agile shapes moving against the sky. "There are birds in the New World no larger than a budding rose; they are too small to have songs. They hover on invisible wings to drink the sweetness of flowers."

"He is often fanciful," said Ettore Colonna to his guest as the two strolled beyond the terrace and into the garden. "He tells tales of the New World that have more to do with the realms of dreams than the world, no matter how New." He studied Ragoczy for a moment. "Did your kinsman tell you nothing of those birds?"

"In fact, he did," said Ragoczy, who had found the humming birds one of the few consolations of his prison cell that looked out into a defile full of tall flowering trees—the little birds had lived there, and Ragoczy had studied them. "He said much the same thing about them, and how bright their colors were."

"Then his wits may not be quite gone, after all," said Ettore Colonna with a sardonic note in his voice. The day was warm and he wore his long brocaded waistcoat over his fine linen camisa; his satin justaucorps was back in the villa. He had also left his wig on its block, and his short-cropped dark hair showed flecks of grey.

"Perhaps not," said Ragoczy uneasily. He, too, was casually dressed in a lightweight riding-coat of fine black Florentine wool over a short silk waistcoat and camisa of glossy white silk, cuffed and banded in lace. His breeches were narrow, of the same material as his coat, and his high black boots shone beneath a new haze of dust. He wore no hat or wig; his dark, loosely curling hair was caught at the back of his neck in a black satin ribband. In spite of the heat, no trace of sweat was on him.

"Would you like to talk to him? He has many stories of your kinsman," said Ettore Colonna as he made his way on the gravel path between the roses.

"Oh, I think not," said Ragoczy with a feigned indifference. "There is no reason to disturb him, is there?" He had no desire to risk having Gennaro Colonna recognize him, for that would be more difficult than he cared to think: Gennaro Colonna could ask questions that would turn scrutiny upon him, a scrutiny that was dangerous to more than himself.

"He isn't easily disturbed," said Ettore Colonna, his long legs covering the ground at a pace many would find difficult to match. "He has few opportunities to tell his tales these days."

"That's unfortunate," said Ragoczy, and waited for Ettore Colonna to say more.

Ettore Colonna walked a little faster. "I suppose it is. But some of his recollections could be dangerous."

Ragoczy, nearly a head shorter than his host, kept up easily. "I cannot recall if you told me before: how long was he in the New World?"

"Oh, decades. He went there in the forties—I forget the year. He says he misses it, though how that can be, I do not know." He glanced at Ragoczy. "What did your kinsman think of it?"

"Wild; sad; beautiful," said Ragoczy, as if reciting from memory. "He found it an amazing place."

"My cousin told me your kinsman was jailed by the Church. He said it was a miscarriage of justice." He waited for a response as they reached the end of the walk, where a plantation of mulberries forced them to turn to the south.

"No doubt my kinsman would agree," said Ragoczy, making no apology for the irony in his voice. The prisons had been no worse than many he had known, and not so bad as some. He had been able to see the world, albeit through small windows; that was preferable to the oubliettes in Nineveh and Babylon, the memories of which could still appall him. The recollection of the cell beneath the Circus Maximus was a more recent recollection, keener for being close at hand, and for Olivia, who had sought him out and saved him.

"And you? What would you say?" Ettore Colonna considered Ragoczy with bright, black eyes.

"I would say that what may be justice to one man is rankest iniquity to another," Ragoczy said.

"Oh, bravo, bravo," said Ettore Colonna, applauding his sarcasm. "Very adroit, my friend." He had reached a sundial set in a small fountain; here he paused again, squinting up at the sun before looking at the angled shadow. "Almost noon."

"So it is," said Ragoczy, aware of the passage of the sun more surely than the sundial could ever be.

"I presume it is useless to ask you to dine with me?" Ettore Colonna raised one emphatic eyebrow.

"You may always ask; I shall thank you and decline," was Ragoczy's punctilious answer.

Ettore Colonna shook his head. "You are so composed, Ragoczy." His amusement was short-lived. "The Church has again begun looking into the lives of my associates. I thought I had better warn you."

"Thank you," said Ragoczy. "But why should they concern themselves with me?" He did not want to reveal the extent of uneasiness this warning aroused in him.

"They need no reason," said Ettore Colonna with sudden bitterness. "If they should decide to suspect you, their suspicions are reason enough. They have only to say that you may be heretical, or blasphemous, or diabolical, or not devout enough, or lacking in faith, or obstinate in sin, or irreligious in conduct, or sympathetic to those who are, or anything they decide will justify their suspicions." He kicked at the gravel, his face set.

"But you are safe?" Ragoczy thought of Ettore Colonna's certainty that no inquiry could touch him, and wondered if this were still true.

"I think so," came his reply. "The Curia knows how much power the Colonnas have in the Church, and they know that I know many things that could embarrass the Church if they sought to harm me. The family may not approve of me, but no one wants a Colonna to fall into the hands of the servants at the Pope's Little House." He laughed without mirth. "I have several written accounts held in France that cannot be opened while I live. The Curia knows this, and it makes for circumspection. If I had not bothered with such precautions, I would be afraid of what might happen to me, Colonna or no. As it is—" His shrug was eloquent and he resumed walking, putting the sundial behind him.

Ragoczy kept pace with his host. "What is the Church looking for, do you know?" he asked, aware that Ettore Colonna was deeply troubled. "Among your associates?"

"Other than our loves?" he countered. "Why, anything that could be used as an excuse to take my associates into custody. If they cannot reach me directly, they will find other means to bring me to heel. I have warned Maestro Scarlatti of this development, and I pray he takes heed of my warning."

"What do you advise we do? your associates." Ragoczy had stopped at a hedge of juniper, his expression expectant.

"Be aware that you are watched. Observe every stricture the Church could wish upon you, and if that is not possible, bring as little attention to yourself as you can." He chuckled. "You are building a new villa and you are enmeshed in a lawsuit. You are not inconspicuous as it is."

"Would I not create suspicion if I were to abandon either project?" Ragoczy suggested.

"Yes; you would. You are a foreigner, and even in this newly liberal Rome, foreigners who are not pilgrims are objects of . . . Shall we call it inquiry? And since Archbishop Walmund is looking for anything that might serve to blacken your character, the Curia has an ally in their efforts." He folded his arms, looking down directly at Ragoczy. "I know I have spoken of this before, but it has become more urgent."

"You have heard something?" Ragoczy asked, making no apology for the tension in his voice. "What is it?" He took a few steps away from the juniper.

Ettore Colonna shrugged. "Nothing specific. But then, I would not hear that in any case," he said, strolling toward a small plantation of rosemary and thyme; their fragrance was as strong as the scent of roses. "No, that is not what troubles me."

Ragoczy was hard put not to demand an explanation. He walked a few steps farther along the path, then said, "You can read these matters better than I, Colonna. I must rely on your comprehension."

"So you must," said Ettore Colonna, stopping beside Ragoczy and looking out across his garden. "And I do not want to alarm you. You have plenty to contend with as it is. But I have heard there are questions being asked about the penitent to whom you have given shelter. Oh, yes. There has been gossip about her. Builders and coachmen talk, and the familiars hear."

Ragoczy managed a nonchalance that he did not feel. "Well, what are they saying? Until her exercises became too severe, she was left in the cell of her own devising." He saw no surprise in Ettore Colonna's long face, and knew this was part of the rumors being circulated. "How can I be suspected for that?"

"She may not be worthy of your charity," said Ettore Colonna; the implications of his words struck Ragoczy as his host waited for a response.

"How do you mean?" Ragoczy asked; as much intrigued as apprehensive.

"How much do you know about her?" Ettore Colonna countered.

"Only that she came to my villa, half-starved, saying she was a penitent, and asking for shelter. I provided a room for her in one of the out-buildings on my property, told the cook to feed her and give her water, and until very recently, left her to her devotions." He paused. "Why should this alarm the Church?"

"What has changed?" Ettore Colonna sounded wary; it was a delicate matter to know how much to learn.

Ragoczy's answer was direct and candid. "She had been using a flagellum as part of her devotions, and the lashes had left unhealed weals; these became pustulant and required treatment, for which purpose I had her brought into the old building and given a room and a maid to care for her as she recovered. She has remained in that room since her treatment began. I see her twice a day, always with the maid present. Anyone who claims anything more has no notion of the truth."

"You provided the penitent a maid?" Ettore Colonna asked, with some sense of relief coloring his tone of voice.

"Per natura," said Ragoczy. "What else could I do that would not bring dishonor upon her, and upon me."

Ettore Colonna nodded. "Prudent as well as adroit," he approved, the severity fading from his long features. "I knew you could not put yourself in so exposed a position as the rumors hint."

"If anyone doubts me, have them speak to my staff." He held up his small, beautiful hand. "And do not tell me that they would lie to protect me: I am, as you say, a foreigner and they are Romans."

"And the penitent? What of her?" Ettore Colonna waited for his answer, a frown returning to deepen the vertical crease between his brows.

"She has told me nothing," Ragoczy said truthfully. "She claims she is no one."

"And what do you think?" his host asked. "Remember, Benedetto Oldescalchi was an attorney long before he was Pope."

"I think she does not wish to be known, whoever she may be." This was also the truth, and Ragoczy was relieved to have it so. "I cannot demand she tell me more than her Confessor would require."

Ettore Colonna sighed hard. "But what if she is a criminal?"

"All the more reason to aid her penitence," said Ragoczy. "The Church cannot object to anyone seeking to expiate sin, can she?"

"You would think not, but—" He stopped. "Lies and half-lies can turn an act of Christian kindness into the deepest vice."

"As well as clothe the greatest depravity in the appearance of virtue," Ragoczy said, recalling the many times he had seen both distortions happen.

"I will tell my cousin," said Ettore Colonna, adding in a lighter tone, "Let us hope this will be the end of it."

"Amen to that," said Ragoczy as he crossed himself. They had reached a crosspath in the garden and they stood for a moment as if uncertain whether to return to the terrace or to continue their tour of the garden.

Their decision was made for them when Celestino Bruschi appeared in the tall doors opening onto the terrace, his hand raised to catch the attention of the two in the garden. "Signore Colonna," he called. "A courier has arrived. He must speak with you. He says it is pressing."

Ettore Colonna had sheltered his eyes with his hand the better to see Bruschi. "Whose courier is he?"

"Your cousin's—the Cardinal's. The man is not a priest." He motioned to Ettore Colonna to hurry. "I have sent him to the dining room. I thought you wouldn't mind."

Ettore Colonna was walking faster now, Ragoczy half a step behind him. "Very good. You did well." He reached the terrace steps and went up them two at a time, making no apology to his ancient cousin as he rushed past him.

Ragoczy was more correct, pausing to make a leg to Gennaro Co-

lonna and say, "With your permission," before following Ettore Colonna into the house.

The courier was eating a wedge of melon served with thin slices
of ham when Ragoczy caught up with Ettore Colonna in the dining
room; the young man wore the mantel of the Guardia Laterana, and
his clothes were dusty from his ride. He had set aside his gloves and
was busy with knife and fork. "I'm sorry, Signore, but I am hungry,"
he said between bites. "I rode out from Roma as quickly as I could."

"Then do not stop eating," said Ettore Colonna a trifle drily. He
pulled a chair back from the table and sat down. "What message have
you for me?"

The courier had a mouthful of melon and could not answer immediately. He gestured toward a leather bag slung over the back of
his chair.

"Bruschi, open it," said Ettore Colonna, and clapped for a servant.
"Wine for my guests. Not Ragoczy: he does not drink wine."

The servant went to fetch a bottle from the pantry while Celestino
Bruschi brought out the letter that bore the Colonna seal; he handed
it and stood back while Ettore read the crossed lines.

"The Pope has sent for his physician. The French are pressing
their advantage to get their Four Points accepted while the Pope is
ailing." Ettore Colonna read on. "My cousin advises me to have no
contact with our French associates, for that would give the Holy Office the excuse it needs to take me into custody for acting against the
Church." He read the rest in silence, saying when he was finished,
"How can the cousins of Cardinal Mazarin pretend to have no associates in France? His nieces married into the nobility, for gli Occhi
della Santa Lucia!" he exclaimed impatiently. "But it would seem that
the French are all devils now."

The courier nodded as he took his last bite of melon. "They are
saying the French are trying to influence the election of the next
Pope." His accent was north-eastern, though not Venezian: possibly
Udinese.

"Innocenzo is not dead yet," Ettore Colonna reminded them all
sharply. "Until he is, his policies are beyond question, no matter what
the French would like to think."

"But he will not live forever," said the courier with a shrug. "We must reflect on what is to come."

Ettore Colonna eyed him, a sardonic glint in his eyes. "You are a bit young to be so indifferent to the end of life."

"He is not indifferent," said Ragoczy. "He is unable to imagine it happening to him, and so he hopes that if he is not distressed by Death, it will ignore him."

The courier jumped as if stung, color rising in his face as he stood up to defend himself. "Who are you to say I am afraid?"

"I do not recall saying you are afraid, only that you would like Death to pay you no heed." Ragoczy's manner was courteous and mild but there was enough of an edge an his tone that warned the courier not to force the issue.

"That's different, I suppose," he said as he sat down again. The servant put a goblet of freshly poured wine into his hand and the courier took a long draught.

"When did the Pope send for his physician, do you know?" Ettore Colonna asked as the courier accepted his goblet of wine.

"Last night sometime; very late, in any case," He drank again, then went on. "They say it could be the mal aria, but that is what they always say in the summer." This time his studied lack of concern went unremarked.

"Last night. Then the news must be all over Roma by now. No wonder my cousin is troubled. The French will be preparing dispatches for Louis." He shook his head. "Difficult times. Even for Colonnas."

"The Pope may rally, and then the French will have troubles of their own; they are already at odds with the Holy See," said the courier.

"No more than any other Kingdom in Europe, if the truth were told; the French are just more obvious," said Ettore Colonna. He put his letter down. "I had better write to my cousin immediately. If you will excuse me?" He rose from his place and left the room without greater ceremony, leaving Ragoczy and Bruschi to deal with the courier.

"My horse is too tired to ride back to Roma this afternoon," the courier remarked to the air. "Signore Colonna will have to remount me."

"I will order a horse be saddled," said Celestino Bruschi with a careful lack of inflection. "There should be fresh horses in the stable." He stepped out of the room briefly.

"They say the Cardinal wants to protect his cousin," said the courier to Ragoczy, an arch look in his clever eyes.

"Such is the way of blood relatives," said Ragoczy, taking an ironic pleasure in knowing this was as true for him as for any Colonna.

"For such a family there is reason to be, for all their long power, they are not always in the shelter of the Pope," said the courier with a trace of bitterness in his words. "Others have no such protection."

"That, too, has its advantages," said Ragoczy, glancing toward Bruschi as he came back into the dining room.

"There will be a bay mare saddled and bridled by the end of the mid-day nap," said Bruschi. "The groom will have her waiting for you."

"The Cardinal will be grateful, I have no doubt," said the courier, drinking the last of his goblet of wine; the servant refilled it at once. "At least this way I can be in Roma by sunset. In this heat no horse can be ridden all day at more than a walk, and for that, I might as well ride a donkey."

Bruschi studied the courier for a long moment, his handsome features marred by a frown. "Bishops ride donkeys," he reminded the brash young man.

"So they do," he agreed, and had some more wine.

Bruschi gave the courier a long stare, saying nothing as he studied the young man; when he spoke, it was to Ragoczy. "In what way may I be of service to you, Signor' Conte?"

"How very gracious," said Ragoczy. "Just at present I would like to retire to the music room." He knew he would be left alone while he played the clavicytherium, for he wanted time to think.

Bruschi made a leg and stepped aside to allow Ragoczy to leave the room, saying quietly as Ragoczy went by him, "The fellow is a fool."

"True," Ragoczy said, "but that is no sin." He left Bruschi with the courier and made his way into the music room; it was on the north side of the villa, with a bowed window overlooking the orchards. There were half a dozen instruments in the room: a violin, a viola da braccia, a viola da gamba, a flute made of silver, an oboe da caccia, and the clavicytherium, its keys polished, its upright case elaborately inlaid with precious woods and mother-of-pearl. Fingering the keys idly to be sure they were in tune, Ragoczy took a short while to adjust a few of the strings, then sat down and began to play; he let melodies meander through his fingers as he put his thoughts to the complexities a new Pope would mean to his efforts on Niklos' behalf. Then he became aware of someone listening from the hall, and he stopped picking out tunes.

"Oh, pray do not stop," said the quavering voice of Gennaro Colonna; the old man felt his way into the room. "It has been years since I heard that song."

Belatedly Ragoczy realized he had been playing one of the songs he had learned in the Americas, and that Gennaro Colonna had recognized it. "I . . . did not mean to disturb you," he said with complete sincerity.

"Hardly disturbing. An old man such as I am has little but his memories to sustain him, and they become sharper and more poignant with each passing day." He found his way to one of the chairs. "Pray do not let me interrupt you."

Ragoczy began to play again, this time deliberately choosing a keyboard reduction of Lully's *Isis*. He knew the old man was disappointed not to hear more music from the Viceroyalty of Peru, but this should help to shift his attention from his memories to the present. He played uninterrupted for nearly a quarter of an hour, then ended his impromptu recital.

"Very pretty," said Gennaro Colonna when the clavicytherium fell silent. "French, I think?"

"You are very kind," said Ragoczy. "Lully may have been born in Firenze, but he is French now."

Gennaro Colonna nodded. "So it seems."

Ragoczy closed the lid of the clavicytherium and swung around on the bench. "It is almost time for prandio; the cooks will have the food ready in a short while. Is there a servant to bring you to the dining room?" The odor of roasting pork had insinuated itself throughout the villa, as successful a signal as any bell.

The ploy did not succeed. "Time enough for that when we are finished here. My cousin tells me you are a man of middle years—perhaps forty-five?" Gennaro Colonna remarked, unwilling to be distracted. "Of average height with a deep chest and small hands and feet?"

"I believe that is my appearance, although I am somewhat older than that," said Ragoczy, staying with what he had told Ettore Colonna, as well as the truth.

"I knew a man, oh, years ago, in the New World. He saved my life, and perhaps my soul as well. I understand he is, or was, your kinsman?" He did not wait for Ragoczy to answer. "Over the years one does not forget voices. Faces may fade, and they certainly change, as my mirror would tell me if I could see well enough. But the voices remain, as much as music does." He said nothing more for a short time, then, when Ragoczy did not respond, went on, "Hearing you speak, I might have thought your kinsman was talking."

"It is sometimes thus," said Ragoczy very carefully.

"And I thought as I listened how much I owe your kinsman, including my silence now," said Gennaro Colonna. "Although I cannot help but wonder: how old are you?"

"Older than you can imagine," said Ragoczy. "All my blood are long-lived."

Gennaro Colonna nodded slowly. "For the sake of your kinsman, you have nothing to fear from me."

"On his behalf I thank you," said Ragoczy, not wanting to say much more to this ancient who, such a short time ago in Ragoczy's sense, had been a hale and active young man.

"You may thank me again when I tell you that when he was finally released from prison I was able to remove the most heinous accusations against him from the records of the Church. I thought he had been unjustly condemned, and I believed it was correct to remove the blot on his name." Gennaro Colonna smiled. "Given how much he helped me, it was the least I could do for him."

"Then on his behalf, I am grateful," said Ragoczy, astonished by this casual admission, on Gennaro Colonna's part to an act that would send him to the Pope's Little House if it were ever discovered.

"Now you may escort me to the dining room," said Gennaro Colonna in a tone that sounded very like triumph.

Text of a note from Alessandro Scarlatti to Ferenc Ragoczy, carried by Maurizio Reieto and delivered on the evening of July 25th, 1689

Mio caro Conte,

I have just received a visit from Giorgianna Ferrugia who has announced that she is with child and will not be available to sing for us until she is delivered of the infant. She apologizes for any inconvenience she may cause and promises her husband will pay for the delay in our opera; he is overjoyed with this news, she tells me. Whether this is true or not, it would be folly to say otherwise, for she knows she must have a child—preferably a male child—if she is to enjoy any of her husband's fortune after his death; she no doubt has pinned many hopes on this pregnancy. She says it is early days yet but she is obeying her husband's wishes and curtailing all activity for the sake of the child. Her delivery should be in late February or early March, and she will be prepared to sing again at the end of March or the beginning of April, assuming all goes well with the baby, and the wetnurse is suitable. She hopes you will not be so angry that you will not wait for her.

The timing of the child is such that you cannot be concerned. More than enough time has passed since their wedding to still any doubts in all but the most vindictive of souls. A young woman of less than noble birth married to such an one as Ilirio must anticipate that the spiteful will use this occasion to discredit her virtue if they can. Try as they will, they will not be able to impugn her honor, for she knows what her risks are. Besides, Ilirio is no Gesualdo, to kill his wife and her lover and then to spend his days composing penitent motets. Ilirio is delighted to get a child on such a woman as Giorgianna Ferrugia, and that she is his wife must delight him almost as much as it must annoy his grown children. You may find that they have rancor toward her which may redound to your discredit, but no doubt Ilirio will soon put a stop to such nonsense.

If you wish to hold the performers for so long a period it will prove costly. I would recommend undertaking some smaller project while waiting for La Ferrugia, such as an Oratorio, which the Church would find pleasing. With the Pope in questionable health, it would be prudent to bring such a work to the fore in any case. Let me urge you to consider it, as it would be to our mutual benefit. We will discuss this situation when we meet again in three days.

With my abiding esteem and highest respect,

> *Your most obedient to command,*
> *A. Scarlatti*

At Roma, by my own hand.

3

Martin, Cardinal Calaveria y Vacamonte, paced the room, ignoring Ahrent Julius Rothofen who sat in disgruntled silence at the table. "He cannot die now. God is not so pitiless as to claim Sua Santita now. There is too much at stake for him to die." He was sweating in the August heat and his crimson garment was darkened at the neck and down the back; not even the attar of roses he had splashed on his body that morning could hide the sharp odor. He slapped at a persistent mosquito and continued to measure out the dining room in predatory strides.

Ahrent Rothofen watched him, his face sullen. "It will help none of us," he said in disgust. "Court will be suspended until the elevation of the next Pope, and who knows what that bastard della Rovere will do in the meantime. He's in the country until September as it is. I had thought the suit would be settled by now. I do not want to give the Podesta any excuse to drag it on." He was miserable in the close air of the day; over Roma the sky thickened and darkened with clouds massive as furniture for giants.

"That suit has been more trouble than anyone anticipated," said the Cardinal without much sympathy. "Do you regret undertaking it?"

"Of course not," Rothofen said curtly. "What I regret is that the marriage between the Archbishop's brother and your sister has been so long delayed." He had intended this to mollify Calaveria y Vacamonte, but his remark had the opposite effect.

"And so do I. Why can we not find my sister?" the Cardinal demanded in sudden fury. "Why is she not here?"

"What does that matter now?" Rothofen asked, still dwelling on his own sense of ill-use. "She is missing and the rumors continue to fly."

"If we can find her before Innocenzo dies, we will be able to have the marriage," he said, as if this were obvious to the meanest intellect. "If we do not, it will have to wait until the next Pope wears the tiara." He glared at his servant who had dared to come into the room unsummoned. "What is it?"

"There is someone here to see you. He is a builder. He has heard you are looking for a missing woman." The servant was staring at his feet as if he could make himself less visible if he did not look directly at the Cardinal.

"What would a builder know of her?" Rothofen asked the air. "And why should he be so impertinent to come here directly?"

But Cardinal Calaveria y Vacamonte did not share his contempt. He stood still for a little time, then gestured to his servant. "This is no time to delay with protocol and propriety. There is no time for it." He clapped his hands to punctuate his decision. "I will receive him—in the smaller reception room. Tell me when you have escorted him there."

"I will, Eminenza," said the servant, and waited for the Cardinal's gesture of dismissal before fleeing the room.

"What do you suppose this fellow wants?" Cardinal Calaveria y Vacamonte asked Rothofen.

"Probably a few coins for rumors that mean nothing," Rothofen replied.

"Very likely," the Cardinal agreed. "Still, he may have stumbled upon something of use. The fact that he dares to come here to speak with me directly lends some credibility to his news."

"Or confirms his impertinence," said Rothofen. He stretched and straightened the wilted lace of his neck-bands. "The weather is horrid."

"The storm should break this afternoon," said Cardinal Calaveria y Vacamonte with supreme indifference. "We will all feel the better for it. It is sufficient that we must hold our breaths on behalf of Innocenzo, but this gathering storm makes it all the worse." He sighed suddenly. "Decadent and sinful as they were, perhaps the old Romans were wise to have their baths. A swim in tepid water would be very welcome just now."

"With the Pope ailing?" Rothofen was sincerely scandalized by such a suggestion. "What would the Curia think?"

"I said it would be welcome," Cardinal Calaveria y Vacamonte told him in a forbidding tone. "I did not say I intended to do it."

Rothofen said nothing for a moment, then slapped his hand on the table. "The Archbishop is growing restive, Eminenza. He fears there will be no wedding, not this year, and not next. The delays trouble him. What am I to tell him?"

"Tell him anything you like," snapped the Cardinal. "But assure him I intend the marriage to occur. You may claim that Leocadia is nervous, or uncertain, or any other reasonable excuse you like. In the end it suits all our purposes that she marry, and when she does, she will be wife to the Archbishop's brother. We must make every effort to ensure the continuing good-will between Spain and the German States, for it is to all our advantages that our old alliances are preserved. My sister is a fortunate woman, if only she would recognize it: she can benefit her family and her country in a single act. And since she must marry, let it be to our greater benefit." He showed his teeth in a lupine smile.

"You are a clever man, Eminenza," said Rothofen. "The girl should welcome your guidance."

"So she should," Cardinal Calaveria y Vacamonte said in self-approval. He tapped his fingers on the back of the chair next to where he stood. "The builder should wait a little longer, I think. He must not suppose I will come at anyone's call."

A figure appeared in the doorway, gaudily dressed and already a bit the worse for drink; Ursellos came a few steps into the dining room. His Italian was slightly slurred, revealing how inebriated he was. "I hear the innkeeper has been paid off. I suppose I have you to thank for that?" He made an effort to adjust his wig and then shook out the ruffles at his wrists.

Cardinal Calaveria y Vacamonte gave his younger brother a hard stare. "What else was I to do? If he had taken you to Court, our family would have been utterly compromised." He clicked his tongue in condemnation. "When will you learn to comport yourself as a man of honor?"

"You should have let me kill the fellow," Ursellos complained. "That would have shown his claim was without merit."

"Oh, yes. If you should be accused of murder, it would be better," said the Cardinal, with such sarcasm that Ursellos blushed.

"If I had horsewhipped him, everyone would know there was no basis for his claim," Ursellos protested with less certainty than he had wanted to show.

"And Roma would hum with gossip for weeks, and the tale would grow more lurid with every telling. What a fine situation that would be," Cardinal Calaveria y Vacamonte exclaimed in condemnation of his brother. "Let me beg you, Ursellos, to curtail your escapades at least while the Pope is in ill-health. What would be excusable when Sua Santita is well would be deplored now, when the duty of all good Catholics is to pray for God's Mercy and Innocenzo's recovery."

"Oh, spare me," said Ursellos wearily. "If you wish to play that farce, I will have to vomit."

"Ursellos!" the Cardinal admonished him. "If you speak so again, I will order you to return to Spain."

"As you did Leocadia?" Ursellos laughed nastily. "Won't the Curia wonder at your motive if both of us are gone at the same time?" He took his quizzing-glass and raised it languidly to his eye. "Do you think such scrutiny will benefit you, mi hermano?"

"Do not press me, Ursellos," his brother warned him. "You have nearly exhausted my patience. If you try me too much, I will be forced to—"

"To what?" Ursellos challenged; the silence that followed was charged with more than the coming storm. "You paid off that innkeeper for your reasons, not for me," he went on when the Cardinal did not speak. "You have your ambitions. Well and good. I have my enjoyments, and I will take them as I wish."

Cardinal Calaveria y Vacamonte sighed. "You have no thought for anyone but yourself, Ursellos. What can I do to show you the errors of your ways?"

"Why, nothing, Martin; nothing." Ursellos made a profound leg to the Cardinal, speaking next in Spanish as a deliberate slight to Rothofen. "And I will not contaminate the sanctity of your presence with my sinful self any longer."

"What's this?" Cardinal Calaveria y Vacamonte demanded. "The only place you should been seen outside these walls is at Confession. Not that you are dressed for it," he added sourly, indicating his brother's flamboyant clothes. "You are not in Paris."

"Confession?" Ursellos scoffed. "With you praying for me, why should I Confess? God must surely pay more heed to the petitions of Cardinals than those of their wayward brothers." He started toward the door. "No, mi hermano, no. The weather is making you testy. So I will not embarrass you with any recitations of my trespasses. Do not fear that I will make you watch me indulge myself while you wait for Innocenzo to die. I am going to the casino outside the walls on the road to Ostia Antica. You need not fear I will return tonight, for I plan to remain in the country for a few days. My friends—debauched though you think them—seek my society as eagerly as you wish to be rid of me."

"This is a difficult time, Eminenza," said Rothofen, his face hardening as he watched Ursellos turn and leave the room without ever acknowledging his presence. "Your brother has the manners of a Turk."

"I would like to be able to leap to his defense," said Cardinal Calaveria y Vacamonte, "but I cannot excuse anything he does. It is a heavy burden."

"So I would suppose," said Rothofen, who was more envious than condemning of Ursellos.

"More than you can imagine," said the Cardinal; he deliberately turned his back on the door through which his brother had departed. "Un-Christian though it is, I hope he is caught in the downpour."

Rothofen shook his head. "That a brother could be so ungrateful. And a sister," he amended. "Both of them do not value you as they ought."

"Perhaps they are testing my faith and my devotion," the Cardinal suggested in a tone of voice that implied the opposite.

"In that case, I pray God sends you fortitude," said Rothofen, and rose from his seat. "I will make an appropriate explanation to the Archbishop. He, too, knows what it means to have an ungrateful brother. If I tell him of Ursellos, he will not be so critical of Leocadia's absence. I may tell him that you have been troubled by the company Ursellos keeps and that you are advising Leocadia to stay away so that she will not be imposed upon by Ursellos' companions."

"An inspired notion," Cardinal Calaveria y Vacamonte approved.

"And one that the Archbishop would understand and applaud. He knows the way of the youth of Roma, thanks to his brother, and he would not want to have a gentle, innocent girl exposed to the unruly men of the city." Rothofen was warming to his own notion, embroidering his idea as he spoke. "You, I will assure him, have been concerned at the life Ursellos is living, and because of that, you have informed your sister to keep well away from Roma until her wedding is set. It is what any sensible man would do." He made a leg. "That should calm his nerves and show him your intentions are genuine."

"Yes, yes. Very good. I thank you for making a reasonable excuse that will not occasion any more doubts." The Cardinal was growing restive. "I had better see this builder. In case he has some information that will lead to my sister." He swept out of the room; in his wake the first ominous roll of thunder grumbled over Roma.

Rothofen wondered if he ought to remain in the dining room or leave. The Cardinal had told him nothing. Therefore, he decided, it would be wisest to remain here, or near at hand, where he might be of use to his Eminence after the builder departed. He was also aware that the builder might have information that he could use, and in this time of flattened wallets and restive landlords, a bit of gossip to sell could be put to excellent use. Satisfied with his decision, he ordered more wine.

The builder was a man in his late twenties, stocky and open-faced, dressed in a dusty smock, and leather breeches. He held his soft cap in his hands; as Cardinal Calaveria y Vacamonte came into the reception room, he dropped to his knee and bowed his head in an appropriate display of humility. When the Cardinal extended his hand, the builder kissed his ring, but remained on his knees while the Cardinal regarded him expectantly.

"You have come to tell me something, my son?" Cardinal Calaveria y Vacamonte asked with deceptive gentleness. He sat down, making his demeanor as serene as possible.

"Yes, Eminenza, I have." The builder coughed and did his best to raise his voice. "I am Giovanni Mandria. I am a mason, and a member of the stonemason's Artei. I ply my trade in building houses. Well, that should be obvious," he said, indicating the dust on his smock. "I am presently working on a grand staircase in marble at the Villa Vecchia, which is owned by Ferenc Ragoczy. He is a foreigner—"

"I know who he is," said the Cardinal. "Tell me why you have come."

"Yes," said the builder, who was beginning to lose his nerve. "Yes. Yes. A very rich foreigner." He shook his head as if to reestablish his purpose. "Eminenza, there is a penitent at the Villa Vecchia, a young woman, I have been told—"

"You have been told?" The Cardinal interrupted.

"Oh, yes. All the workers have been talking about her," said the builder nervously. "Even the servants talk."

"Have you not seen her?" Cardinal Calaveria y Vacamonte interrupted more brusquely. "Report honestly, Mandria, as you would to your Confessor. Consider your words well." He waited while the stonemason visibly brought his dread under control. "Now: have you seen this young woman?"

"I? Oh, no. But I have heard about her. She is young and pretty, they say." He was hoping now to please the Cardinal, certain he had overstepped himself.

"Young and pretty? Who says this?" The Cardinal's questions were sharp now, and any indication of tranquility had vanished.

"The men who made her penitent's cell for her," said the builder, his confidence slipping badly. "I have not seen her myself, as I have said, but all the builders talk about her; I told you that, too. They wonder why a pretty young woman should hide herself a way in a cell like a hermit and beat herself with a whip." He was talking too fast and his face was pale.

"And why do you come to me with this tale?" the Cardinal asked with renewed gentleness.

"I come because I have heard you are looking for a girl, a young one. If you had not found this one, I decided I should tell you of her." He was panting, and not from the heat alone. "I wanted to be of service."

"And what does your employer say?" Cardinal Calaveria y Vacamonte inquired.

"Bonaldo Fiumara?" Mandria was stunned. "What should he say?"

"Not he," the Cardinal interrupted tersely. "Ragoczy. What does the Signor' Conte say of this young woman?"

"He says only that she is a penitent. Nothing more. What would you expect? It is charitable to house the penitent." Mandria sounded ill-used. "I have come to you because I have heard you are looking for a young woman. This penitent is a young woman. Since the Signor' Conte says nothing of her, I reckoned you might not have been told about her—indeed, why should the Signor' Conte say anything of this penitent young woman? She has withdrawn from the world; it would not be suitable for anyone to speak of it. The Signor' Conte is not one to boast of his charities, and who can speak ill of that?" He held up his hands as if to say he was responsible for none of it.

"Who, indeed?" the Cardinal inquired sarcastically. "A woman he keeps at his own villa for his own purposes—"

Mandria was bold enough to interrupt. "The only purpose she serves is prayer and sacrifice. Me, I should know," he went on. "She kept to her cell until her whippings made her ill, and then she was taken into the old house with a maid to guard her." He chuckled. "No one has seen her since. The maid is a dragon."

"But you are sure there is a girl?" Cardinal Calaveria y Vacamonte asked sharply. "This is no tale of bored men working too long in the hot sun?"

"No, it is not." Mandria was offended at such a suggestion. "There is a young woman. Everyone knows this."

"Really," the Cardinal marveled. "Yet you have not seen her."

"The cook has seen her," Mandria protested. "He has made meals for her, and he has given them to the maid."

"And what says this cook?" Now the Cardinal was sounding very bored. "Does he claim to know who the penitent is?"

"No. I have said no one knows." Mandria's patience and his awe were nearly gone. "But if you wonder about unknown young women, this penitent is an unknown young woman. She is at the Villa Vecchia and she has kept to herself. That is all I have to say." He did not wait for a dismissal but trudged toward the door. "Do as you wish about her." He stopped long enough to kneel and kiss the Cardinal's ring.

"Go with God, my son," Cardinal Calaveria y Vacamonte said automatically, and sketched a blessing in the air. "Be thankful that you have not been beaten for your insolence. You carry tales, which is the Devil's work."

This threat, blandly voiced, cowed Giovanni Mandria as he left the Cardinal's presence; he muttered a phrase of thanks, not seeking to worsen the impression he had made.

"One of you footmen, show him out," the Cardinal called out, and paid no heed to see if he was obeyed. "I have nothing but detestation for Ragoczy, but I do not think he would risk the condemnation of the Church just now."

"Not so near Roma," said Rothofen, who had strolled along the gallery and listened to the whole of Mandria's report with a mixture of incredulity and amusement. "He thought he might be able to pry a reward out of you, Eminenza: a reward for a rumor."

"No doubt; unless Ragoczy sent him on this errand for purposes of his own," said the Cardinal, and frowned as he left the reception room. "I see you have more wine."

"Yes," said Rothofen with an unsteady smile. "You have an excellent cellar," he said with a smirk before he drank.

"I am aware of it," said the Cardinal as he walked back toward his dining room, Rothofen in tow.

On the landing below them, Giovanni Mandria stood fuming, inwardly cursing arrogant foreigners who used the Church to better themselves at the expense of good Romans. The Spanish Cardinal might be a Prince of the Church but he had nowhere near the courtesy and manner of Ferenc Ragoczy; he wondered if he had done his employer an injury by coming here. The thought rankled as he prepared to continue his descent. He might have been inclined to fight with the footman approaching him if a young man in ordinary garments had not made his way to the landing, motioning the footman away.

"I will tend to this fellow, Ottavio," said Jose Bruno. His smile was tentative. "I fear I do not see things clearly except when they are very close," he said to the builder. "I am the Cardinal's half-brother, and I am very interested in what you have to say."

Mandria was puzzled, but he did not pull away when Jose Bruno laid his hand on his arm. "You mean about the penitent?"

"Yes. You spoke of a young woman living in a penitent's cell?" Jose Bruno prompted. "I heard some of your conversation," he added, not explaining that his eavesdropping had been deliberate. "I fear my brother is worried about the health of the Pope and so could not give you his full attention: I am interested in what you have to say, if you will tell me the whole."

"Yes. I am a builder at the Villa Vecchia, to the east of the city." Mandria was delighted to have someone listen to him with real curiosity. "I am a stonemason and I am putting in a marble staircase for the Signor' Conte. It is very grand."

"I am sure it is," said Jose Bruno as he made his way down to the loggia. "But about the penitent?"

"Oh," said Mandria as if he had become bored of the matter. "They say there is a young woman in the old villa, one who has been living in a penitent's cell beyond the coach-house. I have not actually seen her myself, but the whole staff talks of nothing else."

"She has been sequestered?" Jose Bruno asked as if the matter were only of passing interest.

"I said she was a penitent," Mandria snapped. "What else would she be? The Signor' Conte would not flout the Church on such matters."

Jose Bruno managed a single nod. "Indeed. And yet how very perplexing. No wonder you came to speak with my brother. I am sorry he did not receive you better." He leaned nearer to Giovanni Mandria so he could see him a bit more clearly. "I cannot help but think that you would be wise to watch your back, good builder."

"Watch my back? Why should I do that?" Mandria asked, becoming suspicious of Jose Bruno.

"Only that Roma is full of spies, and no one who comes to speak with a Cardinal does so unobserved," Jose Bruno said. "God's Hounds have followed the cook to his daughter's wedding. If you are not careful, you will find familiars on your trail as well."

Mandria did his best to look brave but his face was pale. "What would they want with a stonemason?"

Jose Bruno shrugged. "Who knows? They do not have to account for their actions to anyone, not even the Pope." He crossed himself as he reached the loggia. "May God preserve Sua Santita in these times, and return him to vigor and health."

"Amen," said Mandria, crossing himself as well. He stood in the loggia, looking a bit uncertain as to what to do next; the lowering sky was looking thicker by the moment, casting the whole of Roma into a sepia sketch of itself. He lowered his voice. "I do not think I will be followed, but I will use caution."

"Very good," Jose Bruno approved. "I do not like the thought of you being put-upon for so thoughtful an act as coming to my brother." He was able to put enough sincerity into his voice that Mandria actually smiled.

"I have fourteen years as a stonemason, apprentice, and journeyman, and I have never wanted to bring misfortune on anyone who employed me. But the Cardinal is the Cardinal and if he looks for a young woman, I must report that I know of one, must I not?" Mandria looked directly at Jose Bruno, hoping for reassurance. "What could I do, given what I know?"

Jose Bruno patted him on the arm. "Do not fret. Your Confessor would have told you to do this, or carried your message himself." Far likelier the latter, he added inwardly to himself, knowing how ambitious priests could be.

"Just so," said Mandria. He stepped down to the street. "Well. I have done my duty, and that's that."

"Yes, you have," said Jose Bruno, and waved in the general direction of Mandria's voice. "God be with you."

"And with you," said Mandria as he made his way into the desultory confusion of traffic.

Suddenly a pedal E shuddered the air like thunder: the great bell at San Pietro's was tolling, which could mean only one thing.

"The Pope!" Mandria shouted along with a babel of other voices. He dropped to his knees in the middle of the piazza with the rest of the people in the street and crossed himself. The sudden silence was broken only by the sound of whispered prayers and weeping, punctuated by the bell of San Pietro.

Jose Bruno knelt by the pillar in the loggia, aware of the meaning of the bell as well as any Roman: Innocenzo was dead and the Church was in mourning, which meant the whole of the Papal States were, as well. He did his best not to smile, since he knew that Martin's plans would have to be delayed while one Pope was grieved and another elected. During that time he would be able to make inquiries that the Cardinal could not. He began to recite Psalm 88, relishing the despair it expressed.

Inside Martin, Cardinal Calaveria y Vacamonte heard the tolling and cursed inwardly. "Not now! How can he die now? Why could he not have held on for a month more?" he asked as he crossed himself and knelt, beginning his prayers for the dead Pontiff. Beside him, Ahrent Rothofen did the same, crushing the sculptured velvet of his German-cut breeches on the cool marble floor.

"God's Will is mysterious," said Rothofen. He would like to have yelled in vexation at this turn of events.

The Cardinal glared at him. "You are presumptuous."

Rothofen bit back an acidic reply and made himself say, "Surely the Pope's death is God's Will or we are all damned."

For an answer, the Cardinal began to pray more loudly as the bell continued to make its lament. "Everything will have to wait," he said when he had finished his first orison. "Much as it is an imposition on both of us, I will not be available to you until after the elevation of the new Pope."

"And when will that be?" Rothofen demanded as he got to his feet.

"When it is done," said the Cardinal. "The Archbishop will have the same constraints upon him." He closed his eyes as to block out pain. "The marriage will have to wait. Even if we find my sister today, we cannot have the wedding until the new Pope is elevated, and the elections may be difficult. I will try to speak with Archbishop Walmund myself, but he certainly understands that the delay is unavoidable. There is nothing we can do about it now."

"Then I should use the time you are sequestered to continue searching for her," said Rothofen. "My suit will not be heard during that time."

"No, it will not. Very well, do as you think best, but have a care: do not dishonor the Pope or the conclave," said the Cardinal, then clapped his hands loudly. "Ottavio! Order my coach. Have it draped in black. I want it ready within the hour." He turned back to Rothofen. "You will want to be at the Archbishop's service as soon as possible. He may have tasks for you to undertake for him as well."

"Yes," said Rothofen with the kind of automatic piety that made the Cardinal regard him with contempt. "When it is fitting, we will talk again. You may rest assured that I will devote myself to our mutual interests while you are in conclave."

"I cannot imagine how you will do that, given the mourning that must be observed," said Cardinal Calaveria y Vacamonte with the full hauteur of his high office.

"Not all Roma grinds to a halt. The people still must eat, and where there are markets there is information," said Rothofen. "And the tailors will be hard at work making mourning clothes for half the titled residents. They will be busy, and they will hear things. I will listen and do all that I can to act upon my gleanings."

"If you must," said the Cardinal, making a quick blessing in Rothofen's direction. "I will have to leave you now. I must prepare for

Innocenzo's rites. Ottavio will send you a small purse for your expenses while you look for my sister."

"Of course, of course," said Rothofen making a leg; he was not quite obsequious, but the promise of an infusion of money filled him with a gratitude that felt like physical release.

"A pity about your suit," said the Cardinal as he strode from the room. "It should have been settled months ago."

"Truly," said Rothofen to the Cardinal's back, resentment flooding into his soul once more. "I must agree."

The low E sounded again, and Rothofen heard it as being for him as much as it was for Innocenzo. He stood in the gallery door, glowering at the world that had treated him so shabbily. Just when there was a suggestion of progress, the Pope had to die! Why could he not find one opportunity unencumbered by obstacles? The unfairness of it all made him want to curse God. This was hardly the time to do that, he reminded himself. The familiars of the Inquisition would be particularly busy now, ferreting out apostasy and diabolism everywhere. Another somber note, more sensation than tone, rang over the city, and this time it was answered with an ominous thud of thunder.

"Shall I try to find a chair for you?" one of the servants asked Rothofen. "I fear there are few of them available, but I can—"

"No; never mind," Rothofen said. The cost of a sedan chair was an extravagance he could not justify. "It will do me good to walk." His lodgings were closer but the Archbishop would have need of him just now, he was certain of it. He drew his russet-colored cloak around him, thinking it too warm on this close afternoon, but aware that his peach-and-ivory-striped justaucorps was hardly appropriate dress to wear on the street now that Innocenzo's death was announced. He took his hat from a frightened lackey and set out in through the eerily quiet streets toward the small palazzo Archbishop Walmund had recently occupied. He dared not walk too quickly for that might be seen as a sign of disrespect to Innocenzo XI, which could lead to a visit to the Pope's Little House.

He had covered half the distance to the Archbishop's home when the storm finally lived up to its threat, the skies opening with such a deluge that a pilgrim kneeling in the street remarked that the angels must be crying for the Pope. Rothofen had an impious rejoinder in mind, but kept it to himself as he trudged grimly on, knowing he would be drenched long before he made a leg to the Archbishop.

Text of a letter from Narcisso della Rovere to Niklos Aulirios; carried to Senza Pari by Magisterial courier.

To the defending party in the Ahrent Rothofen suit, the formal greetings to Niklos Aulirios, on the sad occasion of the obsequies of Pope Innocenzo XI, whom God honor and welcome into Paradise.

Signor' Aulirios, I know you will understand the necessity for the delay in the final hearing of your case. I will have my clerk notify the Signor' Conte Ragoczy of the necessary changes in the hearing of your case. Until the new Pope is elected and his coronation celebrated, no civil matter may be heard in Roma: any other conduct would require a dispensation issued by two Bishops and an Archbishop, or by the Curia. You will agree that your cause is not so urgent that such drastic measures are necessary, and therefore I have informed the Court that your case will go forward within a month of the coronation of the next Pope. I am certain this is satisfactory to you, as no ships or specifically contested crops are focal items of the suit. As soon as a date is fixed, you will be informed by messenger.

I have been reviewing the material you have provided, and although I am not yet prepared to make a final judgment, unless Signore Rothofen can come up with some proof that Pope Urban's dispensation was countermanded by a later Pope, it would appear to me that your legacy cannot be seized by anyone not specifically designated by the late Atta Olivia Clemens. Of course, if such an order is found and presented, I must uphold the decision of the later Pope, in accord with the authorizations of the Curia. I have informed Signore Rothofen of this as well, to allow him some time to discover any pertinent records that may have bearing on my decision. If you have supporting material, I advise you to present it to me once the official month of mourning is concluded. Any action during the mourning would be seen as possibly heretical, and would carry consequences of its own.

You must understand that I am bound by the law to make my decision within the strictures of our legal codes; I am powerless to do anything that is not in accord with what the precedents set down in the decisions of other magistrates in accord with the laws of Roma and the Papal States. I remind you of this so that you will not be under the misapprehension that I base my judgment on anything more than the laws of the Magisterial Courts, as I am sworn before God to do. Whatever my final determination may be, it will not fail to uphold the example of law.

In accord with the discharging of my office, I commend myself and my recommendations to your consideration, and I pray that God will guide us all to the truth in this most unhappy time,

Narcisso Lepedio della Rovere
Podesta

From Bella Rovere in Tevere, on the 15th day of August in 1689

4

"I cannot linger," said Alessandro Scarlatti as he alighted from his carriage at the Villa Vecchia. He was dressed in mourning for the Pope and wore a spot of ash on his forehead to show his penitent state of mind. Lines of sweat ran from under his wig, leaving damp trails in his lace neck-bands. "This heat is beastly, and there are two more Cantatas and an Oratorio for me to finish before the conclave is ended: who knows how long it will be?"

Ferenc Ragoczy, elegant in his habitual black, with no sign of discomfort from the weather, inclined his head as he indicated his open door. "Then come inside and have a glass of wine and a little cold ham. You can pause long enough for that, certainly."

"Gracious as always," said Scarlatti, shutting the coach door. He patted his black clothing and shook his head at the gloriously clear sky as if deploring its cerulean perfection. "At least it rained the day he died."

"And would have, no matter what the Pope did that day," Ragoczy said with a slight, ironic smile.

"Make sure God's Hounds do not hear you say so," Scarlatti warned, only half-joking. "They are at their most zealous between Popes, and they would not hesitate to act against you if they deemed it advisable."

"I shall keep your warning in mind, Maestro." Then Ragoczy raised his voice. "Matyas! Please tend to this carriage. Signore Scarlatti will want it again in an hour or so. The horses will need water and a handful of grain." Confident that his instructions would be followed, Ragoczy ushered Scarlatti into his villa.

Scarlatti paused in the doorway as his coach rumbled off toward the stable. "Generous, too, Signor' Conte." He gave a sudden, intense stare at Ragoczy's face. "Not a bit of sweat, and you in black from neck to toe."

"More sensible than generous; your horses are hungry and thirsty," he said, responding only to Scarlatti's first observation. He was about to close the door when he hesitated, indicating the new building behind him. "It is more aggravating to pay the Artei for the labor they cannot do."

"Of course. They have provisions for continuing pay during formal mourning; the Artei sees to that," said Scarlatti. "Does it trouble you to have the same arrangement with our musicians?" The interior of the villa was cooler than the day outside but it was still warm enough to make proper clothing and wigs uncomfortable. Scarlatti unbuttoned his justaucorps, murmuring an apology for his lapse in manners.

"Not at all," said Ragoczy. "I know that the musicians continue their practicing while the mourning is enforced, unlike the builders. It may be inconsistent, but there it is. At least they will be allowed to resume work on the thirteenth, the day after—"

"—the month of mourning concludes. Yes, I know. I have two choirs I cannot rehearse with until then. One of them has been singing Requiems and Stabat Maters since Innocenzo died. I know what it is to count the days." He looked a bit impatient. "I would rather be working on our opera. But—" He shrugged. "When a Pope resigns his office for Heaven . . ."

"We knew there would be delays already. Giorgianna has made it inevitable. One more is not significant, not given what has happened," said Ragoczy, directing Scarlatti toward his library with an elegant gesture. "It is the most comfortable room in this old place," he explained. "When the men are working, you can scarcely hear the hammering, and it is never too hot or too cold."

"A pity, then, that it is so much out of fashion. When do you think you will be able to occupy the new villa?" Scarlatti inquired, as he chose a comfortable Turkish chair. "Ah. This is much better than a lurching coach."

"Yes, it is," Ragoczy agreed. "And the builders tell me that, barring a hard winter, I should be in my new villa by the Paschal Mass."

"Good progress, to have a villa of that size built in a year. You must have a large crew working on it." Scarlatti sighed as he pulled off his gloves. "I have not had time to visit my family since the Pope died, although the Queen has offered to procure a travel dispensation for me, for which I am deeply grateful, but I fear that once I reach Napoli, I will find it difficult to return, and that would be very bad, very bad."

Rugerius came into the library through the rear door. "I have told the kitchen to prepare fruit and ham for Signore Scarlatti. I have brought the wine with me: Lachrymi Christi nel Vesuvio." He held up the carafe.

"Ah, you knew what I long for," he said, nodding. "Say what you will about red wines, I like the pale ones when they are as fine as this one."

"If you will pour a goblet for Signore Scarlatti?" Ragoczy told Rugerius, and went on. "I assume you want to know something of Maurizio's progress?"

"Yes, of course," said Scarlatti, a trifle embarrassed at his own candid admission. "I pray he has not been driving you mad while he has been here?"

"Since he divides his time between this place and Senza Pari, there is some respite; he does not spend the evenings here, as you recall, nor his early mornings," said Ragoczy with a trace of ironic humor.

"True enough," Scarlatti allowed. He took the goblet Rugerius handed to him, sniffed the wine, and prompted, "You say he is improving?"

"Yes; he is practicing, which is what you and I both wanted him to do. He is still lax about bowing exercises; he finds them boring, or so he tells me." Ragoczy waited while Scarlatti took a sip of the wine and signaled his approval of it. "The weather has been hot enough to exhaust him, and with the Pope's death I have permitted him some reduction in his practice hours."

"But he is keeping up," Scarlatti asked, seeking reassurance.

"Oh, yes. He wants to impress the young penitent I have been housing: I have mentioned her to you before. She is recovering from the . . . rigors of her devotions, and Maurizio has taken it upon himself to play for her every afternoon." Ragoczy held up his hand to forestall any questions. "He does not enter her chamber, but plays in the garden outside her window."

"It sounds troublesome to me," Scarlatti said, his expression filled with doubt. "He is young and his mind is not disciplined. He is entranced by his own abilities, which are considerable. But an infatuation? This could prove too much of a distraction for him. He has raw talent and believes that it and passion will be enough to carry him through, which it will do for a short time. He needs to steady himself if he intends to be more than a sensation. And if he takes it into his head to fall in love, well—" He made a gesture of helplessness.

"I don't think it has come to that yet," said Ragoczy, "although I suspect he is smitten with the *idea* of her; he does not know enough about her to be more than fascinated."

"Worse and worse; she is a mystery about whom he can weave his own tale, and make himself the hero of it," Scarlatti cried in mock dismay. "What on earth are we to do about his attachment?" He had straightened up and set his goblet aside. "He does not know what folly he—I should speak to him at once."

But Ragoczy shook his head. "I would not recommend it, not to condemn his captivation, in any case. If he thinks his infatuation is dangerous enough to require opposition, he may try to show his devotion by stubbornness, which will suit no one, including that penitent."

Scarlatti nodded slowly. "I take your point, Signor' Conte, and I concur. He is such a hotheaded youngster that he could very possibly decide to behave just as you suggest."

"That is what I think," said Ragoczy, looking up as one of the servants carried in a tray with slices of ham and a bunch of grapes set out on a fine china plate. "This will relieve you."

"It looks wonderful," Scarlatti said. "And I am not one to abstain from meat during the month of bereavement, although some think it pious. This is not Lent, it is mourning, and that is different." He licked his lips in anticipation as the servant put the tray down on the tall stool and moved it to his chair. "Your staff does you credit."

"I hope so," said Ragoczy, adding, "Pray, take what you want. It is not my habit to eat at this hour." He leaned back negligently against a short set of shelves. "I have kept Maurizio busy with a few transcriptions of old melodies, ones he does not know." Ragoczy had played those melodies himself when he had been in the north of France, making his way in the world as a troubador; this he kept to himself.

"Very good," Scarlatti approved. "I will need him to learn a difficult part in this Oratorio I am finishing. You'll like it," he said as he pronged a bit of ham on his fork. "The counterpoint is very innovative."

"I am looking forward to hearing it," said Ragoczy. "Is this for Innocenzo, or for his successor?"

"The successor. I've already completed the various lamentations for Innocenzo, including a setting of the Dies Irae. The Church is inclined to remind the faithful of sin at such times as these. It isn't my best work, but then, I had less than six days to compose it." He chewed busily, continuing to talk as he did. "Do you think Maurizio will complain if I take him away from here for a week or two?"

"He may," Ragoczy allowed. "But if he does go, it may provide him a chance to reassess his passion."

"Ha!" exclaimed Scarlatti. "It is more likely to become more intense." He selected a few grapes and prepared to devour them. "Oh, dear. This is the worst possible time for him to succumb to his heart."

"Very likely," said Ragoczy. "And yet we are too late to stop it."

He refilled Scarlatti's goblet himself, saying to his manservant, "Rugerius, would you be good enough to find Maurizio and bring him to us? Thank you, old friend."

"I shall not be long," Rugerius said, and let himself out the side-door.

"What shall we say to him?" Scarlatti asked, clearly apprehensive. "Do you think there is some way we can address this that will not cause him to cast himself in the role of amorous hero?" He had more of the wine. "It is a pity that you deny yourself this pleasure, Conte; it truly is."

"But there are other pleasures I do not deny myself, and so it balances out," Ragoczy said easily.

"Well, be careful that these pleasures do not *dis*please the Church; I would not like to see such a patron as you end up a guest at the Pope's Little House," said Scarlatti, suddenly very serious. "With the new election coming, the zeal of the Curia is doubled."

" 'Popes come and go but the Curia remains'?" Ragoczy quoted the Roman aphorism with a world-weary humor.

"Something of the sort," Scarlatti agreed. "It is very distressing to think that we will have to do so much to put their attention elsewhere. And pity the poor bastards who claim their attention." He had another sip of wine. "That suit you are trying: there is no reason to think the Curia might be caught up in that, is there?"

"I wouldn't suppose so," Ragoczy said carefully, recalling the many times he had misjudged the tenacity of fanatics: from Obispo Hernan Guarda, who had hunted and imprisoned him in Latin America; to Father Pogner, who had made his mission to Russia so difficult; to Girolamo Savonarola, who had persecuted Fiorenza for being Fiorenza; to Padre Fortunatus, who had so relentlessly pursued Csimenae and her brood; to the Sultan's knights outside Baghdad; to Tamasrajasi, who sought to make a sacrifice of him; to the . . . He forced his thoughts away from the past. "But I am not a familiar."

"At least you have sense enough to be wary of them," said Scarlatti.

"Oh, yes; I have that," said Ragoczy, and looked up as Rugerius scratched at the side-door. "Come in."

Rugerius opened the door and stood aside so that Maurizio could enter the library. "Do you wish me to remain, my master?"

"If you like," Ragoczy said.

"You wish to berate me in front of a *servant?*" Maurizio demanded, his face darkening.

Ragoczy refused to be goaded by this outburst even as Scarlatti set his goblet down with some force. "You see, I have known Rugerius much longer than I have known you, Maurizio," he said mildly. "And it is not my intention to berate you." Before Maurizio could speak, Ragoczy went on in the same affability. "Here is Maestro Scarlatti come to see you at a time his schedule is full. He wishes to hear of your progress."

Maurizio made a hasty, graceless leg to the composer. "I am honored to see you," he said in a flat tone of voice; he had an air of melancholy about him, accented with umbrage.

"Are you?" Scarlatti asked, making the most of Maurizio's confusion. "So how is it that I hear you are devoting your time to something—to some*one*—other than your music?" He rose from his chair and faced the young violinist.

"You are mistaken," said Maurizio, his cheeks flaming. "I occasionally play where the penitent can hear me . . . because we are taught that music brings our thoughts closer to God."

"We are also taught the Devil plays the fiddle," said Scarlatti bluntly, all his intentions of restraint falling away. "Do not tell me you are not acting the moonling, for I will not believe you." He began to pace, and although his voice did not rise, his speech became more clipped. "You think you have been taken with a noble passion, and that you are showing your devotion to an unknown. It is all one to me if you are enamored of a woman, but not at the expense of your studies. You have been given an opportunity to improve your art; if you do not make the most of it, you may regret your inattention in later years." Then he stopped and smiled. "You think I do not know what it is to be besotted with a woman? Do you assume that I am without understanding of your feelings because I am older than you, or because I have a wife and children? You think that because I have work and am married that I no longer have fire in my veins? Not so, young man, not so." He came up to Maurizio. "As long as we are men, we will have these desires, but only a fool lets them overwhelm the things he values in himself." His manner was now avuncular. "I do not wish to set myself at odds with you, Maurizio; I only want you to remember the opportunity you are putting at risk for a woman who, by her very penitence, has put herself beyond your ardor."

Maurizio listened to this recitation with a mixture of emotions that he could not define. He did not look directly at Scarlatti, but kept craning his neck as if to remove himself from the good sense he knew was being imparted to him. "I do not expect you to sympathize: I have no wish to compromise her penitence."

"No, of course not," said Scarlatti, almost maintaining a straight face. "You want only to adore her in her inaccessibility."

"Do not speak to me as if I were a boy!" Maurizio bristled at the implied derision. "I am old enough to comprehend the desires of the young woman, and I would be beneath all contempt if I were to—to interfere with her vocation."

Ragoczy did not appear to be watching; he had given his full attention to the brass astrolabe that stood on a small table at the side of the room. Rugerius remained near the side door, seemingly lost in thought.

"I am not here to castigate you for your affections," said Scarlatti, recalling his purpose. "I have two new pieces that must be ready for the celebrations to welcome the new Pope to San Pietro's Throne. And for this I need your talents." He saw a flicker of interest in Maurizio's eyes. "Yes. Consider well. You have the opportunity to play at the coronation of a Pope. Who knows when such providence will appear again?" He crossed himself to make it clear he did not want such an occasion to occur too soon.

"You want me to play?" Maurizio said with such obvious ambition that Scarlatti chuckled.

"You would have to devote your time to the music. It would mean more practice—practice, not serenading." He came to Maurizio's side. "You mayn't believe it, but I do have your best interests at heart, lad. Talent like yours is rare; it must be fostered if it is to fulfill its promise. I urge you to think of this gift God has bestowed upon you. If the woman were well-connected and returned your devotion it might be another matter, but as it is, I can only encourage you to seize this opportunity to advance your art."

Not wanting to be too blatant in his curiosity, Maurizio asked, "What sort of work are you preparing?"

"More than one. I have an Oratorio that has a Symphonetta in the middle of the work that has a long solo passage for violin, and a longer contrapuntal passage against the rest of the strings. You are the most accomplished player in Roma that I know of; I would be a fool to choose another if I can have you as my soloist," Scarlatti told him with a candor that was as persuasive as it was flattering. "I would like to get the part tomorrow and have you get to work on it at once. My time will not be my own, and so I will rely on the Signor' Conte to assist you in your preparation"—he saw Ragoczy give a single nod of agreement—"and I expect you to devote yourself to mastering the work. I cannot spend my days shepherding you through your ground-work; you are to heed the Signor' Conte in my stead." He flung up his hand as a demonstration of how much he had to accomplish. "You are not accustomed to this kind of haste, I realize it, but you must acquire the capacity to develop a work without extensive rehearsal. It is not convenient for either of us, but we cannot change what is, and therefore we must accommodate our circumstances." He went back to the chair in which he had been sitting and flung himself into it again. "I have more than enough to do in the next days; I will need you to come to rehearsal ready to play. Well?"

Maurizio blinked his eyes. "I cannot turn away from this," he said.

"From what?" Scarlatti demanded. "The penitent or the Oratorio?"

"The Oratorio, of course," said Maurizio, an expression of mild annoyance flickering on his features; his dejection was fading, giving way to the satisfaction of great opportunity.

"Very good," Scarlatti approved. "Excellent. I will provide a copy of the score and your part by tomorrow. Conte," he went on to Ragoczy, "you can do a reduction from the score, can you not?"

"On sight, if I must," said Ragoczy. "I have a harpsichord here; it will do for practice."

"I knew I could rely on you," said Scarlatti. "I will want to hear you play in a week. I only pray that the Cardinals do not elect a new Pope before then." He looked upward as if expecting some response from beyond the ceiling.

Ragoczy preserved his tranquil demeanor though his dark eyes shone with amusement. "We will be ready for you, I am confident of it."

Now Maurizio looked startled. "Could it happen so quickly? Could the new Pope be elected in less than a week?"

"He could be," Ragoczy allowed, "but it is unlikely." He remembered conclaves seven hundred years ago that lasted well over a year; this one, he knew, would not be so long, for the Church could not afford to be without a leader for so long a time. "The Holy Roman Emperor's requirements do not march with those of the Church just now, and there are problems to the east and the west of Roma. It may be they will elect one of the more senior members of the College to fill the post while the factions work out who is to hold the reins over the next decade. The Cardinals will need time to decide which is the most important—the New World, the Protestants, or the Turks."

"Or the French. Louis is still demanding a voice in the appointment of Bishops and other Church officials in France." Scarlatti nodded. "There is much in what you say, Signor' Conte. And whatever God inspires the Cardinals to do, He will need to allow me at least ten days to finish all I have begun to honor His new Pope. I would also like more than a week to rehearse." He reached for the goblet and drank the last of his wine. "So: Maurizio, you must apply yourself."

"That I will, Maestro. I will." He was beginning to look excited, and his face brightened in anticipation. "Is it a very long passage, this one you want me to perform?"

With a sudden laugh Scarlatti turned to Ragoczy. "I am relieved," he said, then directed his comments to Maurizio. "Not only is it fairly long—the solo passage is more than sixty measures, but the counterpoint passage is more than twice that length, with some tricky patterns of emphasis."

"I am looking forward to this piece," said Maurizio, his enthusiasm overwhelming his cultivated melancholy at last. "I will practice five hours every day, no matter how hot it may be. I will master what you have given me to learn, and I will be prepared to rehearse as soon as you have made the proper arrangements."

"Very good," said Scarlatti, adding in a level tone, "And remember, if you would, that this work is for a celebration, a very solemn celebration. None of your flamboyance, if you please—just meticulous technique and solid musicianship."

"Per natura," said Maurizio, his handsome features lighting with pride. "I will not disappoint you, Maestro."

"I knew you would not." Scarlatti clapped him on the shoulder. "And no distractions, mind. We haven't the time for it."

The young man bridled at this reminder. "I have said I will spend my time practicing, and I will not fail in this." He crossed his arms on his chest, affronted that Scarlatti would suggest such a thing.

"Very good," said Scarlatti, soothing Maurizio. "But remember, the builders will be working again shortly."

"If there is too much noise, we will go to Senza Pari. Signor' Aulirios will not begrudge us a place to practice." Ragoczy made a gesture of approval to Maurizio. "You will decide if the noise here is too intrusive."

Maurizio realized it was foolish to be angry. "Do not worry on that account," he said, his expression mild.

"Sta' bene," Scarlatti approved. "Then I will leave you to decide how you will put this to the test. My messenger will bring you the part and the score by mid-day tomorrow." He reached for his gloves, buttoned his justaucorps and drew the gloves on. "I must go. I have two soloists I must speak with yet today—a contralto and a soprano, both castrati, of course. The Church does not like to have women sing sacred music unless they are nuns; nuns do not sing solos in Oratorios, so—" He gestured his exasperation as he swung around to Ragoczy. "Thank you for the food and wine. Both were excellent." He made a leg, then started toward the door.

Rugerius appeared as if by magic, ready to usher the composer out to his carriage. "I have sent word to the stable, Maestro," he said.

"Thank you," Scarlatti said, and continued on toward the front door, Rugerius coming with him. "I am grateful to you for all the opportunities you and your master have provided Maurizio. In time he may realize what extraordinary good fortune he has had in gaining your interest and patronage. For now, I will appreciate it for him, and pray he comes to his senses." He winked at Rugerius. "And do not tell me it is Ragoczy alone who does this. I have played in many great households, and I know if the servants are not in favor of musicians, it matters little what their masters may say."

"I have served Ragoczy for many years; if I did not like music at the start, I have developed a taste for it over time," said Rugerius as he opened the front door for Scarlatti. "May you have a safe journey, Maestro." The afternoon heat made the very air lethargic; even the mosquitos seemed torpid.

"Amen to that. This is not the time for a broken wheel or a foundered horse," Scarlatti said as his coach came up to them; Rugerius opened the carriage-door and let down the steps for the composer. "For good service," he said, handing Rugerius a coin before he got into the vehicle. "Tell your master I will send a messenger tomorrow, as arranged. My poor copyist will have to be up all night, but that is nothing new for Natale."

Rugerius put up the steps and closed the door, signaling the coachman. "Mille grazie," he said, offering Scarlatti a polite salute as the coach pulled away at a slow trot, a haze of dust rising as it moved. As Rugerius stepped back into the villa, he heard the sound of Maurizio's violin as the young man began to practice.

"So what do you think, old friend?" Ragoczy's voice came out of the shadows, and an instant later, he stepped into the wedge of light from the window above the door.

"I think we may have a difficult time for the next few weeks," Rugerius said. "In spite of his good intentions, and his aspirations, I doubt Maurizio will set his veneration aside, not completely. That would be too much of a compromise for him. He is an impetuous young man with more fervor in him than he knows what to do with. And she—she is so alone in her suffering, how can he not want to end her isolation? He is an orphan: he will not abandon her, not even for sixty measures of solo playing."

"I concur," said Ragoczy, falling into step beside Rugerius. "His talent aside, Maurizio is of an edacious temperament, I suspect, and his appetites are never wholly satisfied. I have observed that is often the case when children are deprived—their want lasts a lifetime." He said nothing for a dozen steps, then added, "She is asking to go back to her cell."

Rugerius inclined his head. "Where she will beat herself again?"

"Oh, yes; I think so." He fell to pondering again. "What has brought her to this pass, that she wants to lose herself so utterly?"

"You *could* find out," Rugerius reminded him.

"You mean visit her in a dream and persuade her to reveal the cause to me?" Ragoczy shook his head as he said it. "No. I will not intrude on her. She has been manipulated enough; she will not have more from me."

"You say she has been manipulated: are you certain that she has, or do you only assume it?" Rugerius did not ask unkindly, but there was a bit of doubt in his tone that caught Ragoczy's attention. "She is the sister of a powerful Cardinal, one who is said to be looking to find a husband for her who will add to the strength of the family. She may be as ambitious as he is, or she may be seeking some husband other than the one her brother has chosen for her."

"How *do* you contrive to hear these things?" Ragoczy asked, his incredulity showing itself in a quick smile.

"Servants boast. And they compete in knowing the most noteworthy gossip. Scandal is the finest choice, but political shenanigans are also worth attention. An arranged marriage with so many implications is always fodder for rumors." He made a self-deprecating gesture. "I have little to offer the servants, but I do appreciate what I hear, and I show it with the regular standing of drinks."

Ragoczy's handsome, irregular features were shaped by irony. "I am grateful to you for being circumspect," he said. "And for discovering what may be said about Leocadia. I had supposed it was complicated, but there is more here than we know. This is not simply a negotiation ploy for a political marriage; she has a need for hiding." He caught himself becoming more curious, and he held up his hands to show he recognized this. "She is too much a puzzle, isn't she."

"Unfortunately, she is. It brings her notice for all she tries to disappear. This leads to speculation, and every day a new bit of gossip is added to the whole, and the whispers will grow louder. Eventually they will spread far enough: someone will persuade the Cardinal to seek her out, if not immediately, after the new Pope is installed at the Lateran." Rugerius looked away from Ragoczy. "You have kept away from women since Giorgianna married."

With a single nod of confirmation, Ragoczy said, "And you think it is unwise of me to do this, instead of visiting women in Roma in their sleep, thought you and I both know it would not be safe to make such forays closer to home." He shook his head. "No doubt your reservations are astute, and were we not under such persistent scrutiny, I might look for a more regular connection, but not with the familiars snooping about."

"You spoke of a woman you met two weeks since," Rugerius suggested.

"Adina Bonisoli," said Ragoczy. "Yes. I had not forgot her."

"If she continues her interest, you might find it worthwhile to establish an understanding with her." He nodded once, knowingly.

"My attentions might compromise her; she will want to remarry, and I cannot offer her that," Ragoczy said, his dark eyes distant.

"They will speculate about you and our penitent guest, then," said Rugerius with a certainty born of long experience.

"She has had a maid to keep watch over her since she came in from her cell. I have seen her only to treat her wounds, and never alone." Ragoczy began to pace. "If I make too much a show of caution, it could prove as damaging as if I had failed to show enough." He stopped, his expression distant and troubled at once. "You are right, of course. If she remains here, it could prove dangerous to all of us."

"Is she improving?" asked.

"Yes. She will have scars, but she had some already, old scars that looked to be the results of beatings: most not self-inflicted, by the look of them. I can only guess who has done this to her, and guesses are worth nothing." He rubbed the line of his jaw. "What am I to do? She tells me nothing, and I do not want to demand an explanation from her. If she is determined to maintain her anonymity, I will not betray her."

"No," said Rugerius, thinking of Csimenae and Pentacoste and Tamasrajasi. "You will not."

Ragoczy lowered his voice. "If only she would trust me."

"Why should she? No doubt she is uncertain of your motives for caring for her as much as she is eager to take advantage of them." Rugerius shrugged.

"Do you think she is as deliberate as all that?" Ragoczy said, one brow rising for emphasis. "I have thought from the first that this was a kind of desperate escape, that she is like a hunted animal, crouching in a den to avoid the hounds."

"And if they are God's Hounds, what then?" His austere expression became more forceful. Their kennel is the Pope's—"

"—Little House," Ragoczy finished for him. "How could I permit her to go there."

Rugerius sighed. "You could not. And you can only conjecture about her circumstances while she tells you nothing."

"You recommend waiting," said Ragoczy, his expression revealing nothing beyond what good manners required. "That may be a luxury we can ill-afford."

"And if you force her hand, what then?" Rugerius challenged Ragoczy. "She runs away again, or denounces you as a kidnapper, or worse."

"What would Olivia advise, do you think," Ragoczy said, bemused humor giving a slight curve to his mouth.

"That is hardly to the point," Rugerius said, his exasperation making his voice sharper than most servants would dare to use with an employer. "If Olivia were here, we would not be."

"And our Penitent Guest would be in the hands of a woman, beyond any rumors but the most outrageous ones." Ragoczy nodded, and paused to listen as the first sounds of Maurizio's practicing began. "A remarkable lad."

"That he is," said Rugerius, accepting this adroit shift in subject for the time being.

"Perhaps you could offer him the rest of the ham and grapes?"

Ragoczy indicated the tray that had been brought for Scarlatti.

Rugerius took his dismissal in good part, picking up the tray and saying as he did, "And where will you be?"

Ragoczy's smile was at once sardonic and wistful. "I will be in my apartment; I find the heat of the day oppressive. An hour or so in my bed will restore me."

"I will rouse you at sunset," Rugerius told him, relieved that Ragoczy was finally going to seek his native earth.

"Thank you, old friend," said Ragoczy from the hall door. "You are very good."

Text of a letter from Ennio Lampone in Roma to Ferenc Ragoczy at Villa Vecchia, carried by Antonio Scorda.

To the most Excellent, the Conte da San Germain, the sincerest greet-ings of Ennio Lampone, mathematician, with the fervent hope that this will not be deemed an intrusion on what is so slight an acquain-tance,

Eccellenza, I hope you may remember that I had the honor to meet you at Il Meglio, the palazzo of Giancarlo, Cardinal Colonna, some months past. Your may also recall that my son, Rufio, is currently residing in England, calling himself Rufus Berry, and it is on his behalf, at the suggestion of Ettore Colonna, that I make so bold to address you in this most irregular manner.

It is my understanding that you have occasional commerce with England, and that you can arrange travel for those seeking to make such voyages. I must ask you to receive me before the end of next week so that I may explain how it comes about that I make this irregular request. I am sure you are aware that mathematicians can have enemies as easily as any man may, and that some of them will go to desperate ends to demonstrate their enmity. I fear that has happened in my case, and I am in no position to present an acceptable defense against those things of which I am accused. Flight is igno-minious but it is my only salvation at this point. While Innocenzo reigned, I had little to fear, but now that he is dead, I have learned I am about to be denounced for certain thoughts I have been so un-

*wise as to publish, and which now are to be subjected to the scrutiny
of the Holy Office for the Faith; I am certain some of my conclusions
will not meet with their approval. It is not my wish to bolt in this
unseemly manner, but I am left with no choice but absconding with
all my papers, or staying to be imprisoned as a heretic because of
them. I pray you understand something of the nature of my predicament, for surely an exile is cognizant of these matters.*

*You are reputed to be a man of tolerant character and intellectual
principles. It is in these capacities that I make bold to send this to
you, and pray you will not add it to the condemnations of my work
that are even now being heaped up at the Pope's Little House in the
Via Sacra.*

*If you are willing to receive me, pray tell the messenger who brings
this what time and day would suit your convenience, and I will make
haste to wait upon you then. You may trust this messenger, who has
been my student for nearly ten years, and who shares my peril.*

*I confess I fear for my life. I can offer no account for my thoughts
that have brought me to this dreadful pass but that I have gone where
logic and numbers have led me, for no other reason than a desire to
understand the nature of mathematics. If this is a sin in God's eyes,
I am appalled to think that God could bestow the gift of reason and
then demand it be denied in His Name. If you are willing to help me,
I will sing your praises from my haven in England until God Himself
silences me.*

This brings with it my hopes and my highest opinion,

Your humblest petitioner,
Ennio Lampone
By my own hand and under seal

At Roma, on the 3rd day of September, 1689

5

It was the second day of grape harvest and the air smelled of new wine, an aroma so palpable that the wind seemed inebriated with it. Twilight lay blue and intense over the Roman hills, soft and warm as a caress. Sporadic bits of music drifted up from the crushing sites where tired peasants struggled to go on with their celebrations as long as they could.

"It will be a good vintage," said Niklos Aulirios to Ragoczy as they rode out from Senza Pari toward the road leading into Roma. "The grapes are plentiful and their sweetness balances with their tartness. Olivia would be proud."

Ragoczy laughed. "More likely she would be satisfied. She expected her lands to produce good wine, and would expect an explanation if they did not." He fell silent after he spoke, and so did Niklos. It had been just such an evening when Nero ruled Roma that Ragoczy had attended a dinner at the house Titus Petronius Niger; he recalled he had brought his host a remedy to keep from sneezing at the roses in the garden next door, as well as provided Indian temple dancers to entertain Petronius' guests. That was the first time he had met Olivia, in that long-vanished, lamp-lit garden. "I miss her," he said at last.

"So do I," Niklos agreed. "It has been more than thirty years since she died, and I have not lost the habit of listening for her voice or looking for her. Occasionally I think I hear her speak to me. Often I anticipate a glimpse of her when I come suddenly into a room." He caught his lower lip in his teeth.

A night-bird called overhead, and another answered from some distance away; the drowsy wind hummed with mosquitos.

"Do not fault yourself for that. You served her for well over a millennium. It would surprise me if you could put her behind you in a mere three decades." Ragoczy did not add that he had memories going back to long-vanished Thebes and the Temple of Imhotep which still had a sense of immediacy about them. "In time you—"

"I will not forget!" Niklos said with some heat.

"No, of course you will not," Ragoczy said, unperturbed by Niklos' outburst. "But you will cease to wait for her."

"And you?" Niklos said accusingly. "Will you continue to wait for her?"

Ragoczy's face showed his sadness. "Ah, but for me it is different. She was blood of my blood. I know she is gone, but I cannot lose her."

"But you do not long for her," Niklos said, perversely jealous of Ragoczy's blood-bond, although Olivia had often told him that it was as much anguish as consolation.

"That would be folly," said Ragoczy, and knew he had said too little. "I cannot bring her back again; if I deny her loss, I will lose her utterly: if I accept it, I will have her memory. I prefer the latter, whenever possible."

Five hundred years ago Niklos would have demanded a justification of such a remark, but now he nodded, his handsome features revealing little; he changed the subject. "When do we return to court, do you think?"

"When the new Pope allows it, and we do not yet have a new Pope. Podesta della Rovere will not hear this case one instant sooner than he must." He pointed toward the crossroads ahead. "You are bound for Roma and I am going on to the Villa Vecchia." He sighed. "At least the workers are busy again now that the month of mourning is over. Still, I will have to increase their numbers by half again what they are now if I want the roof on the new building by winter."

Niklos drew in his glossy blue roan. "Are you planning to stay there long?"

"I doubt it; I would have to answer too many questions," said Ragoczy. "But if I fail to rebuild, I will bring attention I would not like. This way I show the world I am wealthy without such ostentation that I would earn the disgust of the old families, and I avoid the suspicions of the Church, at least for a while." He considered this a bit longer. "And I do not like the place looking as it did when Olivia died there; it is too troubling. Rebuilding has allowed me to be rid of all that without causing comment on my purpose."

"I wondered if that might be part of it," he said.

"That, and I suppose all those years in prison left me with a hankering for pleasant surroundings," said Ragoczy, and gave his grey a nudge with his knee as they reached the main road. "This is where we part, I think. I will come again in a week or so to arrange for resuming our rehearsals."

"When will that be?" Niklos asked, starting away down the road toward the city.

"As soon as the new Pope is on San Pietro's Throne and Scarlatti has performed his last Cantata and Oratorio." Ragoczy had to raise his voice to be heard.

Niklos made a broad gesture of farewell as he faded into the dusk; the sound of his horse's hooves carried back to Ragoczy as he continued on his way toward the Villa Vecchia, needing nothing more than the stars to light his way. He had not made up his mind about how he would answer the note brought to him the previous day by a servant of Adina Bonasoli; she was tempting, but he had no wish to create false hopes by his attentions. She was eager to engage his interests, but she was far more eager to marry again, and he would never offer her marriage; she sought a husband, not an admirer. He knew better than to visit her in her dreams, for she might recall just enough of their somnolent tryst to feel the need to ask for absolution: that would never do. His mood was pensive and as he rode along, he let his thoughts drift back, without the longing of nostalgia, over the centuries to when he was Sanct' Germain Franciscus, from Dacia but not a Daci. He remembered Tishtry and Kozrozd, and Aumtehoutep, all dead in the Roman arena so very long ago. He decided that these hills, as much as Niklos' remarks earlier, had evoked the past; Roma had been so different then, and so much the same. Seven hundred years ago while he and Olivia had shared his villa, the city had been halfway to a ruin, but had resurrected itself in the intervening centuries until the explosion that had ended Olivia's long life had also destroyed almost a half of the building. As he made the turning that led to the Villa Vecchia, which in those vanished days was Villa Ragoczy, he saw Matyas coming toward him with a lanthorn in his hand, mounted on a nine-year-old mare. He drew in, his attention on his servant.

"Who's there?" Matyas cried out, lifting the lanthorn and opening its front to shine into the darkness.

"You need not draw your pistol, Matyas," said Ragoczy in a tone of unconcern, and speaking in Matyas' native Hungarian. "I will come peacefully."

"Signor' Conte!" Matyas exclaimed in the same language. "I came looking for you. I was sent to find you." He brought his horse up to Ragoczy's. "The Penitent has been asking for you," he said, lowering his voice as if he expected Hungarian-speaking eavesdroppers in the bushes.

"Has she: I wonder why," said Ragoczy, careful to reveal the full extent of his curiosity. He started his horse to walking again. "When did this happen?"

Matyas shrugged. "Rugerius was summoned by the penitent's maid about an hour ago; she told him she wanted to speak with you. That is all I know." He shone the circle of light cast by the lanthorn on the road ahead of them, making the dark seem greater by contrast with the puny brightness.

"Rugerius sent you to find me?" Ragoczy inquired. "He thought that perhaps I should speak with the young woman as long as she is inclined to talk." It was not so much a guess as a summing-up of Rugerius' nature.

"Yes," said Matyas. "He ordered me to ride toward Senza Pari, to bring you back to your Villa Vecchia." He hesitated before going on. "You have not seen her often, have you?"

"The Penitent? No: I have tended her injuries, that is all." He heard an animal in the underbrush beside the road and calmed his horse at the sound. A thought came unwanted. "Did Maurizio do—"

"No, nothing. He has been playing for her, to help her, but he stays outside her room. He says nothing." If Matyas hoped to provide some reassurance with this additional comment, he missed the mark.

"He leaves his eloquence to his violin," said Ragoczy with gloomy certainty. "And she, no doubt, listens eagerly, hearing his passion. In her austerity, she may find sustenance in his playing, though she may not know what it signifies."

"She says the music comforts her," Matyas said, hoping he was not overstepping any bounds.

Ragoczy tried not to laugh. "How very ... useful, for both of them," he said, feeling his years weigh on him. "If the moon were brighter I would suggest we trot, but tonight that would invite trouble. Keep your mount to a fast walk, as will I. We'll make the best time that way. There isn't much farther to go."

Matyas used his heels and his horse extended his walk. They went some little way in silence, and then Matyas remarked, "She says she wants to see her Confessor."

"And did she say who that might be? Is there someone specific or will any priest do?" Ragoczy asked. The small cypress grove ended and the two villas stood directly ahead, the new one still empty to the sky; Ragoczy did not need to point his horse toward the stable as one of the guard-dogs began to bark.

"That may be why she wants to talk to you," said Matyas. He kept his mare moving in spite of the dog.

"Ah," said Ragoczy as they reached the stable yard. He swung out of the saddle, saying to Matyas, "Ordinarily I would take care of her myself, but tonight, I would count it as a service if you would—"

Matyas had already dismounted and now reached for the reins Ragoczy held. "I will see she is fed and brushed and watered. I'll check her hooves tonight and give them a proper cleaning in the morning, with the turpentine dressing."

"You're very good," said Ragoczy, relinquishing the reins and starting toward the kitchen door. He became aware of a plaintive melody—Maurizio was playing one of the old troubadours' songs Ragoczy had given him to practice on; his style was more flamboyant than anything the troubadors had done, but his expertise was impressive to hear.

"My master," said Rugerius as he opened the kitchen door. "I had not hoped to see you so quickly."

Ragoczy strode past him into the kitchen, removing his hat as he went, and handing it to Rugerius; the cook glanced up from the chicken he was basting with olive oil, basil, and garlic, his brows raised in surprise at the haste with which Ragoczy went through the kitchen. "Matyas found me on the road. Niklos was bound for Roma and I wanted to return before it was so late that everyone here would be asleep." He was almost into the corridor. "I assume Maurizio has some excellent reason not to have returned to Senza Pari tonight." His tone was gently ironic.

"That he does," said Rugerius, catching Ragoczy's inflection precisely. "His horse cast a shoe, and the farrier will have to attend to it in the morning."

"And no doubt the leg in question is being poulticed, for safety?" Ragoczy suggested.

"Certainly," said Rugerius, the humor in his faded-blue eyes belying his stern demeanor.

"Very good," said Ragoczy, continuing down the corridor. "Where is Maurizio?"

"I put him in the antechamber off the main reception room; the one at the back, overlooking the old fountains—you know the one." He slowed his pace as he reached the door to the library. "The maid is with her, of course."

"Of course," said Ragoczy.

"She may say more than we want to her brother," Rugerius cautioned him.

"Old friend, why else is she here but to be eyes and ears for Bonaldo Fiumara? I have known from the moment he suggested she become our penitent guest's maid that he wanted more than safeguarding the young woman's reputation." His smile was tinged with weariness. "You had better tell her I have returned and for our guest to ready herself. I'll have a word or two with Maurizio while you do." He put one small hand on Rugerius' shoulder. "Thank you for all this."

Rugerius nodded his acknowledgment; he turned down the hall, then stopped. "I cannot think how you will want to deal with all this."

"Nor can I, not until I know what our guest wants," Ragoczy paused thoughtfully. "Given what has gone before, I would be glad of candor." He managed a one-sided smile. "Go on. We will talk later."

"Very good," said Rugerius, and continued on his way.

Maurizio was so engrossed in "Jherusalem, Grant Damage me

Fais" that he did not notice Ragoczy until he said, "You play that very well, if a little too quickly."

"It is an interesting work," he said, his face and neck reddening. "It is very old, I think."

"Yes, it is. But perhaps, just at present," said Ragoczy kindly, "you might like to give our Penitent Guest a little silence. Perhaps you would like a rest, as well; you have been playing a long time. You are probably hungry. The cook will have something in the kitchen for you, no doubt: he was preparing chicken as I came in." He kept his demeanor as cordial as possible.

"I am a bit hungry," Maurizio conceded. "But I do not like to leave her."

"You leave her most evenings when you return to Senza Pari. What you do now is an added gift." He managed a wry smile. "She will not mind if you eat."

"She is all alone," said Maurizio, obediently lowering his bow and taking his violin from his neck; the callus on his skin there was brighter than his face.

"And surely you know what that is like," Ragoczy agreed. "But she will not be devastated if you interrupt your playing for a meal. After all, she has had supper by now, and her maid is with her. And usually you are back at Senza Pari by this hour."

"I can explain about that," said Maurizio hastily as he put his violin in its case; the color in his neck and cheeks was more revealing than his assurance.

"The trouble with your horse," said Ragoczy with a gesture of dismissal. "And you did not want to borrow one of my horses for fear it should also suffer an injury. I do understand." His faint amusement was masked by his urbane manner. "We will discuss that later, when you have eaten and I have had a word with our guest."

Something flared in Maurizio's eyes which Ragoczy knew was jealousy. "Of course," he said tightly, doing his best to emulate Ragoczy's correctness. He loosened his bow and laid it in the open case.

"If you want to play after you have dined, do so," Ragoczy offered, making no attempt to criticize him. "Little as you may think it, I have no wish to silence you: I am pleased to hear you practice so diligently."

Maurizio knew his posturing was foolish but he could not bring himself to abandon his aggravation. "You are master here."

"Yes; I am." Ragoczy made a leg and left the young man alone. He went along toward the room given to Leocadia; he brushed his riding coat in case any dust clung to it, touched his wig, and prepared to enter the room. He scratched at the door. "Signorina?"

The maid, Clarice Fiumara, came at once to open the door. "Signor' Conte. Come in. The Penitent has been asking for you."

Ragoczy stepped into the room, moving cautiously, and saw Leocadia kneeling beside her bed, dressed in a long nightrail of cream-colored linen with a grey lawn shawl around her shoulders for modesty, and to keep from shivering in the warm night. She was thin to gauntness, her collarbones standing out enough to make sharp shadows; her skin starkly pale and her dark hair lusterless and lank, as if she had crowned herself with darkness; there were blurs livid as bruises under her eyes and her lips were chapped. He stood as far away from her as the room would allow. "Good evening, my Guest."

She looked up, her face unnaturally composed. "Good evening, Conte." Her voice was little more than a whisper, and she did not meet his dark eyes.

In the short silence that followed, the maid coughed an encouragement to Leocadia.

"You wished to see me?" Ragoczy suggested when Leocadia said nothing more.

"She has been asking for you some time," said Clarice; Ragoczy wondered how much of what she heard was reported to her builder-brother.

"Yes," Leocadia said, and went still again. When he did not prompt her to speak, she sighed. "I must see my Confessor."

"I will send to San Procopio for a priest; it is the nearest church," Ragoczy offered at once, startled that she would make so unremarkable a request of him. "Any of the servants would have fetched one for you."

"No. No. My Confessor is at Santissimo Redentore in Roma; his name is Padre Bartolomeo Battista Tredori. He has been my Confessor since I came to Roma with my brother, nine years ago." Her voice fell to a whisper as her eyes looked into the distance.

"And you would like Padre Tredori to be brought here," said Ragoczy quietly, taking his tone from hers.

"Yes. If you would." She looked up at him with an emotion in her eyes that Ragoczy found troubling. "Tell him he is not to tell anyone, not *anyone* that he knows anything of me."

"I will try to do as you wish, but to bring him out of the city, I must tell him who has need of him, so that he will not think you have summoned him idly, or in contempt for any other priest." He spoke gently, his voice low and musical.

"Oh, no," she said in despair. "Can you not tell him I am a sincere penitent?"

"Certainly he will want to know why he, of all priests, has been summoned. He will have to tell his superior of his mission. And he will ask who you are. You must know this request is unusual, and he will need more than my assurance of your purpose." Ragoczy paused and went on very carefully. "If I tell him no name, he will assume you are my mistress: is that what you want?"

Leocadia crossed herself. "No. Not that."

"Dio mi salva," whispered Clarice, crossing herself. "What a dreadful thought, when you have been at such pains—" She turned away as if to avert scandal.

"Then you will have to tell me who you are and rely upon my discretion to keep your secret," said Ragoczy with all the kindness he could offer without moving closer to her.

She began to shake and Clarice bustled toward her, clicking her tongue in concern. "Signorina, te prego . . . be calm."

"I am calm," said Leocadia, her eyes bright with anger, which faded as abruptly as it had appeared. "I beg your pardon. I am behaving disgracefully, Signor' Conte. I did not mean any . . . any . . . anything." She was out of breath and the veins in her neck showed how rapid her heartbeat had become.

"I did not think you did," Ragoczy said, soothing her as best he could. "You are not one to injure those who do not harm you, are you."

She began to weep. "Signor' Conte, I cannot tell you more. It would be more . . . disgraceful."

Clarice took a shocked breath, and held her breath to listen. "Nothing you could tell me would disgrace you, Signorina. But if I am to help you as you ask, I must know more."

"No. I cannot. I cannot." She shook her head and began to rock herself.

Watching her, Ragoczy decided to take a chance. Keeping his voice steady and tranquil, he told her, "You have no reason to fear your brother will find you if you do not wish it. He and all the Cardinals are still sequestered."

Leocadia clapped her hands to her face as she turned toward him. "You *know?*" She saw him nod. "Por Dios, how long have you known?" she pleaded in Spanish.

Ragoczy answered her in that language. "From the first. You may not recall that we met at Il Meglio, the Colonna palazzo in Roma?"

Mutely she nodded, lowering her hands and waving her nurse back. "Yes," she said. "I remember." She once again spoke in Italian. "You told no one?"

"You did not tell *me*," Ragoczy said.

"Not even Martin?" she asked in astonishment. "You have kept this from him, though he is a Cardinal?"

With a little shriek, Clarice threw up her hands and began, very softly, to pray.

"Why should I trespass on your privacy? You gave me no name when you came here, asking only for what sanctuary I could provide. I have done that, and I will serve you further if you will permit." He studied her face for a short while. "Signorina Calaveria y Vacamonte, you have nothing to fear from me."

"I have everything to fear from you," she countered in sudden vehemence. "You might command me anything: now that you know."

"But I have known from the start," Ragoczy said serenely, trying to communicate a portion of his composure to her. "I have not violated the trust you have reposed in me. Why should I do so now?— nothing has changed."

Her face might have been carved in marble, having no expression whatsoever. "You have done all that is honorable, all that is charitable. You are a most compassionate man," she conceded, her admission made grudgingly and with a hint of condescension. "But it is no longer the same, since you know."

"It may be for you; it is the same for me," said Ragoczy, wanting to assuage the dejection that had claimed her.

"No, no, no, no," she said as automatically as she had recited her penitential Psalms as she flagellated herself.

"Signorina!" Clarice exclaimed, going to Leocadia's side and bending down to hold her for solace.

Leocadia pulled out of Clarice's awkward embrace. "You will say nothing—*nothing*—to my brother, either one. They are not to know where I am. And say nothing to his servants; they will tell in an instant. Say nothing," she ordered emphatically. "You must promise you will say nothing."

Ragoczy bowed slightly. "You have my Word, Signorina."

"You will not tell them?" Leocadia demanded, doubt turning this to a question.

"Of course not: I have given you my Word," Ragoczy assured her, seeing how fragile she was under her attempt at imperiousness. "I will speak to Padre Tredori privately, and all you may tell him will be under Seal. No one will say anything you do not wish." He gave Clarice a stern look.

Clarice returned it. "I know how to keep my tongue in my head, Signor' Conte. Bonaldo will learn nothing of this from me."

"I was maladroit to think you might," Ragoczy said by way of apology. He paused, regarding Leocadia with concern. "If you are so concerned about keeping your presence unknown, you may want to reconsider. Padre Sergio Barzini is from San Procopio, and he will hear your Confession."

She shook her head many times. "No. Padre Tredori: it must be Padre Tredori." Beneath her ire there was dread. "Bring him and no other."

Ragoczy made a leg. "As you wish, Signorina. Will tomorrow morning be soon enough, or do you want me to fetch him tonight? There will be less notice and fewer questions in the morning."

"You are mocking me, Signor' Conte," Leocadia said, pulling her shawl tightly around her shoulders and looking to Clarice for support.

"Indeed, I am not," said Ragoczy.

Leocadia scrutinized him, her head lifted with something of the hauteur Ragoczy had seen that evening at II Meglio. "Perhaps not," she allowed. "If you think tomorrow is best, then so be it."

"I will leave before first light, so that I may bring him immediately after morning Mass. I trust that will be soon enough." He did not add that he would stop on his way to Santissima Redentore to pass an hour with a spinster from Livorno who had the most intense dreams, dreams she never repeated to her Confessor; she would be glad of his ephemeral company, and he would be nourished.

Before Leocadia could speak, Clarice murmured her thanks. "This young woman has need of her Confessor."

Ragoczy would have asked her why this need was so pressing, but realized that if he sought to discover more, his curiosity could put the seal on Leocadia's distrust. "Then I will bring him here before noon."

"May God speed and guide you, Signor' Conte," said Leocadia, with another mercurial shift in demeanor; she was filled with humility and supplication. "I will pray for you tonight."

"What can I be but grateful," said Ragoczy as he slipped out of the room.

Text of a letter of response written in German from Ahrent Rothofen to Archbishop Siegfried Walmund, carried by the Archbishop's personal courier.

To His Excellency, the Archbishop of Oldenburg, Seigfried Walmund, the attentive greeting of his most devoted servant, Ahrent Julius Roth-ofen.

I regret to inform you, Excellency, that I have been unable to find any more information on Leocadia Calaveria y Vacamonte than what I supplied you ten days since. I have done all within my powers to continue the search for her, all without success. The on-going conclave makes it difficult to proceed, for without Cardinal Calaveria y Va-camonte to give his permission for what I am doing, I have no au-thority to pursue the woman, and, should I do so, you know I would attract the attention of the familiars, which neither you nor I would want, not only for the immediate suspicions they would have regarding my intentions in hunting for her, but for the more problematic issue of the circumstances in which the Cardinal's sister might be living, should I discover her. This second consideration perplexes me greatly, for if she has fled to a lover, the whole arrangements for the marriage would be in jeopardy.

There is no progress on my suit, of course, and will not be until the Magisterial Courts are convened again by the new Pope. There are a few things I want to do in this time that may turn the outcome to my benefit. Who would have thought that Aulirios would have such a vast knowledge of the history of the Clemens estate? He has thwarted me at every turn, and because of that, I am at some disadvantage because of the delay and find myself in more straitened circumstances than I could wish. I am at something of an impasse because my advocate is asking for some payment on my account, and I may either do that or purchase a new wig, which I must have if I am to make a proper appearance in the world. It would be a mistake to refuse to pay my advocate, but it would also be an error to make a poor showing, so to obtain a bit more wherewithal, I will gladly undertake any errands or other services Your Excellency may bestow on me.

The conclave cannot last much longer. For one thing Louis of France is increasing his disobedient ways in this unsettled time, and the Church cannot be seen to concede anything to the French, or who knows where it will stop? If the Church continues leaderless for much longer, the French may rally to the Protestant cause, if only to help their King. The sad example of the Protestant turmoil is everywhere before us in the German States, and the Holy Roman Emperor is at odds with the Holy See because of it. I fear that there is more discord to come. Without a new Pope, and soon, this disorder will increase and that can only lead to the disunity Innocenzo himself so decried. Hourly I anticipate the white smoke, as do all Catholics, for the sake of our lives and our souls.

I thank Your Excellency in this uncertain time for the stalwartness of your purpose and I condole with you: if only the marriage between your brother and Cardinal Calaveria y Vacamonte had been cele-brated before this crisis, we might have used this time to secure new alliances for Oldenburg that would give us access to the Spanish col-onies in the New World, which would bring not only gold and silver but land, and the natives to work it for Oldenburg. How much we should rejoice on the day we make this dream a reality. The New World is a treasure, and it is fitting that Oldenburg have a share of it; the Spanish have need of us, whether they admit it or not. They will have to have allies or lose precious possessions to the French, or so it appears to me; I have been watching the activities of the French in the New World, and I know that any of the German States would manage better, had we been given such an opportunity as the French have had in Canada, or in Mexico. If we have learned nothing else in the German States, we have learned the importance of maintaining order amid disruption. We value the firm hand that gives direction and dignity to all endeavors; these are lessons we should bring to the Americas. It is unthinkable that we should be deprived of our rightful place among colonial powers because of the caprice of one young woman.

It is all God's Will, no doubt, but for one such as I, who am no theologian, His Favor seems to be bestowed with little regard for His Church. I do not say this heretically, for I have no doubt that His Purpose is beyond understanding, and I am willing to accept His Will in all things, including His seemingly perverse advancement of Prot-estants.

I will do myself the honor of calling upon you tomorrow at mid-afternoon, unless some news comes from Saint Peter's. Know that I hold you in highest esteem and commend my service to your will,

In devotion and dedication
Yours to command,
Ahrent Rothofen

On the 2nd day of October, 1689

6

"Pietro Ottoboni is Pope!" Ettore Colonna cried out, laughing. He flung the note from his cousin into the air, much to the horror of the young monk who had carried the news from Giancarlo, Cardinal Colonna, to Ettore Colonna. "The French will be celebrating when they hear the news." He swung around to face Alessandro Scarlatti, holding out his hands. "Come drink a toast with me, to the health of Alessandro VIII. You can spare a moment for that, can't you? Such a momentous occasion. It will not make me pay you less for your music." He clapped his hands and one of the footmen came in answer to his summons. "Wine! Bring the best we have. Let us taste the Blood of Christ in honor of His new Pope; let us share in God's joy at this good news. Wine and sweets." He laughed again so that the marble halls of II Meglio rang with it.

Alessandro Scarlatti sighed. "The sheets of music paper are so thick on my worktable they are like a pelt. And the press of work is only just beginning, for now the coronation will be celebrated and I must have new works for that, as well. I will have to be up all of the night to finish the last of the orchestration on my Cantata," he said, then let his curiosity dictate his questions. "Why are you so delighted, Signore Colonna? Do you favor Ottoboni?"

The young monk ducked his head. "I must return to—" He gestured toward the dome of San Pietro.

Ettore Colonna waved him away, then gave his attention to Scarlatti. "I am delighted because Ottoboni is a Venetian. I am more pleased that he is old, and will not reign long, so there will be more confusion among the Cardinals which he will be unable to stop. The disputes of the last reign will not end with Ottoboni, no matter what he tries. At least he will not be locked in conflict with Louis of France. He will care nothing for the Jansenists. He will spend his time trying to keep the Ottomites in check, to stop their advances into Christian lands, when he is able to do anything at all. The Curia will keep him in check, and the Ottomites will be a silent presence in Church affairs again. This should demand more cordial relations with the rulers of the West. The austerities will lessen. The Lampones may come back from England without harm. Who knows, the tax on snuff may come to an end." Ettore Colonna stopped still for a moment. "Ragoczy will have to be informed. Who knows," he repeated "he may even be pleased with the new Pope for reasons of his own: the Turks are greedy for his homeland." He clapped again, summoning another footman. "Bring me paper. Tell them to ready a fresh horse in the stable. And send for Celestino Bruschi. I have work for him."

The bells of Roma began to ring, San Giovanni in Laterano sounding the first peal to honor the new Pope, then San Pietro joining in its bass note, then San Lorenzo Fuori le Mura, then San Clemente, as each of the Basilicas heralded Alessandro VIII, sounding their bells before the churches began. The sound was as powerful as thunder, shaking the air with brazen joy.

Alessandro Scarlatti clapped his hands to his ears. "I cannot *think* in this din. It is going to get louder, of course. I do not know how I will finish my work if I have to listen to this clamor all night; I will have nothing but bells in my head."

"You will accomplish it all," said Ettore Colonna with steady confidence. "You have managed thus far. There is no reason you cannot continue."

"Very likely," said Scarlatti in a sarcastic tone. "You can say so because it is not for you to do."

Ettore Colonna held up his hands in surrender. "I ask your pardon, Maestro Scarlatti." He was still in high good-humor as he said this, his smile unchanged from his first reading of the note. "Habemus Papam," he said: *we have a Pope*, reciting the traditional words of announcement to the world. "Come." He clapped his hands again. "Pour us some fine, red, Communion blood that we may show our gratitude to God, and grow closer to Him."

There was a long moment of silence, and then Scarlatti managed a chuckle. "I do not mean to be an ogre. I am only trying to keep myself from being caught in the madness."

"A sensible thing, no doubt; in your position I would do the same thing," said Ettore Colonna, breaking off to sit down at the wide, polished table as his servant appeared carrying a portable desk. "Very good. Put it here, if you would." He patted the table in front of him and reached for paper as soon as the servant set it down.

"What are you going to tell the Signor' Conte?" asked Scarlatti, his curiosity piqued.

"That there is a new Pope, that the Pope is Venetian and old, and that the Magisterial Courts will shortly be in session again." He reached for a pen and began to trim the quill. "You haven't forgotten Signor' Aulirios' plight, have you?"

"Certainly not," said Scarlatti, who had. "There will be much for him to do in order to prepare to proceed with the case." He began to pace. "And there is the opera. We must resume our rehearsals as soon as possible."

The servant ordered to bring wine appeared, a newly opened, dusty bottle on the tray with the glasses. "I apologize, Signore," he said. "I had to fetch this from the pantry racks." He held up the bottle for approval. "Twelve years old. If you want older, I will have to go into the cellar."

Ettore Colonna beckoned the man nearer and peered at the label on the bottle. "This is an excellent choice for our occasion," he decided aloud. "Open and decant it so that we may show our rejoicing that the Holy Spirit has sent the Church a new Pope. Were it not a heretical notion, I would think that God has a sense of humor— inspiring the Cardinals to elect such a man as Ottoboni to San Pietro's Chair." He winked at Scarlatti. "I am often thankful that God chose good red wine to share Himself with us. He might have settled on seawater or turpentine, and then where would we be?" Seeing that Scarlatti was not laughing, he went on contritely. "Your pardon, Maestro. You were saying?"

Scarlatti fussed with his wide justaucorps cuffs. "I will not be able to get away for a while yet, not with the coronation coming soon, for they will not want to wait many days for the event," he said, his face marked with new dejection. "I had hoped to have time enough to visit my family in Napoli, but it is not going to be possible. My children will not remember me by the time I return."

Looking up from his writing, Ettore Colonna said, "You will have to demand time at the Nativity."

"No," said Scarlatti with a sad shake of his head. "I have too many commissions. I dare not leave until after the New Year." He paused in his lament to watch the servant light the candle to begin decanting the wine. "I miss them all."

"Hardly surprising," said Ettore Colonna, and went on when he saw the startled expression pass over Scarlatti's features. "Do not believe that because I have no wife or children that I cannot understand how you miss them." His face lightened. "Why not send for them to join you?"

"It wouldn't be prudent," said Scarlatti shortly. "Roma being Roma, I must protect my family from the pitfalls of this place." He bowed slightly to Ettore Colonna. "You must understand my concern, Signore."

"Of course I do," said Colonna with sincerity as he signed his name to the note with a flourish and tipped sand onto it. "Where is Celestino?" he asked of the air.

The servant who had brought the desk said, "He is coming, master."

"Very good," Ettore Colonna approved. "Go to the stable and tell them to ready a horse for him." He waved his servant away before returning his attention to the note he had written. After folding the sheet carefully, he struck flint and steel to light the candle on the portable desk, then reached for his sealing wax. "I want this given to Ragoczy before nightfall." He dropped a blob of red wax onto the folded paper and set the impression of his signet ring in it. "There." He looked at Scarlatti as the servant handed the musician a glass of the newly decanted wine. "Taste this and tell me if it is not worthy of a Papal celebration." He accepted his own glass and chuckled as he lifted it. "To Alessandro VIII, may he bring glory to Roma, and with this good Communion blood bring us to the love of God."

Scarlatti stood as he raised his glass, moderately startled that Ettore Colonna remained seated. "Signore?" he ventured.

"The Pope will not mind," he said, and drank. "And if he does not, how can God?" With an ironic laugh he drank down half the glass.

Scarlatti shook his head but acknowledged the toast; he smiled approval as he tasted the wine. "Very good. Truly."

Ettore Colonna opened his mouth to reply, then turned his head as Celestino Bruschi came into the room. "There you are at last," he said in a jolly tone. "As you can tell by the noise there is a new Pope, and one who should be most interesting." He held out the sealed letter. "Here. I want you to carry this to Ragoczy for me. At once. He may or may not give you an answer to bring back."

Bruschi made a leg. "I am all readiness," he said, smiling courteously.

"Let us hope that a horse is, too," said Ettore Colonna. "Barring chaos in the streets, you should be able to reach Ragoczy within the hour."

"The bells will summon the people," Bruschi said just as the noise increased.

"Then hasten," said Ettore Colonna, indicating the stairs. "There should be a horse ready by the time you reach the stables. If there isn't, saddle one yourself. When you return tonight, I will have other errands for you, so come to me before you seek your chambers," Ettore Colonna warned as Bruschi departed. He glanced toward Scarlatti. "He is a most excellent fellow, is Bruschi."

"He seems so," Scarlatti answered carefully; in his long association with aristocrats he had learned it was unwise to contradict them, or to agree too fulsomely.

"How very careful you are, Maestro," said Ettore Colonna, who understood Scarlatti's caution. He indicated the wine in Scarlatti's glass. "If you want more—"

"No; no. Grazie." The last was punctilious. Scarlatti was growing restless; he set his glass down and began to pace. "You say you do not think it will be long until Alessandro's coronation?"

"No," said Ettore Colonna, comprehending the reason for the composer's disquiet. "It would be wise to have the coronation as soon as possible; these interim periods can become treacherous if they are allowed to continue too long."

Scarlatti shook his head. "I hope there is time enough for me to finish the works that have been commissioned, and to rehearse them."

Ettore Colonna drank down most of the rest of his wine. "I do admire your industry, Maestro, and I know I do not share it. Still, given our various gifts, it is probably just as well that God ordered us as He did." He inclined his head. "I will not keep you if you would rather be away; I thought it was wise of both of us to salute our new Pontiff as soon as we heard the happy tidings. Neither you nor I can afford to look laggard in our devotions—for vastly different reasons, of course."

Scarlatti made a leg. "Thank you, Signore Colonna. I rejoice with you." With that, he went to retrieve the cloak he had flung over the back of one of the chairs, swung it around his shoulders and left Ettore Colonna to his private festivities. As he emerged from Il Meglio he saw Celestino Bruschi, mounted on a feisty red mare, heading toward the eastern gate of the city; the composer had a moment's wistful longing that it was he and not Bruschi bound for Ragoczy's villa, but he dismissed such lackadaisical notions from his thoughts and continued on his way, reminding himself that there was work to be done.

Celestino Bruschi rode at a brisk trot—the fastest pace that was safe in the crowded streets of Roma—doing his best to avoid the revelers newly appearing in answer to the clamor of the bells; his short cloak spread out behind him on the rump of his horse. Once he was beyond the limits of the city he gave the mare her head, covering the distance to the villa at an easy canter half the way, and a jog-trot for the rest; the sound of her hooves soon became louder than the bells. Around him the rich Roman sunlight buttered the lovely curves of the hills; a few of the leaves were showing the first burnishing of autumn, but Bruschi hardly noticed, for he was intent on his mission. The mare obliged him, never falling back to a walk until they passed the gates of the Villa Vecchia, where Bruschi found Ragoczy standing in the doorway of his partially completed villa, a slight frown on his attractive, irregular features. "Signor' Conte," he called out as he pulled the mare in and came out of the saddle.

Ragoczy looked around. "Signore Bruschi," he responded, suggesting a leg. "I hope I see you well."

"You see me here on behalf of Ettore Colonna, and with some urgency," said Bruschi, holding the mare's reins with one hand and offering the sealed note with the other. "He sent me to give you this as soon as the announcement was made."

Ragoczy came down the steps, a frown forming between his brows. "Now, what—?" He took the note.

"They are celebrating in Roma," said Bruschi as he watched Ragoczy break the seal on the note. "As I came away, I could not hear anything but the pealing of bells."

"For an old Venetian Pope, I see," said Ragoczy as he read through the missive. "Well, Signore Bruschi," he went on briskly, "you are welcome here, bringing me such news. Now, perhaps, the builders can get back to their work." He gave a single shake of his head, and any trace of annoyance vanished. "Come in and let me ask my cook to feed you. It is the least I can offer you."

"You are most gracious," said Bruschi, pausing as the sound of an expertly played violin came from a short distance away. "Very pretty?" He could not correctly ask for an explanation, so he hoped his compliment would bring some further information.

"Oh, that is the very talented but undisciplined young man Scarlatti persuaded me to tutor; he spends his afternoons practicing; we have become used to him and hardly notice his playing," said Ragoczy at his most affable as he stepped into his old villa; as he held the door for Bruschi, he indicated the corridor. "If you will go along to the library—I trust you remember the way?—I will find my manservant and see about getting you a meal for all your trouble."

Bruschi bowed, and although he was curious to know what else Ragoczy might do, as a guest he was constrained to accept the hospitality he was offered. He made a leg and did as his host instructed him. As he went along to the library, he tried to place the piece the violinist was playing but did not recognize the plaintive strains. Shrugging out of his cloak, he took a seat on the upholstered settee near the window and spent a short while looking out into the small formal garden beyond. Pleasant as the days were, he knew they would not last, for the days were shortening and the weather would not hold; in another week or two the rains would come and the roads would turn to mires, the leaves would fall and the world would be stark and bare. He sighed, deliberately putting such thoughts out of his mind.

There would be time enough to deal with winter when it came, he told himself as he directed his attention from the garden to the library. Idly he picked up a leather-bound volume of botanical prints and thumbed through the pages. He was puzzling out the descriptions of New World aloes when Rugerius came in bearing a tray.

"Buona serra, Signore Bruschi," said Rugerius.

Bruschi nodded his acknowledgment; only then did he notice that the playing had stopped. He rose and went to the trestle table where Rugerius was clearing a space for the tray. "The Conte told you?"

"About the new Pope?" Rugerius asked politely. "Oh, yes. We must be grateful that the wait is at an end." He put the tray in the cleared space. "My master is composing a note to Signor' Colonna. He asks you to indulge him by waiting for it."

"I will do so with pleasure," said Bruschi, and looked at the light meal he was being given: cold duck with pureed raspberries over it, a cup of vegetable broth covered with baked cheese, a wedge of polenta with mushrooms and onions, and sliced apples cooked with cinnamon and covered in heavy cream. "This is an excellent repast."

"I will bring you wine in a moment," said Rugerius, and watched as Bruschi sat down to eat.

"Very good," said Bruschi, both to the meal and to the promise of wine. "I will need a lanthorn to light my way when I leave."

"One will be provided," Rugerius assured him, and went to get the wine, returning with it promptly. "This is from the vineyards of Senza Pari," he said, pouring out the wine from the newly opened bottle.

"The disputed villa," said Bruschi, to show he was abreast of things. "A pity to see it fall into German hands."

"Truly," Rugerius agreed, and left the bottle for Bruschi. He went along to Ragoczy's suite of rooms at the rear of the old building, knocking twice on the heavy oaken door before admitting himself to the six-sided chamber that served as a private sitting room; Ragoczy's cell-like bedchamber was on the north side of the hexagon, and a larger room cluttered with scientific equipment was on the south-east side. Two walls of windows overlooked the darkening pastures, a sight that both men ignored. "He will be ready to leave in an hour," he said to Ragoczy, who sat at a small desk with two sheets of vellum before him; he was writing on each simultaneously, using both hands. He had removed his justaucorps and draped it over the back of his chair; the lace at his cuffs had been tucked up so as not to be stained by the ink, and he had unfastened the bands around his neck. Rugerius went and took the justaucorps, hanging it on a hook by the bedroom door.

"And so shall I," said Ragoczy. "Have the Andalusian mare saddled for me. I should take this to Niklos myself. He and I will have much to discuss, if he is actually at Senza Pari." He sounded distant; all his concentration was on the message he was writing on the two sheets.

"Where might Niklos be, if not at Senza Pari?" Rugerius asked.

"I have no notion," Ragoczy replied. "He has the produce of his fields to take to market and he has other duties. I cannot expect him to wait upon my convenience." He continued to write, his small, neat hand the same on both sheets.

"Which Andalusian mare?" Rugerius prompted. "You did not say which: there are four to choose from."

"The six-year-old," said Ragoczy. "Callista."

Rugerius nodded. "Do you want Matyas to go with you?"

"That won't be necessary: I will have Bruschi for company most of the way; I will not return until very late." He smiled slightly as he signed the two notes.

"You know there is a risk in—" Rugerius stopped himself as he saw Ragoczy's brow lift. "Of course you do." He sighed.

"Considering all Roma is celebrating the Pope's election, I should think all the roughians will make their way to the city to take advantage of the moment." He folded the two notes and prepared to affix his eclipse signet to the wax. "For tonight the roads are safe. But I will go armed; do not fear." He paused and went on reflectively. "Olivia would probably have greeted this night with exasperated amusement. I will do my best to see the occasion through her eyes." He tested the two seals to be sure they were cool. "I will want my Hungarian coat; it is going to be cool tonight. And my riding boots." He bent to remove his square-toed shoes. "My pistols—the French ones with the Florentine locks, I think—and my Japanese sword; bring them here if you will."

"All right," said Rugerius, and stepped into the room with the scientific instruments, to a large leather trunk standing under an ancient red-lacquer chest. "No dirk? No poignard?"

Ragoczy considered a moment. "The francisca," he decided. "If I have to fight from horseback, a throwing-axe is a better weapon than a dirk." His smile was grim.

"Then you are expecting trouble," Rugerius said as he took out the weapons Ragoczy had specified and closed the trunk.

"Not expecting, but I shall be prepared," he said. He had retrieved his boots from his bedchamber and was pulling them on as Rugerius brought him his pistols, katana, and francisca.

"The pistols are charged," Rugerius pointed out as he laid them carefully on the desk.

"I should hope so," said Ragoczy at his most urbane. "My coat?"

Rugerius brought it and held it for Ragoczy. "Thank you, old friend," he said as he fastened the frogs at his neck, mid-chest, and waist. He then accepted a wide leather belt which he buckled into place; the francisca he slid in under the belt at the small of his back, the katana went into a special scabbard that hung from the belt, and the two pistols were put into the deep pockets of the coat's pleated skirt. "There."

"I will tell Matyas to ready Callista," said Rugerius, bowing slightly to Ragoczy as he prepared to leave the room.

"I am sorry that I disappoint you," Ragoczy said quietly as he put his two notes into the top of his boots.

"Disappoint me?" Rugerius repeated, his faded-blue eyes showing faint alarm.

"Why, yes," said Ragoczy. "You do not approve of my riding off to Senza Pari."

"I did not say so," said Rugerius.

"You did not need to," Ragoczy responded. "It is plain that you think I am being reckless; I will have to meet with Niklos in a short while in any case, and there is a greater chance of being watched in a day or two. For now, we may be private." He shook his head. "This isn't Russia, or Peru, or China. I have duties that the Romans expect me to honor."

"Yes, and some will take advantage of that," Rugerius said. "I ask only that you be cautious."

"I have two pistols, a sword, and an axe with me: any more caution and I would need a cavalry escort, which would announce my intentions, as well as my fears, to the world." He had reached for his spurs and was buckling them to his boots. "The Romans laugh at me for using petal-rowels, but the horses prefer them."

Rugerius knew better than to press a point when Ragoczy had so obviously changed the subject. He nodded his compliance. "I will tell Signore Bruschi to ready himself to leave shortly."

"Thank you," said Ragoczy softly. When Rugerius was gone, he went in search of Maurizio, explaining his errand and recommending the young violinist plan to remain at the Villa Vecchia for the night. "Clarice is here, so there can be no impropriety as regards the Cardinal's sister."

Maurizio blushed as if taken with a sudden fever. "I would never do anything . . . not anything that would . . ." He became lost in the tangle of his thoughts.

"I know," said Ragoczy, laying his small, gloved hand on Maurizio's shoulder. "You would never harm her; I have no doubt of that." He added to himself that if he had such apprehensions, he would insist that Maurizio leave with him.

The young violinist attempted to smile, but the expression would not stay fixed. "She will not remain here, will she?"

"Probably not," Ragoczy said gently. "But then, neither will you."

Maurizio ducked his head, muttering, "No, I suppose I won't." He started to turn away, but Ragoczy would not let him.

"I understand your emotions; more than you think." His dark eyes were steady and compassionate. "You want to salve her wounds and rid her of whatever terrible thing haunts her. I sympathize with you. I empathize. You seek to provide the anodyne she so clearly needs. Yet I know—as you will learn—that she does not want deliverance, and until she seeks it within herself, not you, not I, nor God Himself can bring it about."

"So you say," Maurizio said gracelessly.

Ragoczy smiled slightly. "Learn by my experience, if you can, for that lesson was hard-won," he recommended, and let it go at that, despite the myriad swarm of memories that crowded his mind and the many faces that jostled for recollection. "Now that the new Pope is elected, Maestro Scarlatti will soon have need of your services again, so let us make the most of the remaining time we have to work on your technique. If you will pay a bit more attention to your intonation, that will be welcome. I will return late tonight. In the morning I will want to hear your Carissimi variations."

"Very well," said Maurizio, his whole demeanor stiff.

Knowing he could say nothing more to Maurizio that would soothe his injured spirit, Ragoczy made half a leg and left the young man to take out his emotions on his bowing and fingering. To confirm this expectation, an energetic *allegro con fuoco* attack followed him along the corridor to the library where Celestino Bruschi was just finishing his meal. "Good evening once again, Signore Bruschi," said Ragoczy in good form. "I trust you have had a satisfactory repast."

"Oh, excellent, truly excellent," Bruschi enthused out of habit. "You have a most superior cook."

"So I understand." Ragoczy paused. "I have no desire to rush you, but the hour is advancing. You and I would be well-advised to depart together."

"Yes," said Bruschi with less verve. "No doubt you are right." He held back a sigh as he rose and reached for his short cloak. "You have received me very well."

"It was my pleasure," said Ragoczy as he drew his answer to Ettore Colonna from his frogged coat. "For your employer," he said.

"Mille grazie," Bruschi said as he accepted the letter, putting it into the pocket in the lining of this justaucorps. "I will see it into his hand before midnight."

"I can ask no more," said Ragoczy while Bruschi donned his cloak.

A moment later Bruschi professed himself ready to depart, and went with Ragoczy to the stable where Matyas had Bruschi's mare ready, and the grey Andalusian Ragoczy had asked for.

"Here is a lanthorn," Matyas added as Ragoczy mounted.

"Let Signore Bruschi have it," Ragoczy recommended. "I know the road to Senza Pari well; Signore Bruschi will need it before he enters Roma's gates again."

Matyas nodded and waited while Bruschi vaulted into the saddle, then silently offered the lanthorn to him.

"You need not wait up for me, Matyas," Ragoczy told him in Hungarian. "I can tend to Callista myself."

"I have harness to clean," Matyas said, tacitly conveying his intention to remain awake until Ragoczy returned.

"As you please," said Ragoczy, and tapped Callista with his heels to set her jogging out of the stable; Bruschi followed closely behind him, the light from the lanthorn bouncing along slightly ahead of them like an insubstantial toy. The wind had come up, turning the evening chilly and giving the horses an edge to their movements along the well-maintained road.

For a while the two men rode in silence but for the steady beat of their horses' hooves. Finally Bruschi could stand it no longer, and said, "You must be anticipating trouble in dealing with the Magistrate when Court once again opens."

"Why do you say that?" Ragoczy responded politely.

"Because you are calling upon Signor' Aulirios so late at night," said Bruschi.

Ragoczy chuckled. "Both Signor' Aulirios and I are accustomed to staying awake long into the night. There is no significance in the hour that I make this call except for our mutual convenience."

Bruschi was so startled that the light from the lanthorn bobbed like a leaf in a flooding stream. "To be awake long into the night . . . that is most unusual."

"Not for those of my blood, nor for those who serve us," said Ragoczy, glancing over his shoulder to watch Bruschi.

His lapse nearly cost him a serious injury, for as he turned his attention from the road, half a dozen men in dark clothing rushed upon them from the low-growing border beside the road, the men shouting and waving their arms to frighten the horses.

"God Almighty!" exclaimed Bruschi, and dropped the lanthorn as he attempted to keep his frisky mare from rearing and falling over backward at this onslaught. One of the men had caught hold of his cloak and was pulling on it in an attempt to unseat him; Bruschi struck out with his fist in an attempt to break free.

Ragoczy pulled Callista in, bringing her nose almost to her breast-plate; he could feel her tension in the muscles of her back through the saddle as she swung around to face the attackers. Ragoczy drew his Japanese sword and raised it to strike as three of the men rushed toward him, one of them preparing to bludgeon the mare's legs; the katana sliced downward, striking his shoulder and the man with the cudgel screamed and swore as Ragoczy pulled Callista back on her haunches beyond the reach of the adversary's weapon. Unhampered by the darkness, he watched the miscreants roil around him, ready for anything they might do.

"Get the sword!" one man cried in German; Ragoczy used his leg to bring his mare around to face the voice just as a sword struck him in the small of the back, bouncing harmlessly against the hidden fran-cisca under his belt. Ragoczy shifted his grip on the katana and swung it upward, catching one of his assailants under his arm; the sword hardly paused as it severed the limb from the man's body. The third man trying to halt Ragoczy began to draw back.

The fight was not going so well for Celestino Bruschi, who was almost out of the saddle; one arm was flailing, the other was caught in the reins. Two men were hanging on to him, and a third clung to the mare's bridle. Even as Ragoczy pressed toward Bruschi and the men surrounding him and his horse, the mare kicked out with her rear feet, clipping one of the men holding Bruschi on his ribs. The man screamed and fell back, and the mare bolted, with Bruschi hang-ing half on and half off the saddle; the remaining opponents fled.

"Bruschi!" Ragoczy cried, and spurred after the mare and her rider who was now flopping against her side like a sack of grain. Just before Ragoczy caught the mare, Bruschi fell from the saddle with a sick-ening sound of a cracking melon; he crumpled into a heap under his cloak as his mare bolted into the night. Ragoczy halted his Andalusian mare and swung out of the saddle, the katana still in his hand as he went down on one knee beside the courier.

Bruschi was still and limp, and when Ragoczy touched his throat he could feel no pulse there. A further examination confirmed the man's death. As Ragoczy cleaned the blade of his sword on the hem of his coat, he felt sadness for the young man, and wondered how he would explain the events leading to his death to Ettore Colonna; he did not know who had been the cause of the attack, or why it had happened: was it happenstance or something more sinister? for he had sustained two previous, unaccountable assaults. "I cannot answer that now," he said as if to comfort Bruschi. With a sigh he gathered up the body and wrapped it in the cloak, then lifted it into Callista's saddle, securing it in place with the spare set of stirrup leathers he carried behind the cantel of his saddle. Only when Bruschi was thoroughly lashed in position did Ragoczy take Callista's reins and begin to lead her through the night toward San Procopio and the care of the monks sequestered there.

Text of a letter from Padre Bartolomeo Battista Tredori at Santissimo Redentore to Martin, Cardinal Calaveria y Vacamonte, both in Roma.

To the most revered, esteemed Martin, Cardinal Calaveria y Vacamonte, the prayerful and pious greetings of Padre Bartolomeo Tredori.

Eminenza, I write to you in the most humble posture, and with the fervent hope that if I have transgressed, God will be merciful to me for the sin I may be committing in sending this communication to you, for I am not divulging anything sealed by Confession, or I do not think I am. Were I unaware of the absence of your sister, I might not have had the audacity to write to you, but as I know Leocadia has been reputed to be in Spain, I believe it is my duty as a priest to inform you of my recent discovery, and beg you to use the information I am providing judiciously.

A short time since I received a summons from a man I did not know: he sent a messenger to me, begging me to come to his villa to hear the confession of a penitent to whom he had been extending charity for some while. I was perplexed by the request, but I complied, for as a priest, I am bound to serve those who are devout Christians. I had no idea whom I would encounter, but I went to the place with an open heart.

You cannot imagine my astonishment when the penitent turned out to be your sister, Leocadia. She was thin from her religious exercises, and I was told she was recovering from illness, which was the reason she wished to Confess. I could detect no sign of abuse in her beyond what she has done to herself in the name of expiation, which appeared to be stringent. I was able to hear her Confession and to minister to her soul even as her host had ministered to the hurts of her body. She asked that I keep her identity and location a secret, and I pledged to do so; at the time it seemed a reasonable request, given her desire to purge herself of all sin. I had no reason not to give her the oath she sought, and if I erred in allowing her to make such a demand of me, I acknowledge my failing to you. It was her stated conviction that she needed solitude to be absolved, and at the time I believed she was being wise to pursue such a course.

Now I am filled with doubt, and I can no longer support my own vow to keep her location a secret. I have prayed and meditated for several days on this, and I am now certain that is it my duty to inform you, as a Prince of the Church as well as Leocadia's brother, of where she may be found. I do so in the certain conviction that you will honor the rite of Confession and will demand nothing of her that she does not willingly vouchsafe you, and I ask you to be merciful with her even as we hope that God will be merciful to us.

With that as a caveat, I must inform you that you may find her at the Villa Vecchia, owned by the foreigner, Ragoczy, Conte da San-Germain. I have seen nothing that would point to his exploitation of your sister: in fact, I must assume just the opposite, given what I have learned from his household staff. He has provided your sister with a maid and has been at pains to see that nothing transpired that might serve to compromise her honor or the reputation of your family. If there has been any untoward treatment of your sister during her stay at Villa Vecchia, no one has witnessed it, and there are no whispers among the servants to that effect.

May God open our eyes to His Glory and lead us to do His Will. I implore you to consider your sister's suffering, and to forgive her wild imputations and accusations, for this can only be the result of the austerities she has practiced upon herself. No one would find her charges credible, for they are ludicrous in all respects. On her behalf

I beseech you to be forbearing as you welcome her back into your household; she has punished herself severely and would gain nothing from further chastisement.

With my prayers for God's Favor and Wisdom for you and your household, and with our shared gratitude for Alexander VIII, I sign myself,

Your most devoted,
Padre Bartolomeo Battista Tredori

At Santissimo Redentore in Roma, on the day of the coronation of Pope Alexander VIII

Deo Gratias

7

Four men-at-arms accompanied Ursellos Calaveria y Vacamonte to the Villa Vecchia; they arrived under blustery clouds on the morning of the first Wednesday in November. Their arrival brought the efforts of the workmen laboring on the new villa to a halt as carpenters and masons put down their tools to watch events unfold.

"Ragoczy!" Ursellos bellowed as he stood in his stirrups, a horse-whip coiled in his hand. *"Ragoczy!"* His clothes, with their ribbons and shiny fabrics, were more suited to Roman salons than this country villa. He had painted his face the night before and put a patch at the corner of his mouth and had bothered to remove neither; his wig needed brushing and his cloak had four short capes flapping around his wide-brimmed hat. Only his boots were practical: high, narrow-legged and sturdy, at contrast with the rest of him with sharp-roweled, rolling spurs buckled on. He intended to demonstrate his contempt for Ragoczy with his display of negligent opulence and so-cial position and was disappointed that the foreigner was not imme-diately available to have the full impact of his arrival.

If this outburst was intended to cause alarm, it succeeded only sporadically; the door of the old villa opened and Rugerius stepped out. "Buon' giorno, Signori," he said as calmly as if he welcomed a consort of musicians or a group of scholars. "What greeting do you wish me to carry to my master?"

One of the workmen whistled through his teeth, and a few of his fellows chuckled, which served only to fuel Ursellos' indignation; he reddened under his pale paint. "Your master has defamed our family! My brother has dallied and delayed in rescuing her; I am not so political a creature as he, and I have decided to act. Your employer has been laughing us. He will do so no more."

"Do you think so?" Rugerius asked. "Perhaps you would like to discover the truth of it before you shout your assumptions to the world." His bearing was correct, a nice mixture of deference and dignity, just self-effacing enough to provide the new arrivals no reason to take offense, although they did.

"You impertinent buffoon!" Ursellos cried as he scrambled down from his raw-boned, black-spotted gelding. He rushed at Rugerius, flicking the whip as he came, a look of murderous intent about his mouth.

"Señor Calaveria y Vacamonte," said Ragoczy amiably in Spanish, as he strolled around the corner of the new house, coming up behind Ursellos on his left side, "I must ask you not to savage my manservant." He was elegantly dressed for the country, as if he had expected to entertain, in a justaucorps and small clothes of black brocade, a French-style neck-cloth—it was once again safe to wear French fashions—and high black boots; he was fastidiously brushing sawdust from his shoulder as he studied Ursellos and the men with him.

"You *whoremaster!* You *defiler!*" Ursellos raged, swinging around to confront the self-possessed foreigner; he was unimpressed at Ragoczy's use of his language, though the workers exchanged disappointed glances at being deprived of the opportunity to be spectators at a confrontation.

"I have done nothing to deserve your obloquies," said Ragoczy, regarding Ursellos as if the younger man were a ill-trained puppy.

"Nothing? *Nothing?* You have made my sister your harlot, and you claim you have done nothing!" He laid his hand on the hilt of his sword.

"You have no reason to challenge me, Señor, and you will do your sister no good carrying on in this way," Ragoczy said, not quite as pleasantly as before. "I assure you I have done nothing to earn your vituperations, and if you continue to make such unfounded accusations, I will have to take action to vindicate my honor; in the Courts, not with swords."

"Your *honor?* You have the gall to speak of honor!" Ursellos' scorn was so overstated that a few of the workers laughed again, making Ursellos all the more furious. "You have no honor. To have honor, you must have birth and breeding. You are nothing more than a foreign panderer; that title you claim for yourself is undoubtedly false. I will not tolerate such claims as honor and breeding coming from one such as you!"

Ragoczy, who was aware of Ursellos' reputation, resisted the urge to counter these accusations with a similar goad. Instead, he shook his head. "If you wish to discontinue your tirade and come into my house, I will show you the hospitality to which your rank entitles you. For your sister's sake, I recommend you do this. Have your men dismount and water their horses while you and I discuss your complaint." He stood very still while the outraged young dandy made up his mind. "Put the whip away, Señor," he said quietly.

As if suddenly aware of all the eyes upon him, Ursellos flung the whip toward his men-at-arms. "Keep that for me. I may still have use for it." He stalked toward the open door, Ragoczy following him; behind him his escort swung off their horses, prepared to wait awhile. "All right. Where is my sister? I will not be fobbed off by well-mannered phrases. I want to see her," he demanded as soon as he stepped into the small entry area. "Bring her here to me at once."

Ragoczy motioned to Rugerius: he was still speaking Spanish. "Be good enough to ask Señorita Calaveria y Vacamonte if she would like to see her brother." Then he said to Ursellos, "Your belligerence will only alarm her; you must know that. If you wish to persuade her to come with you, then you would be well-advised to take a more reasonable tone."

"She is my sister. She will come with me because I say so!" Ursellos shouted. "If you try to hold her here, you will answer for your—"

"Señor Calaveria y Vacamonte," Ragoczy interrupted his obstreperous guest, "she will hear you. You are shouting loudly enough to be heard halfway to Roma, which I am certain you do not want, for your sister as well as for your errand here. If you do not moderate your tone, you will frighten her. Is that what you want: to frighten her?"

"She *should* be frightened!" Ursellos said. "She has behaved disgracefully. It would serve her right if our brother disallowed her engagement and confined her to a convent." He stalked a short way down the corridor. "This place is very old."

"Yes, it is," Ragoczy said calmly, relieved at the change of subject, but wary.

"You must have bought such a ruin for little more than the land is worth." The contempt in his voice was strong as a noxious odor.

"I suppose I would have, had it not been in my family since it was built, when the Caesars ruled," said Ragoczy.

"A fable, made to impress the gullible," said Ursellos.

"So it may seem to you," Ragoczy said levelly. "Alas, troubles in my native land have kept me from dealing with this holding as I ought—as it deserved, until now. That is why the new villa is going up, as this one seemed too hard to repair and bring to modern tastes." He saw that Ursellos wanted to challenge his assertion, and added a cordial warning: "I have proof of this, if you doubt my word."

Unwilling to hear more of this, Ursellos demanded, "I must see my sister. Bring her to me now!"

"She shall come, if she is willing to see you," said Ragoczy carefully, slightly emphasizing the *she*.

"You cannot keep us apart. I am her brother: she has to obey me, and so do you in regard to her. She will come with me willingly, or the law will force her compliance." He stopped, his eyes narrowing. "Unless you have married her." For a moment the ramifications of this enormity went through him. "You would not do anything so despicable. Not even you would marry her without our permission."

"She remains unmarried, as she wishes to be. She is also my guest, and as her host, I am obliged to acquiesce in her wishes." He kept his voice and manner mild. "You would not ask me to overlook my duties to her, would you?"

"I have authority over her," Ursellos insisted. "The law gives me the right to—"

"As I understand the law," Ragoczy said, daring to interrupt Ursellos again, "the law gives such rights to your brother. The Cardinal is the oldest, is he not? It is his will that the law upholds, not yours." Before Ursellos could answer, Ragoczy indicated a door. "That leads to my reception room. It is small and far from grand, but if you would enter it, I will have my servants bring you some refreshment."

"I will not be here that long," said Ursellos.

Ragoczy shrugged. "It will take half an hour to ready my coach and longer than that for your sister to ready herself to travel, but you may do as you like." He saw the startled shine in Ursellos' eyes. "Or were you planning to carry her back to Roma on the rump of your horse like a wayward peasant wench?" He bowed slightly, his tone ironic, but his purpose was deadly serious. "That would set tongues wagging, wouldn't it? treating your sister like a runaway strumpet."

Before Ursellos could form a rejoinder, Rugerius came down the corridor accompanied by a plain-faced woman in servants' clothing. "She asks her brother to wait awhile," said Rugerius in Italian, without inflection.

"What?" Ursellos was outraged. "You dare to keep her from me?"

"No, nothing of the sort," Rugerius said. "Her maid will explain." He nodded to the servant-woman, giving her permission to speak.

"Her maid!" Ursellos scoffed, also in Italian. "What nonsense is this? Her maid?"

Clarice Fiumara ducked her head respectfully. "I have been maid to your sister since she quit her penitent's cell," she declared.

"And wholly subject to this so-called Conte," said Ursellos.

"No; I have secured my position due to my brother, Bonaldo Fiumara, who is the masterbuilder on the new villa." She stood very straight. "If anything untoward happened here, the Artei would protect me from anything the Conte might require. Not that any such thing has been necessary, for the Signor' Conte has done nothing that

would not be approved by the Pope himself." Her expression sharpened as she made her own measure of Leocadia's brother. "So I tell
you now, little though you may believe it, that your sister has been
treated with highest regard and the strictest propriety, even before
she revealed her name. I shall say the same to my Confessor and any
Magistrate in the land."

Ursellos contemplated the stalwart, unprepossessing woman. "God
knows liars, even in Confession," he said at last, but with less heat
than in his former outbursts.

"Then I have nothing to fear, from you or any man, this day or at
the Last Judgment," said Clarice, unimpressed.

"I am sure you have been paid well to say so," Ursellos sneered.

"I am paid well, yes, but not well enough to lie." She curtsied to
Ragoczy. "She has need of me, Signor' Conte. If you will permit?"

Ragoczy gave a wry smile. "By all means, Clarice; thank you for
your substantiation," he said, and motioned her dismissal.

"It appears, Ragoczy, that you have her fooled," said Ursellos, a
malign curl to his lip. "That, or you have bribed her through her
brother."

For an instant Ragoczy said nothing. "Pray do not attach your own
methods to me, Señor Calaveria y Vacamonte." His manner was still
impeccably polite, but his show of amiability was at an end. Without
giving Ursellos an opportunity to respond, he went on to Rugerius,
"It is nearly time for the mid-day meal, is it not? and the builders
will be stopping work shortly, as will the household staff. Their meal
is being prepared in the kitchen: if you will ask the cooks to put
together a cold repast for the men-at-arms, and make a place for
them in the servants' dining room, I will speak to Matyas and Amerigo
about readying the smaller coach for our guest's—your sister's—use."
All but the last was addressed to Rugerius but for Ursellos' benefit.

"And what of me?" Ursellos inquired angrily. "Since you are such
a stickler for the rules of hospitality."

From the door, Ragoczy turned. "You said you wanted nothing. If
you have changed your mind, your request will be fulfilled at once.
My cooks have excellent reputations, and I am sure they will acquit
themselves well. Rugerius, old friend, see to our guest's wants." He

did not wait for another acrimonious exchange to begin, but left Ursellos in the small reception room, bound for the stables. He had almost reached that building when Maurizio rushed up to him, consternation showing in every line of his body. He halted, partially blocking Ragoczy's way, his hands bunched at his sides.

"Is it true?" he asked breathlessly.

"That her brother has come?" Ragoczy responded. "Yes. He is here."

"And he will take her back to Roma?" Maurizio's voice raised more than a third. "Today?"

"That is his intention," said Ragoczy.

"And you will let him?" Maurizio stared at Ragoczy as if the older man had turned into an asp before his eyes.

"I have nothing to say in the matter," Ragoczy told Maurizio. "He is her brother and the law supports his claim on her. If I were to refuse his request, I would be subject to . . . unwelcome consequences."

"But if she doesn't want to go?" Maurizio pleaded, misery ridding him of everything but despair.

"Sadly, the law is not required to consider her wishes, only those of her male relatives." How different things had been when he first met Olivia, Ragoczy thought—although the protection of the law had had little impact on Olivia herself—at least women had had the right to their own lives. He took a deep breath. "If she has a reason to refuse her brother, she has said nothing of it; I am powerless to interfere."

"*I* would interfere," said Maurizio staunchly. "I would do anything for her."

"I know," said Ragoczy with compassion.

Maurizio was too caught up in his dejection to take comfort from Ragoczy's understanding; he was barely aware of it. "You cannot know how I feel. You're too old."

"Doubtless," said Ragoczy, a sardonic note in his voice.

The impetuous young musician looked up suddenly. "She can run away with me now! I can take her . . . oh, somewhere her brother cannot find us!"

"Have you asked her to fly with you?" Ragoczy was more apprehensive about the answer than his face revealed.

"No. Not yet." Maurizio's answer, defiant though it was, reassured
Ragoczy, although his next remark did not. "But she will come with
me, I know she will."

"Maurizio," said Ragoczy steadily, "there are four men-at-arms
with Leocadia's brother. Assuming that she was willing to do such a
mad thing, and leave with you, how far do you suppose you would
get? And when they caught you—and they would catch you—they
would injure you, possibly kill you: the law would approve their doing
it, for her brother would swear you were abducting her. What would
that do for her?" He read anger and confusion in Maurizio's face.
"Very well: assuming you could get away, what would you do? You
are a musician, not a farmer or a merchant. Your skills do not lead
to hiding. Your very reputation would make it impossible for you to
play anywhere in Europe and not expose yourself, and her, to discovery."

"Then we will leave Europe. We will go to the New World, and
I will play there," he said stubbornly.

"How?" Ragoczy asked. "Maurizio, *think*, just a little, what you
would subject her to. She has trouble enough now. If you are as
devoted as you say you are, do not add to her woes." He paused.
"For her sake, Maurizio."

"I could learn a trade. That would support us, and we would not
be discovered," he insisted. "I would be able to care for her."

"And how do you think she would like the life as a weaver's wife,
or a bricklayer's? Are you willing to give up your music? And where
would you have to go? Not Spain or Spanish territories, certainly, or
any Catholic lands. Where?" Ragoczy asked very gently. "You would
hate it, and so would she."

"But she ran away from her brothers," Maurizio exclaimed. "She
did not want to be with them."

"She ran away from something," said Ragoczy. "If I knew for certain it was her brothers, then I might try to prevent this one from
taking her, and be damned to the law. She has said nothing, and that
limits my actions." He regarded Maurizio closely, telling himself that

his own intuitions had no confirmation, either in word or blood; he had not pressed the matter with Leocadia and now wondered if his reticence had been as reasonable as he intended. "I do not know anything for certain, and my suppositions are only speculation, without foundation or her confirmation. I cannot defy the Church and the Courts on her behalf because I suspect one of her brothers may have exceeded his authority. I could bring calumny on myself, and upon her."

"Then you will do nothing because you are afraid," Maurizio accused.

"Why, yes," Ragoczy agreed without any sign of dismay. "Any prudent man would be. The law is in the hands of the Church, Maurizio, and is more stringent than merciful; you have seen for yourself how justice is meted out in these Papal States. If you do not fear the Pope's Little House, you are worse than temerarious, which does neither you nor Leocadia good." He took a step back, creating more than a slight separation between them. "I must make arrangements with my coachmen."

"For her leaving," said Maurizio sullenly.

"Yes. For her leaving." He could summon up no words of comfort for the young man that would not lead to renewed and fruitless argument, so he continued into the stable, calling for Matyas and Amerigo as he went down the wide, well-swept aisle between the rows of box-stalls. "I have arrangements to make so that our guest may depart in a fashion to which she is entitled. I cannot wait much longer to put them into action. Matyas!" He was rewarded by a whuffle from Callista's stall.

Then "Here I am," called Matyas, coming from the tack-room. "Amerigo has gone to get his prandio." He made it sound as if stopping work for the mid-day meal was a shocking lapse. "He will return when he is done—for his afternoon rest." Again he made this usual routine seem unpardonable.

"Of course. I should have looked for him in the servants' dining room. And you, too, for that matter," Ragoczy said, giving his Hungarian coachman a speculative look. "Is there some reason you have not joined them?"

"I have my own food—not that pap the others eat. Lamb and lentils! What kind of meal is that for a man? Might as well eat clover with the lambs, or hay with the horses." He slapped his chest. "I have my meat with onions and peppers and garlic, to keep my blood strong." His breath attested to this. "I know what gives a man power, and I take care of myself."

"Then ask my cooks to make that kind of dish for you," Ragoczy recommended. "It is their work, as tending to my horses and coaches is yours."

"They know nothing, your cooks," said Matyas, then looked embarrassed. "That is nothing against you, master. It is just that they are not used to appetites like mine. They put rosemary and basil in their meat. I ask you!"

Ragoczy laughed once. "Very well, Matyas. Do as you wish."

"And so I shall," said Matyas. He cocked his head. "Is it true that the penitent is leaving? I heard one of the men-at-arms say so to the stable-boy."

Ragoczy nodded. "Her brother is here."

"Are you certain that he *is* her brother, and not some imposter?" Matyas asked, revealing his distrust of Ursellos.

"Yes. I have met him in Roma. He is her brother and he has the right to take her home." Ragoczy gave a small cough. "We must do what we can to make this as easy for her as we can." He continued down the aisle to the tack-room. "I think it will be best to use the chestnuts, and have them pull the servants' coach."

Matyas bristled. "She deserves your best, master. You know she does."

Ragoczy sighed. "That is true; but it would be poor conduct on my part if I were to put her in my own coach, with my eclipse blazoned on the side and my greys in harness. I might as well announce to the world that she has been staying here, and that I have given her protection. That would make the rumors into a storm of scandal by sundown." He shrugged. "The servants' coach is an anonymous vehicle that might belong to anyone, and chestnuts are not seen as my horses. She deserves to have her return to her family be as unremarkable as possible."

"I take your meaning, master," said Matyas. "No doubt the Romans have already thought of many explanations for her absence, each more outlandish than the last." He pondered this problem. "The chestnuts are a good choice, for they are handsome enough not to look disrespectful of the young woman."

"You take excellent care of them," Ragoczy said, and went on briskly, "You will have the servants' coach brought round, and you will see to the harnessing of the chestnuts. Amerigo will drive the coach. He is a Roman, and he is not so well-known as one of my staff as you are."

"Then you plan to have them leave after the afternoon rest?" Matyas asked.

"I doubt her brother will tolerate any delays beyond that," said Ragoczy drily. "He is already chafing at having to wait."

"Fool!" Matyas spat. "All right. The servants' coach will be ready just after the nap is over, and Amerigo will be on the box." He made a gesture to show his poor opinion of Leocadia's brother. "He has done this badly."

"That he has," said Ragoczy. He signaled his approval to Matyas. "I'll give the orders to Amerigo."

"As you wish," said Matyas, and went back toward his quarters to finish his meal while Ragoczy returned to his old villa, going to the servants' dining room where he found the men-at-arms regaling the staff of Villa Vecchia with tales of their dealings with Ursellos Calaveria y Vacamonte; he stood just inside the door, listening.

"—and so drunk that he could not hold his stirrup to mount," one was saying, nudging his nearest comrade in the arm with his elbow.

Another laughed aloud and struck the table with the flat of his hand so hard that the crockery and cutlery jumped. "His horse . . . his horse had his back up; his neck was swung around and he was showing teeth. You could tell he didn't want any part of his rider." He took a long swig of wine and tried to go on. "You could see he was ready to toss that jackanapes over his shoulder as soon as he managed to get a leg over."

"Probably the same thing with the taproom wench," a third interjected, and howled with hilarity, which was taken up by Ragoczy's servants.

"Well? What happened?" asked Amerigo, who was laughing as heartily as the men-at-arms.

"What do you think? He was tossed into the water trough." The man-at-arms was barely able to get this last out he was so consumed with laughter.

Everyone was enjoying this story, and would have continued to be amused but the assistant cook caught sight of Ragoczy, and made a warning gesture to his companions. "The Conte," he said, and the room became silent.

Ragoczy offered a swift, charming smile. "I would like to have seen that for myself," he admitted; the tension in the room dissipated as quickly as it occurred. "Amerigo, when you are done here, please come to the reception room."

Amerigo ducked his head, proud at being singled out, but mildly embarrassed as well. "Before my nap?"

"If you will be so good to accommodate me," Ragoczy confirmed; he made a gesture of good-will before leaving the servants and going back to the small reception room. He found Ursellos halfway through a roasted capon rubbed with herbs and stuffed with apples and onions; a near-empty bottle of Lachrymi Christi stood at his elbow next to a goblet of Venetian glass.

"Your cook *is* good," Ursellos conceded as he carved off another slice of breast; he looked as if making such a concession cost him dearly.

"Thank you; I shall tell him you said so," Ragoczy replied, and without the usual courteous preamble, said, "I have arranged to have one of my coaches ready for your sister's use as soon as the afternoon nap is over. My coachman will bring the vehicle back, so you need have no trouble on its account."

"After the nap?" Ursellos did his best to summon up indignation at that postponement, but knew that his men-at-arms would insist upon it. "Well, if that is the best you can do, I must be content."

"As I perceive," said Ragoczy quietly.

"That maid will tend to my sister, I suppose," he went on.

"She will accompany her to Roma if that is your sister's wish; she will provide your sister the service she requires. She will return with the coach once your sister is back with your family." Ragoczy did not look directly at Ursellos for fear of giving the young man some new excuse to be offended.

"That will maintain appearances," said Ursellos, downing the last of the wine in his goblet and pouring the last of what was in the bottle into his goblet. He glowered down at the remains of his capon. "I thought about what you said, and it is probably best to behave as if she is still worthy. We have kept her absence acceptable, saying she was in Spain. She might yet be an acceptable bride for Archbishop Walmund's brother."

Ragoczy shook his head. "Perhaps she would prefer another bridegroom."

"Of course she would." Ursellos laughed to show his disdain for such notions. "Most women want handsome, rich, young, chaste men to marry, but they do not often have such opportunities, nor would they have the wits to fix the affections of such a man. You've been about the world enough to know that."

"Oh, yes," said Ragoczy. "I have been about the world."

Ursellos caught the ironic note in Ragoczy's voice and finally looked at him. "She will marry as our brother sees fit. She does not have to like the man, she need only give him the sons the contract stipulates, and then she may secure a separate maintenance for herself; it's a reasonable concession, and she knows it. The contract has been made and it is necessary that she do as we require."

Ragoczy studied Ursellos for a long moment, aware that he could say nothing that would make the Spanish dandy comprehend the unfairness he saw in this arbitrary arrangement. He wished he could speak with Leocadia about this forthcoming marriage, to try to discover if that was her reason for running away; the opportunity for such a conversation was gone now, for he could not have a private discussion with Leocadia without convincing Ursellos that he had been more than a host to Leocadia. For her sake, he would have to keep his peace. "Your brother has the authority to do this," he said at last, because he had to say something.

"That he has," Ursellos agreed smugly as he downed the last of the wine. "That he has."

°   °   °

Text of a letter from Alessandro Scarlatti to Niklos Aulirios, carried by Scarlatti's copyist, Addiso Cicogna.

To Niklos Aulirios at Senza Pari, the sincere greetings of Alessandro Scarlatti, with apologies for the two weeks it has taken me to respond to your note.

Yes, most certainly I am anxious to resume rehearsals for the opera, and now that the flurry around Alessandro VIII's coronation is over, I have only the flurry for the Nativity to contend with, and so have decided to send my copyist to you so that he may begin to make the parts for our musicians. This is a project after my own heart and I long to return to rehearsals on it as soon as such may be arranged to our mutual satisfaction. I have done more work on the score, although not as much as I would like to have done. I suppose we will resume our rehearsals immediately after Epiphany, by which time, Addiso Cicogna should be caught up with his copying. Yes, I have hired a copyist for this opera alone, so that it will not take forever to prepare the parts.

I realize I am asking you to provide Cicogna with room and board, as you have done for Maurizio—when he has not been at Ragoczy's Villa Vecchia. I apologize for imposing on your hospitality in this way, but I am stymied in regard to the necessary copying we will require to continue rehearsals and I rely upon you to assist me in this; it may be an abuse of your good-will, and if it is, I heartily apologize and ask that you forgive me for any impertinence I have shown. Assuming that you will be willing to accommodate Cicogna, I am sending nine gold apostles to compensate you for any expenses you may incur because of his presence. The sum should keep him in supplies until his work is done; he is not a glutton, but if you wish me to provide for his food as well, you must inform me of that. Cicogna is not a demanding fellow. If you put him in the room where we have rehearsed with a writing table, quills, and ink, I doubt he will make a nuisance of himself, for he is a quiet, studious sort of man, not given to any excess except in his zeal for his work. You need not fear for the chambermaids—or the footmen, for that matter—with Cicogna about. His attitude is excellent: respectful and dedicated. If I had the means to house Cicogna here, I would, but my quarters are cramped as it is, and I know he will need more space for his work than I can provide, and more quiet as well. If there is any difficulty, I will speak to Ragoczy and determine some other arrangements.

With your suit coming before Magistrate della Rovere, no doubt you will have much on your mind. I do not mean to interfere with your case, and I pray you will not find Cicogna an intrusion. Make him a nest in a chimney, after his namesake, if he becomes too much of a burden. If my levity offends you, ignore it, and attribute it to a schedule which has left me giddy.

I shall do myself the pleasure of calling on you three days before the Nativity Mass, in order to put our schedules in order for the opera. Badly as I may show it I am deeply grateful for your many kindnesses to me and my musicians in your very difficult time. May God grant you prevail before the Magistrate, and may you relish the fruits of victory.

> *With every assurance of my high regard and esteem,*
> *Alessandro Scarlatti*

On the 29th day of November, at Roma

Post Scriptum: Ettore Colonna is still in mourning for his friend Bruschi, and has canceled his Nativity fete, which is unfortunate for many of us, as he usually employs more than thirty musicians for the occasion; we are therefore wholly at your disposal on that day. However, he has assured me that he will have a small entertainment on Epiphany, so I must honor that commitment for Twelfth Night. If the Nativity is not inconvenient for you, I will be glad to provide the musicians we discussed some months ago. If you have made other arrangements, I wholly understand. In any case, let us hope that the Nativity season is a pleasant one for all of us.

8

"She is thinner than I remember," said Archbishop Walmund to Cardinal Calaveria y Vacamonte as he strolled through central gallery of the Cardinal's palazzo; it was a chilly place this afternoon, as a north wind was blowing, promising rain by nightfall. "You say she is in good health?"

"Her health is excellent. She spent some of her time away in a convent, fasting and praying, so it is not remarkable that she should be thinner than when you last saw her," Martin, Cardinal Calaveria y Vacamonte said smoothly as he indicated the door to his withdrawing room. "She is a most devout girl."

"So it would seem," said Archbishop Walmund. "No doubt she would provide my brother an excellent example." He sighed. "His physician has cupped him twice this month in order to lessen the heat of his passions, but I cannot see that he has improved." He rubbed his chin. "If we did not have the Nativity celebrations in two days, I would recommend we arrange a time for their wedding at once; as it is, we must wait until Epiphany is past, or risk speculation that the wedding was forced upon them because of unchastity."

"Yes," the Cardinal agreed, thinking it was no more than the truth, although not in the way that Roman society would interpret it. "But in the fortnight immediately following, we will have their Nuptial Mass. We will accomplish this binding of Houses with all haste, so that we may put into action the course we have determined." His voice was soft but his intentions shone in his eyes. "You need have no fear that she will not be ready: she will accept your brother without cavil. I will engage seamstresses to make her bride-clothes at once. The time is short, and it is the Nativity, but many women will be glad of a chance to earn a few coins and to help the sister of a man as high in the Church as I, especially at so holy a time."

"Very good," Archbishop Walmund exclaimed. "I am glad to hear this. But if you find it should take somewhat longer to arrange the wedding, I will not be distressed."

"Do you mean you do not think she will be willing?" The Cardinal bristled at the suggestion.

"No; for you assure me that she will do as you bid her. I only suggest that it may take longer to arrange the occasion appropriately, in a manner that would satisfy your King as well as Alessandro VIII and the Count of Oldenburg. We would not want to make it appear that this marriage is a slight to anyone whose good opinion we hope to enlist." Archbishop Walmund put the tips of his fingers together. "On that head: you have confirmation from the Spanish Court that your assurances of preserving our association will be honored no matter who rules in Spain?"

"Of course. It is in Spanish interests as well as Oldenburg's to have a German presence in the New World," said Cardinal Calaveria y Vacamonte tranquilly; he reminded himself that it was near enough the truth not to be a falsehood, for he had the spoken promise of the King's courier that a formal announcement of their terms of agreement would be ready by the beginning of Lent.

"That is welcome news," said Archbishop Walmund. "I will inform my brother that all is in readiness." His smile was nothing more than a spreading of his lips, but the two men understood each other.

"You and your brother may fix the actual date, and I will inform my sister that she is about to become a bride." He folded his arms. "She may be reticent at first, but I assure you that she will be brought to see the need for this union. You must understand that she has long sought to be married with passion, as so many foolish women do. I have told her that if she is wise, she must strive to hold the affection of her husband, and his respect, neither of which will sustain passion for long." His expression showed how willing he was to make allowances for the impulsiveness of youth. "She has had time to consider the situation, and I must say she is now more sensible."

"Very good," the Archbishop approved. "I would not like to have my brother regret his alliance with your family."

"How could he regret our common goals? There is more to be gained for him than sons to bear his name," Cardinal Calaveria y Vacamonte exclaimed. "He must know this alliance will earn him the gratitude of Oldenburg, and the King of Spain?"

"I shall remind him that it will. So we are in accord." Archbishop Walmund bowed slightly to his host. "You will have to excuse me. I am sure you understand."

"You have many things to attend to, as do I," said the Cardinal, his conduct impeccable. "I am grateful to you for sparing me time this afternoon, given the duties of the season."

"Which impinge upon you, also," said Archbishop Walmund. "No doubt we will meet at San Pietro later?"

"No doubt," Cardinal Calaveria y Vacamonte agreed, and stood at the top of his grand staircase in order to watch Archbishop Walmund descend to be escorted to his waiting carriage by two of the Cardinal's footmen. Only when the Archbishop's coach had rattled away from the palazzo did the Cardinal abandon his place at the top of the stairs to go to Leocadia's apartments. He found her kneeling in prayer, her face taut with emotion that was unpleasant enough to make her clench her teeth. As she caught sight of her brother, she paled and grabbed hold of the crucifix she wore on a chain around her neck. "Leave me alone!" she whispered, as if fending off an agent of Satan and not a Prince of the Church.

Cardinal Calaveria y Vacamonte stood in the doorway, his face impassive. "You misunderstand me, Leocadia. I have not come to chastise you, nor to be polluted by your seductions"—he paid no attention to her single cry of protest—"but only to inform you that as soon as possible after Epiphany you will be married to Hubert Christian Lothar Walmund. His brother has just spent some time with it. Due to your long absence there were certain matters we needed to clarify. That has been done and we are agreed upon all the points of your marriage contract."

"I won't do it," said Leocadia, her voice trembling. "How often must I say it?"

"But you will. The fortunes of this House are depending on this alliance. I will not countenance any more defiance from you. I have the right to compel you, and I am prepared to use all the authority the Church and the law have given me." He sounded affable enough, but his eyes glittered. "You forced me to subdue you upon your return, and brought sin upon us both through your obstinacy. I would not touch you if you did not . . ." He looked away from her in order to compose himself; then he said, "If you do not comply, I will have to do the same again, and you will answer for it before God."

Leocadia was visibly shaking, but she faced her brother. "If you do anything of the sort to me again, I will announce in church, before the altar and in the presence of all the wedding-guests, that you have made me your whore, and that no man of honor should touch me." She glared at him, her eyes glazed with fear. "You will have to let me go to a convent then, if only to keep the House from disgrace."

The Cardinal's face darkened. "You will do nothing of the kind. You are not so foolhardy as that."

"We shall see," she said, her conviction faltering.

"You know you will be called a liar, and no one will believe you," he said in a calm, menacing tone. "You have already gained a reputation for precariousness of character: such a denunciation would set the seal on your volatility—it would not harm me. It would be a desperate thing to do—lunacy, in fact."

"I would *make* them believe!" Leocadia forced herself to stand firm, although she was certain that he was right.

"You are a headstrong, willful, unwomanly creature. God surely tested me when He made you my sister." The Cardinal glowered in Leocadia's direction. "You have done all that you can to ruin me, but I will not permit that to happen."

"I have no desire to ruin you," Leocadia protested. "But I do not want to have to marry a man with the pox, though it would bring you the gratitude of ten Kings and all the riches of the New World."

Cardinal Calaveria y Vacamonte laughed in furious incredulity. "You can lie to me in spite of everything? Of course you are determined to ruin me. You have made that your purpose since you first made me forget my vows and my position. You have striven to bring me down, and you have stopped at nothing—no sin was too repugnant for you. If you had not lured me, I would never have touched you, as God knows. No wonder we are taught that women are the handmaidens of damnation." He pointed to her. "You will marry the Archbishop's brother. I will see to it that you receive your separate maintenance when you have provided him an heir. The Archbishop wants two sons, but I know he will accept one."

"And if I have no children? Or if I have daughters? What then?" Her voice had risen in pitch.

"The contract stipulates sons; that is not unusual, and you know it. It will behoove you to pray to the Virgin for sons, so that you may soon have your own establishment." The Cardinal smiled. "You can always return here, where Ursellos and I can provide protection for you, and for your reputation. You know what Romans think of Spaniards: they suppose we are all cut from the same cloth as the Borja y Laras were."

Leocadia swallowed hard, revulsion in every line of her being. "I think that would not be wise," she said at last.

"You still long for the cloistered life? You, of all women? You, who are so full of lust that you incite it wherever you go?" Cardinal Calaveria y Vacamonte asked. "Yet perhaps you are right: you need to devote yourself to God's cause. You have many sins to expiate. If you insist on thwarting my plans, it may be best to send you to the Sisters who care for the mad, for that is what you must be, to act thus." His tone sharpened. "Do not add disobedience to the catalogue. Resign yourself to this marriage and ask God to give you humility so that you may serve your House, your Church, and your King. That will show your submission to His Will."

"God's? Not yours?" She could see the change in his face and braced herself for another attack.

It did not come. "You will soon enough be brought to order by your husband. I will not be lured by you." He made the sign of the Cross and took a step backward.

"If you will leave me alone, I will continue my prayers," she said truculently to conceal her despair.

Her brother was not satisfied. "I know your duplicity of old. I warn you, sister: you will bitterly regret any act of defiance you may be considering. You would do well to keep that in mind." He turned abruptly and left her.

Leocadia sank down on her heels, holding her knees to her chest and shaking all over as if with ague. Without knowing it, she began to weep, her eyes squeezed shut in an attempt to dam the tears. Prayers stuck in her throat and she knew beyond question that she was beyond all succor; no one could help her: Heaven would not intervene and any earthly aid would lead only to the Pope's Little House for any fool attempting to ease her plight. She shoved her fist into her mouth to keep from making any sound. Now, when it was too late, she wished she had confided in Ragoczy, had told him what her brother had done to her, and what he was demanding of her. She wanted to believe that the Conte might have continued to shelter her, or provided her some means of escape, for it was rumored that he had helped that old mathematician to get out of Italy; he might have done the same for her had she appealed to him: even if he had not believed her, he might have taken pity on her unhappiness, and done what he could to alleviate it. She castigated herself for her failure to have courage and for such disloyal thoughts. Gradually, she fell onto her side and remained there, her knees still drawn up against her chest, and still more gradually, she fell asleep.

She was wakened some time later as her maid brought her bread, cheese, and water on a tray; the woman looked abashed as she put this on the table at the end of Leocadia's bed.

"Your brother ordered this for you," the maid whispered.

"No doubt," said Leocadia as she strove to gather her thoughts. "He has ordered me to pray for humility."

The maid shook her head. "You have prayed as much as any nun," she said, doing her best to lend Leocadia her support.

"It would seem I have prayed for the wrong thing," said Leocadia, looking at the austere fare; she feared the taste of it would make her vomit.

"I was told I could not stay with you. I must not linger." The maid curtsied and went to the door. "I will come tomorrow morning."

"Very good," said Leocadia automatically, hardly noticing when the door closed. She looked at the meager supper she had been provided, and although she knew she was hungry, she could not bring herself to eat any of it. She went to her bed and sat on the side of it, staring fixedly at nothing while she tried to reconcile herself to Martin's orders; gradually the long shadows faded into night and still she did not move. She could hear the sounds of the household, but distantly: her brothers were sitting down to their dinner, an elaborate meal that would last for well over an hour; at ten she knew Ursellos would leave to seek his usual evening entertainments. Her thoughts began to drift and she imagined herself far away from this palazzo in Roma.

A melody curled through her visions, plaintive and sweet, and it took her a short while to realize that she was not remembering it—someone was playing the violin in the street below. Brought back to her immediate situation, Leocadia listened intently, recognizing the old-fashioned ballade as one she had heard Maurizio play in the garden at Villa Vecchia. "It can't be," she said aloud, hardly able to give credence to the excitement that welled in her. "He would not do anything so . . . so absurd." Her attempt at laughter failed utterly. She got up from the bed and went to the shuttered window; she adjusted the louvers to listen; the wind that slipped inside was bitterly cold, making her acutely aware of the extent to which the young violinist had gone to comfort her. For a while she let the music envelop her, making a barrier between her and the world. Then she heard Ursellos.

"Here are two silver Emperors. Take them for your trouble and go. You play well, but we want no musicians here."

She could not hear Maurizio's answer, but his playing ceased, and Leocadia felt more alone than before. That fine young artist had been so attentive to her at Villa Vecchia, she thought, always taking time to console her with music. She had not paid much heed then, and only now realized how much comfort she had taken in his kindness. It was tempting to go to the window to summon him back, but she knew that her brothers would then make a point of driving Maurizio off, and would not allow him to come near her again: that, she decided, would be intolerable. She would have to find a way to let Maurizio know she enjoyed his unusual serenade. With this uppermost in her mind, she fell asleep, hoping for inspiration in the night that would give her some occasion for hope.

"Leocadia." The voice was soft and urgent, and the hand on her shoulder was gentle as it shook her.

Gradually she emerged from sleep, from portions of a dream that faded even as her eyes opened to find her room dark but for the candle Jose Bruno held; she was not surprised to see him. She smiled at her half-brother, then yawned. "It's very late," she said by way of greeting.

"Nearly three in the morning," Jose Bruno agreed.

"Nearly three?" she repeated. "Then what . . . ."

He motioned her to silence, saying, sotto voce, "I have a message I could not bring you when the household was awake." He saw the alarm in her eyes and went on quickly. "Nothing unwelcome, I should think."

"Then tell me," she said, sitting up in bed, her face animated.

"A violinist was playing outside last evening," Jose Bruno began.

"Maurizio. Yes, I know," she said hastily. "He was playing an air he used to play for me at the Villa Vecchia."

"So you did recognize it; he was hoping you would," said Jose Bruno. "I talked to him after Ursellos paid him to go away. He told me he came here out of concern for you."

"That is . . . so sweet." Leocadia felt her eyes fill with unexplained tears as she remembered how good Maurizio had been to her. "What is his message?"

"That he is willing to do whatever you may ask of him to deliver you from the tyranny of our brothers," said Jose Bruno. "Those were the words he used."

"How good of him to be concerned for me," said Leocadia, her eyes growing wet. This simple revelation brought home to her the full weight of her dejection. "I did not know he had so much sympathy in him."

"I think he is more than concerned," said Jose Bruno. "I think he is fascinated, or even infatuated with you." He was serious enough as he said this to make it plain he was not teasing her. "That could mean difficulties."

Leocadia bristled. "How could that be? He is someone willing to help me, which is more than anyone else has done. Except you. And the Conte. For all the good it did."

"Don't be petulant," Jose Bruno recommended. "There is no time for it. If you waste time indulging yourself, I will not linger." He went on more gently. "I only think you should be aware that there is more at stake here than keeping you from a political marriage. You could easily break the young man's heart."

Leocadia laughed. "If that is the worst that could happen—"

"It may *be* the worst that could happen to Maurizio." He saw she did not understand. "Listen to me, Leocadia. You are fond of him as you would be of a dog; he amuses you: he is enamored of you, and that is a very different thing." There was a quality to Jose Bruno's voice that made Leocadia listen closely.

"You have known what you speak of," she said quietly. "You have—"

Jose Bruno cut her short. "That doesn't matter now. We must establish what is to be done, or you will be wed in a matter of weeks."

This blunt reminder nearly took Leocadia's breath away. "Do you have any suggestions to make, or are you seeking to torment me?"

"I have a recommendation," said Jose Bruno deliberately. "I have thought about this every day since you returned." He paused to be sure he had her full attention. "I have come up with half a plan."

"Half?" she repeated. "What good is half?"

"Hear me out," Jose Bruno said, and launched into his idea before Leocadia could object. "Tell our Cardinal-brother that you will marry, but after Easter, so that you do not have to begin your married life with the austerities of Lent. Say also that it will give everyone time to arrange the wedding as a splendid event, worthy of Spain and Oldenburg, and not managed in some hidden, hasty way that could only result in gossip no one would like."

"But I *don't* want to marry that man, not with all the pomp or all the secrecy that can be arranged." She stared at her half-brother. "I thought you knew that."

"I do; and I want to help you get some time to arrange the means to leave Roma." He motioned her to listen. "If it can be done at all, it cannot be arranged quickly. You want to escape this place and the husband Martin has chosen. As things are now, that is impossible."

Leocadia stared at him. "How *can* it be done?"

"I have been thinking about that since you came back." He leaned down, lowering his voice. "You show your defiance, which puts our brothers on the alert. The more you resist this wedding, the more restraints will be put upon you." He saw he had her attention, and went on. "But if you will seem to comply with Martin's plans, pretend to accede to him, you gain yourself opportunities you now lack." He laid his hand on her shoulder; she shrugged it away. "Do this, and you will earn our brothers' approval. They will not confine you so closely, and they will permit you to go about with me for an escort." He nodded as her eyes brightened. "Do you begin to grasp my purpose now?"

"I begin to think you have a purpose," she conceded, doing her best to keep from finding fault with this partially formed plan.

"If you are too obstreperous, he will send you to the madhouse; he has said so to Ursellos. Martin thinks that a few weeks with the insane will bring you to your senses fast enough." He regarded her, hoping he had convinced her without terrifying her in the process. "He is completely serious, Leocadia. He intended everything he says. If you thought the cell in the basement was hideous, you do not know what that can be."

"I think I would rather be among the mad than married to Hubert Walmund—he is worse than Ursellos." She pulled her covers up as if they could protect her.

"You think that, but you know nothing of the matter. The maddest are shackled to their beds and left to stink in their own excrement. Some of them howl all night long, like animals, and some lie and stare as if they are already dead. There is only bad food and darkness." He shuddered; he could not keep from saying the rest, his voice a soft monotone making his revelations all the more appalling. "You forget our father confined my mother to such a place, and I know what it is like. I visited her three times. The first time she was still herself, protesting she had been confined wrongly, that there had been a mistake. She begged me to speak to our father, to plead with him to relent. When I did, he had me beaten. It was more than a year before I saw my mother again, and she was then lethargic, indifferent to where she was, more caught up with phantoms than what was around her. She had no message for our father. The third time I went to visit her, she was shackled to her bed because she had been bashing her head on the stone walls, trying to break her skull." He blinked as if to banish his memories. "She may have been nothing more than a tailor's daughter, but she did not deserve to die in that place."

Leocadia swallowed hard. "I . . . I did not know," she apologized.

"No. Only Martin knew; and I." He sighed. "Martin is not jesting when he says he will send you to such a place. He will do it."

This time Leocadia could only nod.

"Tell him you will marry after Easter, and promise him you will not rebel anymore." Jose Bruno paused. "If you are complaint, he will leave you alone, I think."

She understood his meaning. "I cannot bear to have him touch me again," she said, nearly gagging on the words. She rubbed her eyes. "Will he believe me if I say I am willing? I have refused for so long, mightn't he suspect a ruse?"

"You will have to be skillful. Do not change abruptly, but ask for more time to school yourself to his wishes. Tell him you will need a little longer to gain the resolve you need." He managed a lopsided smile. "It is what he wants to hear, and he is vain enough to be convinced."

"And you? What will you do?" Fright put an edge on her question and she began to twist the sheet in her hands.

"I have met a fellow who has sometimes carried more than wine-barrels out of Roma. He trades in the north, in Milano, Torino, and Genova. It is not easily arranged, but he will take you there, to Genova, and you can then find your way to France and any convent you choose. You will be safe in France." He wanted to sound encouraging, though his recitation seemed impossible even as he made it.

"How much does he ask in payment?" Leocadia thought of her jewels, many of which would bring a handsome sum. In spite of herself, she was beginning to presume there would be the means of escape.

"We have not settled on that," said Jose Bruno. He bit his lower lip. "Once you leave, you cannot come back. Not ever. You will have to vanish completely. Think about what that means before you say you are going to do this."

"I want to go. I want to vanish," she said with purpose. "I will thank God on my knees for my deliverance if I can go away forever."

"Think about it," he repeated. "Tell me tomorrow night what you decide to do."

She stared at him. "You are the only one who is good to me," she marveled. "Of my brothers, only you care what becomes of me."

He looked away, saying nothing. When he spoke again, his tone was distant. "What shall I say to Maurizio? He will come to play for you again."

This was so unexpected that it took her a long moment to answer. "Tell him . . . oh, tell him I thank him for his melodies. And tell him not to put himself in any danger on my behalf: Martin and Ursellos will not like having him come again." She shivered, imagining what her brothers would do to the young musician if they thought he was playing for her and not for coins, and what they would do to her for having such a suitor.

Jose Bruno kissed her forehead. "I'll be back at the same time tomorrow." He stepped back. "Remember, do not consent too quickly. Ask for time to prepare yourself."

"Yes. I will," she promised as he closed the door, leaving her alone to think of some way to appeal to Martin and Ursellos to allow her to delay her marriage.

Text of a letter from Ettore Colonna to Ferenc Ragoczy, carried by messenger to Villa Vecchia.

To the Signor' Conte da San-Germain, the belated greetings of Ettore Colonna, who implores you to forgive his long silence through the celebrations of the Nativity and Epiphany, and prays you will not hold this against him.

The death of my friend, Celestino Bruschi, left me so bereft that all I was capable of doing was grieving; I have withdrawn from the haunts of men and kept to myself, in reflection and meditation—and occasionally in a stupor, if I must tell the truth. I was overcome with his loss, and could not bring myself to face anything or anyone. It was wrong of me not to thank you for trying to save him when you were attacked on the road, and so I do this now, with all my heart.

I have heard that Signor' Aulirios' case is finally to be heard on the third Monday in February. You must be anticipating the moment with anxiety as well as relief that the end is nearly in sight. I have no doubt that Podesta della Rovere will have reviewed all the material provided him and scrutinized it most thoroughly. He is basically a cowardly man, and as such, he is most meticulous in his legal conduct, for he has no wish to be found at fault by higher authorities. In your case, I believe his timorousness will serve you well. We must all hope for a happy outcome, for as you have said, the Magistrates' Court is the place of final appeal. It will be settled now or it will not be settled at all, for if it drags on much longer, the Church will intervene and no one will benefit but the Pope.

The small entertainment I attempted for Epiphany did not go well. I am sorry to say that in spite of everything Maestro Scarlatti could do, my guests remained in a state of gloom; in retrospect I am glad you were unable to attend. But I hope you will do me the honor of coming to Il Meglio for Carnival. With Alessandro VIII in San Pietro's, I know that the festival will be kept merrily, unlike many years past when to have true gaiety, one had to go to Venezia. Roma will once again mark the beginning of Lent with the jollification of old, and Il Meglio will be the heart of it. Do me the honor of attending. You need not come masked or in costume unless you would like to; I do not make such indulgences a requirement for my guests, nor do I discourage them.

On a more somber note, I have been thinking about Celestino, as I have mentioned, and I have come to realize that he might have died on my account, because he was my courier; in fact, I have surmised that this is the most obvious reason anyone might have had to waylay him, and you. I have enemies, Conte, and they would not hesitate to act against me if the occasion presented itself. And you have enemies, as well; there is no reason to assume any of them would hesitate to kill anyone in our employ if it would further their enmity. We must both take a lesson from this most tragic incident to be wary of our own safety. A I recall, you have told me of an attack in Roma by street roughians. The men who killed Celestino could have been just the brigands they seemed to be, or they may have set upon the two of you for a purpose. Even if the tragedy was merest chance, you, and I, would be foolish to think it was only that, if for no other reason than we may be marked men. I urge you to be Argus-eyed in your comings and goings, for if the killing was more than happenstance, it is possible that those who oppose us may take inspiration from the slaying and act against us, singly or together. Do not fault me for seeing monsters in the shadows: there can be monsters anywhere.

Enough of these morose maunderings. I anticipate your response to my invitation with pleasure, and I pray on the event we have more to celebrate than the coming of Lent.

This brings my affectionate respect as well as my assurance of high esteem and continuing friendship,

Most cordially at your service,
Ettore Colonna

At Roma on the 22nd of January, 1690

9

As he looked about the courtroom, Podesta Narcisso Lepidio della Rovere was dismayed to see how many people had come to hear the decision he would announce in this most perplexing case; there were nine high-ranking Churchmen among the illustrious curious, and Podesta della Rovere realized with increasing unease that his judgment would be subject to their scrutiny. He sighed as he peered down at the stack of parchment and vellum before him; he wished he could discover another excuse to delay his determination in regard to the suit before him, for he was keenly aware that his findings would not sit well with many of the Churchmen who had concerned themselves in the outcome to such an extent that they were in the courtroom to hear it. But there was nothing he could do about this, and he trusted he would not be criticized for coming to the only conclusion that was possible.

Ahrent Rothofen arrived with Ursellos Calaveria y Vacamonte, who made sure that everyone understood he was representing the Cardinal as well as himself in this gesture of support; both young men were rigged out in their most impressive, formal clothes, one in dark red satin, the other in a somber ochre damask; both wore new, expensive wigs, and both had three tiers of lace at their cuffs and their throats. They carried their display of confidence further by wearing valuable rings in place of gloves; both men had perfumed themselves with attar of roses, and Ursellos had painted his face.

In contrast, Niklos Aulirios looked almost drab: his justaucorps and breeches were of a dull-silver silk twill, and he wore only simple ruffles, not lace, at his neck and cuffs. His wig was of the first quality, but not extravagant, and he had added no jewelry to his ensemble. Besides him, Ferenc Ragoczy was equally austere, elegantly dressed in heavy black silk with white silk bands and unornamented cuffs; his wig was unostentatious in style and his only jewelry was his signet ring, his eclipse device in silver with a round black sapphire at the center beneath the displayed, erect wings, all fitting to the dignity of the Court and the gravity of the occasion. Niklos and Ragoczy remained standing while Rothofen and Ursellos sat down, pointedly ignoring the two men at the other table facing the Magistrate's Bench and the gathering crowd.

A nearby clock struck the hour and the susurrus of conversation faltered and halted as all those attending gave their attention to the Magistrate's Bench. It was the moment della Rovere had been dreading; he met the gaze of his audience with a single, furtive sweep, then stared again at the pages before him. He crossed himself and muttered, "May God give me to see His Will aright," and saw his gesture copied by everyone in the courtroom. He cleared his throat and looked up. "This has been a protracted case, and all parties deserve to have it ended. I will not ask you to wait for my decision, nor will I hear any more arguments from either claimant: we have all had to wait too long for this case to be decided. It will be over now." He sat a bit straighter. "I have examined all the records and testimonies submitted to me in the matter of Ahrent Julius Rothofen's claim on the estate of the late Atta Olivia Clemens and her heir, Niklos Aulirios." He took a long breath, wanting to be done with the task before him as expediently as possible without compromising the dignity of the Magistrates' Court. "I am forced to put primary importance on the dispensation granted to another Clemens woman—also called

Atta Olivia—by Pope Urban III, who, in 1186, allowed that inheritance in the Clemens family would pass through the female line in perpetuity. The records show that this mandate has been followed from that time to this with no deviation: the Clemens estates have gone to nieces and daughters and granddaughters, according to the records maintained by the Clemens family and by the monks at Sacra Carita in unbroken line from the time of Urban III. This fact cannot be disputed. I have information from the monks that show that the Atta Olivia Clemens, who made the Will being contested, was the last of her line, male or female, and so her disposal of her estate was not bound to a female heir: there was no surviving woman in the family who could claim the estate in accord with the terms of the Papal dispensation granted in 1186." He saw that Rothofen's face was distorting with anger; della Rovere hurried on. "Had this not been the case, I would have decided in favor of the Rothofen claim, for the male line, even through an illegitimate heir, must be given precedent over the female in any dispute where there has been no provision to allow the female line to inherit and dispose. In this case, however, there can be no doubt that the claim of Ahrent Rothofen cannot be sustained. The Court must find that the Will of Atta Olivia Clemens must stand, there being no female claimant to the estate." He took his gavel, saying formally, "God grant wisdom to the findings of this Court," before he struck it on the polished surface of his Bench. He rose at once, gathered up the papers, and left the courtroom, bound for his study; he paid no heed to the eruption of noise and consternation behind him.

Rothofen was on his feet, pointing to Ragoczy in fury. "You did this!" he accused. *"You!"*

From the clamor in the courtroom came echoes of this from some of those who had favored Rothofen's claim. A few others shouted their derision for Rothofen. The room quickly became electric with hostility as the men prepared to demonstrate their support; a brawl was brewing, and the guards were uneasy.

Niklos Aulirios stood slowly, a hint of a tired smile on his handsome features. He made a leg to Rothofen and Ursellos, as good manners required. "The matter is settled, Signori."

"Is it?" Ursellos said. "The Magistrate may have spoken, but the Pope has not." His expression was snide; he made no apology for his demeanor. "There are grounds to take this to the Pope for review, I think."

These remarks were overheard, as Ursellos intended they should be. The noise in the courtroom was increasing; the guards were beginning to try to move the crowd out of the building, for it was increasingly likely that fights could break out among the various adherents.

"Do not press your luck," Niklos said, his smile fixed, all amiability gone. "You brought this action in a desperate ploy to enrich yourself. You have failed to gain what you sought. Why compound your error: what can the Pope do, but support the dispensation?"

Before Rothofen could manage an answer, Ragoczy spoke up. His voice was conversational in tone but the purpose behind his words was unmistakable. "And do not add to your folly by trying to find a woman to put forth a claim; you have played that card already in this attempt. The records of the Clemens gens is clear: Atta Olivia was the last of her line, and as such she could dispose of her estate as she wished. Any woman making a claim now would be known as a fraud before she entered the courtroom. The monks of Sacra Carita would prove that, for they have records of all the women in the Clemens line going back to the time of Attila."

Rothofen glowered at Ragoczy. "What makes you think I would employ your methods?"

To Rothofen's vexation, Ragoczy chuckled. "I think nothing of the sort, Signore Rothofen. That is why I trust you understand my meaning." He made a leg in good form, took up his small portfolio, and prepared to make his way through the crowd.

"You cannot walk away!" Ursellos challenged as he managed to get in front of Ragoczy; his face was flushed and his breath smelled of brandy. He stood with arms akimbo and legs apart, as if expecting an onslaught.

"But I can," Ragoczy said coolly. "The Magistrate has ruled. It is fitting that Signor' Aulirios and I leave. As should you."

Ursellos did not budge. "You have much to answer for."

Ragoczy motioned Niklos to keep back. "No doubt. But not here, and not to you."

The guards had succeeded in getting half the crowd out of the courtroom and were jostling them along toward the stairs, making a point of keeping them moving so that there was no opportunity to escalate their disputes; the rest of the crowd continued to swarm in the courtroom, a few of them hoping to see something more dramatic than Podesta della Rovere's announcement.

"You are contemptible," said Rothofen, sneering at Niklos. "Hiding behind the Court for your protection."

Niklos stiffened, and murmured something in Greek; Ragoczy replied in the same tongue, then looked at Rothofen. "If you believe you have been imposed upon, you may seek another trial, but I would advise against it. The evidence presented will not change."

"Of course you would advise me to capitulate," said Ursellos, and spat at Ragoczy's feet.

This deliberate insult held the full attention of those remaining in the courtroom; even the remaining guards stopped their efforts in order to see what the foreigner's response would be. The silence was taut.

Ragoczy studied Ursellos a moment. "You demean this Court, Signore."

"I demean *you*," Ursellos persisted, unwilling to give way; beside him, Rothofen was grinning. "And you demean the Court."

A guard came up to the rail. "Spitting is forbidden," he said. "I will have to escort you from the building."

For a long moment it seemed that Ursellos might fight the guard. Then he shrugged. "Why should I sully myself with this charlatan? He is not worth the time he has already taken from me. Why should I give him anything more?" he asked the air, moved his leg as if squashing a bug underfoot, and shouldered his way past the guard, gesturing to Rothofen to follow him.

The tension in the room ended as abruptly as wine ran from a broken glass. The crowd became subdued, almost sheepish, as they began to disperse, opening up to let Niklos and Ragoczy leave.

"He is not going to be willing to let this go; he will try to find another way to get Olivia's estates," Niklos said in Greek as he and Ragoczy made their way down the corridor, a dozen men in pursuit.

"He may not want to admit defeat, but he would be stupid to do anything direct, either in the Courts or in the streets, for the finger of blame would point directly at him if you should come to harm." Ragoczy paused to acknowledge the congratulation from a young advocate while a Barone whose land marched to the west of Senza Pari clapped Niklos on the shoulder and declared that he had always known that Niklos would prevail. As soon as these two well-wishers passed on, Ragoczy continued. "I know there is reason to be careful, for Rothofen is not beyond plotting vengeance. You and I would do well to be heedful of our surroundings for some time to come, I think." He nodded ahead to the foot of the stairs where Rothofen and Ursellos were getting into the Calaveria y Vacamonte carriage. "They will not forget a slight, I fear."

"This is hardly a slight; the case was founded on a lie," said Niklos, starting his descent as the Spanish carriage pulled away. "Rothofen had no claim, illegitimate or otherwise."

"They would not agree." Ragoczy started down the stairs, his thoughts far away. As they reached the bottom, he held up his hand to summon his coach. "Come. I will take you home."

Niklos smiled. "It *is* home, isn't it? truly my home." He glanced up into the sky where heavy clouds scudded in from the west. "It will rain before night."

"So it will," Ragoczy said as Amerigo brought Ragoczy's best carriage, drawn by his best team of greys, to a halt before them. Ragoczy himself let the steps down for Niklos, and climbed in behind him; this show of respect was not lost on those lingering around the Magistrates' Courthouse; there would be tales all over the city by nightfall that the foreign Conte da San-Germain had made himself a lackey for Niklos Aulirios.

Roma was crowded and the Ragoczy carriage made slow progress toward the Porta Pia; inside neither passenger had much to say as the Magistrate's decision was mulled over in silence. Finally, as they passed the ancient church of Santa Constanza, some distance beyond the walls, Niklos said, "Thank you. I should have—"

"You have nothing to thank me for," said Ragoczy quickly. "Think of this as an obligation I have owed Olivia for many years." His dark eyes were distant. "What else could I do for her, but this."

It was a difficult moment for Niklos, who wrung his hands and coughed delicately. "I still feel in your debt. What can I do to show my gratitude? It is useless to offer you money, and you would be offended by such an offer."

"How well you know me," Ragoczy said, ironic amusement shining in his dark eyes.

Niklos sighed. "There must be something you would accept. I do not want it said that I ignored your goodness."

"Then continue to allow the opera rehearsals at Senza Pari and we will consider the debt discharged." Ragoczy was doing his best to divert their discussion.

Niklos did not protest. "Very well." He leaned back. "I suppose I should make some effort to celebrate this occasion."

"There would be comment if you did not," Ragoczy observed. He let Niklos consider his new situation without offering further prompting.

"There will be comment in any case," Niklos said with a trace of bitterness in his voice. "Still, it will be less if I behave as if I am vindicated than if I do not."

Ragoczy gestured his accord. "You know the Romans of old."

They went on to the turning near San Procopio. "You do not have to remain here now," Niklos pointed out. "There is no reason for you to remain in Roma."

"If I leave before the new villa is complete, I will have more questions to answer than I would care to deal with, and I would leave behind speculation that could redound to you. After this case, I doubt you would welcome further scrutiny into your life; something might be discovered that would lead to official investigations," Ragoczy said drily. "Besides, the builders are eager to finish the villa; if I abandon the project, they will complain."

"You need not be here for the builders to work and be paid," Niklos said. "I could take care of such things for you."

Ragoczy smiled slightly. "Maestro Scarlatti would never forgive me. The opera is incomplete; he is looking forward to its premiere."

"Oh," said Niklos. "That is another matter."

They fell silent again as the coach rattled on.

The reaction at the Calaveria y Vacamonte palazzo was not so sanguine: Ursellos had arrived with Rothofen, both in filthy moods. Neither had been civil to the other during their fairly short carriage-ride, and now they had settled into a vitriolic quiet that boded ill for any who crossed their path.

Ursellos had demanded brandy as soon as he was at the top of the entry stairs, and had gracelessly given a glass to Rothofen in the same manner that he might toss a coin to a crossing sweeper. "You have as many sorrows to drown as I," he remarked as his servant brought their drink to them in the larger reception room.

"I have more," said Rothofen contentiously; he was spoiling for a fight and was not fussy about whom he fought.

Ignoring this, Ursellos took his glass and drank deeply. "To have that impudent foreigner gull the Magistrate in that way!"

"If he did not bribe him. They say Ragoczy is made of money." The resentment Rothofen felt made his words sound like cursing. "He could purchase ten Magistrates to do his bidding, and he would not dress in rags."

"A dispensation from a Pope no one cares about anymore. Whoever heard of such a thing?" Ursellos flung his half-empty glass across the room, grinning as it shattered. "More brandy, Salvatore," he shouted. "And clean up this glass."

"Do you think Alessandro VIII would set aside a dispensation of Urban III?" Rothofen suggested, a brightening in his eyes. "It was given so long ago, when the Church was trying to take back Jerusalem. If a dispensation from then were forgotten, who would care?"

Ursellos had a disgruntled answer. "The Curia would care. Never forget the Curia, Rothofen: they never forget anything. And they hold all Papal decrees as sacred and untouchable. There is no power sufficient to make them give up a position once it has been taken. Unless there is some overwhelming reason not to; and money is not overwhelming enough," he added cynically. "This dispensation is not enough for them to bother with so it will stand."

"That Ragoczy should hide behind an ancient Pope!" Rothofen took another long sip of brandy, relishing the heat it added to his choler. "I want him shamed! I want him *ruined*."

"An excellent notion," said Ursellos with malignant glee. "Let us have him sent to the Pope's Little House as well. That would make up for what he has forced us to endure because of him. That knowing demeanor, the affectation of black clothes, as if he had some right to wear a priest's habit."

"Not Ragoczy—Aulirios," said Rothofen. "He has done this to me. He is the one who has deprived me of the money and lands of the Clemens estate. Without Aulirios, there would have been no reason for Ragoczy to come to Roma, and no cause to take this before the Magistrates' Court. If the Clemens estate had been left to the hands of the Magistrates to begin with, I would only have had to show my information and they would have brought it all to a happy end."

"For God's sake!" Ursellos exclaimed. "You need not rehearse it again. You aren't going to be tiresome, are you? trotting out your grievances at the least invitation? No one will want to entertain you, if you do that."

Rothofen was not quite finished. "Aulirios is the one who has offended me: Ragoczy is only his tool." He held the glass more tightly. "Not that I would object to seeing him brought down along with Aulirios." He tried to cross the room and staggered as he went; the brandy was only partly responsible—his outrage made him clumsy.

Ursellos watched Rothofen closely. "You're not going to do anything impetuous, are you? That would be as tiresome as publicly nursing a grudge." He was annoyed at the possibility and made no attempt to conceal his feelings.

"Not impetuous, no," said Rothofen. "Anything I do will be carefully considered."

With a dramatic sigh Ursellos pointed directly to Rothofen. "If you take action against either Aulirios or Ragoczy, you will be the first man suspected of any crime against those two. You will have to leash your indignation for a time. Let other enemies become uppermost in the public mind, and then you can act."

"That could take months and months. I do not want to wait so long." Rothofen drank more of his brandy as he dropped into one of the upholstered chairs near the marble-fronted fireplace. "I want satisfaction."

"Do not fear: you will have it," said Ursellos grandly. "Must you do the damage yourself, or are you willing to let others do it?"

Rothofen thought about this for a short while. "I would be content to have it done, if the punishment meted out was severe."

"How severe?" Ursellos asked, enjoying himself hugely.

"Deadly," said Rothofen just before he drank the last of his brandy. "Utterly deadly."

Ursellos considered this reply. "I think I can make an arrangement that would please you." He clapped to summon the servant to bring more brandy.

"I doubt it," was Rothofen's glum response. "I have paid men before to set upon Ragoczy and they have failed to harm him." He watched as his glass was refilled. "They cost me good money, too."

"Well, we shall have to find men who are more reliable, if you are to have your justice," said Ursellos, then paused as the significance of Rothofen's last remark struck him. "Whom did you pay, and when?"

This question brought back Rothofen's sense of ill-usage. "I paid men twice: once to disable his carriage—that was early in this matter—and once, much more recently, to waylay him on the road. They managed to kill the man with him but could not subdue Ragoczy. You would not think that such a bookish fellow could fight, would you? But they say he can. I had intended to have my hirelings ambush Aulirios, but I knew that I would be under suspicion at once. I knew I had to do something to stop Aulirios. So I thought that if his advocate was badly injured, Aulirios could not muster enough of a case to prevail against my claim." He shook his head several times. "Perhaps I should have had Aulirios dealt with directly, after all, and not bothered with Ragoczy."

Ursellos barked a laugh. "That foreign miscreant! He has more to answer for than the decision in Court today. He will be taken down." Then he pointed a finger at Rothofen. "You cannot have found very dangerous men if all they could do was kill a catamite. How bold they must be." His sarcasm was intended to sting. "You must exercise better judgment if you are to cause Aulirios to regret his victory."

"He has no victory—he has surmounted through trickery." He paused, frowning with concentration. "Is *surmounted* the word I want?"

"I have no idea," said Ursellos, who was finding Rothofen's complaints tedious. "He has made the law accommodate him. If that is what you intend to remark upon, then that is the word you want." His eyes were aching, he realized, and his mouth felt dry; he had more brandy and told himself he had a little improvement.

"What shall I do?" Rothofen asked suddenly. "I gambled on getting the Clemens estates. I have debts. What am I going to do?"

Ursellos laughed. "Debts—everyone has them. Do not let them trouble you."

"All very well for you to say, with a Cardinal for a brother and lands in Spain earning you money." Rothofen was pouting now. "But I have no such lands, or riches, or any other income but what the Archbishop settles on me. Once your sister is married to his brother, I will receive a commission for my part in the arrangements, of course, but it will be a paltry sum: such commissions usually are."

"Do your debts exceed the commission?" Ursellos was distantly interested, as if hearing of these misfortunes would ease the ache in his head.

Rothofen waved his hand to show that the disparity was vast. "Naturally. I was sure I would have the Clemens—" He stopped himself before he repeated his woes yet again.

"That was foolish," said Ursellos. He pinched the bridge of his nose but the headache did not abate.

"Perhaps it was." Rothofen said forlornly. "But who would have thought that those damned monks had kept records of her estates?"

"For a woman!" Ursellos laughed aloud at the absurdity. "For a woman."

"Yes. Her ancestors must have paid the monks well to do this." Rothofen narrowed his eyes as the magnitude of this perfidy struck him. "For generations, they surely spent a fortune to have the monks maintain such records."

"Unfortunately there is no law against gifts to monasteries," said Ursellos.

"But if it is a bribe . . ." Rothofen's protest trailed off.

"They're all bribes, either to the Church or to Heaven. Why else would anyone pay a stranger to pray for him?" Ursellos wagged a finger at Rothofen. "Do not repeat that; the Pope, even this Pope, would not like it."

Rothofen laughed a little. "Dangerous sentiments, even in a Cardinal's brother. You don't mean that, surely."

"Who better than a Cardinal's brother to see the Church for what it is?" He drank more, and made a reckless gesture.

"And who better than a drunken man to speak of it?" Rothofen was feeling nervous because he knew he could be questioned by the Holy Office for the Faith in the Pope's Little House for hearing such heretical—such blasphemous—opinions. He stared at Ursellos as if he could force his companion to talk of less troubling things. "The wedding? It is to be at the end of April, so I am told."

"That it is. The Count of Oldenburg wishes to attend, and he cannot spare the time until then." Ursellos looked put-upon. "My sister pretends she does not think this is a reprieve but it is obvious that does. Not that I blame her; Hubert is no prize. But he is the means for advancing his family and ours, so she owes it to us to go through with it. She owes it to Oldenburg and the Pope as well, not that she admits it." He swung around to face Rothofen, a smile wreathing his face. "You might be able to have the Count of Oldenburg take you on. You can address him while he is here for the wedding. He'll be in a festive mood, no doubt. It isn't the same, being a courtier in the German States, but it may be more lucrative. For a man in your position, Roma can be ruinous."

"The Count might be better-pleased with another set of eyes here; a set outside of the Church, if you see my point," said Rothofen seriously; he began to turn Ursellos' flippant suggestion over in his mind, as if mentally tasting the possibilities.

Ursellos made a face to indicate his disgust with Rothofen. "You are nothing more than a merchant. You deal in whispers, innuendos, and rumors, but you are a tradesman." It was a terrible insult and both men knew it.

Rothofen made himself laugh. "That is the brandy speaking, not you."

"*In vino veritas,*" said Ursellos. "And doubly so when the drink is distilled." He raised his glass. "To trade."

This insult was too much for Rothofen, who set down his glass and rose stiffly. "I will spare you the pain of my company, Signore." He made a leg and prepared to leave, his face blank with fury.

"I was jesting, Ahrent—*jesting,*" Ursellos protested with an indulgent chuckle. "You must not be offended by what I say."

"Why not—I would demand satisfaction of any other man," Rothofen said bluntly.

"I didn't *mean* it," Ursellos cajoled. "You take me too much to heart." He held out his hand. "Come. We must continue as friends, if for no other reason than to move against our common enemies."

Rothofen paused. "You said that there was truth in wine just now. Do you now disclaim that?"

"Most certainly," said Ursellos. "I often disavow myself." He did not quite laugh. "Any number of tavern wenches will attest to that."

"Are there many Calaveria y Nessuna infants in Roma?" Rothofen gibed, grinning to show he was joking.

"The women cannot use my name when they have their bastards— my brother sees to that. So they are Nadie y Nessuna." He beamed at this witticism. "Nobody on both sides."

"Does that never trouble you?" Rothofen asked. "Bastards can be a problem for those in the Church."

"They are not my brother's, and that makes his position a powerful one; as for the infants, he pays well to have them forgotten." Ursellos coughed and changed the subject abruptly. "I am going to Napoli for a few weeks. If you want to join me, I would expect my brother will pay for it. He prefers me to have company."

Ordinarily Rothofen would have leaped at such a chance; now he took a deep breath and said, "May I tell you in a day or so? I have certain . . . arrangements I must make."

"Not against Aulirios or Ragoczy?" Ursellos demanded. "That would be—"

"No," Rothofen cut him off. "I must make some arrangements for my more pressing debts, and that means . . . I must arrange to sell certain possessions. I would prefer not to have to, but as I must, the sooner it is done, the better." He rubbed his face as if to shape his expression to a more content one. "Once those matters are settled, I will be wholly at your service."

"How much is involved?" Ursellos asked at his blandest.

"I do not think it concerns you," said Rothofen. "Suffice it to say that it exceeds my resources." The pleasant glow brought on by the brandy was fading rapidly.

"Would two hundred gold Angels be enough to cover most of them?" Ursellos asked in an elaborately offhanded way.

"Two hundred gold Angels?" Rothofen repeated, enthralled by the amount.

"I have a few wagers that I have recently won, and I am just now very plump in the wallet, as the English say. If you would take that sum from me, and pay it back as you can, or earn it in occasional private services for me, I would be glad to put it at your disposal." Ursellos let his offer dangle. "You need not tell me at once."

Rothofen cocked his head. "Is this another jest?"

"Not at all. I am completely serious." He waited while Rothofen thought this through, adding, "With the wedding coming, I promise you I will make you earn it."

The amount was too much to refuse. "What murder do you want done?" He laughed to show he did not expect such a commission.

"We will talk about that, later," Ursellos said as he summoned his servant to bring more brandy to seal their bargain.

Text of a letter from Bonaldo Fiumara to Ferenc Ragoczy, Conte da San Germain.

To Su Eccellenza, Abbe and Conte, the greetings of Bonaldo Fiumara, masterbuilder, regarding the current state of work on the villa currently being built for your use.

As you are no doubt aware, we have reached the point where work must begin on the inner walls and decorations. Your generous payment has made our work progress rapidly; as a result, it will be pos-

sible to put the roof on the building by the end of March, and then to tend to the finishing of the inside, including flooring and wall decorations, before summer. It will be useful to discuss with you any and all plans you may have for ornamenting the interior of your villa, for the appropriate craftsmen will need to be engaged, and their Artei contacted in regard to payment for their work.

Thus far you have acquitted yourself most honorably in regard to recompense for labor, and with so sterling a record, I would be loath to see any smirching of your admirable record. Therefore I would recommend that you plan to meet with me and various representatives of the Artei in regard to what you will require for your villa. I will superintend all such work, and hold the results accountable to you, as the means of demonstrating your good-will, and our compliance in it.

The deposit of fifty gold Apostles with the upholsterers' Arte is necessary before suitable furniture can be made, and another fifty gold Apostles paid to the drapers' Arte is required before any draperies can be installed. We will require another forty ounces of gold to pay the glazers for the installation of windows, as well as one hundred ounces of gold for the laying of floors. The price is high, I agree, but you know that as a foreigner you must pay in advance for all the services you seek to engage. I have offered to vouch for you, so that only half the amount need be laid out, but this is not acceptable to the Artei in question, so I will stand by their order and require that you do all that the Artei demand, and in a timely manner. I do not doubt your probity, but I am a member of my Arte, as the others are of theirs, and we all abide by the strictures of our contracts.

Incidentally, I have been informed by four of my men that officers of the Holy Office have been asking questions about you. They were under the impression that the clerics were seeking information on the events surrounding your Penitent Guest, for that was the primary thrust of their inquiry, although one of my men was questioned extensively regarding your status of Abbe in Transylvania. My man thought that Pope Alessandro VIII might be trying to determine the amount of support he would receive if he ordered another drive against the Turks. That is only a guess, but it is in accord with all the stories one hears coming from San Giovanni in Laterano; being

Venezian, the Pope is eager to do what he can to lessen the power of the Ottomites. Whatever the purpose of the Holy Office might be, I am sure you should know about the questions that have been asked. You will be well-advised to prepare yourself to address the Holy Office, or resign yourself to the hospitality of the Pope's Little House.

In that regard, my sister has asked me to thank you for your generosity—paying her a full year's salary for the time she waited upon your Penitent Guest was lavish indeed, and I must join with her in expressing the gratitude of our family, for such magnanimity is rare, and it is fitting to acknowledge it where it is found. She has said that if you have need of her services again you have only to ask and she will be willing to put herself at your disposal once again. My family is deeply obliged to you, Eccellenza, and we do not forget our obligations.

As soon as the monies required are received and the terms endorsed, I will begin engaging such craftsmen as you need for the continuing work on your villa. I must soon be in contact with roofers so that as soon as our outer work is complete, the roof may be installed. Whatever amounts their Arte will demand, I will tend to the matter of making arrangements and the transferring of monies in the sums the Arte will ask of you as a deposit on the work to be done. The spring rains are persistent but not so heavy that our work has been much delayed. If the weather does not worsen, you may expected your roof to be in place by July.

With my most sincere respect and the high regard of all those who have the honor to work for you. May God send such ethical conduct to all men wanting villas built in and around Roma. Our Artei would not have to be so strict in the matter of deposits if half the world conducted their business affairs in as forthright a manner as you do.

Believe me, Eccelenza,
Yours to command,
Bonaldo Fiumara
Masterbuilder

At Roma, on the 13th day of March, 1690
A true copy of this letter is on file with the Console dei Artei.

10

Her wedding dress was nearly complete, a heavy garment lavishly shining with gold embroidery and gems, a visible declaration of the importance of the marriage it was intended to grace; Leocadia sighed as two of the seamstresses worked on the corsage, sewing pearls to the points of lace that made a frame for her face and bosom. She told herself that she would not have to go through with the ceremony, that Jose Bruno would indeed find a way to save her from that fate, but her certainty of deliverance was fading fast. Realizing she was weeping, she motioned the seamstresses to stop their work.

"Did I prick you?" the younger seamstress asked, holding her needle as if it had suddenly caught fire. The sewing-room was littered with fabric and lace, with several boxes of jewels and beads standing open on the long cutting-table, along with measuring tapes, scissors and shears, and papers riddled with pins. A bolt of fine muslin lay at the end, chalk marks on a section of it showing the pattern that would later be cut in silk.

"Yes," said Leocadia, knowing it was not true. "I'm sorry. I am very tired." She touched her only jewelry—the antique golden crucifix that hung on a golden chain around her neck. "I must ask you to excuse me."

The older seamstress, a plain woman with a knowing eye, said, "Best to rest now, for once you are wed, you will not have an hour to call your own. We'll leave you for now, Signorina." She made a knot and snipped off the thread. "We will return tomorrow morning. We have another three or four days to go before the dress is finished. Plenty of time before the great day."

The younger woman was making a knot as well. "Some brides have to be sewn into their dresses, they have so little time to prepare." Her laughter was genuine but had a cynical note to it. "Here. Turn so I may unfasten the laces."

Leocadia did as she was told, waiting patiently while the ties were opened and the impressive garment was lifted up and over her head. She stood in her underclothes, her corset biting into her flesh, while the seamstresses hung the dress on a mannequin, then gave her her jonquil-satin wrapper. "Thank you. You are very patient with me." She wanted her corset unfastened, too, but that was task for her maid.

"Nothing of the sort," said the older seamstress. "In our work we see all sorts. You're not the worst—not at all." She found her shawl and wrapped it around her shoulders. "Four hours of this is enough for any bride. Besides, the light will be gone soon enough. We will use the rest of the afternoon to work on your negligee; we have six tiers of lace to sew on yet."

The younger woman sighed. "Lace is always difficult to work on; the threads are so fine and they must be made to lay smoothly."

"Yes," the older agreed. "Put lace on poorly and it appears as if the bride's neck is surrounded by caterpillars." Laughing at her own description, she went on, "You don't know how often we have to take extra stitches just to make it appear that we have taken none at all."

Leocadia nodded, not really hearing the two seamstresses. There was nothing she could say that would show the women that she prayed their efforts were for naught; if her hopes were realized she would never have to wear it. Her hands felt leaden and her body might as well have been put together from scraps of wood for all it seemed to be her own. "The embroidery is beautiful," she said at last, knowing that her silence would be seen as a rebuke.

"We hope that it is," said the younger woman as she made ready to leave. "The Cardinal has been most specific about his desires, and it is our wish to do as he has commanded. He will see it when it is complete." She glanced at Leocadia. "Is the dress to your liking?"

"It is splendid," said Leocadia, hoping neither woman would notice she had not answered the question. How much more she longed for a nun's simple habit and quiet, cloistered life! The seamstresses would not understand her emotions, and she knew it was useless for her to speak of them. She secured the sash of her wrapper and sat down on the chaise near the window where the watery early-spring sunlight provided illumination in the late afternoon. Leocadia gazed out at the thin film of clouds that veiled the blue expanse over Roma, making it pallid and flat-looking; it all looked like a sham, a trick from

the theatre, or a painter's illusion; the slanting beams gave the buildings an artificial patina, as contrived as the sky. As the two seamstresses left her alone, she began to think that she was no longer
anything more than a figure in a game. The crucifix she wore was no
comfort to her; of late she had begun to fear that God had deserted
her, and that prayer was empty. She closed her eyes and let her
thoughts drift as she sought a respite. So lost was she in her reverie
that she did not notice when the music began. At first she assumed
her memories had evoked the melody; only gradually did she realize
that she was hearing Maurizio, and that he was playing in the passage
that led from the street to the stable behind the palazzo.

With a stifled cry, Leocadia surged to her feet, the pinch of her
corset forgotten, and her sense of futility fading with her daydreams.
She was glad now that she was alone, for she did not want to have
to account for her sudden delight. No candles had been lit and so
the window where she sat was dark, a fortunate accident. Risky
though it was, she opened her window to listen more easily. After a
short while, she decided she must show her thanks; she looked about
the sewing-room and noticed a knot of gold ribbons. She seized this
and flung it out, hoping that Maurizio would find it and know it for
what it was. The music went on, and she hummed along with the
tune she had heard so many times at Villa Vecchia.

The playing stopped abruptly in the middle of a phrase, and Leocadia heard the rough sound of the steward ordering Maurizio away;
she could not make out Maurizio's answer, which frightened and saddened her. Closing the window, she looked about for flint-and-steel
to light the candles; when she could not find them, she began to
pace, going the length of the cutting table and coming back to the
window; she was unaware that she was still humming the song Maurizio had played to her. Finally she made up her mind and called for
her maid to dress her. "Feve, ask Jose Bruno to wait upon me as
soon as I am dressed; and light the candles when you return," she
ordered, and pointed to the bronze silk ensemble hanging on a hook
near the door. "That needs cleaning, by the way. There is a stain on
the sleeve."

"I'll attend to it. Jose Bruno is presently assisting the cook," said her maid. "When he is through, I will ask him to come to you."

"Assisting the cook?" Leocadia asked in surprise. "How should he do that?"

"Even the simple can help sort herbs," said Feve primly.

"He *isn't* simple," Leocadia said, defending her half-brother vehemently. "He has something wrong with his eyes. He has told me himself. He does not see the world as you, or I, do."

"And that makes him simple," said Feve, setting the matter to her satisfaction. "But I will ask him to come to you. After you are dressed."

"Then help me; I want to be ready as soon as may be," said Leocadia, unfastening her sash and making an urgent gesture. "Bring me the deep-rose taffeta, I think, the one with the square neck."

"As you wish," said Feve, and hastened away to Leocadia's room to fetch the gown in question, a fashionable toilette with a double skirt, the outer one pulled back to form a train and revealing a lining of shadow-striped rose-and-burgundy Siam-cloth. The garment was heavy, but in cool weather it was suitable for evening entertainments. Gathering up the ensemble, the maid hurried back to the sewing-room where she found Leocadia had become agitated in her absence. "God save us, Signorina, what is the matter?"

"My brother wishes to see me." She crossed herself. "He is angry about something." The room was in twilight, just enough brightness was left to allow her to read the words on the paper she clutched tightly.

"Jose Bruno?" asked Feve, who could not imagine it.

"No. Never Jose Bruno. My brother Martin." She began to shake. "His manservant just brought me a most . . . uncompassionate note."

Feve put the taffeta gown on the cutting-table in a glorious heap before she went to Leocadia. "You must be mistaken, Signorina. There is no reason for your brother to be unkind to you."

"He does not agree," she said, and opened the hastily scrawled note she had been given a short time ago. "Look. See here? He says that I have been duping him, that I am conniving with his enemies to dishonor our House and that I am . . ." The words were lost as she began to cry in earnest.

Feve took her hand, patting it soothingly. "It is nothing. He is piqued about—"

"He is piqued," said Leocadia between sobs, "because a musician . . . played outside the . . . this palazzo an hour ago. . . . He is cruel and . . . he is . . . he is . . ."

"He has the weight of the Church upon him. Occasionally the burden makes him testy with those to whom he should show only kindness. You must forgive him for his outbursts." Feve did her best to smile a little encouragement to Leocadia; she had seen for herself that Martin, Cardinal Calaveria y Vacamonte, could be capricious and ruthless.

"How? Why?" Leocadia asked, trying to contain her tears. "He does not . . . care about me. He cares only . . . that I am marrying . . . the man he wants . . . me to marry." She lowered her head into her hands in utter dejection.

"Signorina, Signorina, no. Do not cry. You are overwrought." She took the crumpled note that dangled from Leocadia's fingers; taking care to smooth it, she saw that some of the words were written in capital letters, but since she was unlettered she could not read what they said. "Come. Sit down. You will need to compose yourself," she said, half-supporting Leocadia to the chair by the window.

"Why should it matter . . . if . . . if someone plays music outside this palazzo?" Leocadia demanded of the air. "It is common enough in Roma. Musicians are always playing in the streets. Why does Martin assume the musician was playing to me? How would anyone know I am here?" She knew she was babbling but she could not stop; she had to keep Maurizio a secret. "Roma has many musicians who come to the great houses, thinking there will be better opportunities there. The musician is like any other, seeking money for his art. He was probably hoping to gain a few coppers, or a meal, or a commission to play for . . . for the household's entertainment." She was wiping her eyes now with the sleeve of her open wrapper; her hands trembled.

"Do not . . . you must not, Signorina. Do not be distraught." Feve continued to try to calm her. "Speak to your brother. Tell him that his note was hurtful. I am sure it was not his intention to cause you pain."

"Oh, yes it was," said Leocadia, in the voice of one in the midst of revelation. Taking a long, uneven breath she finally stopped her tears. "He intended that I should be miserable. He has done it deliberately. He *wants* me to be unhappy so I will not mind wedding a debauched husband." Saying this aloud made it more real, more accurate. "Yes. I see it all clearly: that is his plan." She became very quiet. "Well. Now I know." She found the sash to her wrapper and pulled it around her waist. "He says he wishes to see me. Let it be now, and let it be here."

"But Signorina, you are not dressed," Feve protested, shocked.

"He is my brother and a Cardinal. If he demands to speak to me at once, I will accommodate his demands." Her dismay was gone; in its place was a cold-burning anger that frightened her maid.

"He should come to this room?" Feve asked, looking around its gloom. "Let me light the candles."

"Leave me your flint-and-steel. I will attend to it," said Leocadia, sounding as if she were speaking in a dream. "This might as well be settled."

Feve was confused; she had not been in the household long enough to comprehend the undercurrents that ran in it, but she had heard the servants whisper about things that were too outrageous to be true. She took her flint-and-steel from her pocket and handed them to Leocadia as she sidled to the door, "I will tell him you are waiting to see him," she said before she made good her escape.

Leocadia was unable to move as she waited for her brother to enter the room. She wondered if she had set a trap for herself and was now caught in it. All the courage she had summoned up to insist that he come to her was lost as quickly as it had arisen; her pulse was loud and weak at once, and she could not convince herself that he would be content with excoriating her. When his wrath took hold of him, he lost all semblance of virtue and did these things that would send them both to the innermost circle of Hell: he had forcibly lain with her three times since her return from the Villa Vecchia, and no importunities on her part had kept him from possessing her; he had told her that she was the cause of his sinning, and had been the cause from the first. As much as she denied it, she was afraid that he was right, for the Church taught that women were intrinsically more sinful than men. His recriminations echoed in her mind as she strove to keep her purpose uppermost in her thoughts.

His knock on the door seemed loud as cannon-fire. "Leocadia!"

"I am here, brother," she answered, hating the whine she heard.

The door opened and the Cardinal stepped inside, very grand in his red satin. "You must know why I have to speak to you."

"No," she replied, seeing the glint in his eyes.

"Do not be coy with me," her brother said in an edgy voice that told her that he was already lost in his litany of reproach.

"I . . . don't know," she said, trying not to be cowed. "I suppose it is about my forthcoming nuptials."

"So willing you are that you are pleased with your arrangements, or you have tried to make me believe you are." He shook his head in an exaggerated kind of sympathy. "How much of an idiot do you take me for?"

"I would be the idiot, to try to deceive you," she said, hoping she could placate him. "How could I hope to succeed?"

He took a hasty step toward her. "You are flippant with me?" His disapprobation became more marked. "You are pretending innocence—to *me?*"

Leocadia felt sick; she had seen this pattern before, too often, and knew that it boded ill for her. "You baffle me. I have done nothing to earn your condemnation, I swear by the Virgin and the Saints." She crossed herself, as much for her own protection as to demonstrate her piety. "Whatever you have discovered that you attribute to me, I cannot guess: it is not mine to own." As she did her best to summon up other protestations of her rectitude she tried to back away from him, to get out of reach. "If someone has spoken against me, it is a falsehood or a mistake—"

"Do not be sly with me, sister. You are a font of deception." He took two brisk steps toward her and struck her a sharp blow across the face. "Now, think. Tell me what lies you have spoken. Do not suppose you can hide your mendacity from me: I know the black depths of your soul."

"I have not lied!" she protested as she brought up her hands to shield her face from more blows.

He lashed out again. "You have plotted and schemed, and you will stop at nothing to ruin me. You have made it your purpose to bring ignominy upon me. You have!" His fist landed on her hip, hurling her back; she struggled to stay on her feet.

This was worse than she feared, for his wrath was growing so quickly that she had no way to circumvent it. "Feve is coming," she said desperately, wanting to forestall any greater damage. "You do not want her to witness this."

"She will not come," her brother panted. "I have sent her to supper. What would she see but a chastisement you have brought upon yourself?"

"But I have done nothing," she cried out, and hated the lie she knew it was, for she had been planning her escape for weeks. Had he discovered her plans?

"You are perfidy itself," the Cardinal exclaimed, pursuing her; there was a glaze to his eyes that Leocadia dreaded. He reached out to grab her arm and snagged the front of her wrapper; the fabric tore, revealing her corset beneath. "There! You see how you—how you exploit your charms to my ruin." He lunged for her, but she eluded him.

"Martin, don't do this. I pray you, do not do this," she whispered, moving back along the cutting-table. "You are in error. Someone has misinformed you." She was as consumed with fury as much as with fear. "You shall not do this to me!"

The Cardinal laughed. "You delight in compromising me, in turning me away from my chastity in the most execrable way. That is bred in your bones from the time of Eve. You are one with her. Desecration is the heritage of all women." He nearly caught her in a sudden lurch that caught the edge of the cutting-table and made it shift, scraping hideously as it moved; her deep-rose dress slid off the edge and onto the floor between them. "The very color of shame! Your own garments condemn you!" he exulted.

"You are wrong to accuse me," said Leocadia, her voice rising in pitch. "No, Martin, do not—"

He snared her near the fireplace; his arm went out around her, and he shoved her around so that he pinned her against the cutting-table. "You are made of prevarications. Mendacity is your virtue. You corrupt and debauch everything you touch. Ursellos is depraved because of you, and I have fallen into sin at your temptations." He began to fumble with her clothes. "You sought this of me. You received me as the loose woman you are. It is your nature to defile those who strive to live Godly lives."

Leocadia struggled against him. She wanted to scream, but knew if she did, it would gain her nothing but a beating, for in this palazzo, no one would dare to answer her calls for help. Tears smarted in her eyes and she tried to wriggle free of him. "Martin, let me go. For the love of God, let me—" She got no further.

"Trollop!" he raged at her. "How can you—you are appalling!" He struck her face several times.

"No! *No!*" She flailed at him, trying to kick him or shove him off of her, but he landed a blow to the side of her head that dazed her and left her feeling nauseated and dizzy. She began to swing her arms, trying to find some vantage-point to hit him; she was as angry as she was frightened now, and she could not bear the thought that he would use her yet again—not when he was forcing her to marry a degenerate. Her eyes stung and the back of her mouth tasted of bile. She wanted to escape, to vanish from this room, from Roma, from the world. "Martin," she begged. "Don't."

He was beyond listening; already he was fumbling with his clothes while trying to keep her pinned against the table. When she was able to strike him with her fists, he took her by the hair and banged the back of her head against the table, smiling at the sound of the impact and her shrieks.

Dazed and hurting, Leocadia squirmed and flailed; behind her the fabric was bunched and wrinkled, and occasionally she touched pins and other sewing gear, but all of them were useless. She shouted curses as she began to weep. "You have no right—no *right!* You are a priest, a *Cardinal!*"

Her brother grunted as he tried to hold her down in order to penetrate her; his features were mask-like and ugly. "Lie. Still." He struck her again, so hard that she felt a tooth loosen. "Lie still," he repeated.

All the resistance went out of her as if she had lost her breath. Disgust and hatred immobilized her: if Martin could become something alien, then so would she, she told herself, letting her hands fall back, no longer resisting.

"Good," her brother grunted, leaning over her and beginning to thrust.

The back of her hand struck metal; it took a moment for her to recover from her apathy to realize that the object was the pair of wedge-bladed shears. The enormity of this—its possibilities—banished her indifference in a heartbeat. She turned her hand and grasped the metal loop of the handhold, then in one rage-driven motion, swung the shears around, open, to ram the shear into the place between his neck and shoulder. Her scream of outrage and triumph was scarcely human.

The Cardinal spasmed, his eyes bulging. He pounded on her breasts with one fist as he tried to pull the shears free with the other. As soon as he had the shears out, blood fountained out of the wound. "You *whore!*" he bellowed, and tried to slash her face with the blade; he left a long furrow in her cheek, and grinned. Then he went pale and sweat stood out on his face. "Por Dios," he muttered, and began to fall.

Leocadia seized the shears and pushed free of him as he collapsed. Then she straddled him and began to plunge the gory blade into him over and over again until the blood ceased to spurt from his wounds and his chest no longer rose and fell. Her breath hissed through clenched teeth. Abruptly she was cold, wondering what was wrong with the room. What had been so carelessly spattered about that the walls and floor and even her wedding dress was full of it? "Martin?" she whispered, dazed and now shaking with a rush of nausea that was as intense as it was sudden. The acrid odor of vomit mixed with the hot-metal smell of blood; Leocadia was now stupefied by what she saw. What in the Name of God had happened? She stood up, shaking severely. The shears fell from her hands as she perceived the red stain on her hands and ruined clothing for the blood it was. She wanted to scream, but the only sound she made was a mewing cry.

Then the door opened; Leocadia yelped and crouched down behind the cutting-table, shaking and doing her best not to weep.

Jose Bruno could not see well enough to discern the magnitude of what had occurred, but he knew from the odor that violence had been done. "Leocadia?" he whispered, half expecting her not to answer.

She rose unsteadily. "Oh, Jose Bruno," she murmured in relief, and clung to the edge of the table.

"What happened?" Jose Bruno asked as he came a little farther into the room. He was able to make out shapes now, and color. "Dear God," he muttered, and crossed himself.

"Martin is dead," Leocadia said, and began to wail.

Jose Bruno went to her and clapped his hand over her mouth. "Hush. We must not let this be discovered." He peered closely at the body on the table, at the bloody shears, at the gaping wounds in the Cardinal's chest and neck. "Did he attack you?"

Leocadia could only nod. "He was . . . It was my fault. He . . . he . . ." She broke down, sobbing wretchedly.

Abruptly Jose Bruno made up his mind. "You cannot stay here. If you do, you'll end up in the Pope's Little House."

The very name made Leocadia cringe. "No. No. No." She punctuated this by striking herself on the breast with every word.

"Stop it," Jose Bruno ordered. "You can do that later." He looked at her ruined wrapper and blood-stained corset. "You cannot leave this room like that." He looked around, concentrating in an effort to see as clearly as possible. Finally he noticed the bolt of muslin. "There. We can drape you in that."

"Oh, yes, yes," said Leocadia without any trace of understanding.

"Now, you must be quiet," he told her very gently. "You cannot make a sound. Will you do that?"

Leocadia nodded repeatedly, her hands knotted together, her eyes vacant. She would not face in the direction of Martin's body, nor would she look toward the door; she put one hand over her mouth as if to keep the words in.

It was the best he could hope for; Jose Bruno went and tore off a length of muslin, then brought it back to Leocadia and wrapped her in it as if it were a blanket. He moved slowly and carefully, not only because he could not see well, but because he was afraid of what Leocadia might do if she were startled or frightened. "Now, I am going to take you out of here. You are not going to say anything to anyone. If we are stopped, let me do the talking."

"You talk," Leocadia agreed, and passively let him lead her away.

He took her down the servants' stairs and into the stableyard at the back of the palazzo. They met no one on their short journey; so far as he knew, they were unobserved. As he shoved her into a empty box-stall, he said, "Lie down and make no noise. I'll come back in a little while."

She was listless as she sank down on the straw bedding. "He's gone."

"Yes," said Jose Bruno with deep compassion. "He's gone." He knew she would have to find sanctuary, and that might be difficult in Roma. He frowned as he closed the stall door.

He had no idea of where he should look for sanctuary for his half-sister. He would need an ally for that. Perhaps, he thought as he made his way back into the palazzo, that musician would come back again, and perhaps he would know how to protect Leocadia from the wrath of the Church and Ursellos.

Text of a letter from Giorgianna Ferrugia, Marchesa di Scosceserto, to Ferenc Ragoczy, Conte da San-Germain.

To the esteemed, the excellent Conte, Ferenc Ragoczy, the affectionate greetings from Giorgianna Ferrugia, Marchesa di Scoscescerto.

Ilirio, my good husband, is overjoyed at the twin boys I delivered ten days ago. He is boasting of his prowess to anyone who will listen, from the scullion to the Bishop. I am glad that I have fulfilled my obligations so well, for now I am at liberty to see you once again, for purposes other than musical.

And I do wish to see you, for though Ilirio is a worthy man, and kind in his way, he has all the subtlety with women that a bull has with a cow. It has got him what he longed for—male children—and I am pleased that God was willing to have it so. But I have languished for you, and all the wonderful things you know to do to please women, or this woman. I have had no spasm of joy with my husband, nor did I expect to have it. Ilirio is a realistic man, and he knows that I have a temperament that he cannot fathom, and so he is willing to permit me to reestablish my affaire with you, providing you have done as you have in the past and do nothing that would bring dishonor upon him, his family, or upon me.

I hope you will want to see me again, and to be my lover, for I know it would make me happier than any music you might compose for me. My husband will not embarrass you if you are discreet—I think that in his heart of hearts he would be grateful to you for providing me with what he cannot give me. But I have one condition to impose upon you, my dear, dear Conte: you must tell me nothing you would not want my Confessor to know. You have hinted that you have information you must convey to me. While I appreciate your concern, I do not want to have to reveal anything about you that the Church could hold against you. If this is satisfactory to you, I will look to see you at the Villa Santa Lucia on the Ostia Road five days from now. I pray you will come, for I long to hold you again, and to know the passion you and only you have found in my soul.

If you will meet me, send me a page of music—any page of music—and I will be filled with delight. If you will not meet me, then I will see you at rehearsal when we resume our preparations in two weeks' time. And if prayer will persuade you, I implore you on my knees to say you will come.

Your most devoted, most beseeching, most longing
Giorgianna

On the 22nd day of March, 1690

PART III

FERENC RAGOCZY, CONTE DA SAN-GERMAIN

Text of a letter from Ahrent Julius Rothofen to Ursellos Calaveria y Vacamonte.

To my most revered friend, in his time of trouble and grief, with every expression of the most profound sympathy, I set pen to paper to offer you what comfort I can in the wake of calamity and holy celebrations of your brother's soul.

The death of your saintly brother must surely have been a dreadful shock to you, coming as it did when you had every hope of seeing your sister successfully wed to the brother of my patron, Archbishop Walmund. I know how profoundly shocked I was when I first heard the terrible news. To think that we had all planned to attend a wedding and not a Requiem. The funeral itself was as full of pomp as the Cardinal could wish, and his virtues were extolled even as his memory was given a cherished place among the Princes of the Church. To have the promise of Resurrection follow so closely on his obsequies must alleviate your most desperate grief. At that dreadful occasion I offered you any help I could provide you in this most crushing time, and I wish to reiterate my intentions now. Three weeks have passed and it seems to me that you may have recovered from the initial stupefaction that so great a tragedy must surely cause.

It is my understanding that your sister is still missing, and your half-brother as well. I know it is assumed she was kidnapped, and he along with her, by whomever murdered your Cardinal-brother. Rumors being what they are, all manner of outrageous suggestions are now bruited about: some say that your half-brother did the murder and forced your sister to flee with him; others speculate that it was your sister who fled upon discovering the body of your brother, and your half-brother went with her to provide protection. More ludicrous tales are being whispered but no one believes them, for which God must be thanked. If half of what you told me is true, it would cause a scandal such as Roma has not seen since the most outrageous of the Anti-Popes of the Avignon Obedience. That would never do, for the Archbishop has said that scandal would serve to sever all ties to your family, and all the plans that your brother and the Archbishop made to their mutual benefits and the benefit of their respective homelands would be for nothing.

Surely you cannot wish such a thing to happen. You must see it is best to do all that is possible to determine how your brother died and who performed the abomination so that justice might be meted out to the despicable miscreants who brought so noble a life to an end. I cannot urge you more strongly than this to summon up your courage and your duty in order to salvage as much as may be of the alliance that would have been realized by the marriage of your sister and the Archbishop's brother. If your sister can be found and is shown to be innocent of any part of the murder of your brother, then the wedding might still take place and the goals for which your brother labored so long could be fulfilled.

The longer your sister remains missing, the greater the chance that her reputation will be stained beyond all amelioration, and that would be unfortunate for your family as well as for any hopes that the Archbishop holds for being able to see his brother well-married. You have your family's dignity to vindicate and nothing would accomplish that half so well as seeing your sister cleared of any whisper of calumny. I hold myself ready to serve you in any capacity that may lead to that happy resolution.

You and I have been boon companions, Ursellos, and I hope I may, for the sake of our friendship, prevail upon you to permit me to assist you as you endeavor to bring this sad time to an end. I understand why you have been haunting the taverns and gaming houses since your brother's funeral, for I know how you must need distraction from your grief; you have endured more than most men have had to bear. But it may be more efficacious to take action to bring the criminals who committed these foul acts to the Church's Court than to attempt to blot these catastrophes from your thoughts through excess.

I will do myself the honor of calling upon you in three days' time when I pray you will receive me for the purpose of establishing a plan whereby your sister may at last be found so that she may answer the inquiries of the Holy Office.

Your most truly dedicated friend to command,
Ahrent Rothofen

On the 9th day of April, 1690, at Roma

1

As the musicians put away their instruments and began to make their way out to their waiting carriages and horses in the front of Senza Pari for the return to Roma, Alessandro Scarlatti took a moment to pull Ferenc Ragoczy aside. "I need a word with you, Conte; in private."

Ragoczy glanced at Giorgianna Ferrugia, sitting demurely at the keyboard, picking out the new aria that had been added to her role. "Is this private enough?"

"I fear not; it's not about the opera," said Scarlatti. "You will have to spare me a few moments—perhaps outside, where we cannot be easily overheard?"

This suggestion was unusual enough to alert Ragoczy. "If you think that best, then by all means, we shall step outside." He turned to Giorgianna and made a leg. "I shall be back directly; of your mercy, wait for me."

"Of course, Conte," she said with an impish smile; she went back to reading the score she held, softly humming the melody.

Ragoczy led the way to a side-door that opened onto a small neglected stretch of garden almost taken over by berry vines. A narrow footpath led to four pear trees that were just coming into bloom. "Is this private enough, Maestro?"

"An excellent choice; no one will be tempted to hide in the shrubbery," said Scarlatti, winking at his pun on Ragoczy's honorific of Eccellenza; his good humor faded at once. "This is most difficult." He stared at the blooming pear trees as if seeking inspiration. "I wish I did not have to speak of this at all."

"Of what?" Ragoczy did not let his impatience sound in his voice. "Tell me, what has you so upset?"

Scarlatti did not answer; he walked along the path a few steps beyond the trees, as if that additional distance would increase their privacy. "I swore I would not speak of this, but the young fool has made such a mull of it—" He gestured his exasperation as if he expected a musical accompaniment to the emotion. "He needs help, Eccellenza. There is nowhere they can turn if you deny it them. If he says anything to his Confessor, or she to hers, they will all pay dearly—"

Although Ragoczy had surmised the identity of Scarlatti's provoking young fool, he said only, "If you would tell me what the trouble is?"

"It's Maurizio," said Scarlatti, rolling his eyes upward. "Who else? And that penitent. The one you kept at your villa?"

For the first time, Ragoczy was distressed. "Yes? The sister of the murdered Cardinal?" he asked sharply. "What of them? Do you mean they are together?"

"Maurizio has been hiding the woman and her half-brother. There's nothing improper. The half-brother will swear to it. No one could be more gallant than that young upstart has been, at least that is what the woman's brother says. Maurizio is very much afraid for them all. He thought he would be able to arrange something before now. When I saw him last, he was almost distraught. He says the Holy Office will put them both—brother and sister—in prison if they are found, and himself as well. In that he may be right." Scarlatti was speaking very fast, and just above a whisper. "He wants to carry them out of the country—to England or the Lowlands, anywhere the Church cannot easily reach. He would even take them to the New World if he could find passage for them all on a ship."

Ragoczy closed his eyes for a moment. "He has got himself, and all of them, into real danger," he said at last, speaking very calmly. "Tell me the rest."

"The rest?" Scarlatti asked in unconvincing bafflement.

"Someone has been shielding these three," said Ragoczy, looking directly at Scarlatti. "Tell me you have better sense."

"I? Oh, no. I could not, even if I wanted to, not with a wife and children; it would mean putting them in danger, and I could not, even for so gifted a musician as Maurizio. No. They have been in a hunting-box on Ettore Colonna's estate, the one outside Sezze. No one uses it at this time of year. They could get to the shore in a day, if it were necessary." This last was hopeful. "If they could get aboard a ship?"

"One of mine, you mean," Ragoczy said slowly.

"Yes; that is what he hopes," Scarlatti answered with an honesty that compelled Ragoczy's reluctant admiration. "There is no one else they can trust, and no one who has been willing to offer passage to those who are—"

Ragoczy held up his hand. "Before I founder in encomia, I must tell you that what Maurizio wants may not be possible," he said at last. "I regret to tell you this, but I do not want to create hopes where there can be none."

"Iddio mio, why can you not?" Scarlatti's distress made his large eyes seem huge.

Ragoczy shrugged slightly. "I am being watched, and anyone who comes to me will also be watched. The Holy Office already suspects me because I provided a retreat for the Cardinal's sister. Now that she is missing, the hunt is on. If she is not, in fact, a captive, they would expect her to come to me again, and if she does, they will apprehend her. Not everyone is satisfied I only gave her shelter and would like to find their worst suspicions were confirmed."

"Did you . . . do anything?" Scarlatti asked, looking worried. It had not occurred to him that the rumors might have some foundation after all.

"Of course not," said Ragoczy, so flatly that there was no doubting him. "If Maurizio wishes to avoid the risk of capture, it would be better to use other ships than mine," he recommended. "Also, if you know I have used my ships in this way, then you must reckon that the Holy Office does as well." He sighed. "This could be toilsome. What possessed Colonna to do this?"

"I have no idea," said Scarlatti, although his expression suggested otherwise. "They cannot stay there much longer, whatever Colonna might think."

"No, they cannot," Ragoczy agreed, frowning with concentration. He began to pace, not too quickly, as he considered what he had been told. "The Cardinal's murder makes Leocadia's position very dangerous. The Holy Office must act in some way, if only to show the killing of Cardinals will not be tolerated." He rubbed his chin. "Did Maurizio plan to make this complicated, or is this only an unfortunate result?" he asked of the air in exasperation.

"He wanted to help her," said Scarlatti simply.

"Very likely," said Ragoczy. His brows drew together. "Where did you see Maurizio?"

"With Ettore Colonna," said Scarlatti. "There was a garden breakfast and Maurizio played for it. I had no idea that there was more to it than a well-paying job until Colonna told me that Maurizio needed to talk to me."

"I presume this accounts for Maurizio's absence at our rehearsals," said Ragoczy.

Scarlatti nodded. "He understands the risks here; he does not want to be followed, or to implicate you." His thick brows lifted in wry amusement. "He does not understand that asking for your help might be more risky than anything, but you are the only hope he has."

"I see," said Ragoczy, his tone mildly sardonic. "Well, I suppose I must hear him out, if nothing else."

"Then you will talk to him?" Scarlatti looked so hopeful that Ragoczy did not want to dash his expectations.

"I have been invited to call upon Ettore Colonna on Saturday, and I have accepted his invitation. Doubtless there is some connection between your message and the invitation." He caught sight of the copyist, Addiso Cicogna, who was coming toward them at a steady pace, and he went on as if they had been discussing music the whole time. "—and I think that adding another viola da gamba might make the bass too prominent. That would be as distorting as adding more violins, and drown out the lyrics. However, I am willing to consider you adding another flute for the two choral laments."

Scarlatti took up the subject with immediate comprehension. "It is only my concern that the strength of La Ferrugia's voice may make the balance of the whole too much to the treble." He glanced in Cicogna's direction for the first time. "Ah. We may be creating more work for you, Cicogna, I regret to say."

"I am willing to work," said the very self-contained copyist. "Signor' Aulirios sent me to fetch you. I apologize for interrupting your discussion." He sounded just curious enough that Ragoczy provided an explanation.

"I learned long ago, Signore, that one does not discuss the music for singers in front of them." Ragoczy saw Scarlatti gesture in agreement. "It seemed wisest to speak privately, and the day being so pleasant . . ."

"It *is* a fine day," said Cicogna, glancing somberly up through the branches of the pear trees. "They say a wet spring leads to more mal aria in the summer." He bowed slightly to the two men. "Well, I have delivered my message. I will not linger." Nor did he. He went off down the path, not looking back.

"That was . . . not quite what it seemed; or perhaps precisely what it seemed," Ragoczy said. "Thank you for your help, Maestro."

"My honor, Eccellenza," Scarlatti replied with a bit of a flourish with his lace-edged handkerchief. "Although he might not have been spying on us."

"And then again he may," said Ragoczy. "Well, we should start back, in any case. To put suspicions to rest, if nothing else."

Scarlatti strolled along, about half a stride behind Ragoczy. As they went past the berry vines, he ventured, "About the matter—?"

"I will think about it," said Ragoczy. "Do not despair. Something can be done." He went on as if on the same subject. "We will balance the sound of it all somehow."

"And remember, the theater where we perform it will shape the music differently than this chamber where we rehearse. When we go there, we will have to balance again." Scarlatti smiled, taking up his tone. "So day after tomorrow we may discuss the changes?"

"Before rehearsal, of course," said Ragoczy as he walked across the narrow terrace to the villa.

"Very good, Eccellenza." He made a leg. "Thank you for hearing me out."

Ragoczy cocked his head. "Very flattering, Maestro."

"And to a good end," said Scarlatti playfully. He went off toward the side-room where his remaining musicians were putting away their instruments and enjoying the wine, cheese, and ham set out for their delectation.

"There you are," said Giorgianna as she looked up from the keyboard. "I was beginning to fear you had forgot me."

"Never," said Ragoczy as he came to her through the empty chairs and music stands. He stopped behind her, bent down, and kissed her shoulder. "No one could ever forget you, Giorgianna."

"You flatter me, Conte," she said flirtatiously. "You went off with Maestro Scarlatti and were gone so long." She sighed prettily.

Ragoczy slipped his arms around her under her breasts. "Then I was a fool," he said and kissed her shoulder again; her pearl earring pressed against his cheek as he did, and the lace of her corsage was under his chin.

"Have you missed me?" She played a minor arpeggio on the keys, the very turn of her wrist seductive.

"Constantly," said Ragoczy, knowing what she wanted to hear. "You have been the one solace amid many tribulations." His expression was as extravagant as the times demanded, but the sentiment was genuine. "I am still astonished that your husband should be willing to allow you to resume with me."

"Well, I promised him you would do nothing that could or would endanger the succession, or that you never have in the past and I am prepared to believe you will not," she said with a pert smile. "So long as that is the case, he will have no objection to our dalliance until I am pregnant again."

"And do you intend to be pregnant again? I recall you intimated it was not to your taste." He neither condemned nor condoned her; he was only seeking information.

"For now I will be satisfied with my twins. But in time it may be wise to have more children." She sighed, this time with some regret. "It is ever the fate of women to have to prove their worth through their bodies. Well, that duty is done, and now I will have my reward." Her perfume was modern, combining two fragrances most daringly—an intense compound of rose-and-jasmine; she had put it on her wrists and elbows as well as between her ample breasts. As she leaned back into his embrace, she sighed luxuriously. "You have no notion how much I have missed you, Conte."

"I have certainly missed you," he murmured, caressing her breasts through the taffeta and lace of her corsage.

"Not even Adina Bonasoli has tempted you?" she asked archly. "I have seen her watching you; the poor woman has tried everything to catch your notice." She reached over her shoulder to touch his face. "That widow is enamored of you."

"She is enamored of not being a widow anymore. If I had a squint and was missing a foot, so long as I had my fortune and my title, she would be interested in me." He said it more sadly than harshly, and his voice was kind. "What else is there for her to do, but marry again?"

"True," said Giorgianna, no longer interested in the Widow Bonasoli's plight. "I am greedy enough to have a husband *and* a lover. Why should I not, if my husband does not forbid me? He understands that artists are not like other people. If I cannot find all I need in one man, then I will have two." She stopped her desultory playing and swung around to face him. "It is a wonderful thing to be with you again."

He bent to kiss her lips, very softly, very persuasively. He did not rush, letting their sensations play out before he spoke again. "There is a very pleasant room upstairs. Niklos Aulirios has prepared it for our use. Would you do me the honor to come there with me?"

"Since you ask me so prettily, how can I refuse?" She held out her hand so that he could assist her to rise from the bench without snaring her profusion of skirts on it; this also provided her a plausible excuse to lean against him while he swept her petticoats free. Once beyond the instrument, she swung around to face Ragoczy; pressing herself into his arms, she kissed the corner of his mouth. "You are a lover any woman would dream of." She took his hands in hers and guided them around her waist. "Do you want me? Do you want to do all those wonderful things we did before? Do you want to try something new?" she asked playfully, but with an underlying urgency that startled him.

For an answer he kissed her lips, lingeringly and thoroughly, re-learning his sense of her in the nuances of her response to him. She was then all the reality in the world to him, the beginning and ending of time. The scent of her perfume seemed to penetrate everywhere, heady and seductive, an outward sign of her rising passions; he drew her even closer, ignoring the profusion of lace at her elbows and corsage, and lace extravagance of petticoats. Beneath all the clothes and corsets there was the utterly genuine flesh of a passionate woman. He could feel her ardor in the restlessness of her hands on his shoulders, in her breath on his cheek, in her quickening pulse. "Come with me, Giorgianna. We should be private."

She was a bit dazed as she stared at him. "Oh, yes," she admitted. "The servants."

"And our host," Ragoczy added. "You will be more comfortable with a bed to lie upon, and not the floor." His chuckle was sympathetic. "And so would I. I am no longer so young that I see no virtue in lying at ease."

Her hand slipped into his. "Then let us go there, and quickly. I have been hungry for you since I came back from my honeymoon."

They went into the corridor, where three servants were studiously busy with minor duties, then along it to the stairs that led up to the second floor. He took her to a room about halfway between the stairs and the end of the corridor. "This has been my apartment for many years. Niklos readied it for me—and you."

The apartment was filled with the pinkish light of a spring afternoon, making the elegant outer chamber glow. Two upholstered chairs covered in damask silk with rosewood legs sat in the alcove of the louvered windows; three fine paintings adorned the walls, one of them by Velasquez, one by Titian, one a faded fresco section that showed a view of Roma as it had looked fifteen hundred years earlier;

on the far side of the room was a sumptuous divan of authentic Turkish design, covered in heavy, iridescent silk. Ragoczy led her toward this, saying, "You will find this a pleasure to lie upon, dolcina."

"They say the Turks are very decadent," Giorgianna said, smiling like a cat. "To have such a thing as that, they would have to be debauched."

"You may put that to the test," said Ragoczy, and slipped his arms around her again. "Shall I be your maid?" He touched the lacing down the back of her dress.

"Now and after?" she teased.

"Of course," he said, his voice soft and mellifluous. "It would never do to have you leave here looking like a ragamuffin. You must leave as you came, nothing out of place." He found where the ties were slipped under the bodice just above the skirt. "Do you want me to loosen these?"

"Yes, please," she said, her face and bosom flushing in anticipation. The knots slipped easily, and the taffeta corsage and bodice fell away, revealing the satin-and-whalebone corset beneath; embroidered flowers twined the stays and ornamented the edge of the garment. "Now the skirt," she said, slipping away from him so that she could unfasten it herself; she let it drop, then raised her arms as if to acknowledge applause. "Illirio doesn't ask me to take off more than this. He says he likes to play with the petticoats."

Ragoczy was unsure if she approved or disapproved of her husband's tastes. He touched her shoulder with the tips of his fingers. "If he keeps you clothed, he is depriving himself of much joy." In two steps he was beside her; he reached behind her and tugged out the whalebone latch that held the corset together.

With a gleeful cry, Giorgianna wriggled out of her petticoats and was left standing naked but for her white silken hose gartered just below the knees, and her brocaded shoes with wide silver buckles. "There! Oh, yes!" she exclaimed, flinging up her hands again, and then, with another shriek of pleasure, cast herself back onto the divan; the furniture creaked as it shifted to support her body, accommodating the movements she made. "Oh! I wouldn't have thought— This *is* marvelous," she purred as she slid about on it.

Ragoczy went down on one knee beside the divan. "The saddlers make them on flexible frames, and they have eight layers of padding, so that they are always soft." He took her hand and kissed each finger, then the palm, then the wrist.

"How clever," she murmured, but whether in praise of the Turkish saddlers or Ragoczy's kisses was impossible to tell.

At her elbow, Ragoczy paused, alternately kissing then using his tongue before making his way up to her shoulder; her skin was lovely and flawless, as enticing as the silken divan. His need answered hers as his lips touched her mouth; Giorgianna arched her back as Ragoczy's fingers brushed her throat, her breasts, evoking bliss.

"Thank all the Saints you know what you're doing," Giorgianna said when she had the chance to speak. "I am so tired of being nothing more than a . . ." Ragoczy flicked her nipple with the tip of his tongue and she forgot all her complaints. She was too eager to be pliant in his embrace, too hectic in her carnality to achieve the abandon she longed for. She was moving so he could touch as much of her as possible as quickly as she felt the impulse. She sighed and strained, wanting to make up for the long months without this fulfillment.

Ragoczy drew back a bit. "Giorgianna, dolcina, *un poco adagio,*" he said, smiling at his musical joke. "If you hurry it, you will miss what you want most. You are rushing to the last movement before the first is hardly done. There is much to delight in in between. The gratification will be all the greater if you give it its full crescendo."

"Your metaphor is very good," she remarked impatiently. She squirmed, her face a bit flushed. "But it's been so long," she protested quietly. "I can feel my desire all through me. I am afraid I will burst with it."

He stroked her side and hip, then down her leg; his touch was light, just enough to cause a frisson as it went. "Go a little slower, and I promise you, you will not regret it."

"Oh, all right," she said, not as petulantly as she would have liked. "You have never disappointed me before." There was an underlying note of doubt in her assertion, so she added, "It's just that I have missed this so much."

"As have I," said Ragoczy candidly. He did not add that visiting women in their dreams offered only a dim reflection of what a knowing partner gave him. "You have had other things to occupy your mind; I have not. Do not assume I do not know what you desire, for I do, and I treasure it." He bent to kiss her again, this time tenderly, persuasively, allowing her to reach her arousal more gradually, with more rapture and less frenzy. His hands soothed, coaxing her trembling out of her and replacing them with shivers of ecstatic anticipation as he rekindled her passions, finding places on her flesh that she never knew could feel so deliciously keen, so deeply defined in every fiber of her being as his touch traveled all the hidden byways of her body.

Gradually her tension drained out of her to be replaced by an ardent languor, and she was content to indulge all her senses, savoring each caress of his hands and lips, his understanding of her joy. When her release came, it surprised her with its suddenness and its intensity, pulsing through her in blissful jolts that made her cling to him, small, high sounds like the cry of birds escaping her as she held his head pressed to her neck. Finally she sighed with profound contentment and let go of him. "I was afraid it wouldn't be good anymore," she confessed as she stared up into his compassionate, enigmatic dark eyes. "They say after you have children, it isn't the same."

"Who says this?" He stroked the damp tendrils of her hair back from her brow.

"Old women. Priests. They all say the pleasure is less." Her faint frown began to fade. "Everyone."

"And was it? the same?" The warmth in his gaze was tinged with amusement.

She stretched, lithe as a cat. "It was *better*." Catching his hands in hers, she smiled up at him. "You smell of me."

"I taste of you, too, dolcina," he responded gently. "You have become part of me. You will always be part of me."

The frown was back. "Is that because you . . ." Before he could speak she shook her head, her frown deepening. "No. Don't tell me. I don't want to know anything that could be compromising when I Confess."

A thousand years ago he might have insisted she tell him why: now he only nodded slowly. "If that is what you wish."

"It is," she said, and attempted a light-hearted giggle which caught in her throat. "I'm sorry, Conte. But it would be so difficult . . ."

"For both of us, no doubt," he agreed. "Yes, dolcina, you are right." How this concession tore at him, the certainty that knowledge of his true nature would be as deadly to her as it would be to him, filled him with a chagrin he had not realized he possessed. He bent and kissed her lightly on the forehead. "Never mind. You and I must make the most of what we can have together: mustn't we?"

"Yes; oh, yes." She ducked her head against his shoulder. "I am so sorry that . . . that I cannot . . ."

"Never mind," he repeated, his arms around her now for comfort. "You have two little sons whom you must guard. In your place I should probably do the same thing."

"Would you?" She leaned back and studied him, her expression changing to a defensive one. "Tell me, did you grow bored, waiting for me to deliver, and did you have your way with that penitent? Did you grow tired of being alone, and—"

"No," said Ragoczy, quietly, gently, but with such conviction that she could not doubt him.

"I have no right to be jealous, of course," she went on, trying to amend the blunder she had just made. "I am married, and we can never be more than we are now."

"I've understood that from the first," Ragoczy reminded her, no touch of blame in his demeanor. "If you had been unwilling to come back to me, I would not have held it against you. I have learned that only those who are willing can be loved." There was a distant look in his eyes, and an unfathomable sadness.

"Oh, no, no, no." There was a timorous quiver in her voice; an instant later she began to weep. "Conte. Conte. Do not be angry with me."

"Angry with you?" he echoed. "Why should I be?" His concern was more than she could bear; he was struck again with how ephemeral joy was and how enduring pain could be, and this realization reawoke his private anguish which he sought to assuage by consoling her.

"Giorgianna, I have no reason to be angry, believe this." He saw she was made more miserable by his compassion, so fell silent to allow her to speak.

"Then you should. Because I'm spoiling this," she sobbed, struggling to break free of his embrace. "It's all going to be lost."

Ragoczy drew her toward him, comforting her. "Dolcina, do not. You could not diminish anything we have had if you wished to; no matter what comes, it will not change what we have now," he said as he soothed her, and all the while, Laurenzo's lyric of two hundred years ago rang in his mind: *Chi vuol' esser lieto, sia; / Di doman' non ch'e certezza*—Who wishes to be merry, be so; / Of tomorrow there is no certainty.

Text of a letter from Padre Bartolomeo Battista Tredori to the Holy Office of the Faith, Via Sacra, Roma.

To the most esteemed, most truly reverend holy Fathers, the obedient greetings of this most humble, troubled priest, with my fervent prayer that God, Who guides us in all things, will show me Grace and Wisdom in my answers to your questions. Amen.

First, I must report that I have seen the young woman you seek but once since the shocking death of her brother. That was perhaps a day after that hideous act. There were scandals whispered all over the city, and the Guardia Laterano was out in force, making inquiries on behalf of Sua Santita, for it was feared that an attack on a Cardinal might well portend more outrageous assaults. The young woman came to my church in the company of her half-brother, who is simple and lacks clear sight. How often we see the Hand of God laid heavily on those already afflicted. He had the care of his sister, and as diligently as he could he attended to his duty, bringing her to me so that she might Confess.

Second, I fear all that she said to me is under the Seal of Confession, but I will tell you that in my judgment, whatever it was she witnessed must have unhinged her reason, for she made such accusations against her martyred brother as could not be heard without disgust and revulsion. All men sin, for we are the children of sin, but those of known worthiness, who have vowed to keep from sin, as the

Princes of the Church must, could not do such things as this deranged woman uttered. I gave her penance for lies and prayers for the soul of her slain brother, and entrusted her once more to Jose Bruno. I told him that his sister was overwrought and would need some time for meditation and reflection before the balance of her mind was restored and her soul could be cleansed of all guilt and grief. I warned him that it would be best if she were encouraged not to speak of the things she had Confessed, for in time, she would come to be ashamed that she spoke so, whether in her turbulent state she may now believe it.

Third, I encouraged the two to return to Spain if at all possible, for I could not countenance her marriage after her brother's murder, particularly given her state of mind. Jose Bruno told me he had money enough to keep them reasonably well, and said that he had a friend who would help them to leave Roma without any greater upset than what they had already suffered. He pleaded with me to say nothing of this to Ursellos, their older brother, for the young woman unaccountably holds him in fear, for which I cannot account. I agreed that I would offer no information, but added that I could not lie for her or anyone. Jose Bruno said he was content with that, and left a donation before he and his sister departed.

Fourth, I know nothing of the friend Jose Bruno mentioned: the name of the friend was carefully avoided, I have supposed not to tempt me into the sin of prevarication if I was questioned. There was no indication of the friend's age or rank or gender—nothing that would hint at the friend's identity, or where that friend might abide. My own suspicions are only that: suspicions. But I cannot help but recall when last the young woman absented herself from her brother's house she took refuge with the foreigner, Ferenc Ragoczy, Conte da San-Germain, at his estate, the Villa Vecchia to the north and east of the city, and that having found sanctuary there before she might well find it there again. It is incumbent upon me to say that it may be that he is the friend to whom Jose Bruno referred. I have no confirmation of this, but it does strike me that if he would shelter her once, he might well do so again. If I have erred in this assumption, may God forgive me for creating suspicions of a guiltless man.

Fifth, I have no doubt that the killing of the Cardinal is a twice-damned act, and that his blood, shed so mercilessly, has brought him a crown in Heaven. Any suggestion of improper conduct in regard to Sua Eminenza must be laid to the rancor of the Germans who had so many hopes riding on their association with him. I, for one, believe that it suited Archbishop Walmund's purposes very well to have the wedding of his brother to the Cardinal's sister postponed, for it is known that the Archbishop's brother has been in the care of physicians in order to restore his manhood which the curse of syphilis has so cruelly blighted; until the Archbishop's brother is whole and capable again, any marriage would be unconsummatable and therefore invalid in the eyes of God and the Church, which the Archbishop must not want. That it is being bandied about by certain unscrupulous persons that the Cardinal was all but whoring his sister to the Germans to further his own worldly schemes is a calumny not to be borne, and I ask you, Good Fathers, to undertake what acts you deem appropriate to silence all such malicious speculations. Women must marry, and if they can marry to the advantage of their families, it is their duty to do so, as Scripture teaches us.

I am ever conformable to the Will of God and His Church, and stand prepared to present myself to you, most holy Fathers, whenever you should advise me that such is your wish. As you do, I grieve for the loss of so exemplary a Cardinal as Martin, Cardinal Calaveria y Vacamonte, and I pray diligently for his soul, as I pray for the souls of all good Christians.

Your most submissive and devoted servant
Padre Bartolomeo Battista Tredori
Santissimo Redentore

In Roma, on the Feast of San Marco, the 25th day of April, 1690

Deo Gratias

Blossoms blurred to smears of color in the soft rain; the gardens were coming into their full glory as Ettore Colonna led Ragoczy down the same path they had trod in the past; the exuberance of spring was all around them in spite of the mizzle. Although it was just past noon it was cool but not truly cold, and both men wore cloaks, as much to stay dry as to keep warm. "It was good of you to come, Conte," said his host as they stopped between two beds of roses.

"How could I not?" Ragoczy countered, his expression cordial. "It strikes me that you and I are long overdue to talk."

Ettore Colonna nodded. "Of course. You are concerned about this development with Maurizio."

"If it were only Maurizio," said Ragoczy, smiling a little. "You know as well as I, that is just the beginning." He bent to sniff one of the blooms, the scent of it reminding him of Giorgianna's perfume.

"That it is," said Ettore Colonna. "I may have put us all at a disadvantage; I pray not, but it is possible. If I have, I offer you my deepest apology. I could not sit by, doing nothing: I know what it is to have the might of the Church marshaled against you, and I could not leave those poor, hapless—" He cut himself off. "I took them in. And now I rely on you to find a way to get them out."

"I hope I am flattered?" Ragoczy said quizzically. "It will not be easy. I know you are aware of that." If he had learned nothing else in the last millennium, he had learned that the arm of the Church was long, and that it had more than one weapon in its grasp.

"Oh, yes: none better." The corners of his mouth turned up, but it was not a smile he showed his guest. "Yet I must make some effort—and so must you—or I will be in disgrace with myself until I explain myself to God—assuming I'll need to."

Ragoczy cocked his head. "Do you think that will be necessary?"

"Not if God is as omnipotent and omniscient as the Church insists He is," said Ettore Colonna, his tone tinted with sarcasm. "Even when I was very young, I wondered how God could be so all-loving and all-understanding and yet be such a petty tyrant, granting favor and misfortune with the caprice of a madman. Nothing I've seen since has changed my mind in that regard." He nodded in the direction of an ornate gate. "There's a belvedere at the far side of the ornamental lake. You've never seen it before, I think?"

"No, not that I can recall," said Ragoczy, wondering where Ettore Colonna was leading him—for surely he was leading him just as if he had taken him by the hand. "And a belvedere by a lake in the rain must be most—"

"—damp," Ettore Colonna finished for him. "It couldn't be helped, my friend. Something has to be arranged, and this has been our first opportunity. We must make the most of it, inclement weather or not." He had reached the gate, opened its lock with a key, and swung it open on complaining hinges. "I find the sound provides an excellent warning; no one can open it without this metallic braying. It is only oiled once a year." Stepping aside, he bowed Ragoczy through it. "Just keep on the path. I'll be right behind you."

"Very good," said Ragoczy, following the instructions he had been given. "When was this built?"

"About eighty years ago, when the villa was enlarged," said Ettore Colonna. "The original plans were more lavish, but my great-great-great-uncle ran out of money before the whole of his vision could be realized. He had wanted to put up a kind of village, but the cost was outrageous."

Thinking what he was paying for his new villa, Ragoczy could only say, "I am not surprised."

"That's right," said Ettore Colonna. "You have to deal with the Artei, don't you? They're most demanding. Particularly where foreigners are concerned." He pointed to an artlessly placed bed of rare irises. "Old Tancredi was one of the first to import these varieties from the Lowlands. Of course, the religious situation wasn't so convoluted then as it is now, and no one took exception to his planting them so near Roma; if you did it today there would be an uproar. Still, we were lucky, for once the Lowlands became troublesome, cousin Giuliano had been made Jules Mazarin and was Minister of France and so the bed could be left as it is without occasioning criticism." He indicated a fork in the path ahead. "Bear to the left."

Ragoczy did as he was told; he was enjoying the garden, thinking the misty rain enhanced it, sharpening the smells even as it smudged the colors. "Did you choose this place for its unapproachability?"

"In part; no one can come upon us by accident," said Ettore Colonna. "I believe it will be wise of us to take as much care as possible when we approach the belvedere. I don't think we are being watched in this weather, but prudence is advisable. We do not want to make it appear that going there is anything more than a whim."

"What makes you so very cautious, my friend?" Ragoczy inquired. "I should think that you could be reasonably safe on your own property." He knew better, of course; his own household was filled with servants more eager to show themselves loyal to the Pope than to their foreign employer.

Ettore Colonna sighed. "I would like to be as reasonable as you are, and look upon all these precautions as nothing more than an overanxious mind. But I fear that ever since Celestino was killed, I've not been able to forget how easily that happened." He inadvertently splashed himself with mud as he took a hasty step, landing in a puddle Ragoczy had just managed to avoid. "There are too many men in Roma who believe it would bring them credit with God and the Church if they should hit upon some means of disgracing me so that my family could not protect me."

"I am aware of that," said Ragoczy, squinting ahead through the mizzle. "That is why I am perplexed by your willingness to help Maurizio, and Leocadia, and her half-brother. Yes, I recall what you have told me, but I am still in a quandary."

"You doubt my motives?" Ettore Colonna challenged.

"No. They have never been unclear to me. But since Leocadia witnessed the murder of her brother, she might protect herself with her testimony, and none of this would be needed." He saw the pale marble pillars of the belvedere ahead of them.

"That is the very heart of the problem: her testimony," said Ettore Colonna. "Mind the steps down; they're slippery." He followed his own advice, saying nothing until the two of them were in the entry of the hexagonal building. "I am afraid there is good reason for concern."

"Any time the Pope's Little House is a possible residence, there is reason for concern," said Ragoczy. "Is there anything about Leocadia's situation that makes it more so?"

Ettore Colonna smoothed his moustaches. "I think there may well be. You see, according to what Maurizio told me, *she* killed her brother." He paused. "With scissors."

"She?" Ragoczy repeated, not nearly as surprised as he thought he would be. "Leocadia killed the Cardinal."

Ettore Colonna muttered confirmation, continuing, "From what I have been told, the Cardinal attacked her carnally, and she killed him to stop him. Jose Bruno confirms the story, though he is not a very good witness, considering he is reputed to be a half-wit. Maurizio says they told him it wasn't the first time the Cardinal had done it, that it had long been the Cardinal's practice to make his sister his whore." He spoke flatly, with less emotion than he had shown when he pointed out the irises. Under his wide-cuffed boots the herringbone pattern of the floor was shiny wet.

"You believe her?" Ragoczy asked, curious as to the answer he would receive; as he recalled her stay at Villa Vecchia, he knew beyond cavil that he did; he had sensed the anguish in her penance that was more than rebelliousness or madness: this served to confirm what he had perceived without defining. He had a brief, poignant memory of Xenya, whose life had been blighted by a rape she could not have prevented, and another of Olivia, whose husband had forced her to submit to brutal men for his own gratification.

"You mean do I think a Prince of the Church would try to force himself incestuously upon his sister? Of course I do." He lifted his arms in a gesture of helplessness. "When you live as near the Papacy and all its adjuncts as House Colonna does, nothing surprises you, except, perhaps, sanctity."

"I see," said Ragoczy, who could not argue the point with him; in his long, long years of life he had seen Popes of every nature and disposition, and Cardinals with the same range of character.

"It's the power; I saw that even when I was very young," said Ettore Colonna, flipping back the hood of his cloak and slightly adjusting his curling wig. "They all come to think it belongs to them instead of God. There is no one to stop them doing as they like, and so they tell themselves that their satisfaction is God's Will. They decide that their position makes them capable of acting in God's stead, and from there, it's an easy step to convincing yourself all you do it right as long as you have power enough to do it."

Ragoczy said nothing for a long moment, then told Ettore Colonna, "I hope you do not tell others this is what you think?"

"Of course not," said Ettore Colonna, crossing himself. "I have not got to my present age by being a trusting fool." He studied Ragoczy's composed features. "Nor have you."

"Precisely," said Ragoczy, and looked at the lake. "Your ancestor did a splendid piece of work."

"Or his builders and gardeners did," said Ettore Colonna, by way of agreement. "There have also been decades for the place to weather. The rain helps." He walked to the edge of the belvedere. "You have nothing like this at Villa Vecchia. Are you planning to add formal gardens?"

Whatever Ragoczy's reply might have been was lost as Maurizio stumbled onto the uneven marble floor of the belvedere. He was dressed in a traveling cloak and the most ordinary clothes, as if he were a draper or an ordinary clerk; his kinky hair was tied back and without powder so that he would hardly attract any real attention. "Signor' Conte!" he exclaimed as he came up to Ragoczy. "Thank God you have come. You did not have to, so I am doubly grateful you did: I did not think you would . . ." He stopped himself. "But you are here and you will listen to me." His words tumbled out in a rush. "I have no other way to say it but to plead with you. Please, please, you must help us! It is imperative that we . . . I was afraid you would refuse to see me. I was about to despair." He dropped on one knee. "This is a most difficult petition to make, but I beseech you to hear me out. Our lives are in your hands. You must help us," he repeated in a frantic rush. "You must!"

Ettore Colonna remained where he was, near the edge of the open building, staring out into the rain. "Welcome, Maurizio," he said over his shoulder.

"Oh! Signor' Colonna, you are so very kind to us. I cannot tell you how much your kindness means to us," Maurizio said, looking mildly embarrassed that he had neglected to acknowledge his host.

"Do not bother about me, lad," said Ettore Colonna. "It is Ragoczy you must convince."

Maurizio nodded, swallowing before addressing Ragoczy once more. "We must leave Roma, and the Papal States. We must go beyond the reach of the Holy Office, or we will all pay a terrible price for remaining. We have done nothing deserving of punishment, not really. We will be imprisoned if we remain, and we will rot in prison. You have ships and you can get us away. I beg of you to do this for us. If we remain in the Papal States, we might as well die at once and spare the Holy Office the trouble." He noticed that Ragoczy was listening intently, and pursued his point. "I know I shouldn't just blurt it all out like this. I would do this better if we were not so wretched. Conte, we are abject." He steadied himself, trying to appear more self-possessed. "This is not the way to approach you. I know I should present myself more properly, and ask your support in the approved form, but I haven't *time*. We must get away before we are discovered or all will be lost."

"While that may be true," said Ragoczy in a manner intended to calm the young musician, "is it really so urgent? I do not deny that you would be well-advised to leave, but why now? You make it sound as if you must be outward-bound in a fortnight. I am aware that you have good reason to want to get away, but just now the hunt is on for you, and the ports are more carefully watched than usual, which would make your departure more hazardous; I am being watched, as well, and so I must be provident in making any plans. It would be better to wait awhile longer, until the hunt is called off. By midsummer, there will be other problems to occupy the Holy Office, and you may slip away with far less risk than now." He did his best to sound encouraging. "I can probably arrange to find you a place on a ship, but it would be better if I have a month or two at the least to—"

"No. Oh, no," Maurizio interrupted, his features distorted by the intensity of his despondency; it sagged his face, making stark lines at odds with his youth. "You don't understand. We cannot wait any longer. We must be away from here at once."

"Are you in danger of discovery?" Ragoczy asked, knowing that would be more than enough reason for haste.

"No," said Ettore Colonna before Maurizio could answer.

Maurizio rose and began to pace, his steps impetuous and uneven. He held his hat in one hand and twisted it with the other. "We cannot remain here any longer."

Ragoczy watched the young man move, recognizing the tumult he could not contain. "It certainly is inadvisable, I agree, but in this case—"

"You don't understand," Maurizio burst out. "She is with *child*. *His* child." He stopped still, aware that Ragoczy and Ettore Colonna were staring at him. "Her last courses were in December, and she is increasing."

"Cristo in Croce," Ettore Colonna with more piety than he knew. "She will deliver in August."

Maurizio shook his head repeatedly. "And we must be gone well before then. The longer we wait, the harder our travels will be. There is something more: she will not marry me, not while we are in the Papal States. I have asked her and asked her and *asked* her, but she refuses. She is too frightened to go to a church, no matter what I promise to do. I cannot persuade her that she must do this. Nothing will change her mind, and if she will not consent to marry, her child will be known for what it is, and . . ." He waved his hand in dismay. "She says that the priest would betray us, and we would be taken before the Holy Office at once. If we are gone from here, in a Protestant country, then she will marry me."

"Is that what you want?" Ragoczy asked quietly.

"More than anything. No matter how she got that baby, I will see she and it have a home. I am an orphan. I would not permit her child to live as I did, not while I have strength to care for it, and for her." His voice was more subdued but there was no lack of fervor in his avowal. "Jose Bruno will help, too. He has sworn that to me."

Ragoczy nodded once. "I assume Jose Bruno is with her now."

"Yes," said Maurizio, and stood as if abruptly out of words.

Ragoczy went up to him. "Does she know you're doing this?"

Maurizio could not meet Ragoczy's dark eyes. "She knows I have come to speak to Signore Colonna. I said nothing about you. She would have forbidden me to leave if she knew you would be here." He tugged at his hat. "She does not want anyone more to know what happened. She is afraid someone will tell the priest, and the priest will inform the Holy Office." He crossed himself.

Ettore Colonna was watching Maurizio with increased concern, his heavy dark brows drawn down over his deep-set eyes; he said nothing but his silence was eloquent.

"You have no reason to fear me on that account; I will say nothing to anyone but Signore Colonna and Maestro Scarlatti, who know something of your plight already, and may be relied upon to keep silent," Ragoczy said quietly, though to his mind, too many men knew of this already. There was a remaining uncertainty nagging at him. "What does she say about the baby she carries?"

The question struck Maurizio as if it were a stone, for he flinched and pulled back. "She says it will not live, that it is so tainted, it is not fit to live."

"I see," said Ragoczy, vast compassion in those two words. "So she does not share your hopes for your escape."

"Of course she does," said Maurizio, the heat back in his voice. "She is just so scared, and so . . . so filled with worry, that she cannot let herself believe we can win free."

"Just so," said Ragoczy, who suspected that the situation was more precarious than Maurizio was admitting. "Then, as you say, there is some urgency. That makes it more problematic from my point of view. It may mean improvising." He saw Maurizio's shoulders droop, and went on more heartily. "But I am fairly resourceful; I can find some way to accomplish what you ask." He paused. "I am troubled about what you tell me of Leocadia's state of mind."

"She is upset," Maurizio said quickly. "Anyone would be."

"Yes. Anyone would be," Ettore Colonna agreed, unexpectedly. "A pregnant woman, all the more so, for they are then subject to the humors of childbearing. I do have sisters, you know," he added. "And nephews and nieces."

This was the current wisdom and Ragoczy was not going to be

distracted by the remark; he kept his gaze on Maurizio. "Is she in good health? given that she is with child? Has she weakened at all?"

"I don't know," said Maurizio, becoming upset. "She says nothing about it, or not to me; she may speak with Jose Bruno. She fasts on Wednesdays and Sundays. Her face is wan, but she has many terrible memories to weigh upon her, so . . ." He shrugged the end of his thought.

Ragoczy knew better than to show the alarm he felt. "This is not wise, not if you are going to travel. She must be strong for her voyage, or she and the babe will suffer for it. She can fast when she is delivered." He saw the wariness in Maurizio's face. "Tell her you have spoken to a midwife, if you must account to her in some way."

"That is what my sisters have always been told," Ettore Colonna confirmed. "If she starves herself, she starves her infant."

Maurizio ducked his head in a show of compliance, but his unease continued. "There is trouble with . . . You must understand, with the baby what it is, she has no . . . She . . . She is not . . . she doesn't want . . ."

"That may be," said Ragoczy. "But it is too late for her to be rid of it without grave risk." He saw the startled look Ettore Colonna gave him, and said, "A child is no blessing when it is got as this one was."

"And apothecaries do a thriving business in such philtres as will end unaccountable babies, yes," Ettore Colonna said. "But this is no mere beginning, when such things are easily managed. She is well along in her breeding. You said her last courses were in December, and any remedy she sought now could be harmful. She would not want to try stopping it now, not if—"

"Stop it!" Maurizio cried, forgetting himself. "She had such a chance and refused it. She said if God had sent the babe to her, He could take it away." His face was wet from more than rain. "Jose Bruno pleaded with her to see the herb-woman, but she would not and now it is too late." He began to pace again. "If she does not leave this place, I do not know what she might do to herself. Or the child she carries." He looked directly at Ragoczy. "When we are far away, she will be able to restore herself once again. If she remains here, she will be in as much of a prison as if she were in the Pope's Little House."

"That would not be advisable," said Ettore Colonna at his driest. "Not with what the good Fathers would require of her."

Ragoczy's memories of Church prisons were still sharp from his long incarcerations in the New World; he could hardly bear to think of such hardships imposed on Leocadia, who had endured so much suffering already. "No. You are right. She must not be abandoned to the Church." He stared at Maurizio. "I will do my utmost to secure you passage to the Lowlands or England. The voyage to the New World is too long and the conditions there too harsh for a woman in her condition."

"England would be best," said Ettore Colonna. "Maurizio will find work there. The English love music because they can so rarely make it themselves."

Paying no attention to this slight to the English, Ragoczy agreed. "There are many opportunities in London for talented fiddlers, at the theatre as well as the palaces and halls." He did not want Maurizio losing heart now. "Your gifts will be amply rewarded if you seek out opportunity to perform."

Maurizio bowed. "I will. And I will take care of Leocadia and her child. And Jose Bruno, too, if he will come with us. He isn't simple, you know. He's half-blind, but he isn't simple." This last was said as if he expected contradiction. "He knows a great deal, but he is not able to see much unless it is immediately before his eyes. It isn't as if he would be of no use. Leocadia depends upon him."

"All right. You want passage for you, for Leocadia, and Jose Bruno, and it must be soon," said Ragoczy, his somber expression showing his determination. "I will do what I can, but you will have to do your part."

"Oh, yes," said Maurizio, his eagerness compounded of renewed hope and profound dread. "Tell me what you require and I will see it is done."

Ettore Colonna held up his hand. "I will have to be part of this, for I have no messenger I can trust now that Celestino is dead."

"Very good," said Ragoczy, who was glad that their secret would spread no farther. "When I have the arrangements made, I will send you word through Signore Colonna. You will have to leave at once. There will be no time for packing or gathering provisions. All that must be ready as soon as you are told to depart. I will make sure you are on one of my ships, from the company I own in the Lowlands, otherwise any officer of the Pope could board the ship and demand the Captain hand you over." He tried to recall which of his ships would be available in the next week, and thought only of the *Avond Roos*, currently bound for Venezia. Then he remembered the *Sorella Agnesca* that was due at Malta in a few days; it could be intercepted if he sent a fast ship to meet it. Most of her crew were non-Catholic Italians, as he recalled, and could be relied upon for discretion.

"Can you give us no warning?" Maurizio asked. "I don't mean to demean anything you can do, but I am afraid that Leocadia will need time to prepare."

"A warning to you is also a warning to those looking for you," Ragoczy pointed out. "It would be best to prepare what you will need to travel now, and keep it all readily to hand, so that when I have everything in place, you can depart promptly."

The rain was falling in earnest now, the last downpour before summer; it rattled on the roof and hissed off the lake, dulling the garden to soft shades of grey. A wind sprang up, whipping at the flowers and making the afternoon cold.

Maurizio glanced out between the pillars. "It will be a hard ride tonight."

"Change horses at the *Bue Giallo*; you know the place. They will not notice anything if you toss them an Apostle or two." The inn Ettore Colonna referred to was not on the main road; most of its patrons were farmers traveling to market. "I would offer you a place here, but that would destroy the very secrecy we seek to preserve."

"You will want to get back quickly," Ragoczy added. "But take care. If your horse comes down on you, no one will be able to tell Leocadia." He saw Maurizio bristle in near-panic, and did his best to assuage it without lessening the seriousness of his caution. "If you are truly going to get out of the Papal States, you must be conscientious at all times. You cannot afford even the smallest misstep. So do not push your mount, change horses at the inn, and do nothing to attract the notice of other travelers."

"I will do what I can," said Maurizio. "And I will await word from you, Signor' Conte."

Ragoczy clapped the young man on the shoulder to show his approval; this familiar gesture was so unusual that Maurizio stood absolutely still while Ragoczy said, "It will take me a few days to put all in order. Use that time wisely, for it will make the difference between success and failure."

Ettore Colonna added, "Heed what the Conte says to be ready and to travel light. You cannot go lugging everything you possess with you."

"We possess very little," said Maurizio, his face almost blank. "She left it all behind when she fled her brother's house; what she has Jose Bruno took for her, and for himself. I, so long as I have my violin and a change of clothes, I can go anywhere." It was a kind of unhappy boast, one that made the corners of his mouth turn down.

"All the more reason for you to keep yourselves ready," said Ragoczy, thinking back to all he had left behind in Egypt, in Greece, in Baghdad, in China, in Fiorenza, in the New World, in . . . He shut his retrospections away and turned his attention to the immediate problem.

"That I will," said Maurizio, his face less strained than it had been. "It is good of you to do this for us, Signor' Conte, and you, Signore Colonna. I . . . I have nothing to show you my thanks. I wish that I did." He twisted the points of his hat again. "I will remember your kindness in my prayers until I die." This time he bowed deeply. "I am under obligation to both of you; I will not forget that."

"Let us do something of your dedication first," said Ragoczy, his brows lifting slightly in sardonic amusement. "When we deserve your appreciation then you can reaffirm your devotion." He squinted at the rain. "You had better depart, Maurizio. The storm will be worse by nightfall."

"Yes," said Ettore Colonna. "And mind you prepare as the Signor' Conte has asked you." He waved at the sodden expanse of the ornamental lake. "Best to leave by the way you arrived, over the old wall."

"That's where I left the horse," said Maurizio, bowing again. "I will await word from you. Thank you, thank you, thank you." With this repetition he bowed himself out of the belvedere and vanished into the rain; they marked his progress by the thrashing of the hedges.

When Maurizio was out of earshot, Ragoczy turned to Ettore Colonna. "Is the old wall easy to climb?" he asked nonchalantly.

"Why, yes, if you know where to go," said Ettore Colonna, then nodded once. "You mean someone could have followed Maurizio over the wall?"

"It is a possibility," said Ragoczy, his expression revealing little.

"Well, yes, it *is* a possibility," Ettore Colonna allowed. "But it is unlikely that anyone would know to follow Maurizio, or to watch that part of the wall."

"That you know of," Ragoczy amended.

Ettore Colonna sighed. "As you say: that I know of."

Text of a letter from Bonaldo Fiumara to Ferenc Ragoczy, Conte da San-Germain.

To the most Excellent Conte, Ferenc Ragoczy, da San-Germain, the most sincere greetings of the Masterbuilder, Bonaldo Fiumara;

Eccellenza, I must take pen in hand to address you on a most pressing matter, and one which I must discuss with you in the next few days. I hesitate to impose upon you, but I find that my conscience demands it, although custom frowns upon such matter. You must forgive me for what surely appears to be impetuosity and a deliberate flouting of the conventions that govern our live, and to which we adhere for the good of ourselves and others.

You should know that I have recently been summoned to answer questions by the Holy Office in regard to the Cardinal's sister who last year took refuge at Villa Vecchia; I was required to swear that you had not made her your mistress, or was giving her shelter at your estates now. I had to answer them to the extent of my knowledge, for to do otherwise would endanger my soul and the lives of my family. The reply I made to them was that so far as I knew, you had not made any attempt to entice, compel, or seduce the Cardinal's sister, that you had made sure she was chaperoned once she left the cell you provided for her penitence. I told them that my sister had served as the Cardinal's sister's maid and would testify to the truth of what I said. I doubt they will question Clarice, since she is a woman and therefore of reduced reliability, but I have done what I may to make it possible for her to speak if the Holy Office, if they decide to require her to appear before them, which I pray they will not do, for Clarice would be overcome with terror in such an event, and could not be relied upon to be prudent. I also informed the good Fathers that you had not taken the Cardinal's sister into your villa since her brother came to claim her, and that so far as I could discover, there has been no contact between you since that day.

Along with the questions of your conduct toward the Cardinal's sister, there was also some interest as to your whereabouts on the day the Cardinal was murdered. I had to tell the good Fathers that you were away from your villa for several hours, but that I did not know where you had gone, nor did I know your purpose in going. I would like to have been able to deny any such knowledge, but for these Godly men, I could not give even the appearance of mendacity. I offer you my sincerest apology if I have inadvertently compromised you in any way; that was not my intention. I pray you will understand why I had to be at pains to give them an accurate account of what I know of your actions that day. Others will tell them the same thing, and if they suspect I have not answered them as fully and honestly as I can, they will demand I explain myself, and their methods of exacting information are too stringent for me to contemplate.

Three of the men working under me have also been summoned to address the Holy Office in regard to your conduct. I have informed our Arte that the testimony has been given freely, so that nothing can be held against the rest of our members if the good Fathers are dissatisfied with what my men tell them. It is upsetting to all of us working on your villa to have to do this, for you are a fair and generous employer. But the Holy Office is powerful; all the Artei of

Roma are subject to the Pope, and through Sua Santita, to the Holy Office.

In regard to the villa we are building, the Holy Office has ordered that our work be stopped for ten days so that officers of the Secular Arm may inspect it, to be certain you have done nothing in your planning that would be against the Church. I have submitted the plans we have been following, and I have had my crews stipulate, to a Notary, that the plans have been accurately adhered to in our construction. It may be that the Holy Office will examine your villa closely, or their inspection may be cursory: I cannot tell which. But I advise you to be present while the men of the Secular Arm are making their observations, for they may have questions that only you may properly answer. If you are not present, the good Fathers may take that as an indication of deception—they have done so in the past.

As soon as it is permitted, my builders will resume their work. The carpenters involved in finishing the interior will be summoned as soon as the Holy Office authorizes the resumption of labor. The Arte already has your deposits in hand, and so there will be no delay on that account. I have also taken the liberty of arranging for plasterers, and will need thirty gold pieces from you before they set to work. All the records of your deposits to the various Artei have been reviewed by the Holy Office; so far there have been no questions about the sums required of you, but that could change. If it does, I will inform you of it. I am sending the official requests for deposits with this letter, for I do not wish to have copies on file with the Artei, or the Console, for all of our sakes.

It would be advisable to burn this once you have read it, for I do not want it to seem that I am telling you more than I should: perhaps I am, and if that is the case, you might be held accountable for my lapse in conduct. I hope this will not be the outcome, but I think you should be aware of the possibilities.

Again, I apologize for putting myself forward in this way and for having to bear witness in what might be a complaint against you. It is not my intention to do you any disservice, for you have done noth-

ing I am aware of to deserve suspicion or condemnation, and so I
have told the Holy Office.

Your wholly yours to command,
Bonaldo Fiumara
Masterbuilder

At Roma, on May 7th, 1690
By the hand of my cousin, Giovanni Brunelli, Notary

3

The hall was filled with the most elegant personages in Roma; two
Cardinals and three Bishops had made it a point to attend this first performance of Alessandro Scarlatti's new opera, for it was reckoned to be
the most exciting event of the spring. In the fourteen box seats, men
and women in their greatest finery looked out over those in the upholstered seats set up under the shining chandeliers where tall candles
shone, occasionally dropping wax on the audience beneath. Most of the
women wore masks, many of which were elaborate, painted and jeweled more than the faces beneath. The afternoon heat was fading, and
first breeze of evening made the hall almost pleasant; servants carried
wine to those in the audience who signaled for it—not for the decorous
Romans the antics of orange-girls that the English allowed—and provided fans for those who had failed to bring their own, or who used
this as subterfuge to pass covert messages to others in the crowd.

It was almost thirty minutes after the appointed hour to begin that
Maestro Scarlatti stepped onto the stage carrying a tall, thin cane
with a pearl-studded head; he waited while the buzz of conversation
faded as the audience turned their eyes upon him, whereupon he
made a flourishing leg to those who sat in anticipation. "Welcome,
one and all, to this first performance of *La Lyra di Nerone*; the text
of tonight's opera was written by Ferenc Ragoczy, Conte da San-
German, who will also play the clavichord." The title was a last-

minute decision, issued by Church censors, and one which Scarlatti
was still uneasy about. "The Vestal Virgin will be sung tonight by
Giorgianna Ferrugia, her maid will be sung by Renata Merlo. Sapienza will be sung by Annamaria Marenzio, Follia by Gaetano Strada.
Giove will be sung by Andrea Puntello, Nerone will be sung by Tancredi Guisa. Patrizio Gentile is the chorus director. The staging is by
Egidio Tedesco." He made a leg again, and signaled his musicians to
come into their narrow seating area immediately at the foot of the
raked stage; there were nineteen of them, a large ensemble for such
a performance. When they were all in place, Alessandro Scarlatti
made his way down the steps at the side of the stage and took his
place at the front of the musicians. He gave a signal, and Ferenc
Ragoczy sounded an A on the clavichord which the other musicians
took up for tuning.

Then Scarlatti tapped the floor with his cane and the heavy curtains billowed open to reveal Giorgianna Ferrugia in a grand modern
gown with a swath of silk draped over her shoulder to suggest the
garments of ancient Roma. She held up her arms in supplication and
began:

> *I, my soul given to Roma, fear for her*
> *Such things I have seen!*
> 　*Such things I have seen!*
> *Great and mighty Giove, spare Roma*
> *From the horrors of my dream!*
> 　*From the horrors of my dream!*

The innovative orchestration caught the interest of the audience
at once; a whispered obbligato of commentary provided a counterpoint to the unusual composition; this was not going to be an ordinary
premiere, and everyone now understood that, a comprehension that
leant its own excitement to the evening. The audience grew quiet as
Giorgianna launched into her first aria, a long petition to Giove to
guard Roma from the tragedies she had seen in visions. She was in
particularly good voice tonight, her famed warmth of sound aug-
mented by thrilling flexibility that made for bravura singing. At the
end of her first aria there were cries for an encore, so she sang the

last verse and refrain with more lavish fioriture than before, and gained excited applause; she stood for a short while acknowledging the ovation with small, gracious bows of her head. The adulation of the audience filled her with a gratification almost as intense as anything Ragoczy had experienced with her; he recognized this with a sad, wry smile to himself as he played the next measures.

O Vestal, O Virgin, I hear your plea

Andrea Puntello's deep bass was not fully warmed up, so his sound was a bit muffled, but that was not a disadvantage for the declamation he was about to deliver. The opera was properly under way at last. By the end of the first act, which concluded with a duet between the contralto Sapienza and the castrato mezzo-soprano Follia, the success of the opera was assured, if only for all the controversy it was bound to create.

Scarlatti removed his justaucorps as soon as he got backstage; the waistcoat and camisa revealed were both shining with sweat. He took off his neat, white wig and rubbed a cotton cloth over his head. He glanced around as Ragoczy stepped into his line of vision. "I always sweat like a pig, but look at you: not even so much as a damp upper lip. How do you do it?"

"Those of my blood rarely sweat," said Ragoczy, and did not add that they did not weep, either.

"How fortunate. I am going to have to change clothes, I fear, or drown myself in scent." He chuckled at his own recommendation. "If you will excuse me?" Without waiting for any response, he began to undress.

"I should have brought Rugerius with me; he would be useful. Yet I may be able to make myself useful." Ragoczy went to the small chest standing open and pulled out a camisa and waistcoat not unlike the ones Scarlatti had been wearing. "Here, Maestro. I will be valet for you."

Scarlatti was so shocked at this offer that he went quite still, his face set in hard lines. "No. No, Eccellenza. It isn't fitting." He took a step back.

"Do not be silly, Maestro," said Ragoczy. "We are not at Court, where such forms matter, and I certainly will not tell anyone that you permitted me to help you. We are backstage, where everything is pretense anyway; and I am a foreigner—who knows what strange things I might do?" He held out the camisa. "Give me the one you are wearing. I may not perform this duty well, but I have seen Rugerius manage enough times that I hope I can do him credit."

Baffled, Scarlatti accepted the camisa and dropped his soggy one on the floor. "You are too good, Conte."

Ragoczy shrugged. "When you have been a soldier in the field, as I have," he said levelly, "you become pragmatic about such things."

"Pragmatic," Scarlatti repeated as he took the waistcoat and shrugged into it. "Very well, in the spirit of pragmatism, I thank you for your courtesy." He began fastening buttons and adjusting neckbands.

"Just by way of curiosity, why is your valet not with you tonight?" Ragoczy asked as if he had no interest in the answer beyond the dictates of polite form. He bent to pick up the discarded camisa so that his face was hidden as Scarlatti answered.

"He sent word that he was unwell and feared that he might pass his infection to all those performing. He fears it may be the mal aria, although it is early in the year for it." Scarlatti peered into the small mirror that hung from a nail on the wall. "It will all be rumpled in the next hour and half, in any case," he said to his reflection.

"How unfortunate," said Ragoczy, who could not help but wonder if the valet had been entirely truthful. It was not a matter he wanted to bring up, so he strolled away to the makeshift dressing room where Giorgianna Ferrugia was adding rouge to her cheeks and mascara to her lashes. She was radiant, her face almost glowing beneath her heavy makeup. "You are divinity itself tonight, dolcina," he said softly.

She glanced at him and went back to her maquillage. "I always end up with runnels down my face." She took her powder puff and tried to blot up the tracks through her pale makeup. "I shouldn't be talking, not to you or anyone."

"Yes," said Ragoczy, knowing she was right. "Save your voice. There is a long way to go yet, especially if the audience continues to demand encores."

She nodded with an exaggerated sigh. "But it is flattering," she said sotto voce. "Ilirio is in the center box, as proud as any man could be, for tonight all his friends envy him."

"And deservedly so." He went to the rear of the backstage area, behind the backdrop with its fanciful depiction of Corinthian capitols and long colonnades that were meant to represent the Roman skyline at the time of Nero; this was much at odds with the city as he remembered it, sixteen hundred years ago, before Olivia came to his life, when he had been Ragoczy Sanct' Germain Franciscus.

There was a flurry of activity as half a dozen members of the chorus hurried by to get into their costumes for the scene in the second act where Roma burns and Nerone serenades the flames with an heroic account of the Trojan War; Patrizio Gentile trotted along beside them, shepherding them so that none would stray.

"I wish Maurizio were still with us," said Scarlatti, coming up to Ragoczy; he was buttoning the top buttons of his justaucorps and fussing with his neck-bands. "I could use him tonight. Aroldo is all very well in his way, but he lacks Maurizio's verve."

"True enough, but at least he plays what is on the page," said Ragoczy, referring to Maurizio's gift for improvisation.

"Yes, that he does," said Scarlatti. He drew his watch from his pocket. "Ten minutes more at least. I hate this waiting. Why should we give them so much time? All that happens is that half the orchestra and all the audience drinks too much wine." He replaced his watch. "It is going well, I think."

"So do I, although I am not in a good position to tell." Ragoczy allowed himself to give a bit of a smile; he recognized the nervousness underlying Scarlatti's complaints.

"They've stayed fairly quiet and they have demanded encores. That's encouraging." The composer fingered his tall cane. "If they remain excited for the second half, we may be sure of success."

"Then Santa Cecilia guard and aid us," said Ragoczy, crossing himself at this pious wish.

"She has done well by us, thus far," said Scarlatti, also crossing himself. "And on such a subject, too."

Ragoczy said nothing, then changed the subject. "When this is over, do you return to Napoli?"

"For a time, yes. I am summoned to the north, into Toscana, and

I will have to go there soon or lose any chance of acquiring a position there. I would like to have my situation more settled than it has been." His eyes were distant. "This has been too long an absence. I miss my family."

"Then why did you not bring them with you?" Ragoczy inquired. "When you realized you would be here for some time."

"I told you some time ago, Conte. There are too many dangers in Roma, so close to the Pope. I would prefer my wife and children not be exposed to what goes on here." He looked about as if wary of eavesdroppers; his manner became slightly furtive. "In that regard, I have been asked by the Holy Office to answer some questions about you. I must do it, little though I want to."

"Of course you must," said Ragoczy with a sinking heart but an unaffected tone. "Refusing to accommodate the good Fathers would benefit neither of us." He managed to preserve his self-possession but it was more of an effort than he had anticipated. "Did they tell you what they want to know?"

"No. Only that it concerns you." Scarlatti hitched up his shoulders. "I hope I can put to rest any misapprehensions they may have about you."

"So do I," said Ragoczy, his tone light but his dark eyes unreadable.

"It's just that the Cardinal's sister is missing, and because you sheltered her before, they suspect you may know where she is." He flexed his hands. "I can tell them that you provided her a kind of sanctuary, which should be sufficient. I am not worried that they might decide to demand more of me than what I know."

Aware that they might be overheard, Ragoczy said, "The Holy Office would not suborn any witness; that would contravene all their sacred duties and trust."

"Amen, and benedicamus Domino." Scarlatti pulled out his watch again. "Four more minutes."

"You will have a triumph tonight, Maestro," said Ragoczy, returning to safer matters.

"It is more La Ferrugia's triumph than mine, but, yes: this will be remembered for some time to come," said Scarlatti, beginning to look satisfied; he went on magnanimously, "The story you tell in the libretto has gained some of the approval that accounts for the favorable reception."

"Roma has always been ambivalent about Nerone," said Ragoczy as if that accounted for his verses. "Little as the Church may approve him, he has captured the imagination of the people of Roma: they are all fascinated by him." It had been true when the young Emperor was alive: handsome, charismatic, and spoiled, he had been loved by the citizens, mistrusted by the Legions, and loathed by the Senators; Ragoczy had been cautious with Nero, knowing how capricious he could be.

"Do you think the Church will approve your depiction in the libretto?" Scarlatti asked.

"The censors approved it," Ragoczy said, as if he had no concern about it. "Surely that is sufficient."

Scarlatti did not answer. He took hold of his cane and said, "It is time we resumed the opera. Come, Conte."

Ragoczy went with Scarlatti, motioning the other musicians to join them as they reached the small door that led to the foot of the stage. "May this act be as well-received as the first," he said to the composer as they prepared to step into public view once again.

"Yes. That would please me," said Scarlatti, some of his edginess returning.

The audience was not yet back in its seats; the promenade of fashion and fashionables was continuing even as the musicians took their places. The few servants who were still bringing wine to those who wished it, pointed out that the Maestro was ready. For several minutes no one paid any attention. Then, gradually, they all sat down again, not quite as attentive as before but willing to give the performance some attention.

Tancredi Guisa held center stage as the curtains parted. He wore a laurel wreath over his russet-colored wig, and carried a prop lyre which he pretended to pluck as he sang of his devotion to art and poetry. When he was finished he acknowledged the applause in good form before the chorus surged onto the stage to tell him of the Vestal's prophesy.

From his place at the clavichord, Ragoczy kept a covert watch on the audience, particularly the two Cardinals; he gauged their approval by their enthusiasm and was relieved that the Princes of the Church were enjoying themselves, for he knew their good report would be added to what the Holy Office was recording about him. As he played the continuo with the violas da gamba he made a mental note to be sure to speak to one of the Cardinals at the next Papal banquet, scheduled for San Onorato di Amiens' Day, in order to show that he was not avoiding high-ranking Churchmen.

The highlight of the second act was the burning of Roma and Nerone's long declamatory serenade to the fire. Tancredi Guisa poured his voice into the demanding aria, and followed up in the cabaletta with a series of spectacular variations that served as a challenge for Giorgianna Ferrugia when she came to perform the long thredony that ended the opera; she embellished the second and third variations far beyond anything they had rehearsed in a display of artistry that was thrilling to hear. When she was finished, the audience went wild, applauding her and begging for more.

By the time the evening was over, she had sung three encores of the thredony, and was panting from the effort her virtuosity had demanded of her. She stood in front of the curtain, curtsying deeply in appreciation for all the praise being showered upon her, her jewels glinting in the light of the candles in the chandeliers. Because she was married no one offered her flowers, for that would have insulted her and her husband, but the cries of approval that rang as loudly as any of the music served as bouquets better than posies might have done.

When the musicians were finally released to leave their seats, the crowd in the hall was thinning and some of the candles were guttering; wax splashed down from overhead, but no one paid any attention to it. Lackeys opened the tall windows overlooking the street, and those who remained in the hall suddenly realized how warm they had been.

"You did well tonight, Conte," said Scarlatti as he came up to Ragoczy backstage. "I did not know if the audience would confuse you."

Ragoczy gave a slight bow. "I have had some experience perform-ing in public," he said, thinking back to his time as troubador and his years of playing instruments in Spain, a thousand years ago.

"That served you well," Scarlatti approved. "I will not worry when we perform three nights hence." He was grinning. "Half of Roma will try to hear this work, I think."

"Which should please you," said Ragoczy.

"And you, as well. It is your libretto and you have been the patron of the work." He coughed diplomatically. "I feared for a time we would not have the opportunity to perform it at all, but, thankfully, I was wrong."

"Why would we not have done this opera?" Ragoczy asked, his voice sharpened more than he intended; he made himself pause and then went on. "I have gold enough to endure a year's delay."

"It might have been longer," said Scarlatti darkly, "had they elected another Pope. This Venezian is not one to behave as if the faithful should take no joy in this world, although there are Cardinals who have such convictions—although they may not apply them to themselves." He chuckled to show this was a joke. "Operas might have been found to be too frivolous and that would have meant this could not have been performed anywhere in the Papal States if the Pope had disallowed them. I would have had to leave, and promptly, as would many other musicians, in order to avoid any possibility of imprisonment."

On the far side of the backstage area, Giorgianna Ferrugia was preparing to depart, her husband hovering near her, glowing with pride. Half-a-dozen courtiers were with him, fawning on Giorgianna, complimenting her outrageously. She had a new bracelet of pearls and rubies on her left wrist; she made many gestures so that she could show them off without actually demanding that anyone admire them.

"Surely the most stringent Pope would not go so far," said Rago-czy, but with great reservations. "Nothing of that sort has happened since the Middle Ages."

"That does not mean it could not happen again." Scarlatti said. "As long as the Pope rules Roma and the Papal States, no one can think himself shielded from Papal decrees." He began to peel off his justaucorps. "The King of France has his Ministers to keep him in check; the Pope has the Curia, but the Curia is not like Ministers." He looked at Ragoczy. "You should not delude yourself, Signor' Conte: Roma is in the hands of the Pope and those who want to be Pope. France's Ministers cannot become King."

Ragoczy understood the warning he was being given, and he took it to heart. "I understand. I will reflect on what you say."

"Va bene," said Scarlatti, and dropped his justaucorps over the back of a chair while he gave his attention to the buttons of his waistcoat. "Our success is assured for the moment, and that is a good thing for all of us. It may not last, however."

"I will remember that, my friend." Ragoczy bowed slightly, then picked up the composer's justaucorps. "Where do you want this?"

"You aren't going to serve as my valet again?" He sounded genuinely alarmed. "Once was fine; I am grateful for your help. Twice, and it could be seen as more than it is."

"How do you mean?" Ragoczy had a fairly good notion that he grasped Scarlatti's intent, but he thought it best to ask.

"Any sign of favor to anyone of lesser rank can be seen as suspicious, Signor' Conte," said Scarlatti, using Ragoczy's title with heavy emphasis. "Of those who are well-known, much scandal is spoken: only a fool provides fuel for that fire."

Ragoczy put the justaucorps back on the chair. "Then I will do nothing to bring you into jeopardy." He could not suppress an ironic smile. "No doubt the good Fathers will ask you about such lapses on my part."

"Yes," said Scarlatti, sounding sad. "And more than they."

"You might tell them that in all the years I have fought to defend my native earth, I have come to think less of titles and more of allies than many who have not had to carry on this long battle. I do not think that a minor courtesy will upset the order of the world." That his first campaign had taken place more than three thousand five hundred years ago he did not mention, nor that he had continued to defend his corner of Transylvania from various invaders in the intervening centuries; his recent actions against the Turks were known in Roma and he depended upon them to maintain his reputation in such matters. He had a quick, hard recollection of the demands of fame, and knew that Scarlatti's warning was not unfounded; as much as he strove to maintain a good public reputation, for anonymity often led to suspicion, he was aware that fame could become a dangerous burden: that had happened often enough in the past.

"You have done much to oppose the Turks," Scarlatti said with apparent relief. "And with this Alessandro VIII, action against the Turks means more than it did with his predecessor." He managed a faint smile. "That will be a most useful reminder."

"Then use it as you see fit, Maestro," said Ragoczy, not quite making a leg. He glanced about at the diminishing confusion, and said, "Will you be bound for your lodgings, or are you going to dine and celebrate?"

Glad for this change of subject, Scarlatti replied, "I am a very tired man. Evenings such as this leave me exhausted. I will go home, have my landlord order up a tub of hot water, and I will soak in the bath for as long as the water is warm while I long for the embraces of my wife. Then I will have a meal—a small one; nothing more than pasta with onions and bacon and a spring soup—and a bottle of wine. I shall sleep until eleven in the morning, and take a meal with my friends at noon." He bowed slightly to Ragoczy. "I would ask you to join us, but it would only add to the—"

"—problems you face because of me," Ragoczy finished for him. "And I have chores to do between now and our next performance."

"You are a most gracious man, Eccellenza, and I thank you for it. Would that more patrons were so perceptive." He bowed more properly, looking a bit ridiculous in his open camisa.

"Perhaps I have a better appreciation of your circumstances than you think, Maestro." Ragoczy answered his bow with a profound leg. "Enjoy your meal. You have certainly more than earned it."

"And you, Signor' Conte? Where are you going now?" The question sprang from good manners rather than from any desire for information.

"I am planning to ride home," said Ragoczy. "I may have something to sustain me along the way, or I may not. I, too, will sleep well into the morning."

"I thank you, Signor' Conte. You made this evening possible. If no one else values that, I do." He cocked his head to the door through which all the performers left the building; Giorgianna had departed a few minutes ago and now only a handful of choristers remained there, waiting for carriages or sedan chairs to take them away from the hall through Roma's dangerous streets. A few of the stage-hands were still busy storing the flats and props in anticipation of the next performance, but otherwise the hall was nearly empty.

"Then, Maestro, I will accept your kind words and I will leave you. Until three days hence." He turned away from Scarlatti and made his way to the small cloakroom where he claimed his cloak and his sword before he went out of the building, going directly to the stables across the street where his grey gelding was stalled. He took his time tacking up the horse, for he wanted to inspect the breastplate and girth before buckling them onto the saddle. He checked the bridle and reins, satisfying himself that no mischief had been done. He secured his rolled cloak to the cantel with two narrow leather straps, for he had no need of it this night. Then he picked the gelding's hooves, and on the rear off-side hoof, he found what he was looking for: a nail had been driven in between the shoe and the wall of the hoof. In a short distance the gelding would have come up lame or cast the shoe. Ragoczy removed the nail with care and rubbed some turpentine salve into the hoof. He would not stop tonight to visit the young Widow Poggi in sleep; he might be followed and observed. His esurience would have to wait.

A drowsy lackey took Ragoczy's payment and mentioned that there would be an extra charge at the city's gates for leaving so late. Ragoczy asked nothing about anyone going into his horse's stall; he did not want to alert the culprit that he was aware of what had been attempted.

Ragoczy nodded his acknowledgment and started off toward the north-east. He rode slowly, not only to save his mount's hoof, but in order to determine who was following him: for someone must have intended to follow him when he left the stable or there would have been no attempt to disable his horse. After a short distance he was rewarded when four large men slipped out of the shadows and made a grab for his reins and at the same time struck out with a knobbed stick; the grey sat back on his haunches and whinnied in distress. Ragoczy brought the gelding under control, drew his sword, and prepared to fight off the men; his blade flashed in warning.

"Get him off the horse!" one of the men bellowed as he struggled to hang on to the reins he had seized.

Ragoczy signaled his horse to rear and turn slightly; the man holding the reins was thrown aside by the force of the movement, as Ragoczy had intended. Two of the man's comrades hesitated; Ragoczy swung at them with his sword, catching the nearer of the two in the upper arm.

The man swore and fell back, dropping the dagger he carried and bolting back down the side-street. A moment later one of his fellows followed him as Ragoczy's sword came perilously close to his ear.

Ragoczy swung his sword again as his horse came down onto all four feet once more, fretting as Ragoczy held him in check while he pinked one of the remaining men; he fought with the expertise and pragmatism of experience, and the attackers recognized this. As the third man ran off, Ragoczy steadied his mount. Then he turned on the man who had led the assault, deliberately setting his horse cantering at the man just as he tried to flee. "No. You will tell me who set you on this." Ragoczy reached out and grabbed the man's collar, tugging him off his feet. Although Ragoczy was smaller and lighter than the roughian he captured, he held the fellow easily, undeterred by the man's struggles and oaths. Forcing the miscreant to jog clumsily along in an awkward kind of dance, Ragoczy found a piazza with an old fountain a short distance ahead. Holding his captive as he dismounted, he confronted the man. "Who told you to waylay me?" he asked conversationally.

The man spat and swore. "You can't make me talk!"

"Can I not. Well, we can wait here until the Guardia comes, and you can explain yourself to them." Ragoczy kept his affable manner. "Or you can tell me and I will not force you to tell the Guardia anything."

"Whoreson turd!" the man shouted.

"If you raise your voice you will bring the Guardia all the sooner," Ragoczy reminded him. "But that is up to you." He pulled a length of leather from the cantel of his saddle and with a strength that astonished his captive, swung the big man around and pulled his wrists together at the small of his back, securing them with the length of leather. "Now, if you will sit on the edge of the fountain, we may continue."

"There is nothing to continue," said the man, but with less vehemence than before.

"Perhaps," said Ragoczy. "And yet, I cannot persuade myself that you came upon me by accident, for a number of other men on horseback must have passed you by. I am not so much better dressed, nor is my horse so showy that you would settle upon me by caprice."

"You!" The man spat again. "You have . . . You have much to answer for."

"No doubt I do, as do all men living," he responded in the same infuriating calm. "I wonder who put such a notion into your head."

"Everyone knows you have—" He stopped, having already said too much.

"Knows I have what?" Ragoczy asked gently. "What is it that everyone knows I have done."

The man stared at the wall on the far side of the piazza. "Everyone knows," he muttered, refusing to look at Ragoczy.

"Then there can be no harm in telling me, as it would seem I am the only person in Roma who does not know." Ragoczy regarded the man, and when he remained obstinately silent, Ragoczy said, "Let us try an easier question, one you have heard before: who set you upon me?"

"Someone I do not know," the man answered quickly, and with a touch of smugness that suggested that he would not readily change his story.

"Ah." Ragoczy strolled a short distance from the man. "Was the man Roman?"

The attacker barked a laugh and spat. "Not he."

Something in the man's demeanor caused Ragoczy to ask, "A foreigner, then: was he, perhaps, German?" He suggested, recalling the fury he had seen in Ahrent Rothofen's eyes when they had been in the Magistrates' Court. "Tall, lanky?"

The man's manner became evasive once again; he squinted, fidgeting with his bonds. "I will tell you nothing."

"It would be like him, to hire street toughs to do the work he is afraid to do," said Ragoczy, flicking a bit of invisible dust from his cuff. The more he considered this incident, the more likely it seemed that Rothofen was behind it; he looked around at the man he had caught. "I want you to carry a message to your sponsor, ragazzo," he said in an amiable tone.

Now the man was suspicious. "How do you mean?"

"I mean what I say," Ragoczy told him, his calmness concealing his growing sense of perturbation: was Rothofen truly so petty as this? "Tell him that if he continues to send men against me, I will have no choice but to settle the matter directly with him. If any trouble should befall any of my friends, I will make their cause my own."

"How am I to deliver this message?" The question was surly.

"I will release you, of course, and give you an Apostle to do this." The amount was more than the service warranted, and both men knew it.

"All right," said the man as Ragoczy came back to his side and untied the leather strap around his wrist. He rubbed his hands together. "What is to stop me from gutting you here and now?"

Ragoczy smiled in genuine amusement. "Do you think you could?" He took an Apostle from his purse and handed it to the man. "You and I have no quarrel, ragazzo. Do my bidding with my thanks."

The man took the coin and studied Ragoczy for a long, silent moment. "I will," he said at last. Then he hurried away as if he feared Ragoczy might change his mind or accuse him of stealing.

Watching the man depart, Ragoczy felt an overwhelming dismay: how had he overlooked Rothofen as an enemy? How could he have assumed that the man would cease to act against him simply because the suit was over? And how many of the previous attacks he had sustained had come at Rothofen's instigation? He considered capturing the hired roughian again, but thought better of it: the man would reveal nothing more useful than he already had. Castigating himself mentally for not suspecting Rothofen before, Ragoczy remounted his grey and with these unhappy questions for companions, went on toward the gate that would lead to the road back to the Villa Vecchia.

Text of a letter from the Captain of the *Sorella Agnesca* to Ferenc Ragoczy, Conte da San-Germain.

To the most distinguished Conte da San-Germain, patron of my voyages and owner of my ship, the greetings of Benedetto Pace, Captain.

Eccellenza, I have received your letter of last week, which came swiftly on your ship, Canzone di Sorrento, *and I will do all within my power to comply with your orders: one of my longboats will wait for a fishing boat at midnight just off the coast at Lago di Folgiano, on the Saturday two weeks hence. We are to signal with two lanthorns in the bow of our boat, and will see three lanthorns on the fishing boat. The Captain of the fishing boat will present your eclipse device as token of his purpose. Our departure from those waters is to pass the Isola di Ponza, where Papal ships do not patrol, and the Sicilian ships avoid. We are to take aboard two men and a woman and carry them as unknowns to England. We are not to call at Anzio or Genova, but go directly to France and then on to England.*

Your payment for this service is in my hands, and it is generous, as always. I am proud to perform this deed for you, and I swear no sailor on this ship will speak of it until we are in Protestant ports. Those of us who adhere to the teachings of Peter Waldo are always willing to do what we may to help those oppressed by the Pope and the Church, and have done so for centuries.

No one who has seen the prisons of the Holy Office can want to see anyone, no matter how heinous a criminal he might be, given into the care of those who maim and torture in the name of God. We will protect these unfortunates to the limits of our strength.

May we have fair winds and good seas to carry us to England.

Your most obedient,
Benedetto Pace
Captain, Sorella Agnesca

At Malta, by my own hand on the 20th of May, 1690

4

Putting his hand to his aching head, Ursellos glared at Ahrent Roth-ofen. "This had better be good news." He was in his dressing-gown and wigless, having been wakened at Rothofen's insistence less than twenty minutes earlier; his eyes were gummy and his mouth tasted of mold. He distantly remembered arriving home shortly before dawn, two plump prostitutes for his escort; they had been paid by his servants and sent away.

"It is nearly noon," said Rothofen urgently. "You must bestir your-self, man." He was dressed for riding. "I have only just learned of how they are planning to—Listen to me, you ungrateful sot!" he expostulated. "I know where your sister is, and your half-brother. But if we do not hurry, they will beyond your reach." He pounded on the dressing-table in a complete lapse in manners.

Ursellos glowered. "What are you talking about?" Had his head not been hurting so much that he felt rats were gnawing the insides of his skull, he would have demanded satisfaction of Rothofen, though he was in no condition to fight a duel.

"I have been trying to find your sister. You remember we agreed I would look for her? You *do* recollect that conversation, don't you?" There was so much sarcasm in his voice that Ursellos bridled at it.

"You forget yourself, Rothofen." He made himself sit up straight. "I recall you said you would undertake to search for her, and I did not forbid it." The memory was vague just now, but he was aware that he had made some agreement with Rothofen. "I gather you have had some success."

Rothofen made a leg. "I meant nothing to your discredit." Then he took a more determined tone. "But I did tell you I could find your sister, and you said you would pay me twenty gold Angels if I did." He hated to have to remind Ursellos of the payment, but he was so lacking in money that he felt he had no choice in the matter.

"You say you know where she is? Is that why you ordered me from my bed?" Ursellos was dubious, and therefore resentful. He signaled to his manservant. "Bring me chocolate and a biscuit, will you? and quickly!"

The interruption annoyed Rothofen, but he concealed his emotion. "I do not like to think that she may escape for lack of action."

"And is there any chance of that?" All Ursellos wanted to do was to lie in bed for another hour or so, drinking chocolate and letting his head improve. This call to action did not please him. "Or is this only a tale?"

"She will be gone by tomorrow night, and that is no tale. I found out from a gardener at Ettore Colonna's estate that Colonna has extended the use of his hunting-box outside Sezze to your sister and her companions. You may be sure it is true. Your sister has hidden there, the gardener swears to it: I paid him well for this information, and he rewarded my largesse with news that your sister is to go aboard ship tomorrow night, bound out of the Papal States." He spoke with heavy emphasis, weighting each word with all the force he could summon up. "If we do not act now, she will be gone."

Ursellos toyed with the sash of his dressing gown. "You believed a gardener? You say you paid him well. No doubt he is attempting to get more from you by this report." He pinched the bridge of his nose, but it offered little relief.

"He knows that I will beat him if he lies to me," Rothofen blustered. "I warned him that I would not tolerate being lied to."

"How very brave of you," said Ursellos with indifference worthy of a cat.

"I know he is honest," Rothofen protested. "He said that the ship they are to meet is owned by Ragoczy." He saw Ursellos' head come up. "I thought that might put another complexion on the matter." Doing his best not to gloat, he went on. "It would seem that Ragoczy has been party to this from the first. He may have been the one to ask Colonna to make the hunting-box available—I wouldn't put it past him."

"Nor I," Ursellos said sulkily. "Very well; go on."

Stirrings of pride made Rothofen sound boastful as he continued. "I have made inquiries: the hunting-box is to the south of the village of Sezze, about two leagues. There are two caretakers to act as guards, but nothing more formidable than that. Colonna made the place available to them because of Maurizio, the violinist. He is with your sister."

Ursellos cursed in Spanish and flung his patch-box across the room. "What a whore she is!" His headache was fueling his rage, making him ready to fight about anything. "And that upstart *musician!* To make himself her companion!"

Rothofen was secretly delighted to see that Ursellos was no longer disinterested in his information, but he managed not to smile: no saying what Ursellos would make of that. "He is impertinent, but so is Colonna, and Ragoczy."

"But at least they are men of position, and consequence. The musician is only that, hardly more than a craftsman or merchant." He snorted in disgust. "Whatever made my sister turn to such a creature as that?"

"Women are fickle, feckless creatures, ruled by whims," said Rothofen.

"Um." Ursellos saw his servant bringing him his chocolate. "Very good. Put it down and make ready to dress me for riding. It seems I will have to be on the road today, and possibly tomorrow. Put clothes and other necessities in my saddle-pack. Get to it, man!" This last was sharply condemning; he touched the cup containing the chocolate and had an instant of heat on his fingers. He would have scolded his servant but the man was already following his orders and preparing his clothes for overnight on the road. "And when that is done, tell the stable to saddle my roan—she has the most staying power." He glanced at Rothofen. "I suppose I should supply you a horse, too."

"If you want my company," said Rothofen, his face growing ruddy from acute embarrassment. "I came on a horse from a livery stable, and it has no bottom."

"I'll need a brace of pistols, and my sword, as well," Ursellos called out to his servant. "I may have to fight." The prospect was not unpleasant. "And the blood-bay for Rothofen. Do you have your own saddle, or is that rented, too?" As Rothofen turned a deep-plum color and muttered that he had his own saddle, thank you, Ursellos added,

"Put his saddle on the bay, and anything buckled or strapped to it."

The servant interrupted his packing to bow in obedience, then went on selecting clothes and readying them to go into the leather saddle-pack he had taken from the chest by the door.

"We will need to remount on the road," Rothofen reminded him.

"My brother had arrangements all over the Papal States. We will have no trouble in changing horses as we go at any of the posting inns." He drank his chocolate; it was too hot but for once this did not annoy him. He pushed himself to his feet, making an effort to shut out the pain that roared around his skull. "If I find that that trollop has done anything more to disgrace the family, I may help her to go, if only to save us from more shame. She has done more than enough already. If she had only cried out when our brother was attacked—" He stopped, turning to Rothofen abruptly. "You are to keep all of this to yourself, or you will answer for your folly."

"Do you think I am so foolish?" Rothofen demanded with all the heat such an insult demanded.

"Not foolish: venal," Ursellos said, untying the sash around his waist and letting the dressing gown drop to the floor; his night-rail was askew but he paid no attention to it. "You would bargain your mother's soul if you thought it would add to your position, or line your pockets. Do not pretend otherwise."

"If you have so poor an opinion of me, I wonder that you bother to employ me," said Rothofen, his attitude a huffy one.

"So do I, Ahrent; necessity makes for odd company," said Ursellos, wholly unaware that he had increased the insult he had given. "If you will wait downstairs, I will order the cook to prepare food for us to eat on the road; he will give it to you and you may carry it on your saddle." It was a gesture that turned Rothofen to his servant.

Not trusting himself to speak, Rothofen made a leg and stormed out of Ursellos' room, almost tripping on the stairs, he was so distracted by his fury. It had not abated when, a short while later, a lackey brought him a wicker box of provisions. Rothofen excused the lackey with a curt oath, and then weighed the basket, trying to think how best to attach it to his saddle. It was galling to have to be grateful for the loan of a horse; the thought of the injustice of his position made his stomach churn and his body tighten as if for a fight. To keep from becoming locked in a cycle of resentment, he considered the basket again, and how he was to carry it on the road. He had just made up his mind how to attach it to the cantel above his cloak when Ursellos appeared, fully dressed for riding, his wig perfectly in place, his face pale and his lips rouged, the ruffles at his wrist freshly laundered, his boots shining. Rothofen made a leg and said, "I have the food."

Ursellos shrugged. "And wine, I hope. I won't do this work while thirsty." He pointed to Rothofen's dusty justaucorps. "Is that all you have?"

Choosing to misunderstand the question, Rothofen said, "My cloak is buckled to my saddle."

"Is it?" With a chuckle Ursellos began to pull on his leather gauntlets. "It will do for where we are bound, I suppose."

Rothofen took umbrage at this deliberate slight. "You may say what you want, Signore: I will not attract notice on the road, you will be remembered."

Ursellos glowered at Rothofen. "Do you expect me to admire your discretion?" He clapped his gloved hands, and although the sound was muffled, it brought an immediate response. "A stirrup-cup for both of us as we depart. I should be back tomorrow or the night after. If anyone inquires about me, tell them I am gone to visit friends. I will want to know the names of all who ask."

The servant bowed and withdrew.

"Do you think you will have so many callers?" Rothofen knew he sounded snide and did not care.

With a reproachful glance, Ursellos said, "I think that Ragoczy may come, or Colonna." He made an obscene gesture. "Once they learn their plans have miscarried."

Rothofen swore. "Perdition to both of them."

"Amen," said Ursellos, crossing himself and starting along the gallery to the stairs. "Well? Are you coming? Your saddle—with your cloak—will be on one of my horses. You can take care of that." He pointed to the basket. "I don't want you trying to impress me. Do what I tell you and all will go well."

"That I will," said Rothofen, offended but determined not to let Ursellos embarrass him again. "She is your sister," he added, enjoying the wince he saw Ursellos make.

"And therefore my responsibility," he reminded Rothofen. "Now, where did you say we are bound?" He started down the marble stairs, his boots slapping smartly on the stone.

"A hunting-box near Sezze, one owned by Ettore Colonna." Rothofen was right behind Ursellos, pleased that the Spaniard was acting on his advice, no matter how churlishly he did it. In future, Ursellos might be willing to pay for more help, and Rothofen had a plan in mind as to the reward he would ask. They reached the loggia at the foot of the stairs, and found two grooms holding horses for them. Without delay, Rothofen went and pulled the straps holding his cloak tight and slipped them through the handles of the basket, securing the buckle to keep it pressed against the cantel. Then he vaulted into the saddle and took up the reins. He felt a stab of envy that Ursellos, debauched wastrel that he was, should have such covetable animals, when he could only afford to rent what the livery stable provided. Hating to admit his straitened circumstances, he said to the groom holding the bay, "Take the horse I rode back to the stable across from San Zaccharia in Porto; the owner is Milanese—you will know him by his accent." Reluctantly he handed over two silver Caesars, hating to give up even so small a sum as that. "Keep one for yourself." The other would have to be handed over with the horse.

The grooms stepped back, and a lackey went first to Ursellos, holding up a tray with two pewter mugs on it. Ursellos took one, drank down the contents, and slammed the mug back on the tray; the lackey then went to Rothofen, who did his best to consume the hot brandy-sherry-and-cream as quickly as Ursellos had. When he was done, he handed the mug to the lackey. He knew he ought to give the fellow at least a silver Duca for the service, but he had none to spare, so offered the disgusted lackey a salute instead as he legged the blood-bay around to follow after Ursellos through the bustle of the Roman streets.

Ursellos rode without regard for others in the way. Difficult as it was to move so quickly, he kept his roan at a trot. He overtook pedestrians and donkeys without apology. Once he knocked over a tradesman's cart, and once he nearly sent a toddler hurtling into the air when the child did not move out of the way; Rothofen was forced to ride in the same disdainful manner which he began to enjoy once he got over the recklessness of it.

At the city gates Ursellos drew in and informed the Guardia officer, "We are bound for Anzio," before he paid the necessary fee for them both to depart Roma.

"Do you think he will make a record of your lie?" Rothofen asked as they pressed their mounts through the throng at the gate.

"Probably not. We are too well-dressed to be questioned." He laughed, a nasty edge to his mirth. "Who knows, we could be procurers for one of the Cardinals, or for the Pope. No one in the Guardia wants to know such things."

Rothofen had been in Roma long enough to no longer find such a suggestion shocking. He grunted a response and steadied himself for their long ride; the blood-bay he rode was a strong animal with powerful shoulders and a magnificent neck, but the beast had a trot rough as a mountain stream-bed, and he knew the journey would leave him aching. He set his teeth and followed Ursellos along the road that had grown up beside the ancient Via Appia.

The afternoon was warm, and the breeze that came off the distant sea was slow enough to do little to cool the air. Soon the horses were sweating and blowing; for a league they slowed from a trot to a walk, Ursellos angry at even this minor delay. He swung around in his saddle and called back to Rothofen, "Do you know exactly where we are going?"

"Yes, I do," said Rothofen, although it was not entirely true; he had only the directions supplied by the gardener to go on. "Sezze is the village, and from the central crossroad we take the road to the west, and then follow the southward track." He was glad he sounded so confident, for he had no wish to have Ursellos question him.

"What about the hunting-box? How big is it?" Ursellos seemed more annoyed than he had been earlier. "Will we have to search it?"

"It is small. Two stories, one large room below, two bedrooms above, or so I have been told." He was glad he could be so specific, for he was not eager to have Ursellos take his dissatisfaction out on him.

They went on for a short distance in silence. "We will get fresh horses at Alcano Nuovo. The Shepherd's Pipe there has my brother's horses stalled. If we must, we can change again at Doganella. That's two leagues from Sezze, according to what I recall from traveling with my brother." Ursellos was beginning to look grim, his dissipated features showing a kind of sullen determination that Rothofen found unnerving. "I have never been to Sezze, but I know where it is."

"I have been there, once," Rothofen lied; he had been past the village but had not entered it. "It was some time ago."

"Do you think we can reach it before dark?" Ursellos was testing Rothofen; luckily the German recognized this.

"I doubt it. Even if we change horses, we will not be there before nightfall." He had calculated the distance and thought that they would arrive between ten o'clock and midnight. Not wanting to discourage Ursellos, he said, "We might be there by nine."

"I will order lanthorns for us at the Shepherd's Pipe. They will supply them." He turned around in the saddle and urged his horse back to a trot. "Don't lag behind, Rothofen!"

"I won't!" Rothofen shouted. He was starting to feel hungry, but doubted that Ursellos would allow them the chance to eat until they changed horses at Alcano Nuovo; that was at least two hours ahead— possibly three. Their whole ride would take more than six hours to accomplish, and seven was more likely. With half an hour to change horses, they would be at Sezze between nine and ten. He considered praying, asking God not to let the three escape, for fear of what Ursellos might do to him in revenge.

They passed three drovers herding cattle toward Roma which slowed them down once again. Ursellos did his best to get past the cattle as quickly as he could, but that proved to be difficult; the cattle were being kept close together and that did not make it easy to get through their numbers. A league farther on they had to pull to the side of the road as a carriage and outriders in Papal livery rattled by, bound north at a brisk trot; the six horses pulling the carriage were flecked with foam and the carriage was dusty.

"It must be urgent, to demand so rapid a pace," said Ursellos, mildly interested. "The horses will be blown before they reach the city if they are kept on that way."

"That may be," said Rothofen, not wanting to argue the point. "I trust they will change teams soon."

Ursellos started his horse moving again. "We will, soon. Alcano Nuovo isn't far ahead. We should be there in under an hour." He gave Rothofen no chance to speak; he nudged his roan to a trot.

Rothofen did his best to ignore the bone-jarring gait, posting grimly as a means of lessening the impact. He tried to admire the steady regularity of his mount's action, but he took little consolation in it. Please God, he thought as they rode on, an easier trot for the remount.

Alcano Nuovo was a village dominated by a small piazza and a church dedicated to Santa Barbara that was not much more than a century old. The Shepherd's Pipe was on the south side of the piazza, an establishment with some pretensions to graciousness; the stable attached to the inn had five noble devices blazoned on the doors, indicating the patronage of the families represented by the arms. Third among them was the crowned skull and the red cow on a green mountain of Calaveria y Vacamonte. An ostler lounged by the water-trough, his attention on a young woman crossing the piazza toward the church; he did not notice as Ursellos and Rothofen rode up.

"Ragazzo!" Ursellos shouted when nothing was done to make them welcome. "Remounts!"

The ostler glanced around, nettled by the interruption. "Who are you to demand that?"

Ursellos swung out of his saddle, and holding the reins of his exhausted roan, advanced on the ostler. "I am Calaveria y Vacamonte," he announced, pointing to his family's device. "You have my horses stabled here. I want two of them saddled and bridled and ready to ride in half an hour. I want these horses fed and watered and stabled until I return tomorrow." He poked the ostler in the chest. "Say it will be done."

"It will be done," the ostler declared, and caught the gold Apostle Ursellos tossed him negligently.

Ursellos held up his hand in warning. "When you choose the re-mounts, make them the most strengthy horses in the string."

"Of course, Eccellenza." He bowed, tugging his forelock. He had no notion if the young dandy deserved a title, but it seemed safest to give him one.

"What of the basket?" Rothofen asked as the ostler reached for the horses' reins. He got out of the saddle, preparing to loosen the straps holding the basket.

With a chuckle and a nod, Ursellos said, "We'll have it later. For now we can eat a real meal." He turned, leaving the ostler to his work as he led Rothofen into the inn, shouting to the landlord, "Wine and something to eat. Quickly!"

The landlord, a saturnine man with an obsequious manner, bowed deeply to show his compliance, his face revealing he did not regard Ursellos' presence as a blessing to his establishment. He clapped his hands and issued terse orders, then said, "The second private dining room is available, Signore."

"Is that the best you have?" Ursellos demanded, paying no attention to the pained expression on the landlord's face.

"Cardinal Pignatelli has commanded the use of the larger private dining room, Signore Calaveria y Vacamonte. I regret that I must honor his earlier claim." From the tone of his voice, he did not regret it in the least and did not care if Ursellos knew it.

"Cardinal Pignatelli?" Ursellos said, as if he could not place the powerful man. "Very well. For the memory of my brother, I will defer to Cardinal Pignatelli. But let him know that I did."

"The door on the right, Signore," said the landlord, pointing Ursellos in the direction. "You will have your food promptly."

"Very good," said Ursellos, motioning to Rothofen to come with him. The room was well-appointed but a bit stuffy, having been shut up for several days. The hearth was cold, but with so warm an after-noon, no fire was needed to make the two men comfortable. A table large enough to seat six stood in the middle of the room, with chairs drawn up to it. Shutters on the window turned the light to dusk. Ursellos flung the shutters open. "That's better. Sit down, Rothofen. You might as well be comfortable."

"If you do not mind, I will stand until our drink arrives," said Rothofen, grateful to be off the hard-trotting horse. He could feel the tension in his back that would tomorrow become a solid hurt.

"As you like," said Ursellos, and flung himself into the nearest chair. "My sister had better be where you say she is. I don't want to have come all this way for nothing."

"You have cautioned me on this point before." Rothofen sighed. "Why would I want to make such a ride with you if I doubted my information?"

"That is the only reason I have come with you on this mad venture, that I do not—not entirely," said Ursellos, looking up as a young man in cook's clothes came into the room. "What is it?"

"There is pork, capon, and lamb hot just now. Tell me which you want." He bowed as he finished speaking.

"A capon for me, and lamb for my companion. Bring plenty of bread, and any soup you have." Ursellos pointed at the young man. "And send in a bottle of good wine, a Lachrymi Christi nel Vesuvio."

The young cook bowed again and went out of the room.

"He will be back directly," said Ursellos, leaning back in his chair. "You make me nervous; sit down, Rothofen." Although he said it genially enough it was clearly an order.

"If you insist," said Rothofen, reluctantly lowering himself into a chair.

An employee of the inn brought a bottle of Lachrymi Christi and put it on the table. "I will open it if this is what you want."

"Go ahead," said Ursellos, watching avidly as the cork was drawn and a generous amount poured. He drank, and said, "You may leave it. See that our food is brought quickly." As soon as they were alone, he poured wine for Rothofen, saying as he did, "It's better than I thought it would be."

Rothofen took the glass and drank; the wine was good, which made him worry: Ursellos could be counted upon to drink a lot of it, and that could work against them. He was trying to think of some way to express his worry when the young cook returned bearing a tray with two platters, a basket of bread, and a tub of butter upon it. "Signore, keep in mind we have far to go."

"All the more reason to eat quickly," said Ursellos, shoving Rothofen's platter in his direction. He bowed his head for thanksgiving, then reached for the fork and knife the young cook had given him; he ate greedily, paying no attention to Rothofen.

Resigned, Rothofen consumed his lamb in silence; ordinarily he would have found it tasty with its garlic and rosemary flavors through the meat, but now, with so many apprehensions weighing on him, the food lacked savor. By the time he was finished his meal, Ursellos was on his second bottle of wine. "Signore, it is time we left."

"In a moment, Rothofen. I don't want this to go to waste," said Ursellos as he poured himself another glassful and drank half of it down. "The horses should be ready."

"That they should," said Rothofen, getting to his feet; he did not care how impolite this was, for he was determined to be away from the Shepherd's Pipe before Ursellos could drink himself into a stupor.

Ursellos tossed off the last of the wine, pulled four gold Apostles from his purse and flung them on the table, and strode for the door. "I am ready. Come, Rothofen."

Hurrying to keep up, Rothofen went out of the inn to find two horses waiting and ready; their saddles and possessions firmly in place. This time he was up on a dappled mare and Ursellos was given a chestnut with a fiery eye. The ostler gave each man a leg up and accepted a silver Duca from Ursellos before stepping back from them. As they set out, Rothofen decided to use the time to think, for he was determined not to let this chance pass him by. There had to be something he could do that would salvage everything for him, and he vowed to himself he would find it before they found Leocadia.

The road to Sezze branched off from the main way some four leagues below Alcano Nuovo. This was not the same fine old highroad that they had traveled on; this one was narrow and rutted, and forced them to drop back to a walk in order to keep the horses from stumbling on the rough surface. That meant it was dark when they finally entered Sezze, and were greeted by the barking of two dogs.

"Where is the road?" Ursellos asked; the euphoria the wine had provided had vanished about sunset and he was now in a sullen state of mind.

"There," said Rothofen, who had been shining his lanthorn about the darkness, looking for the signpost. "There. We are not far from them now."

"Very good," said Ursellos, dragging on the chestnut's head to send him down the country lane toward the hunting-box; they still moved at a walk, a pace that was wearing on Ursellos. "Why don't they keep their roads up?"

"I cannot say, Signore," Rothofen said, keeping his lanthorn moving so he could not miss the turn for the hunting-box. As it was, he almost missed it in the shrubbery that lined the road: that would have been unbearable, and he made sure that Ursellos saw the gate. "There. That is the way."

The approach was lightly graveled, allowing the horses to trot safely in spite of the moonless night, a development that mollified Ursellos enough for him to say, "This is better."

There was a light burning in the upper window of the hunting-box, and two mules waited below, boxes loaded on their pack-saddles. Someone was hauling a fifth box from the house as the two men drew rein.

"God and the Saints!" cried Jose Bruno, hearing the horses but unable to see them. "Is it time yet?"

"More than time, you ingrate!" shouted Ursellos as he vaulted out of his saddle.

"Ursellos!" Jose Bruno raised his voice, intending to give a warning, but his half-brother reached him and struck him a sharp blow to the head, sending him reeling.

Rothofen dismounted more carefully; he took the chestnut's reins and drew that horse and his own mount up to the rail where the mules waited, and he secured the horses before following Ursellos into the little house. He could hear Ursellos bellowing Leocadia's name and kicking what he hoped was furniture about.

"Run! *Run!*" The woman's voice was high and shrill, filled with fear and something else that Rothofen could not identify. "You can't save me. Go!"

Ursellos was pounding up the stairs, screaming imprecations and vowing murder; Rothofen stepped into the lower room only to find it a shambles, tables and chairs and benches all overturned and wax puddling under the overset candles.

There was another shout from upstairs, a scuffle, and another shriek. *"Go! Save yourself* It's me they want. Go. Go! *Go! For my sake!"*

A moment later a wild-eyed young man with kinky hair came rushing down the stairs, almost knocking Rothofen over as he swung into the room. "He's mad. He is going to kill her. He's mad," Maurizio said in an appalled voice; a welt as long as a finger and red with blood stood out on his cheek.

"Did he do that?" Rothofen asked, stepping back as he saw what he thought was a plank in the young man's hand.

"No, no. *She* did." Tears shone on his face. "She said she would kill me if I stayed." The despair in his voice was greater than any emotion Rothofen had ever heard. Maurizio pelted away, out the door and into the night before Rothofen realized that what the young man carried was not a weapon but a violin case.

Ursellos was cursing again, accompanying the sound of blows and the whimpers that became a wail. Hearing this, Rothofen could not summon up the courage to climb the stairs; he did not want to witness whatever Ursellos was doing to chastise his sister. Beyond the building he was vaguely aware of the sound of donkey's hooves and the snorting of the horses. He would have liked to flee with the young musician, but could not make himself do it. Very slowly he put his foot on the first tread of the steps, and began the hideous ascent to the floor above.

Leocadia was huddled on the floor in the larger of the two bedrooms, her arms over her head in protection. She was quite obviously pregnant, though she was gaunt from fasting. Her clothes were in disarray, and a knife lay near her on the floor. She was weeping and praying softly as her brother bent to strike her again; Rothofen saw his chance and determined to seize it, certain such an opportunity would never come again.

"NO!" Rothofen yelled, so loudly that he managed to stop Ursellos from hitting her. He knew he had found the thing he had sought. "No, Signore. No more." He was amazed to hear the authority in his words.

"Get out of here!" Ursellos commanded.

"No," said Rothofen, doing his best to sound determined. "I cannot let you harm my affianced wife."

"Your what?" Ursellos exclaimed, swinging round on him, his expression ugly.

Rothofen managed to stand his ground. "Look at her, Signore. She had better be *someone's* affianced wife or your family will be disgraced."

Ursellos laughed aloud. "Roma is full of bastards." He prepared to go on beating his sister. "What do you think Jose Bruno is?"

"I think your sister is not like you, and her disgrace would be felt in Catalonia more than it would in Roma." He pointed to Leocadia. "We can say it was arranged between us, when the marriage between her and the Archbishop's brother became uncertain. She has admitted she ran away because she disliked the marriage. When her brother, the Cardinal, was murdered, she sought to put the whole thing behind her. She fled in the company of her half-brother and a retainer. The child she carries we will say is mine. She and I will marry and there will be no disgrace."

"Have you lost your senses?" Ursellos demanded. "What nonsense are you talking?"

Rothofen put himself between Leocadia and her brother. "I am giving you a means to salvage something worthwhile from this coil. Think about it. If you let the story out that she and I have long loved each other—"

Leocadia's laughter screeched as she began to rock where she sat. "How could I?"

But Ursellos had gained enough control of his temper to realize that Rothofen was right. "It could work. There would still be an inquiry, because of the murder, but if you and she were married, it would be less severe." He kicked Leocadia. "It is more than you deserve, you whore."

"Martin's whore," she said, and laughed again.

"None of that," Ursellos told her. "Show your gratitude, woman. This man is going to keep you from infamy." He faced Rothofen. "Go on."

"We will have to arrange the wedding at once," said Rothofen, his thoughts racing, and began to explain the plan he had worked out as they rode toward Sezze, certain his future was going to be secure at last.

Text of a note from Padre Bartolomeo Battista Tredori to the Holy Office of the Faith in Roma.

Most worthy and reverend Fathers, in the Most Holy Name, in compliance with your expressed commands, I wish to inform you that I have heard the Confession of Leocadia Perpetua Dulce Calaveria y Vacamonte, and I report to you that she will marry on special license in four days.

The sins she entrusted to me for absolution she has said nothing of, and says instead that while she was away from her brother's palazzo, she was with her half-brother and a friend who sought to keep her away from the brother of Archbishop Walmund so that she would not be compelled to go through with a marriage that she found repellant, but which her brother, the late Cardinal, wanted, for the benefit of Holy Church and the Kingdom of Spain. She acknowledges that her flight was wrong, but after so gruesome a murder, she had not the heart to remain in Roma. I have told her she was wrong to do so, for her testimony as a witness to murder is much needed by you and the Guardia. She has accepted my rebuke with Christian meekness.

I will appear before you as soon as you summon me, but I must tell you that this is the sum I of what I can impart to you without breaking the Seal of Confession.

In all ways I am ever the most obedient servant of Holy Church,
In utter devotion,
I am
Padre Bartolomeo Battista Tredori
Santissima Redentore

At Roma, by my own hand, this 3rd day of June, 1690
Pax vobiscum

The new villa was nearly finished; the window-shutters had been put in place two days ago and the carved front doors were leaning beside the opening where they would be hung the following morning; the next week the glazers would arrive—after their Artei had received a deposit of forty gold Apostles. In the soft, pre-dawn light, the place looked as splendid as an ancient Emperor's tomb, or so Ragoczy thought as he stood in the courtyard and looked up at it, his eyes little hampered by the dark.

"You are not pleased with it, are you?" Rugerius said as he came up behind his employer.

"Not as much as I hoped I would be," said Ragoczy with a hint of a sigh. He was in a neat justaucorps of brocaded black silk with lace neck-bands and ruffles at his wrist; his eclipse signet was incised on his silver ring. He had no other ornamentation, but he was decorous enough to make it apparent he had just come from a grand occasion in Roma: he had attended an entertainment at Il Meglio earlier that night, but had spent two rapturous hours with Giorgianna Ferrugia before coming back to the Villa Vecchia. "I thought it would make me less lonely, to be in a home that Olivia had never known, but it only serves to make my solitude worse. It has made me more acutely aware of her absence than if I had done nothing." He sounded more puzzled than sad; he began to walk toward the broad, shallow, marble steps leading up to the gaping front door. "Perhaps if Giorgianna were willing to know me for what I am, and to accept my true nature, I would not be so desolate; but she is wise: there is danger for both of us once she understands what I am. But it still brings me . . . I don't know how to describe it: not pain, but not unpainful." He stood in the doorway, staring into the vacant interior. "Two months more and it will be complete."

"And you do not wish to live in it," Rugerius said quietly.

"No," Ragoczy admitted. "I never thought until now I would not feel some relief when I could leave the old building behind. But so it is; it will be a double burden."

"Will you stay to see it finished?" Rugerius asked.

"I do not know: no doubt it would be the wisest course." He stared up at the villa. "It seems a shame not to, but—" He shrugged. "It would insult Bonaldo Fiumara, and all the men of the Artei who have built this place to leave it." He came to the edge of the stairs; he was still framed by the doorway. "They have worked hard to make this a showpiece."

"As you asked them to do; and paid them well for their labors," Rugerius pointed out.

"Oh, yes," Ragoczy agreed ironically.

"It is what you wanted, is it not?" Rugerius said. "Half of Roma will want it when you finally show it to the world."

Ragoczy managed a smile. "That has been my intention," he allowed. "To have an establishment that would provide some compensation for my foreignness. And to indicate that I have wealth enough to protect myself from malice. That at least should make opening it rewarding in its way." He stepped off the top stair and came down to Rugerius. "You will say I am never satisfied, old friend."

"It is not your satisfaction that gives me concern, my master," Rugerius said. "You have done the thing you came here to accomplish: Niklos Aulirios has vindicated his claim to Olivia Clemens' estate. You have fulfilled any obligation you have here, and yet you remain. No one will accuse you of running away if you go now."

"There was the matter of the opera," said Ragoczy quietly, with a hint of amusement in his dark, enigmatic eyes.

"Which is finished, and has been acclaimed as a masterpiece," said Rugerius. "There is no more to be done with the opera that Maestro Scarlatti cannot do. You know that better than I do." He cocked his head. "Is it Leocadia? It is not as if you have been her lover. She has no claim upon you."

"No; she has not," Ragoczy said distantly. "Not as one of my blood, and not even so small a hold as Giorgianna can claim—certainly not since she had the great good fortune to marry Julius Rothofen." His sarcasm surprised even him; he took a long breath. "No wonder she longed to be a nun."

Rugerius looked surprised, his austere features revealing more than he knew. "Surely you did not want her for yourself?"

"By all the forgotten gods, no," said Ragoczy, his voice quiet but intent. "But she has needed an ally, and she has been thrown to the wolves."

"You offered her your protection, and she did not take it. Why do you continue to . . . to . . ." He could not find the words he sought.

"You wonder, after all the years I have spent in Church prisons? At least mine had walls and locks; hers is built in her soul." He shook his head. "Poor woman. Between the Cardinal and Ursellos, she has received only harm from her family."

"Which you cannot undo," Rugerius reminded him.

"True enough," said Ragoczy.

"She is more like Estasia than Xenya, or Acanna Tupac," Rugerius warned him. "For all that she has suffered, she is more like Estasia."

"And more like Cismenae than any of them; so I think, too—you need not worry yourself that I am deceived in her," said Ragoczy. He lowered his eyes and regarded a place on the ground about two paces ahead of him. "At least Maurizio got to the ship. He will be in England soon."

"Do you think he will be content to remain there?" Rugerius wondered. "He has an impulsive nature and the urge to be a hero."

Ragoczy gestured his agreement. "But he is not foolish. No one who has grown up an orphan as he has is willing to sacrifice success for so ephemeral a promise as Leocadia is to him, particularly now that she is a married woman. Let him have a taste of fame and fortune, and she will become a bittersweet myth in his past."

"Do you think he will have fame and fortune?" Rugerius was moving ahead of him now, making ready to open the door to the old villa.

"Oh, yes. His playing is excellent and he has just enough wildness about him to make him a sensation. He is foreign and therefore exotic, the more so for having an African father. Give him two or three years of performing and London will make him one of the Olympians." Ragoczy spoke wholly without cynicism. "Maurizio is exactly what the English like to embrace in foreign artists: he is talented, flamboyant, a fugitive from persecution; all in all, very un-English. When next we go to London, I expect we will find Maurizio steeped in royal favor and wallowing in luxury."

"You sound as if you are tired, my master," said Rugerius, a hint of a question in the end of the phrase.

"Yes, and world-weary. I have been thinking of Acanna Tupac and Doña Azul." He glanced up at the sky.

Rugerius held the door wide. "It will be light soon."

"And I need rest; yes, you are right." He smiled once at his manservant. "Can you tell me this place does not play upon you as well as it plays upon me?"

"It does," Rugerius said. "You brought me back to life here. Sixteen hundred years ago."

For a moment Ragoczy stood silent. "Do you ever regret that I did?"

"No," said Rugerius. "For all that we have endured over the centuries, I do not regret that you restored me to life. Occasionally I miss my family, but they were lost to me well before you found me." When Ragoczy gave no response, Rugerius pointed the way to his apartment. "Your bed is ready. I will waken you in three hours."

"That is good of you," said Ragoczy. "I must meet with Maestro Scarlatti this afternoon; he wishes to discuss certain matters with me regarding the opera. He has asked me to join him in Roma." He ambled down the hall, pausing before the library door. "The books will have to be crated soon. And all the other goods."

"It will be done," said Rugerius. "I have made arrangements for those tasks to be done."

"Reliable as ever," said Ragoczy in approval. "You are very good to me, and I know how fortunate I am, though I apologize if I have failed to show it these last few months."

They were nearing the door to his apartments. "I have no doubt of that, my master."

Ragoczy offered a slight bow. "Thank you."

"Get some rest," Rugerius recommended. "You are tired."

"And not even two hours in the lovely arms of La Ferrugia can change that," said Ragoczy, deep sadness under his frippery manner. He held up his hand to catch Rugerius' attention. "Perhaps I do not want to be run off again: perhaps this time I would prefer to choose for myself when and how I leave."

"Just so," said Rugerius as Ragoczy went through the door. Only when the door was closed did his faded-blue eyes fill with worry.

In his elegantly appointed sitting room, Ragoczy undressed quickly, hanging his clothes over the backs of chairs, and placed his jeweled rings in the small chest on the narrow table against the wall. That done, he opened the armoire and took out his sleep-wear; he pulled on a black silk dalmatica in the style of Imperial Roma. Then he went through to his bedroom, where his bed was made up on a chest filled with his native earth. He lay down upon it, pulling the light coverlet up to his shoulders and in a short while lapsed into that stupor that among vampires passed for sleep.

The sound of builders hard at work greeted him as he woke; Rugerius was nowhere in sight, so Ragoczy assumed some sudden noise had jarred him awake. He sat up, stretched, was remotely pleased that he was somewhat restored from his short sleep. He swung around and got off his bed, all the while listening intently to the shouts and scrapes and hammering and trundling that marked the labor on his new villa. Nothing suggested any reason he should have been so disturbed, and this troubled him. He straightened his bedding, then went into his sitting-room to dress, noticing that the day was hot and close, its heaviness promising a thunderstorm before sunset. The clothes he chose were grander than what he usually wore for a meeting with Scarlatti, but he had promised to visit with Giuseppe, Cardinal Trasilvi when he was done, and that made him decide upon formal elegance instead of more ordinary garments. His boots, tall and thick-soled, were glossy with polish. He dressed quickly, unperturbed by the heat, for weather—hot or cold—had little effect on him. He found the lack of mirrors no inconvenience: he had not seen his reflection in more than three and a half millennia; by now, its appearance would have been more disconcerting than useful.

A short while later Rugerius knocked on his door. "Bonaldo Fiumara is here, my master. He wishes to speak with you."

"Then, of course, he shall," said Ragoczy, taking a lace handkerchief and pushing it under the ruffles at his wrist so that the lace cascaded beneath his hand. He then secured his eclipse pectoral, placing the black sapphire in the middle of his chest. Satisfied, he left his chamber, strolling into the hall with an air every dandy in Roma would strive to emulate. "Where is Fiumara?"

"In the library. He is watching the books being taken from the shelves." Rugerius indicated the corridor. "What would you like me to bring to serve him?"

"Some wine and cheese should be sufficient," said Ragoczy, his face showing nothing more than mildly polite interest. "Thank you again, old friend."

Rugerius stepped aside and watched as Ragoczy went along toward the library, no indication of any apprehension in his demeanor.

Bonaldo Fiumara was staring at the books as Ragoczy let himself into the room; his smock was stained with sweat and the smell of him was a sharp presence in the room. "A most astonishing collection, Conte," he said, not turning to face his host for a short moment. When he did turn, he stared, and bowed.

"You need not bother with such courtesies," said Ragoczy. "I am dressed for Roma, not for this place." He paused. "What did you want to see me about?"

"It's about the room on the second floor—the one with the tall windows and the double doors?" He looked acutely uncomfortable. "A familiar from the Holy Office has requested more information on that room."

It was Ragoczy's alchemical laboratory, but Ragoczy knew it would not be wise to admit so much. "Surely the Holy Office knows I dabble in the sciences. That room is set aside for any work I may decide to do."

"That is what I told them, but I don't think he believed me," said Fiumara, looking quite miserable. "He insisted that you send them a statement of the use you intend. If you fail to do so, it would be the worse for all of us, for we have built your villa." He held on to the hem of his dusty smock. "I don't like to have to say any of this to you, but my Arte must accommodate the Church or lose the right to bargain for our wages."

"I do not blame you for anything the Church may do; I comprehend the way these matters are handled." He gave a short, aggravated sigh. "Very well. I will prepare a report to be submitted to them. You need not worry that you will be held accountable for what I have had you build for me."

"You are very good, Signor' Conte." He shifted on his feet, his expression more apologetic than ever. "The glazers will not be allowed to come until the room is given the approval of the Holy Office."

"Dear me," said Ragoczy in mock distress. "What motive do they assign me? What do they imagine I will do with such a room, with windows everywhere." He saw that his question was not amusing Fiumara, and he made a gesture to show he had intended no distress. "Forgive me: I am maladroit."

"Nothing of the sort, Conte, nothing of the sort," said Fiumara, too hurriedly.

Ragoczy shook his head. "You need not coddle me, Masterbuilder. I have given you dismay, for which I ask your pardon." He began to wonder what the familiar had said that was so troubling to Fiumara; it was useless to ask the man directly, for that would serve only to make him more upset. "Of late I have often thought," he said as if discussing a theory, "that Pascal was right when he said that men never do evil so wholly or gladly as when they act from religious belief." That he had come to a similar conclusion many centuries ago he did not mention.

Fiumara paled. "You must not say such things, Eccellenza. Truly, you must not."

"Which only serves to show that it is true," said Ragoczy, turning as Rugerius came into the library with a tray. "Something for you, Masterbuilder. I hope it will make your labors easier."

"You are always generous, Signor' Conte," said Fiumara, glad to have a chance to refresh himself and to turn their discussion to less dangerous subjects. He reached for the wedge of cheese and a slab of bread, and ate eagerly. "We will have a long nap after our mid-day meal," he said through the food.

Rugerius filled the goblet on the tray with wine and set it down for Fiumara. Then he put the tray on a crate and, bowing slightly, left the two men alone.

"A very good man, Rugerius," said Fiumara, putting down the bread and reaching for the wine. "I didn't take to him at first, but now I am convinced he is a most worthy fellow."

"As am I," said Ragoczy.

"Been with you a long time?" He drank and set down the goblet.

"Almost half my life," said Ragoczy. "I first met him here in Roma." That it was about the time that Vespasianus became Caesar he kept to himself.

"Long enough to know the value of the man, then," said Fiumara. He chewed the cheese, not able to talk, and glad of the respite. "The familiar—"

"I will deal with the familiar. As I am bound for Roma, I will prepare the material for the Holy Office and take it with me. If I give it to Cardinal Trasilvi, he will doubtless see it gets into the proper hands." He read relief in Fiumara's face. "You have nothing to worry about, Masterbuilder." He paused. "I trust your sister is well?"

"Clarice?" Fiumara was mildly surprised. "She is. How good of you to ask, Eccellenza."

"She did me good service while she was here," said Ragoczy, knowing it would please her brother to hear this, particularly since the Holy Office had been asking information of them.

"That she did," said Fiumara, actually smiling. "It's good of you to say so."

Ragoczy bowed slightly. Then he said, "I am dispatching the money to the Arte of the glazers today. They will be able to work next week."

"Very good," said Fiumara, a bit apprehensively. He did not want to doubt anything his patron said, but he was certain the Holy Office would have something to say about the glazers.

"You have done well by me, Fiumara. You will have no reason to fear me." He inclined his head again and turned toward the door. "I am going to prepare the report for the familiar. Then I am riding to Roma. You may tell your men that I have taken the action needed. That should make the day easier for all of you." He paused in the doorway. "Enjoy the wine, Masterbuilder. I will have more of it delivered to your crew at day's end."

"After such heat, we will be glad of it." Fiumara was looking more at ease now.

"Very good," said Ragoczy, and left the library to return to his own apartments. In his sitting room, he went to the small secretary that stood at the far side of the room, took out a sheet of vellum, a goosequill, and the standish, then began to write an account of his intended use of the room in question. He spoke of his known interest in science, and his intentions to grow medicinal plants, and to make observations of the heavens, all of which was true enough: he did not, however, mention any of the alchemical equipment he would install there, for the Church disapproved of alchemy; instead he told the Holy Office that he might do chemical experiments, which, again, in a limited sense, was the truth. When he was done he signed the report in his neat, small hand, set his eclipse device below it in hot wax, then folded and sealed the vellum. As soon as the wax was cool, he slipped the report into the pocket inside the front of his justaucorps, took up his hat and strode out of his room.

Matyas was waiting in the stable, his old, seamed face flushed from the heat. "Devilish time to be on the road," he said as he saw Ragoczy approaching him.

"I hope that is what all the robbers think," said Ragoczy. "Don't worry. I will not press the horse, not in this weather."

"There will be a proper storm," Matyas remarked as he went to the stall of the dappled seven-year-old mare Ragoczy would ride. "She's going to be fresh. I could run her a bit before saddling her up, to get the frisks out of her."

"Never mind," said Ragoczy. "She will need it for the ride. I can handle her."

"I don't doubt that, Conte," said Matyas. "But it would be an easier ride if you'd let me run her a little."

"It would not be easy if she became exhausted," said Ragoczy, indicating his best saddle. "Use the lightest saddle-pad you have. I do not want her sweating after half a league at a walk."

"As you wish," said Matyas. "I will be here when you return tonight, in case she needs walking." He went into the stall to brush and saddle the mare, leaving Ragoczy to amble out into the stableyard, where he stared up into the clouds overhead. Ordinarily he would have saddled his horse himself, but Matyas took umbrage at what he saw as the usurpation of his duties and had insisted that he be given the opportunity to do the work he was paid for. When Matyas led the grey out a short while later, he was scowling. "She'll need new shoes in a week."

"I'll keep that in mind," said Ragoczy, mounting the mare and taking her reins. "You're right. She's fretful."

"She's fresh and the weather makes her spooky," said Matyas. "Be careful with her as you go."

"That I will," said Ragoczy, and rode away from Villa Vecchia toward the road leading to Roma. Centuries ago, before the barbarians sacked the city, there had been another road, a straighter one that cut the distance he traveled in half; but a thousand years ago such roads, with the exception of the old military roads, were torn up, and a long, outer ring-road built around the city, to make the approach to it more easily controlled. On days like this he missed that old road. The mare was sweating, but more from the heat than the activity; Ragoczy could tell that she would tire quickly. He kept his eyes on the turns ahead, his ears alert to any sound that might indicate danger; today the worst that happened was that the mare was startled when a large hawk suddenly swooped from the top branches of a trees, passing not much more than an arm's-length overhead. The mare snorted and curvetted until Ragoczy pressed insistent knees into her, holding her steady and putting her at ease once again.

Scarlatti was waiting for him as he drew rein in front of the very respectable rooming-house where he had taken lodging some time ago. The composer was well-dressed, aware that he was known throughout Roma and therefore had to make a creditable appearance at all times. He made a leg as Ragoczy dismounted. "There is a very good inn a short distance from here. Fiorello will take good care of your horse." He indicated the young servant standing near the end of the building. "He tends to all the mounts of those living here." With a snap of his fingers, he called the young man over. "This man is my guest. His horse needs a stall for a few hours."

Ragoczy handed him a silver Leo and gave the lad the reins. "She should be given water when she is cool, and an armful of hay. Loosen her girth, but do not unsaddle her, or remove her bridle."

"Sta bene," said Fiorello, doing as he was told.

Scarlatti motioned to Ragoczy. "Come with me, Signor' Conte. I am glad of your company."

The streets were crowded but almost everyone moved lethargically; there was a warning rumble of thunder in the distance, but no sign of rain. Scarlatti moved more quickly than the rest of those on the street. He looked about with the kind of curiosity that revealed he was afraid they were being watched. As they reached the inn, the La Piuma Nera, Scarlatti said, "I have already reserved one of the private dining rooms. The staff will not disturb us there."

"Do you think such precautions are necessary?" Ragoczy asked, although he would have done the same himself in Scarlatti's position.

"I think they are sensible," said Scarlatti as they went into the small reception area between the taproom and the private dining rooms. "You would think the same yourself if you thought about it for any time."

"No doubt you are right," said Ragoczy, following Scarlatti down the narrow corridor and into a good-sized chamber with windows propped open. Two lavish sconces of candles framed a mirror of Venezian glass, giving the room a brilliant glow; Ragoczy took care to keep away from the line of sight for the mirror. "This is a handsome place."

"Yes. So I thought. And one where we may be private." Scarlatti took his seat at the foot of the table, reserving the head for Ragoczy. "The servants know how to keep their mouths shut. It's one of the many things I approve of here."

"And what is it you do not want them to overhear?" Ragoczy asked in his mildest tone.

Scarlatti paused. "I want you to know that I am leaving for Toscana in two days. I know I said I would delay a bit longer, but I find that I cannot. So this will have to serve as our farewell." He looked embarrassed to say this much. "With Cicogna and Cervetti asked to give their testimonies to the Holy Office, I do not think I can postpone my departure without—"

"—without putting yourself at risk. So you have indicated before, and I cannot dispute your decision. Yes, it is apparent to me, as well, that you would be wisest to put some distance between you and Roma just now." Ragoczy did his best to smile. "Were I in your situation, I would probably do the same thing."

"My wife and children will join me in a few months' time," Scarlatti went on as if afraid that if he fell silent, he would not be able to speak again. "You see, Conte, those of us who survive on the patronage of the great cannot have the Holy Office poking about our work, or we may find ourselves unable to secure a living anywhere in Catholic lands. You must know this, after the help you gave to Maurizio. Were I a young man like him, it would not matter so much. But I have my family to consider."

"And your career, which you do not want to compromise," said Ragoczy. "I understand completely." He looked up as someone scratched on the door.

"Enter," said Scarlatti, and smiled at the cook who appeared. "Te prego, Eccellenza, tell this good man what will please you."

"I will dine later, thank you; but have what you would like," Ragoczy said. He tossed a gold Angel to the cook so the man would not be offended by his refusal of food.

Scarlatti shrugged. "Then I will have the Spanish soup, cold; the fish in olive oil and garlic; the veal stuffed with mushrooms in cream-and-wine; the ripe cheese with red wine and walnuts." He glanced at Ragoczy. "You won't change your mind? The kitchen here is superb."

"I do not doubt you," said Ragoczy. "But it is best if I decline."

"As you always do," said Scarlatti heavily. "Very well. You will have to endure the torture of watching me consume an excellent meal."

"I am resigned to it," said Ragoczy with a touch of amusement; he saw that Scarlatti was uncomfortable, so he added, "And I hope I will not interfere with your enjoyment." He waited, knowing there was more Scarlatti wanted to tell him; he knew it was pointless to hurry the man.

"Let me tell you how grateful I am to you for your efforts on behalf of our violinist," he went on. "I know I have expressed my feelings before, but I sense them more keenly now that I, too, am leaving."

"It was a privilege to help him," said Ragoczy, still curious what Scarlatti might say.

"The familiars of the Holy Office have decided that it was the violinist who murdered the Cardinal. They have come to the conclusion that the Cardinal disapproved of the attention the violinist was paying to his sister, and when the Cardinal ordered him to go, the violinist killed him in a rage. They have been demanding that those of us who know him confirm what they have decided is the truth." He had lowered his voice and spoke all in a rush. "That is what they believe."

"As they have every right to do," said Ragoczy, loudly enough to be overheard by whomever was listening.

"But that puts a double burden upon you, Eccellenza, and upon me," said Scarlatti apologetically. "I would not have wished this predicament upon anyone, but it is apparent that your role in his escape is not unknown."

"How do you hear these things?" Ragoczy marveled.

"People talk." Scarlatti cleared his throat. "They do not pay attention to musicians; they speak in front of us with never a thought that we might listen, though they would not do so before their servants." He looked about uneasily. "So. I happened to overhear two Franciscans talking at the gala for which I performed two nights since. They say there is some mention of your kinsman in the New World in their records which they would supply to the Holy Office. No doubt Ettore Colonna can confirm what I say; he hears everything."

This last brought Ragoczy fully alert although there was no change in his comportment. "Franciscans, you say?"

"Yes," said Scarlatti. "At least it isn't Dominicans. Or Jesuits." He was doing his best to cheer his foreign guest. He looked up uneasily as thunder blundered through the lowering sky.

"Or Passionists. Small comfort," said Ragoczy, then did his best to look unconcerned. "You are very good to tell me these things, Maestro. I thank you for it." The memory of Church prisons, only a few decades behind him, came back to him full force; he made himself show nothing of this outwardly.

"It was what any man in my position would do; I am sorry that I will not be able to remain here to help you, but you understand why I am leaving," said Scarlatti, and called out as there was a scratch at the door, "Enter."

The cook and one assistant came in with the soup, bread, and wine, all of which were presented with a flourish. "The fish will be brought when you call for it," he told Scarlatti, bowing deeply to the composer while completely ignoring Ragoczy.

"Thank you, thank you," said Scarlatti, grateful for more than the meal. "The aroma is heavenly." He took up his spoon to show his enthusiasm as the cook and his assistant withdrew. But once the door was closed, he put the utensil down again. "I seem," he said to Ragoczy as if confessing to a sin, "to have lost my appetite."

Text of a letter from Niklos Aulirios to Ferenc Ragoczy, written in Byzantine Greek and carried by private messenger.

To Sanct' Germain, my hurried greetings.

The Holy Office has summoned my houseman Cervetti to testify, and has said that others of my servants may be called as well. From what I can determine, this is part of the investigation into the death of Cardinal Calaveria y Vacamonte as well as the flight of Maurizio Reietto, events that are thought now to be connected. The inquiry has also extended itself to you, as you are aware, for it is now understood that the young violinist left on one of your ships. The Holy Office would seem to be looking for a conspiracy, or at least a larger plot than what they originally thought was the case, and are trying to discover anyone who might be implicated in the Cardinal's death. This is a most ominous sign, or so it appears to me. I must urge you to consider leaving, for your own sake, if for no other.

I do not say this out of ingratitude: were it not for you, my own situation would have been extremely difficult. You have done all that could reasonably be asked of you—far more, if the truth were told. I never intended to put you in danger, but it would seem that I have, and for this I most earnestly beg your pardon. Had I understood what was involved in this ordeal, I might have tried to find another way to protect my inheritance, but I confess I cannot imagine what that would be.

No doubt I will be asked to reveal what I know of the matter of the Cardinal's death and Maurizio's escape, and if the Holy Office should seek me out, I will not attempt to deceive them: ghoul I may be, but that does not make me immune to torture. As soon as the most pressing part of the inquiry is over, I shall find my way to France, to Olivia's horse-farm there. King Louis will provide me some measure of protection against the Church, and that is what I will be glad to have.

Olivia would not ask either of us to remain here in danger to no purpose. She herself often left Roma precipitously when trouble loomed. I know you do not want to increase the burden you carry, nor do I wish to throw more suspicion on you, but as I am bound to France, I am convinced you would be well-advised to develop a plausible reason to leave Roma as soon as may be. The Pope will not object if you express a desire to return to your homeland to fight the Ottomites: as a Venezian, he is looking for leaders to hold off the Turks, and you have already proven yourself a worthy ally. If you appealed to him as a protector of the Carpathians, he would give consideration to removing any barriers that might hinder your departure.

You have been all that is kind, all that is gracious in circumstances neither of us anticipated when I first asked you to come to Roma. I am in your debt. Yet I would be worse than craven if I did not now do my utmost to persuade you to leave. I cannot say enough to impress upon you the seriousness of the danger which is increasing around us steadily. Follow my example, and be gone from here before July is over, I beseech you. Once Leocadia's child is born, I do not think you will have an opportunity to go unhindered, for it is said that when she is delivered, she will be examined again by the Holy Office, regarding the murder of the Cardinal. From what Cicogna and Cervetti have said, the good Fathers are hoping to place the blame of this on you as much as on Maurizio.

Heed my warning, for Olivia's memory.

Your most indebted, in haste

Niklos Aulirios

By my own hand at Senza Pari, on the 19th day of July, 1690

6

Still pale with rage and terror, Giorgianna Ferrugia looked directly at Ferenc Ragoczy. "They kept saying I should tell them the truth, over and over and over," she said, her voice shaking. "I had no idea which truth they meant, and they would not tell me. They were so cold, so unfeeling."

The small palazzo her husband had engaged for the run of the opera was nearly empty: Ilirio himself and their twin sons had left nine days earlier to join his cousins for the summer in the north at Lago di Como; only a small staff remained to look after Giorgianna, and to pack up the household.

"Did they hurt you?" Ragoczy was very still, and his words were filled with compassion, but there was something implacable in his enigmatic gaze.

"No. No. They did nothing, and said nothing to threaten me." She shook her head. "But they had these . . . these *things* on a table before me, and I knew they were used to do terrible—" She began to weep, shivering. "They were smooth, as if they were carved statues and I nothing more than . . . than . . ." Her afternoon gown of green-and-cream-striped taffeta was the very height of fashion and her hair was dressed in great style, but she looked as desolate as the poorest widow in Roma. "I am certain if I were not a Marchesa and well-known, it would have been otherwise."

Ragoczy went to her side at once, taking her in his arms while she cried out her fury; he said nothing more than soft, loving words to give her comfort until she sniffed, quivered, and stopped. "They should never have done this to you, dolcina."

"No. They should not." She fixed her attention on the far wall. "I was so *ashamed*. And I don't know why."

"Nor do I. If anyone should feel shame, it is the men of the Holy Office who have used you so disgracefully." Some of his anger was in his voice, and he felt her wince. "It is their disgrace, Giorgianna, not yours. They are the ones who have dishonored themselves. You have done nothing to deserve such treatment; you have never." Not that any zealot was ever stopped by such considerations, he added to himself.

Her fingers pressed against his lips. "You mustn't say such things. It isn't safe."

"I say only what is true and just," he told her, aware that her caution was well-founded.

"But if they call me again, I must report your words," she said in a small voice. "I cannot refuse, for the sake of my children."

Ragoczy bowed his head. "I have put you in danger again. I apologize, dolcina, from the depths of my soul."

"You don't have to. Just don't say anything more. It is best if I am ignorant." She dabbed at her eyes with the trailing lace at her sleeve. "It was *humiliating*, to be treated so." She was trembling again. "I . . . I never thought a priest could be so cold."

"Those men are not priests, no matter what they think, or what vows they have taken," Ragoczy said softly. "They are only masquerading as priests." He smoothed her hair back from her face. "The most reprehensible thing is, they do not know it."

Her smile was brief and tight. "I hated them. May God have mercy on me, I hated them."

"So must God, if He is what the Church claims He is," Ragoczy told her as he held her face in his hands.

"Do you think so?" Her eyes brimmed again and her attempt at another smile was so forlorn that she gave it up at once.

"If you believe that Christ is love, how could the Holy Office serve His purpose? Those who claim sanctity in suffering when it is they who cause it—" He saw the flicker of panic in her eyes. "Very well. No more of this." He took her hand and brought it to his lips. "This time is too precious to fill it with dread."

"Thank you," she whispered, and leaned her head on his shoulder. "I am glad you are still here. I thought you and I would never be private together again, but I was wrong. This is something I have longed to have, but did not hope to enjoy." Her wonderful voice was seductive now. "With Ilirio away, I would be alone if you were not here. Maestro Scarlatti left two days ago and now my only friend is you."

"I have not been the friend I should be, if you are in such travail," he said as he drew her closer to him in response to the need he felt within her. He was strangely glad to be with her, and to have this last, unexpected chance to know her love.

"You are always so kind to me, Conte," she murmured as she clung to him. "You have never been cruel."

He kissed the curve of her neck, the froth of corsage lace against his cheek, and the emerald-and-diamond bauble of her earring. "No man should ever be unkind to you, Giorgianna."

Her sigh was deep and heart-felt. "If only that were true," she said, shifting in the curve of his arms so that she could kiss his mouth more easily. The kiss lasted a long time, going from consoling to something more urgent, more carnal. As she broke away from him, she stared into his dark, compelling eyes. "One final time, Conte. I do not want to part without loving you one last time."

"Nor I." He answered her kiss with his own; one that summoned up the passion of her music and the desolation of her heart. With his arms around her, slowly he unfastened her lacings and slowly he slid the shiny taffeta off her soft, rounded shoulders; he held the fabric in one hand as he caressed her neck and back with the other as she sighed in anticipation. Her stiff corset held her opulent body rigidly, but he released the laces on that, too, all the while continuing their evolving kisses. Only when she was naked to the waist did he step back. "I will miss you, Giorgianna."

"You will miss my body, you mean?" She was trying to coquette now, but sadness took all the mirth from her.

"Yes, for it is part of you. I will miss your laughter and your singing and your art. I will miss the smell of your perfume and the touch of your hand." He let her clothes fall over a low stool. "I will miss the silences we have had."

"Oh, Conte," she whispered. "How good you are. You are never clumsy. You always know what I seek." Her hands came to rest on his shoulders. "There is one thing I would want from you, one thing I have not had."

Ragoczy shook his head. "As much as I may do, I have done already."

"Not that. I have a husband for that," she said, almost playfully. "You have not undressed for me, though. Before you go, I would like to see you naked, just once. Please. I want to have that for a memory."

He did not respond at once. "I have many scars, dolcina. I fear they would distress you."

"Scars?" She was perplexed. "Are they so horrible?"

"Well, they are very large, very wide," he said, holding her eyes with his own. "You might be repelled by them."

Her laughter was a bit too bright, but she did not stop. "What man reaches twenty without a scar or two." She touched his shoulder. "You see my flesh. This one time let me see yours." Her plea seemed to have been set to music for it worked upon him as if it were more than words.

He shrugged a little as he considered her request. "Why not, if it would please you?" His expression was affable; concern lurked in his eyes, so he looked away from her in order to spare her any distress. "But I must warn you that they are severe." He loosened his neckbands and began to unfasten the frogs of his justaucorps; she batted his hands away.

"No. Let me. I have wanted to do this for . . . for ages." She took over his task, working the frogs from their fastenings. When she had opened the justaucorps, she started on the small ruby studs closing his waistcoat. These were a bit harder-going, and it took her a little longer to undo them all. Then she was down to the camisa. "No sign of sweat, and on such a hot day."

"I regret, dolcina," he said as she took hold of the ties holding his camisa closed, "that those of my blood do not sweat—or weep." He stood very still as she tugged his camisa open and began to slide it down his arms. Then she loosened his small-clothes, exposing the whole of his torso.

"Oh," she exclaimed in a small voice as she saw the wide swath of white tissue stretching from the base of his breastbone to the bottom of his pelvis. She crossed herself. "God and San Egidio!"

"I said they were bad," he reminded her as gently as he could. "If you find them too repulsive—"

"Yes," she said distantly. "But I had no idea . . . These are . . . they are . . ."

Ragoczy met her gaze. "They are from old wounds—very old." They were the last scars his body had acquired, from his execution by disemboweling.

"But, Dio mio, Conte . . ." She struggled to find words to express what she saw. "No wonder you do not often go naked."

He saw the distress she felt; he pulled up his breeches and closed his camisa. "There. You need not look at them again."

"No," she said, pulling his hands away and then reaching to the small of her back to unfasten her skirts and petticoats. "No, I want to touch you, all of you, and your scars." She gave a sudden giggle. "No *wonder* you cannot do the act of men."

Although the scars had less to do with it than his undead nature, he echoed, "No wonder."

"How long have you—" She stopped herself. "Forgive me, Conte. I should not ask."

"A very, very long time. I was . . . quite young when it happened." He said it calmly, no lingering trace of dismay, and this seemed to reassure her.

"Oh." She stared again. "They look almost . . . fatal." Her fascination was intense. "How could you live through such wounds?"

He was tempted to tell her that he did not survive them, but that would impose knowledge on her she had sought to avoid, so all he said was to repeat, "It was a very, very long time ago."

She looked at his face once more, then flung herself into his embrace. "Appalling," she exclaimed. "You have endured so much, Conte."

He held her as if sheltering her from a storm. "Everyone has much to endure," he whispered as he began to kiss her again.

"Oh yes, oh yes," she answered. "Everyone." She knelt down before him and began to stroke his scars, her face rapt. Occasionally she touched his penis, and once she licked it, watching to see if there was any response in his flesh; she circled his flaccid organ with her hand, squeezing as if to force it to stiffen, and when this did not happen she resumed her attentions to his scars, although she continued to glance from time to time to discover if he was reciprocating her excitement with his own. She rubbed the head of his penis against her breasts, and fondled him with a determination that puzzled him. When she made a gesture of frustration, he touched her hair.

"Giorgianna," he said tenderly, "dolcina, I have told you that I cannot take pleasure in that way; believe this. It is I who should be giving pleasure to you."

She stared up at him, her eyes dazed. "But you have given me so much. I thought that I should do as much for you."

He lifted her to her feet. "Dolcina, I have pleasure in your pleasure. As you are fulfilled, so am I." He took her face in his hands, looking deeply into her eyes; there was excitement there, and something else: regret? grief? chagrin?—he could not tell. "If you would let me love you, I will be amply rewarded."

There was the sound of a slamming door a room or two away. Both of them looked up, startled out of their splendid privacy.

"It's the servants. Packing." She laughed a little breathlessly. "How good you are," she said. "If it is what you want, then love me. Love me."

He sensed her desperation as he kissed her eyes, her cheeks, her mouth, her throat, her bosom; her response was rapid, febrile. As he bent to take her nipple in his mouth, she cried aloud, her head flung back, her whole body quivering. She showed her excitement in a number of ways that were new to him, in giggles and sighs and purrs. This was a greater arousal than any she had shown before, and for a moment it troubled him. Then he was caught up in her frenzy as it grew with every kiss, every touch he squandered indulgently upon her; as he slipped his hand into the apex of her thighs, she achieved her release with high, clear sounds like the calls of birds tossed on the wind. Her spasms were so ecstatic that she nearly knocked them from their feet as she held his head pressed to her throat.

"What did you do to me?" She blinked as if she had been wakened from sleep. "I have never felt anything so . . . so *complete.*"

He kissed the corner of her mouth. "You were exquisite, bella mia, dolcina." The ephemeral rapture was fading but enough of it remained to intoxicate him.

"How do you know what I want? How do you know when to do it?" She gave him a hug that was almost playful.

"I know from you," he said, no longer caught up in her passion.

"Was it because this is the last time?" she asked, sadness returning to her voice. She moved out of his arms, her face averted. "You do not need to console me. I understand, better than you know. There will be nothing more between us." Looking down at the tangled pile of their clothing she said, "Gran' Dio, what will the servants say?"

"If I help you dress, they will say nothing," Ragoczy replied; she was pulling away from him as surely as if she had placed a screen between them.

"If we hurry," she agreed as she reached for her petticoats.

Ragoczy left the palazzo half an hour later, as impeccably dressed as if he had just come from the hands of his manservant. He left by the front door, going quickly to the stable one street away where his horse waited. He was preoccupied with his thoughts and so did not notice Giorgianna leave by the side-door.

There was a sedan-chair waiting for her, one with curtained windows. The bearers took her up and carried her to the Gesu, where three priests received her; she had covered her head with a lace-edged shawl but otherwise was in the same clothes as those she had worn when she received Ragoczy. She was taken to a small study near the vestry and told to wait inside.

"You would do well to occupy your time in prayer," advised the tallest of the priests.

"Of course," said Giorgianna, going through the door into the stuffy chamber. There was a writing table with a Savonarola chair behind it, and a stool in front of it; she sat on the stool, folded her hands and did her best to look pious when she was actually frightened.

Some while later the door opened and the three priests entered the study, going behind the writing table. One of them—the oldest—

took the chair and took a sheet of vellum from the table drawer, then set a quill and a standish out.

"Signora Marchesa," the shortest of the three said. "Have you done as we have ordered you?"

"I have tried, Padre," she said, barely able to keep from shaking.

"You spent time with Ragoczy da San-Germain as we ordered you to do?" the oldest demanded.

"This very afternoon. Not two hours gone, Padre," she answered; the vein in her neck revealed the speed of her pulse. "I did my best to rouse him, as you told me I must do. I could not do it." She saw the skeptical expressions and hurried on. "I am not inexperienced in these things, Padre. I used all the skill I have, but he could not stiffen."

"He had no desire," said the tallest.

"He had desire enough to make love to me without union," she responded shortly. "He is a passionate man. But he does not . . . he cannot . . . He is impotent. He does not . . . rise." This last was difficult for her to say. "He is as generous a lover as any I have known, but he has never done the act that generates life in the womb." Her face was burning now, and her chin was up. "After what I have seen, I do not think that he can."

"What have you seen?" asked the oldest. "And remember, your salvation is lost if you lie to us."

Giorgianna nodded and crossed herself. "Then God knows I tell you truth: the Conte is badly scarred. Very badly. I have never seen anything so hideous on a living man." She swallowed hard. "From the base of his ribs, all down his abdomen, and across it from one side to the other, he is scarred. I tried all that I know, but I could not stir his manhood to life. After seeing his scars I do not believe he can be made erect."

The three priests leaned together and whispered in Latin. Finally the shortest one looked at Giorgianna again. "What did you do to try to waken him?"

"Please." Giorgianna shook her head. "Must I say?"

"This is for the sake of your soul, Marchesa." The oldest priest pointed to her. "If you would save yourself from the Sin of Eva, you must tell us."

She huddled down on the stool; she felt smirched and belittled, but she answered. "I touched him, in many ways. I stroked him, squeezed him. I used my hands and . . . and my mouth to try to stir him. There was not so much as a twitch. A eunuch would have more life in him . . . there." Her face was scarlet and she was sweating; she could smell the odor of her body and it disgusted her.

"But were you sufficiently ardent?" asked the tallest. "Did you do your work with a will?" He flicked his tongue over his dry lips. "Did you offer yourself with hunger?"

"Yes. Yes!" she responded, despising herself for saying so much. "I offered myself as eagerly as a whore on the Via San Giacopo."

"You were wanton?" the oldest inquired, making the word filthy as he wrote on the sheet of vellum in front of him. "You plied yourself in a way to fire a man's deviltry?" He held the quill poised.

"Yes," she answered, her voice dropping to a near-whisper.

"Were you, perhaps, too forward?" asked the shortest. "Did you distress him with your sluttishness?"

"He did not kiss me as if he were distressed," she said, wanting to be gone from this place, from Roma, from the world.

"Then he *did* kiss you," said the tallest. "How many times?"

"I did not count them, Padre. Many times. And I kissed him." She hated them for making her last time with Ragoczy a thing of depravity rather than apolaustic gratification.

"You encouraged him?" the oldest persisted.

"Yes." She did not want to admit how much she desired him, or how great her culmination and transports had been, for that would cheapen them forever.

"And he was captivated by your charms?" The oldest priest was watching her from the tail of his eye.

"He seemed to be," she said. "He caressed me . . ." She almost said *tenderly* but that would have revealed too much. "He caressed me fervently."

"You made no protestation," said the shortest.

"No. You said I was to excite him. I did all that I know to do from the times I have been with him, the things that have always brought the greatest fulfillment to us both, as much as he has fulfillment. He has never insisted I do anything that does not gratify me. If I had refused him, he would have done no more to me. He is not one to demand more than I am inclined to give." As soon as she said it, she wanted to take it back; she had said too much, exposing their intimacy to this condemning scrutiny.

"Oh, come. You make him sound a model of seduction. Would not a little resistance have sweetened the chase for him?" prodded the tallest. "What man does not like to conquer a woman, after all?"

"That man does not," Giorgianna said hotly. "He is not one of those grand gentlemen who live only to force themselves on women. He is no rake."

"So you claim," said the shortest.

"I have been his lover long enough to know that he would not use a woman—any woman—against her will. What he gains from a woman can only come with her consent." She folded her arms as if to keep the three priests from staring at her; she felt shame increasing within her, for telling these priests what they insisted they hear.

"You believe this?" The tallest studied her as if she were as foreign as Ragoczy.

"I have experienced it for myself," she said. How much she wanted to get away from this place and from these men! She was beginning to despise herself for doing their bidding and compromising Ragoczy. Her head was aching and she had to fight the urge to urinate.

"You claim he used you well," the shortest said. "How are we to think of you, if that is the case? Have you not declared yourself an adulteress?"

"I have not performed the act that would make me so," Giorgianna protested. "If I were a virgin, his loving would not make me less so. My virtue is untainted." She knew it was useless to say that her husband had given her permission to have Ragoczy for a lover so long as they were discreet and she brought no cuckoos into the nest.

"Does your Confessor say so?" asked the oldest in sharp disapproval.

"He has given me a penance to perform, and I have done this in humility." She did her best to sound submissive when she longed to shout her anger. "As I have done the thing you ordered me to do. No doubt you will also impose penance upon me for doing as you required me to do."

"You have done what was needed for you to be redeemed with the Church," said the oldest of the three. He regarded her with sharp, unforgiving eyes. "Women have always been a source of ills in the world. No one is more aware of that than I am. Every day we see how men are turned from love of God to the carnal passion of women." He crossed himself. "I have been spared such tribulation, through God's Mercy."

The shortest priest nodded, adding, "That you have used the thing that damned you, to reveal greater evils than your own, exonerates your sin." It was apparent by the way he spoke that this was supposed to be encouraging.

"Then I will thank God for it," said Giorgianna, hoping her acquiescence would end her interrogation. "I have done what you have asked. I have told you all I know."

"And God will reward you as you deserve," said the shortest as he looked down to glance over the record that had been made. "Sign this for us, and you may go. The sedan-chair will return you to your palazzo."

The suddenness of this decision almost took her breath away. Giorgianna got up from her stool and went to the table. She was shown the place she had to sign, and was given a quill for the purpose. "But . . . I haven't read . . ."She silenced her protestations and took up the quill, putting down her signature quickly; she was shocked to see how crabbed and unsteady her writing was.

"You will say nothing of this," the oldest ordered her. "If you speak of what you have done, no sin of yours can be absolved."

She curtsied, grateful and outraged at once. "I will say nothing," she vowed, and turned as she heard the door behind her open. At a signal from the oldest priest, she hurried out of the chamber, only to be confronted by a monk, who pointed down the corridor. Hoping this was truly the way out, she went where the monk indicated, and emerged into blazing afternoon sunlight. A sedan-chair waited a few steps beyond, and she hastened to get into it, praying as the bearers took it up that she would indeed be returned to her palazzo and not carried to the Pope's Little House.

Back in the little room of the Gesu the three priests looked over Giorgianna's account. "What do you think?" the shortest asked.

"It is at odds with what the Spanish woman says," the oldest remarked.

"The Spanish woman says her Cardinal-brother made a whore of her," said the tallest with a look of contempt. "Why should she not lie about the father of her child as well?"

The oldest tapped a lean finger on the vellum. "Much as I deplore women who display themselves in public, I find the testimony of this singer more credible than that of the Spanish woman." He sighed. "We had better summon her again. She can travel; she was delivered four days ago."

"The infant is undersized and hare-lipped," said the tallest. "Her brother has supplied us with the midwife's information. The delivery was not at full term, and the girl is not expected to live."

"A hare-lipped infant—and a female at that—speaks to the perfidy of the mother," the oldest declared. "Yes. Have her brought here so that we may discover what took place between her and Ragoczy. Before she arrives, we should have the testimony of all those questioned brought to us." He tugged the bell-pull and repeated this to the monk who answered the summons, adding, "Tell her husband and her brother that either or both may accompany her here, but they may not listen to our questioning."

"Do you think that wise?" asked the tallest.

"Her brother is a hot-headed man, and would be inclined to try to discover our purpose if we did not permit him to accompany her." The oldest sighed. "That Cardinal Calaveria y Vacamonte should have been burdened with such a family: it is a most unsatisfactory thing."

The two other priests exchanged knowing glances; the shortest crossed himself. "God imposes burdens on us all."

"Amen," said the other two, and sat down to wait for the records and the arrival of Leocadia.

It was two hours later when she was escorted into the study, still wan from childbirth, her eyes red with weeping and exhaustion. She wore a simple dark-brown gown without lace or other ornamentation over petticoats of simple muslin. Facing the writing-table, she dropped to her knees.

The three priests looked up from the various records of interrogations they had been reviewing. The oldest pointed to the stool where Giorgianna had sat. "You may."

Leocadia did as she was instructed, her manner subdued. She crossed herself and pressed her hands together, waiting.

"Did your husband and brother come with you?" asked the shortest.

"My brother. My husband . . . is occupied." She spoke just above a whisper; the priests had to strain to hear her. "My brother's carriage brought me. My brother is across the piazza."

"He will be attended to," said the oldest as he held up a vellum sheet. "This is your accusation of Ragoczy da San-Germain as your seducer and the father of your child. Do you recognize it?"

"If you tell me that is what it is, I believe you," she said, trying to make herself heard.

"And you stand by this accusation? that it was he who got you with child?" The oldest stared at her, his old eyes keen.

"I swore before God that it was so, more than once," she said, her voice faltering. "I have nothing else to add."

"You say that Ragoczy used you in the way of men, against your will. That he forced himself upon you carnally while you sought refuge at his villa, and where he pretended to provide you with sanctuary all the while demanding that you accede to his desires." The tallest priest rapped the table with his fingers. "You said this on more than one occasion. Your answers were taken down and you declared them to be accurate."

"They are," she said; she was sitting hunched over as if to warm herself in a room that was close and hot.

"Do you still hold to that testimony?" asked the shortest priest.

"Why should I not? It is the truth." She glared at the floor.

"But you also swore it was true that your murdered brother, Cardinal Calaveria y Vacamonte, had ravaged you for his carnalistic pleasure. Then you said that it was not so, that Ragoczy had compelled you to lie," the shortest said, holding up another sheet of vellum. "You swore you had to obey him, or he would do harm to your family."

"He killed my brother," she muttered.

"No, he did not," said the oldest. "We have testimony from three different men, none of whom knew the testimony of the other, that puts him at Senza Pari at the time the murder occurred. Whom do you suspect, other than Ragoczy?"

Leocadia shook her head several times. "No. No, no. It was Ragoczy. I saw him. He swore he would kill Martin, and he did." She began to rock on the stool, her eyes half-closed, her shoulders up.

"Good, trustworthy men say otherwise," said the shortest. "They reported what they knew, and put their hands to it as truth. Do you say they lied?"

"They lied," Leocadia answered in sing-song tones.

"Why should they lie? They swore on their souls that they reported honestly." The tallest drummed the table again. "You say they lied, when it is you who have lied."

"I have *not* lied," she said, opening her eyes and staring at the three priests with a look compounded of indignation, distress, and effrontery. She straightened up on the stool. "He made me his unwilling mistress, and would not permit me to return to my family until he knew his seed was planted within me."

The oldest priest leaned forward. "The midwife says the female infant you delivered came before term. That would mean that she was conceived in December or January, according to her testimony." He indicated another sheet of vellum. "Your brother provided us with her account of your delivery and the condition of your daughter. God has struck a heavy blow."

Leocadia winced. "She is not perfectly formed." This concession brought tears to her eyes.

"If your brother brought you back from Villa Vecchia before December and the infant you have is unfinished, how do you account for that?" The shortest priest pointed at Leocadia. "Do not add to your lies, woman. The time in which a woman is delivered was established with the birth of the three sons of Adamo and Eva. The Devil may expel an infant from the womb before time, but only the ignorant Ottomites believe that the baby will slumber in the womb for more than a year when a wife is widowed."

"I do not lie," Leocadia said again. "I have been made pregnant by Ragoczy, and the baby I have delivered is his."

"His," repeated the oldest. "You say he lay with you, that he penetrated you as a man penetrates a woman. You swear that only he has had access to your body, and that no other man impregnated you."

She nodded. "He did."

The tallest looked directly at Leocadia. "When he lay with you, could you see his body?"

Her mouth trembled. "Some of it," she said carefully.

"What part did you see?" the tallest pursued.

"The front part, of course," she replied in a burst of temper. "He had to undress in part to do the act."

The tallest nodded. "And did you take note of anything that would identify him more certainly? Did he have marks on him that you can describe?"

"I . . . I did not notice any," she said, and saw something in the glances the priests exchanged that put her on alert. "I did not see all his body."

"But what you did see was unmarked," said the oldest, nodding once.

"You are certain it was the man Ragoczy," said the tallest. "You could not be mistaken."

"Yes! It was he! I should know who ravished me!" She made each accusation as if she were delivering blows.

"But you said your brother ravished you," the oldest reminded her. "You said he had made you his whore. Now you say it was Ragoczy. You said you thought Ragoczy killed the Cardinal, but we have good evidence that he could not have done it. We also have testimony that he could not be the father of your child. We must investigate more thoroughly before we can consider all you have revealed to us."

"You have told your Confessor that Ragoczy offered you protection and used you with charity and respect," said the shortest priest. "You said as much out of the Confessional, so the Seal is unbroken." He held up his hand. "Which are we to believe?"

"But I *was* ravished!" Leocadia exclaimed, reaching out as if to grasp the priests across the table. "The infant I bore is proof of it."

"Yes. It is proof that someone lay with you," said the oldest severely. "We cannot establish who that person was. We must be cautious in these matters." He folded his hands. "We will let you go back to your home, where your brother and your husband can care for you." He tugged the bell-pull. "We will take no further action for now. For which you should give thanks to God; a false accusation is as much a sin as the sin named in the accusation."

Leocadia staggered to her feet. "No! *No!* You must punish him."

The tallest priest gave her a long, cold look. "Be grateful we have not. Your soul could be forfeit." He looked up at the monks who came into the study. "Escort this good woman to her brother, that he may take her home. You will find him at Il Cacciatore."

The monks nodded, and came to flank Leocadia, paying no heed to her outburst of prayers. Without speaking, they moved her out of the study and toward the side-door through which Giorgianna had left, and took her across the piazza to the very select gambling den where they knew Ursellos would be. Every step of the way Leocadia recited Psalms or called out imprecations, none of which fazed the monks; only Ursellos' threat of a beating succeeded in quieting her while they waited for his carriage, and her stillness was born of her wrath as much as her despair.

Text of a letter from Jean-Louis, estate manager of Olivia Clemens' horse-farm near Tours, to Niklos Aulirios.

To the most well-regarded heir of the widow Olivia Clemens, the greetings of Jean-Louis, son of Perceval, the manager of this place.

Good Sieur Aulirios, it was with joy that I learned of your coming visit. I have alerted all the staff that it will soon be our very pleasant duty to welcome you to your home in France. All of us at this establishment are delighted to learn that you have prevailed in your claim

in the courts, for it would have be the cruelest injustice to see all
Madame Clemens' holdings pass into the hands of a bastard, and a
German at that.

The land, I am overjoyed to tell you, is in good heart, and I am
further happy to inform you that our orchards have been especially
bountiful in the last two years. The vineyards are not quite as ample
in their yield as the rest of the crops, but this is more than made up
for by the quality of the wines that we have produced in the last four
years. I know you will be satisfied with the standards we have established in that regard. In terms of grains, the wheat has done relatively
well, but the barley has been excellent, due in part, I think, to our
regular tathing of fallow fields. We have tried rye in one field, but it
has not been a very promising crop thus far.

The damage to the house has long since been repaired, and all
neglected rooms have been put in order. During your absence, and
the absence of Madame Clemens, we have had the honor of housing
Louis le Roi not once, but twice. He brings a vast household with
him, and our resources were strained, but not beyond limits. My father supervised the first of these visits, and I supervised the second.
We have kept the memoranda of commendation he was gracious
enough to leave with us, so that you, too, may see how well the King
was satisfied by our service.

You say you will leave Roma at the end of August, which will likely
bring you here toward the end of September, as you will be traveling
by coach with a good-sized staff with you. You say you have made
arrangements for new teams along the way, but we will send horses
to the places you have requested, so that you will be brought to your
house by your own horses.

Currently we have nineteen mares in foal—fewer than last year.
There are thirty-one yearlings, thirteen colts and eighteen fillies in the
paddocks, and a total of sixty-two mares, eleven stallions, and forty-
nine geldings in the stables. This is a smaller number than Madame
Clemens maintained, but we have thought it advisable not to expand
the herd until you can review the stallions and their get.

I send to you my most sincere esteem, and on behalf of all who
are your household, I anticipate your coming with inestimable cheer.

May your journey be swift and safe, may you make the journey without illness or mishap, and may you be as elated to return here as we will be to greet you.

> *Your most devoted*
> *Jean-Louis*
> *Manager*

By my own hand on the 7th day of August, 1690

7

Heat hummed on the air like a vast, invisible mosquito; Roma was stifled by it. Along the streets traffic moved lethargically where it moved at all, and for those hardy few who ventured out, they were hotly enveloped as if in an oven. The marble-fronted buildings shone, baking streets and interior alike; Il Meglio was no exception, and even in the second-floor salon with all the windows opening, it was sweltering.

"If only there were a breeze," said Ettore Colonna as he fanned himself; he was reclining on a Turkish sofa, his head back against the rolled-and-padded arm. He had taken off his wig, justaucorps, and waistcoat, but even his fine linen camisa was too heavy a garment in this surly weather. Glancing at his newly arrived guest, he said, "Not a hair out of place, and your brow dry as a brick. You astonish me. Does nothing ruffle you, Ragoczy?"

"Yes. But fortunately not the heat." Ragoczy was dressed in a Hungarian dolman and mente of black damask silk; his eclipse device hung on a ruby-studded silver chain, making a striking pectoral. He wore his own slightly-wavy dark hair clubbed at the nape of his neck and secured with a small, neat bow. His shiny high boots were laced Hungarian-fashion and he carried a small staff in one hand to indicate his rank, and wore a rapier in the scabbard that hung from his belt; his appearance was very elegant and very foreign.

"Then you are blessed among men," said Ettore Colonna with a sigh. "Only two o'clock. In another hour I won't be able to breathe. God must be sending us this foretaste of Hell as warning. Or the Devil has already taken up residence here." He pointed to Ragoczy with a languid hand. "Why on earth have you come to Roma on such an impossible day?"

"I received a summons from the Holy Office. I am to present myself at the Gesu at four o'clock, to answer their questions, which, for the moment, are only questions, as they made a point of telling me in their missive." He gestured to show he was more annoyed than upset. "It is more of the same: they are determined to find out how correct their information is regarding the parentage of Leocadia's daughter."

"Not that still!" He sat up. "They are trying to fix some blame on you, my friend. Mark my words: they will not be satisfied until they have reason to condemn you."

"That is what Ursellos Calaveria y Vacamonte would like, and probably his brother-in-law as well." Ragoczy's tone was drily sardonic, but his expression was sad. "And Leocadia is caught between them."

"How can you defend her, after her accusations?" Ettore Colonna asked as he sank back down on the sofa. "I can comprehend Christian forgiveness to a point, but this is absurd."

"Oh, I do not forgive her," said Ragoczy. "I understand her." He saw the puzzled frown settle on Ettore Colonna's brow and went on. "She has been a tool all of her life, and it has made her lose her knowledge of herself. She now only defines herself by what she opposes. If I had grasped that earlier, she would not be in the predicament she is now."

"And you are not in a predicament?" Ettore Colonna batted his fan in Ragoczy's direction. "What do you expect me to believe? that you are allowing her to blacken your reputation because she has suffered?"

"She has not blackened my reputation," said Ragoczy with the hint of an ironic smile.

"Not for want of trying," said Ettore Colonna mordantly.

"Perhaps." Ragoczy went to stand by the open window and looked out on Roma. "I am sorry to have to leave this place."

"You mean you have come to your senses at last?" Ettore Colonna did not wait for an answer. "And not before time. The Franciscans and the Dominicans have sent to the New World for the records of your . . . kinsman's . . . incarceration there. They have already asked my cousin Gennaro for testimony, which should give you some indication of their intentions." He held up his fan, now closed, as if it were a warning finger. "You may think that they will not try to tie you to that other Ragoczy, but that would be a foolish assumption. The Holy Office does not want to be proved wrong. Ever." He rolled onto his side to face Ragoczy. "Your case is no exception."

"Then it is my good fortune that they have not yet defined their suspicions sufficiently to be proved wrong." He turned his back on the open window and the city beyond. "That, and the Pope has uses for my troops in the Carpathians."

"My, my. You are almost as cynical as I am," marveled Ettore Colonna.

Ragoczy shook his head. "Not cynical: experienced." He shut away his recollections of the cells in the New World, only to have it replaced by images of Anastasi Shuisky, of Girolamo Savonarola, of Eudoin Tissant, of Obispo Andreas de Zaragosa, of . . . In order to interrupt his memories, he said, "You have more reason to be cautious with the Church than I do."

"Cynical *and* naive," remarked Ettore Colonna. "Oh, yes," he went on at his most urbane. "I have my differences with the Church, but so far I am not in harm's way, nor am I likely to be as long as the current Pope reigns; Alessandro VIII is more concerned about Turks than he is about how I, and men like me, spend my time. If we have another Innocenzo on San Pietro's Chair, then I, too, may need your help to leave the country. Only where would I go?" He reached out for his wineglass that stood on an end-table at the head of his sofa, and lifted it in a silent toast.

"You must have plans," said Ragoczy, deliberately indirect.

"Of course I do, very practical ones, but I never expect to use them." He drank the butter-yellow wine and smiled. "That is undoubtedly idiotic, but—"

When Ettore Colonna did not go on, Ragoczy said, "Roma is your

home; you do not want to leave it." He chuckled. "I am familiar with
the draw of native earth; few bonds are stronger than those of earth,
or blood."

"Then it might be best if you sought out your native earth. In the
Carpathians, is it not? Transylvania?" Ettore Colonna smiled at Ragoczy. "A long way from Roma."

"And the Holy Office, you mean?" Ragoczy sat down on the chair
facing Ettore Colonna's sofa. "I suppose you are right."

"Then heed your own advice and leave here." He propped himself
on his elbow. "You have friends here, but none of them will favor
you over the wishes of the Holy Office—not even I will do that."

"I appreciate your exhortation," said Ragoczy at his most affable.
"I have no doubt you are right. But I am the oddest creature: I do
not like false accusations against me to go unchallenged." He studied
Ettore Colonna for a short while. "I am exasperating; I realize that.
Yet I think this trouble with Leocadia must be settled."

"It may be beyond settling, if half the gossip I hear is correct,"
Ettore Colonna warned. "I hear *everything* that is whispered in this
city, from the urchins to the Cardinals, and the Cardinals are the
worst."

"Gossip is inconvenient," said Ragoczy. "Sometimes it reveals tid-
bits of worth; most of the time it is nothing more than babble." He
made himself appear less concerned than he was.

"But they are saying that Leocadia has said dreadful things about
you," Ettore Colonna said, summoning up more energy than he had
earlier. "She is in a position to cause you harm."

Ragoczy held up his hand to make a point. "Only if she is believed."

"You are not afraid?" Ettore Colonna was incredulous.

"No; not of her." Ragoczy hesitated before adding, "The Holy
Office troubles me. I would not like to end up a guest at the Pope's
Little House."

"So you have not wholly abandoned good sense," Ettore Colonna
approved. "You relieve me."

Ragoczy inclined his head, saying nothing as a footman came into
the salon to announce that Sergio Lombardi had arrived and wanted
Ettore Colonna's advice on the plans for the restoration of his country

villa. "He says it is urgent, Signore Colonna," the footman said expressionlessly.

"It must be, to bring him out in such heat; Sergio is a most indolent man, for all he fancies himself an artist," said Ettore Colonna. "Show him up, and bring more wine. And some of that rose-jelly on soft cheese." He waved the footman away and turned apologetically to Ragoczy. "You will have to excuse me, my friend. Sergio can be obstinate, and never more so than when he is unsure of himself."

"Of course." Ragoczy rose. "I thank you for receiving me."

Ettore Colonna swept his arm as if making a leg. "You will forgive me if I do not rise? You're very kind."

Ragoczy made a leg and made his way out of the salon and down the broad stairs; as he descended, he met Sergio Lombardi coming up. Ragoczy offered him as much of a leg as the stairs would permit, and noticed that Lombardi gave only a minimal nod in response; Ragoczy wondered what the man had heard that resulted in such cursory politeness. Reaching the loggia at street level, Ragoczy looked about in what seemed idle curiosity: he took note of three men lounging where they could watch the elaborate front of Il Meglio. Without any sign of being aware of them, he signaled for his horse. As he rode off, he noticed two of the three men were following him at a discreet distance.

Arriving at the Gesu, Ragoczy was asked to hand over his weapon before he was ushered into the same study where Giorgianna and Leocadia had been received, and was confronted by the same trio of nameless priests.

"You are early," said the tallest. He offered no other greeting, no polite phrases that would usually be required of men in their circumstances.

Ragoczy took his tone from the priests. "I finished my tasks in Roma more quickly than I had anticipated, and so I hoped you would be willing to advance the hour of my interview." He was courteous, conducting himself as befitted a man of his high rank, but making no concessions to elaborate social forms.

"Very few come to us in haste," said the oldest in what might have been amusement. "Yet you are here an hour before the appointed time."

"If it is an inconvenience for you, I will be willing to wait," said Ragoczy, and regarded the three men with what seemed mild interest.

"It is no inconvenience," said the shortest. "God willing, this can be settled quickly, and the lie uncovered." He pointed to Ragoczy. "Remove your garments."

Ragoczy did not attempt to conceal his surprise. "I beg your pardon?"

"Remove your garments," the shortest repeated in a tone of voice that was suddenly very stern.

"Good Fathers, may I ask why you wish me to do this?" Ragoczy inquired politely.

"You may not," said the oldest. "If you refuse, we will summon aid and our servants will undress you."

For the first time, Ragoczy felt a twinge of fear, though he concealed it: the Dominicans and Franciscans in the New World had made a record of his scars; if these priests compared the description with what they saw, they could discover more about him than Ragoczy wanted them to know. "You do not need to summon your servants. I am shocked by your request, but I will comply," he said, giving no hint of capitulation. "It is my intention to cooperate with your investigation. He turned away and began to unfasten his clothes. "Shall I remove my boots as well?"

"No need," said the tallest, an assurance that spurred Ragoczy's apprehension.

It did not take him long to remove his dolman and mente, and as soon as he did, he made himself turn to face the priests, expecting harsh condemnation from them as soon as they saw the scars on his abdomen. "The injury is an ancient one."

The oldest priest crossed himself, not in shock but in acknowledgment. "Per l'anima!" he exclaimed. "It is as the singer said."

"He is deep-chested and strongly built," observed the shortest eagerly. "He is not a feckless adventurer, not with such a body. Of average height, well-formed, and most compact; the scars do not detract from his physical prowess. No wonder the woman was taken with him."

Ragoczy closed his eyes in a rush of sorrow. That Giorgianna had been in the hands of the Holy Office on his account—he could not imagine how terrified she must have been. He made himself remain silent as the shortest priest came up to him and began to examine the scars. Had Ragoczy been much younger, he would have been tempted to fight with the man, certain that his vampiric strength would allow him an easy victory over the priest, but in his long life he had learned that such impulsive acts were usually more dangerous and foolhardy than strategic; now he kept still and paid close attention to what was happening around him.

"The scars go to the base of his hips," the shortest priest announced. "The wounds that left these were severe."

They were fatal, thought Ragoczy, his feature expressing only the aggravation that these men might expect. He took a step back as the priest touched his penis. "I think not," he said sharply, authority in his voice.

"It is essential that we confirm the report," said the shortest priest, a bit too eagerly.

"What report?" Now Ragoczy was confused: did this inquiry stem from the South American records, or some others?

"You may not ask that," said the oldest. "You are to answer our questions." He leaned forward. "Well?"

As the shortest priest continued his examination, the tallest said, "According to Amerigo, your coachman, you have sometimes been alone with a woman in your coach."

Trying not to let the shortest priest distract him, Ragoczy said, "Yes. Occasionally Giorgianna Ferrugia has been good enough to accompany me in my coach. Not since she became a married woman, of course."

"Of course," said the tallest. "When you were alone together, did you never press your advantage with her?"

"What advantage do you mean?" Ragoczy asked, already guessing.

"The advantage a man has over a woman," said the oldest.

Ragoczy shook his head. "If you mean did I kiss her, or fondle her, yes, I did, as long as she was willing I do so. If you mean did I force myself on her, no I did not. It is no easy thing to . . . take a woman in a moving coach when you have her full consent; if she resists, I doubt it would be possible."

"Your coachman supports your assertions," said the oldest, and asked nothing more.

The shortest priest was manipulating Ragoczy's flesh, his ministrations as expert as a courtesan's; the other two remained quiet and attentive. "There is no life here that I can find," he said a short while later, sounding disappointed.

Ragoczy kept his voice level. "Had you asked, I would have told you I am impotent."

The shortest priest went back to the writing table. "But that is a thing a man might readily lie about if he is accused of rape." The last words crackled in accusation.

"Rape?" Ragoczy said, too baffled to be insulted. "Whom am I to have raped?"

"That we cannot tell you," said the oldest, seeming to be satisfied by Ragoczy's outburst. "We hold all such accusations under the Seal of Confession."

"The matter we must determine is if it is possible for you to commit such an outrage, for it is very evident someone has." The tallest priest tapped his fingers on the table; it was an irritating sound that Ragoczy suspected was intended to increase the distress of the person being questioned.

"If that is what you seek, good Fathers," said Ragoczy as civilly as he could, "then I fear you must look elsewhere. I will always disappoint you in such crimes." His bow, in his undressed state, would have been ludicrous had he not had a subtle air of command that was usually seen in much taller men.

"You are unmoved by a woman's caress, and a man's," said the tallest priest, his lips nearly smirking. "You should be one of us."

The very idea revolted him; Ragoczy inclined his head slightly. "I have not had a calling, good Fathers, and I understand that such a calling is essential."

"Amen, et benedicamus Domino," said the oldest with a kind of habitual piety that made Ragoczy uneasy. "You may put your clothing on again."

"Thank you," said Ragoczy, and began to dress, not hurriedly but with efficiency.

"Do you need a mirror?" asked the shortest snidely.

"You are good to offer it, but it is not necessary," said Ragoczy, adding, "I have dressed on campaign so many times that I have learned to manage without." He was gratified that this was at least partly true.

"Ah, yes. You have fought the Ottomites," said the oldest, putting the tips of his fingers together and regarding Ragoczy over the peak.

"Yes." He said nothing more, not wanting to appear boastful.

"You have defended your homeland and your faith," said the shortest.

"As much as I have been able to do," Ragoczy said, once again enjoying the irony of truth. "There have been many battles in those mountains."

"Your troops have been put into the service of the Pope," said the tallest.

"Yes," Ragoczy agreed. He was almost dressed now, and he put himself in order with minimal fuss.

"Are your neighboring nobles of the same mind you are?" The oldest leaned forward.

"Some are, some are not," Ragoczy replied, certain they knew the answer already. "The region has long been troubled, and there are those who see their survival in siding with whomever they reckon is the most powerful."

"But you do not," said the shortest.

"I do not side with the Turks," said Ragoczy. He stood very straight. "My homeland deserves my allegiance, and I am bound to do all that is in my power to protect it."

"Admirable," said the oldest. "And yet, you are here in Roma, not with your troops in Hungary."

"The eastern borders of Hungary are far from secure," said Ragoczy. "Those of us wishing to preserve our lands have need of the support of Papal troops." He looked at the three priests. "And I had an obligation to fulfill here in Roma, as you are most certainly aware." He saw that he had surprised them again. "Atta Olivia Clemens was a blood relative, and I came to ensure her Will was upheld."

"We have reviewed the case provided by the Magisterial Court," said the tallest.

"Then you understand why I came," said Ragoczy.

"When you arrived, you bore the title of Abbe as well as Conte," said the shortest. His eyes narrowed. "Did you not?"

Ragoczy was prepared to answer this accusation. "In lands where the Ottomites are powerful, often the only way for the old nobility to maintain some authority is to become the head of a monastery. The Turks usually leave such places alone, and as an Abbe a man of my heritage may continue his duties to his homeland. I am not the only one who has made himself an Abbe—without final vows—for the preservation of the legacy of his blood. Had I young sons, that would be another matter, but as I am childless and will remain so, I have found a bastion in the monastery."

"It is irregular," declared the oldest. "But it is in service to God."

"And others have done it before him, and will do it after," said the tallest. "Any man who has paid so high a price in his flesh for his faith cannot be faulted for using such means to preserve the honor of his blood."

Ragoczy found this unexpected defense perversely amusing but maintained a somber demeanor. "I am grateful you understand."

"That does not resolve the matter of the accusation made against you," said the shortest.

The oldest lifted his joined hands. "There is an injustice being done, that is beyond doubt. That must be addressed." He glowered at Ragoczy. "You have enemies, Signore."

"Most men do," Ragoczy responded carefully.

"That you could be held accountable for such an outrage as has been claimed you committed is a most grave error. Someone seeks to use the Holy Office as a weapon for personal vengeance." The tallest priest crossed himself. "I pray that we will be given the power to rectify this sin."

Ragoczy remained very still, listening intently to the priests and hoping that they would not demand he reveal more in order to enable them to apprehend those they would hold responsible for false accusation. He kept his eyes lowered so that the priests would not decide he was challenging them.

"There is much we must do," said the oldest. "Our tasks are laid before us." He glanced significantly in Ragoczy's direction.

The shortest addressed Ragoczy. "You may go. But do not leave Roma without permission. There are still questions that have not been answered that we must put to you."

Ragoczy went down on one knee as a demonstration of acquiescence. "God give us to know right."

The three priests crossed themselves to show agreement with Ragoczy's sentiment, never aware that his intention was ironic. "You have been tested, Signore," said the oldest. "Your test is not over." He indicated the door. "We will send for you when we need to know more."

The dismissal was beyond question; Ragoczy rose and left the study, his emotions in turmoil: he was elated that the Holy Office had apparently not yet examined the records of the Dominicans and Franciscans, but he was apprehensive that they clearly intended to do so; he was saddened that Leocadia—for his accuser had to be Leocadia—could have spoken so viciously against him; more than that he was sickened at the thought of what Giorgianna had endured because of him. Most of all, he felt a light-headed relief that he had a short time to act in order to head off the worst of what the Holy Office could do; he had to do as much as he could manage in the time remaining to ensure neither woman would suffer again on his account. As he buckled on his sword again and took his staff, he decided Leocadia was in the most immediate danger, so that when his grey was led out for him to mount, he headed toward the palazzo that had been hired by Martin, Cardinal Calaveria y Vacamonte, where Ursellos now shared his lavish household with his sister and her husband; drawing up in the piazza before the palazzo, he knew better than to try to speak to Leocadia, but he hoped that Jose Bruno might talk to him.

There were sounds of excitement coming from the palazzo's open windows as Ragoczy approached it. The worst of the heat was over but the stone walls retained their oven-like warmth, dragging out the lassitude of the afternoon and delaying the activities of evening for most Romans—but not all; the squeal of eager, feminine voices rose above a rowdy chorus of male singing; Ursellos was entertaining again, Ragoczy thought. He drew in his horse across the piazza and dismounted, giving an Angel to a youngster to hold his horse, and another to the child's comrade to go ask Jose Bruno to come outside.

Clutching the coin in his hand, the boy ran to the palazzo and ducked into the alleyway that led back to the stables and coach-house behind. His companion, holding the grey's reins in his fists, said, "You don't worry. Lucio knows where to find the half-wit."

At another time Ragoczy would have done his best to explain that Jose Bruno's apparent dimness was caused by his eyes, not his wits; but today he was too preoccupied with the more immediate dangers which the Holy Office represented. "Then pray he hurries."

The youngster fidgeted, as if this would urge on his friend. "It is too hot."

"That it is," Ragoczy said, and kept himself from pacing by idly counting the windows in the fronts of the houses and two other palazzos facing the piazza. It was a fairly successful diversion, and it kept the boy occupied as well, once he figured out what Ragoczy was doing and joined in the counting.

It was almost half an hour later when the young messenger returned, leading Jose Bruno by the hand. "Here he is. He was sleeping in a stall." He laughed to show his opinion of those who did such things.

"Who is it?" Jose Bruno asked, squinting in a vain attempt to see more clearly.

"It is Ragoczy, Jose Bruno. From the Villa Vecchia." He held out his hand to the young man, moving it toward Jose Bruno's when he could not make it out. "I need to speak with you." He made his tone as soothing as he could. "I am afraid the situation is precarious."

"Because of Maurizio?" His manner grew nervous. "I told Leocadia I would say nothing about it."

"No; not about Maurizio." He took Jose Bruno by the elbow and drew him away from the two curious boys. "I believe I should warn you, and your sister, that there may be trouble."

"You think we have had no trouble?" Jose Bruno asked sarcastically.

Ragoczy knew there was no point in arguing. "I am sure you have, and I would like to do what I can to spare you more." He had Jose Bruno's attention now and made the most of it. "I think she—and you—are going to have more unless you prepare for it. You do not have much time." He paused, looking across the piazza, but focusing on something far more distant than the front of the Calaveria y Vacamonte palazzo. "The Holy Office has been asking questions of you and your sister."

"How do you know?" Jose Bruno's voice rose a major third. "Who told you?"

"Indirectly the good Fathers themselves did," said Ragoczy quietly. "There is something in Leocadia's information that the priests are not satisfied with; they were not specific, but I did what I could to discern the cause of their disapprobation." He spoke in an undervoice, leaning toward Jose Bruno. "They would not tell me what it is, and I was in no position to ask, but I surmised that their uncertainties may have something to do with my appearance."

"Why should that concern Leocadia?" Jose Bruno whispered.

"She can answer that better than I." Ragoczy noticed Jose Bruno's introspective frown. "I suspect they have conflicting accounts about some aspect of my person. That would explain why they required me to undress." He paused to let Jose Bruno consider what he had said. "If Leocadia has not been entirely truthful with the good Fathers, she would do well to revise her testimony."

"Why should she do that?" Jose Bruno was defensive now. "She won't, and I can't persuade her." He began to chafe at his sleeve as his discomfort increased. "I know she ought to be grateful to you, that you helped her when no one else would. But in the end, she has got nothing for herself but suffering."

"For which she would like me to pay?" Ragoczy let the question hang. "If she has said anything to the Holy Office that can be held against her, she will have to endure yet more suffering. I do not believe her brother Ursellos will do anything to stand between her and harm: do you?"

Color rose in Jose Bruno's face and he shook his head no. "She does not lie; that is not her intention."

"I am not accusing her of lying," Ragoczy said very gently. "But the good Fathers are more absolute than I am."

"You are not going to betray her, are you?" He was growing frightened.

"If I were going to do so deliberately, I would not seek you out this way. I would let the priests continue their investigation unchecked. I would say nothing to you, and leave Leocadia to be caught in whatever misrepresentation she has made to support her accusations. Yet I have to tell you I had the strong impression that some of the reports the good Fathers have gathered contain information that does not agree with what your sister has told them." He waited, and when Jose Bruno began to fret, he said, "I would not want this inquiry to be prolonged."

Jose Bruno shook his head. "No. She would not deal well with more questioning. Since our brother's death, she has been overwrought. Even before then, she was upset; well, you know she was. Who can blame her? With all her wretchedness, it is not remarkable that she would . . . Our brother demanded so much of her: too much. Some of the things she has claimed have been born of her shock at his murder." He had pulled two threads loose on his sleeve and now busied himself unraveling them.

"Then urge her to revise what she has said. For the sake of her daughter if not for herself." Ragoczy saw the discomfort in Jose Bruno's face once more. "What is it?"

"The child has been given as an oblate to the convent of Santa Euphemia in Ostia," Jose Bruno told him. "Ursellos thought it would be best, and Rothofen said he did not want the baby about to remind Leocadia of her sins."

"An oblate," said Ragoczy, appalled that the infant should be made a gift to the Church to grow up a virtual slave to the nuns of Santa Euphemia. He had seen oblates often over the centuries and his compassion for them was as boundless as it was futile.

"You have not seen her." Jose Bruno crossed himself. "You don't know what her face is like. She would not be a wife, not with such a deformity. Eventually the Church would be her haven. Better it should be now, when she has not had to endure the unkindness of the world and the disgust of those around her." He repeated this as if reciting a lesson learned many years ago.

Ragoczy was tempted to ask if Ursellos or Rothofen had been the more insistent but realized this would be useless. He shook his head. "Poor little girl."

"Well may you say so," Jose Bruno murmured.

The was a quality to the remark that engaged Ragoczy's consideration. "What do you mean?" He laid one small hand on Jose Bruno's shoulder. "Is there any reason the child does not deserve sympathy?"

"No . . . no." Jose Bruno looked about awkwardly. "But someone might interpret your solicitude for something more."

"And why is that?" Ragoczy would not be denied a truthful answer.

Jose Bruno capitulated. "She told the Holy Office that the child is yours," he muttered, looking away and ruining the cuff of his sleeve.

Ragoczy stared in amazement. "How can she think that?" he asked, deliberately calm.

"Because the Holy Office calls the truth a lie," said Jose Bruno with a burst of spirit.

"That the baby is the Cardinal's," said Ragoczy, knowing that he was correct. "Of course the Holy Office would not tolerate such an assertion; they would not—they could not entertain such a possibility." He paced a few steps away from Jose Bruno, then paced back to him. "She told them what she decided they wanted to hear, is that it?"

"Yes," said Jose Bruno; he was neither belligerent or servile.

"So she has named me the father." He achieved one sad crack of laughter. "No wonder the priests were so insistent."

"What do you mean?" Jose Bruno asked, growing pale about the mouth.

Ragoczy shook his head. "If you have any influence with your sister, advise her to withdraw her accusation. It can lead to nothing but tragedy for her."

Jose Bruno peered at Ragoczy. "It would help you, too, wouldn't it?"

"Not as much as you suppose," he replied. "Jose Bruno, talk to her. She must rescind her testimony. She can claim she made it in the throes of grief; the priests will accept that. But if she persists it can only bring more hardship upon her." He came close to Jose Bruno. "I was unable to give her the succor she desired when she put herself in my hands; now I can, at least, spare her more—"

"I'll talk to her, but it will be useless. Ursellos and her husband are satisfied with what she has told the Holy Office and they will not tolerate any change she may decide to make." He lowered his head. "She will not defy them."

Remembering what he had said to Niklos Aulirios when he first arrived in Roma—*here, everything I am is dangerous*—Ragoczy shook his head slowly as he started back toward his horse. "Then I fear," he said as kindly as he could, "that her travail is not yet over."

Text of a message from Ursellos Calaveria y Vacamonte to Ferenc Ragoczy da San-Germain, carried by private courier.

Ragoczy:

You vile scoundrel, you have made your last attempt to corrupt my sister. How despicable of you to impose on my half-wit brother to accomplish your loathsome purpose. On her behalf and on behalf of the honor of our family and her husband, I tell you now to name your second. You and he will meet me at midnight three days hence, on the 30th of August at the crossroads of the Roma-Trefonti and the San Zaccharia–Belcampo Roads. My brother-in-law will act as my second. You have the right to choose the weapons, of course, but I remind you that men of courage fight with rapier and dagger; only cowards insist on pistols. Still, the choice is yours, and I will await your reply. Should you fail to send me word by sunset tomorrow I will know you for the craven, disgraced debaucher I have always maintained you are.

I leave it to you to arrange for a physician, as you are the one most likely to need his services.

Until midnight of the 30th, when only one of us will see the dawn of the next day.

                                    Ursellos Calaveria y Vacamonte

By my own hand, this 27th day of August, 1690

8

Amerigo cursed as the coach rumbled over another deep rut; the bull's-eye lanthorns fixed on the sides of the vehicle did little to illuminate the way ahead on this cloudy night, or to help guide the coach that followed after them, which Matyas drove. A rainstorm earlier in the day had eliminated the dust but had created a thin film of mud in the ruts of the road which slowed their progress up the long slope.

"You did not have to accept the Spaniard's challenge," Ettore Colonna said, repeating himself for the fourth time since they left Villa Vecchia. "His sister's testimony is discredited and she has been given a year of public penance for bearing false witness; she is to be beaten every Sunday for her mendacity. No one will believe anything she says of you."

"She has never been believed, more's the pity," said Ragoczy. "No one wanted to know the truth."

Ettore Colonna shook his head in exasperation. "So you have taken it upon yourself to show that you—what?—think she should be excused her lying about you?"

"No." He laid his hand on the hilt of his rapier. "But her brother and her husband have much to answer for."

"Given that pair of miscreants, I have no doubt of it. But what good is a duello? It is so secret that no one will know." Ettore Colonna waved his hand out at the night. "Not so much as a whisper."

"Do you really think so." Ragoczy's face was hard to see in the darkness, but there was a sardonic cast to his attractive, irregular features.

Ettore Colonna gave a hard, short sigh. "Yes. Of course. Everyone always finds out about duels, though the Saints alone know how." He swore as the coach jounced over some small rocks. "You'll break a wheel and we'll be stuck out here until a farmer comes along to carry your coachman to a blacksmith."

"Ettore," said Ragoczy, "you will not change my mind. I would rather have this settled once and for all than have to spend all my days wondering when and where my enemies will strike next. After tonight this is over."

"You do not truly think a duel will put an end to it, do you?" Ettore Colonna shook his head in amusement. "Rothofen has made several attempts against you, and his lack of success has not discouraged him. With what has happened to his wife, he will resent you more than ever." He hung on to the looped strap as the coach swayed over another bad section of road. "No one will try to interrupt your engagement, Conte; rest assured the Guardia will not come to stop your duello. Who in his right mind would travel such a terrible road at night?"

"You are here," Ragoczy pointed out.

"Ah, but I am not in my right mind, not according to the teaching of Mother Church." He looked out the window. "No wonder Ursellos wanted the meeting at that crossroad. There isn't even a farmhouse for half a league in any direction."

"It will suit his purpose very well," said Ragoczy, leaning back against the squabs; he was feeling tired and old. "This is such a senseless thing."

"But you are going to do it, aren't you?" Ettore Colonna asked rhetorically.

"I must, if I am to have any peace. If I refuse the challenge I will have to endure greater suspicion than I have already encountered." He smoothed the front of his long, black waistcoat and fingered the unruffled cuffs of his camisa. "I rely on you to make sure that all the niceties are observed. Observe every point of honor, and be painstaking about it: so that my opponent can have no grounds for complaint."

"Complaint? From someone like Ursellos Calaveria y Vacamonte? Or Ahrent Rothofen?" Ettore Colonna scoffed. "Those men could not be trusted to present a petition in proper form."

"Then your role as my second is all the more crucial," said Ragoczy, going on steadily, "If anything should happen that cannot be mended, see that the physician is paid off." He cocked his head to indicate the coach behind them. "Then talk to Rugerius; he knows what to do with my body, which is why he is riding with the physician. He also has all you will need to place my Will in the records of the Magistrates' Court. I would not like to see another fiasco like the one that brought me to Roma."

"You speak as if you do not expect to survive," said Ettore Colonna in genuine concern.

Ragoczy inclined his head. "It is always wisest to be prepared." He lapsed into a thoughtful silence, recalling the many, many times he had prepared himself to face the True Death. "I have survived thus far," he said a bit later.

"The crossroad is ahead, Signor' Conte!" Amerigo called down from his box. "We'll be there in a moment."

Ettore Colonna took his pocket-watch out and held it up outside the coach-window to light its face in the beam of the bull's-eye lanthorn. "We're ten minutes early. I expect Ursellos will see poor conduct in that."

"Why?" Ragoczy prepared to get out of the coach behind Ettore Colonna.

"He will claim you have used the time to take advantage of him," was the answer.

"That is probably a good thing," said Ragoczy. "We can walk the ground, to be sure there are no surprises underfoot." He felt the remote calm taking hold of him that he had long associated with fighting.

"A wise precaution," said Ettore Colonna sarcastically. "Just as this is." He patted the low pocket of his justaucorps.

"What have you there?" Ragoczy asked as the coach slowed down.

"A charged pistol, of course. To make sure the duello is fair."
Ettore Colonna flourished his hand as if to bow.

"Do you expect treachery?" Ragoczy asked as if he had no interest
in his companion's answer.

"No. If I expected it, it wouldn't be treachery." He half rose as
the coach came to a halt. "I will step out first, in case there is anyone
hidden in the trees with a weapon."

"Calaveria y Vacamonte would not go to the trouble of challenging
me if all he intended to do was ambush me," Ragoczy said, wondering
as he spoke if it was true.

From his place on the driver's-box, Amerigo pointed down the
slope. "There is another coach coming. Listen!"

The rattle and thuds of the third coach came through the night.

"Persistent devils, aren't they?" Ettore Colonna asked as he took
one of the bull's-eyes lanthorns from its bracket on the coach and
began to shine it about the crossroad. "It could be worse. Having the
two roads crossing has worn down the deepest furrows." The light
struck a small stone shrine containing a badly weathered statue. "I
don't know what Saint guards this place, but—"

Ragoczy came to scrutinize the figure in the shrine. "Persephone,"
he said at last. "How fitting."

"Don't let the Holy Office hear you mistake a heathen goddess for
a Christian Saint," Ettore Colonna warned in mock indignation. "You
have just eluded them for the moment. Saying this is not a Saint
would give them reason to call you back again."

"First I must survive the duello," said Ragoczy, lifting a warning
finger. He moved away from the shrine and had a look at the ground
of the crossroad: it was as he had assumed—the footing was uneven
but worn enough to be less rutted than either road going through it,
as Ettore Colonna had remarked. The night did not hamper his vision, and he made the most of the little time before the third coach
drew up, horses steaming and blowing.

Rothofen was the first out of the coach; he lowered the blazoned
panel and used the built-in steps to come down. He made a very
minor leg to Ragoczy and Ettore Colonna. "At least you had the
stomach to come," he sniffed as he turned to offer his hand to assist
Ursellos to emerge.

The Spaniard was dressed in dark colors, too, but he had kept the ruffles and elegancies of dress fashion demanded including wide buckles on his spur-leathers. He gave a single, contemptuous nod in Ragoczy's direction. "Did you think to bring a priest?"

"You did not request one," said Ragoczy as he bowed in good form. "If you would prefer to have one present, I will send my servant Matyas to fetch one. It shouldn't take more than an hour to bring a priest here."

Ursellos glared at Ragoczy. "I do not think I will require one." He laid his hand on the hilt of his sword to make his point.

"It may be just as well that the Church know nothing about this encounter," Ettore Colonna said flatly. "The Pope does not approve of dueling."

"He does not approve of whores, either, but Roma is full of them," said Ursellos. He began to pace out the crossroad. "Large enough for a good fight, but not so large than you can escape me." He smiled and motioned to Rothofen. "You can watch from the box of my coach, to be sure the fight is proper."

Rothofen gave an answering smile. "That I will. You may rely on me." With that, he went back toward the coach, giving no sign of noticing Ettore Colonna; this deliberate slight was noticed by the coachmen as well as by Ragoczy.

"I thought our seconds were required to inspect our weapons," said Ragoczy as if he knew nothing of the matter and sought only information.

"And I assumed we would mark the beginning of the fighting together," said Ettore Colonna.

"Surely even a butterfly like you, Colonna, can scrape our rapiers for us: as to your weapons, Ragoczy: are yours inferior, or are they unacceptable?" Ursellos asked with elaborate and insulting condescension.

"They are as stipulated—a rapier and a dagger." He did not mention that his concession to Ursellos' preference in weapons was far beyond what most challenged men would accept.

"Rapier and dagger," said Ursellos, indicating the ones he wore. "Do you want any changes in ground?"

"I have no recommendation to make," said Ragoczy; he stood aside as Ursellos walked over the ground. "Will the darkness trouble you?"

"Why should it?" Ursellos' saunter turned into a swagger. "I know how to fight in the night."

"Waylaying helpless gamblers and sots on the street at night, no doubt," said Ettore Colonna. Nudging Ragoczy's shoulder, he whispered, "He is up to something."

Ragoczy nodded. "And not for the first time." Over the centuries he had seen many men readying themselves for battle; only a few had been as overtly confident as Ursellos.

"Watch him." Ettore Colonna stepped back, going to the shrine and taking up his post there. "I will set you on as soon as you ask."

Ursellos continued to move about the crossroad. "You do understand this is to the death, don't you?"

From far down the slope a single, tuneless bell began the six chimes of midnight.

"That did seem to be your intention," Ragoczy said.

"Nothing less will not vindicate my sister's honor. Since you are the one who ruined her, you must give up your life, as you have stolen hers." Ursellos turned abruptly, holding up his gloved hand and ticking off his grievances with his fingers. "You got her with child. You sent your assassins to kill our brother. You have poisoned the Holy Office against her. For that only your death will answer."

"Her child was your brother's. I do not know who killed him." Ragoczy was growing weary of this posturing. "You are the one who insisted on this duello. Do you intend to fight, or do you only wish to revile me." His tone was courteous enough but the purpose in his dark eyes would have unsettled Ursellos had he bothered to look at them.

Ursellos spat. "You are execrable."

Ragoczy stood very still. "You are the one who demanded this meeting. If you have no heart for it, say so, and we will all return home."

This was more than Ursellos would tolerate; he drew his rapier and rushed toward Ragoczy only to find that Ettore Colonna had stepped between him and the target of his odium. "Move!"

"When you have saluted each other, I will, when my part in this is complete. Until then, I must insist you abide by the code of honor you invoked when you issued your challenge." He held his ground while Ursellos cursed and took a step backwards. "Sta bene. Signore Calaveria y Vacamonte, if you will stand here?" He pointed with his rapier to his right. "And you, Signor' Conte, if you will stand here?" This time he indicated a place to his left, about two arm's-lengths from Ursellos. "You must begin properly, or there will be those who would say we conspired in murder."

"This is foolishness," muttered Ursellos. He shot a quick look toward Rothofen, who was taking his place beside his coachman.

"Perhaps, but it is the foolishness you chose, and you will accept the strictures of the duello," Ettore Colonna reminded him. "If you will draw your weapons?" He waited a bit nervously while both men complied. "Gentlemen, salute each other, then place your blades en garde."

"Still time to withdraw, foreigner," said Ursellos, whipping his rapier so that it sang on the air.

Ragoczy drew his rapier without flash, holding it in his left hand, and drawing his dagger with his right. "When you give us the office, Colonna," he said.

"You should hold your rapier in your right hand," Ursellos complained, shifting his stance to block a left-handed attack.

"You chose the weapons," Ettore Colonna said, watching as the two antagonists saluted each other; he brought his rapier up between their crossed blades, lifting the two apart. "Begin!" he ordered and jumped back as Ursellos rushed at Ragoczy.

Shouting incoherently, Ursellos ran forward, slashing with his rapier and stabbing down with his dagger, determined to overwhelm Ragoczy with the ferocity of his attack. But Ragoczy was not where he had been a moment before; he had stepped aside and swung neatly around to face Ursellos, who had stumbled to a halt. "Craven!" Ursellos bellowed and rushed toward him again, and once again discovered Ragoczy had eluded him. "Fight me, you gutless old man!"

Ragoczy took up his fighting stance. "At your service," he said coolly; long, long ago he had learned to fight silently, reserving all his concentration for fighting, not for adding insults to the conflict. His attention was so fixed on Ursellos that he could almost feel him breathing.

This time Ursellos closed with him in a more workman-like way, relying less on a single dramatic burst than on a tactical approach, moving less precipitously than before. His rapier work was rapid but without finesse, and hampered by trying to parry a left-handed opponent. He used his dagger to keep Ragoczy from moving any closer to him, flailing out with it as his rapier flicked along Ragoczy's blade. His anger gave him strength, and he squandered it in lashing assaults that Ragoczy turned aside with what appeared to be no more effort than swatting a mosquito, which enraged Ursellos all the more. He became increasingly irate, the veins standing out on his temples. "You cold-blooded poltroon!"

In response to this insult, Ragoczy stepped up his swordplay, catching Ursellos off-guard; he faced the Spaniard and in a brief, dazzling series of seemingly effortless feints, drove Ursellos back half the distance of the crossroad. Then he stopped, giving Ursellos room to find new footing. "Colonna?"

Ettore Colonna had been watching as closely as the darkness would permit—the light from the lanterns provided little useful illumination, creating little tunnels of light in the dimness—and now left his place by the shrine. "Momentino," he called, striding over to the two combatants to once again separate their crossed blades.

"You shall fall!" Ursellos shouted, lunging at Ragoczy, only to find his rapier parried neatly and Ragoczy's dagger pointed at his belt. With a yelp he jumped back, slamming his rapier through the air as if it were an axe. As he recovered himself, he swiped out at Ragoczy's legs, following this foul cut with an upward jab of his dagger aimed at Ragoczy's ribs. His exclamation of triumph was brief.

Ragoczy slipped away, leaving Ursellos to try not to be overbalanced by the force of his strike; taking up his fighting stance, he kept on the flattest ground, avoiding the most uneven places that could trip him up. "I have done nothing to compromise your sister," he said as Ursellos prepared to charge him.

"Liar!" Ursellos hewed the air with his dagger and then his rapier, infuriated as Ragoczy deflected the attack. He stood panting, peering into the night for Ragoczy, who was not standing in the light of any of the lanthorns. "You want to hide from me?"

Off to his right, Ragoczy said, "I have no reason to hide from you." Ursellos shouted and drove his rapier in the direction of the sound. "I'll kill you!"

Ragoczy did not bother to answer; he moved deliberately into the light and readied himself for another onslaught. When it came, he slipped his rapier inside Ursellos' thrust and swung his dagger out and in a long curve upward so that Ursellos could not reposit in time to hurt him; he disengaged and stepped back.

"Very prettily done," Ettore Colonna approved.

Paying no attention to his second's remark, Ragoczy moved lightly aside as Ursellos rushed at him again; he was glad of the night, when his strength was at its greatest and his endurance was enhanced. He felt Ursellos' dagger catch on the sleeve of his camisa, ripping the fabric; he managed to tear it away so that no weapon would be entangled in the loose flap of cloth, all the while moving warily so that he could watch Ursellos at all instants: he had no wish to kill the obnoxious man, for that would leave Leocadia with only Ahrent Rothofen to protect her.

"God will send you to Hell!" Ursellos yelled, making an ill-considered run at Ragoczy; he plunged beyond the place where Ragoczy had been standing and very nearly tripped on his spurs in his haste to swing around to continue his assault. He struck out and nicked Ragoczy's cheek with the tip of his rapier; he howled with delight at the sight of blood. "That is just the first."

Ragoczy did not bother to touch the little cut: he could feel it, cold and hot at once, as well as the thin trail of blood sliding like tears down his face. He did not speak, but his dark eyes grew flintier as he prepared to take the offensive. There was a subtle shift in his attitude as he met Ursellos' next charge: this time he did not slip away, but caught Ursellos' rapier on the basket-hilt of his own, at the same time pinking Ursellos' shoulder with his dagger.

Now it was Ursellos who staggered back, furious astonishment distorting his features. "You *turd-fucker!*" he brayed, slapping at

Ragoczy with his rapier as he retreated almost to the edge of their dueling-ground.

Ragoczy pressed his advantage just enough to shake Ursellos' angry confidence. Then he stepped back, once again allowing Ursellos to find a better position before summoning Ettore Colonna to recommence their contest.

"I can stop this," Ettore Colonna said before he released their blades.

"Ask Calaveria y Vacamonte," Ragoczy recommended. "He issued the challenge."

"I will not be satisfied until I have his life," Ursellos growled, his Spanish accent much stronger than usual, revealing his faltering control.

"You won't be able to get it," Ettore Colonna said, a bit waspishly, as he scraped his rapier upward between theirs.

"What does that fop know?" Ursellos sneered, slashing horizontally with his rapier and following with an abrupt thrust with his dagger.

But again Ragoczy pivoted away, using Ursellos' own momentum to throw the Spaniard off-balance while he set himself for the next paroxysm.

"You *offal!*" Ursellos ran at Ragoczy, his face red, his mouth an open square, his weapons pointed forward like lances or spears.

Instead of stepping away from Ursellos' advance, Ragoczy took the brunt of it, parrying both rapier and dagger so swiftly that none of the observers could say how it happened: one moment Ursellos seemed about to bowl Ragoczy over and run him through, in the next heartbeat, Ursellos' rapier was spinning through the air, he was lying on his side and Ragoczy had pinned his dagger-hand to the ground with his heel. "This can end now; I have no wish to kill you."

"*I* have a wish to kill *you*," Ursellos said in Spanish. "Let me up, I order you!"

Ettore Colonna strolled forward. "You are no longer the one making the rules, Calaveria y Vacamonte. You have been bested." He glanced at Ragoczy. "Do you want to run him through?"

"Not particularly; he is not worth the trouble that would bring." Ragoczy went down on one knee, his attention wholly on Ursellos, whose wrist he still kept pinioned. "I am willing for this to be finished between us."

"You whoreson bastard," Ursellos grumbled; he was breathing hard, some of it because of exertion, some from the intensity of his emotions.

"That is no answer," Ragoczy said calmly. "I do not think you quite understand." He was about to lean forward when he heard the bark of a pistol behind him, and in the next instant a hot furrow dug itself the length of his thigh.

In the next breath, Ettore Colonna had drawn his pistol and shot Ahrent Rothofen, sending him sprawling back on the roof of the Calaveria y Vacamonte coach; as soon as he was sure no more shots would be fired—Amerigo and Matyas had brought muskets and now held them at the ready—he turned to Ragoczy. "Are you all right?"

Through clenched teeth, Ragoczy answered, "It's damnably painful, but it will heal." And, he added to himself, would leave no scar.

"Can you get up?" Ettore Colonna ignored Ursellos who was writhing in an attempt to pull his arm free.

"You're getting blood all over me," Ursellos burst out, slapping at his clothes with his free hand.

"I thought that was what you wanted," said Ragoczy, his voice still tense, but his manner formally correct. He looked up at Ettore Colonna. "If you would be good enough to lend me your arm? And ask the physician to see to Rothofen. He is moaning dreadfully."

"You are the one who is hurt," Ettore Colonna said as he helped Ragoczy to rise, keeping himself between Ursellos and Ragoczy as he did.

"Not as badly as Rothofen." He looked past Ettore Colonna to Ursellos, saying, "You have what you want. Leave it at that."

Ursellos cursed extravagantly, but took an unsteady pace backward. "This is not over yet." In the confusion of the lamplight, he stumbled, and screeched as his hand was bent back.

"But it is," said Ettore Colonna, rounding on him. "You demanded blood and you have had it. Ragoczy has the victory, and you should be glad to be alive. If you make any more attempts on this man, the story of this evening will get out, and you will have to bear the condemnation of those who matter in Roma."

Ursellos hung on to his wrist. "I think it's broken," he said, and started away toward his coach.

"The physician will look after Rothofen," Ragoczy called out, steeling himself against the stripe of agony down his leg. "He was probably aiming for my back." There was an ironic note in his voice that mixed with the stress of his pain; a bullet in the back would have meant the True Death for him as surely as it would for any living man.

"Let the blaggard bleed," said Ettore Colonna as he began to help Ragoczy gingerly make his way toward his coach. "It's no more than he deserves."

"But I do not need it whispered that I conspired in his suffering," said Ragoczy, wincing as he limped. "It will be bad enough when this duello is talked about."

From his place on the driving box of Ragoczy's coach, Amerigo kept his musket trained on Ursellos, prepared for trouble.

Ettore Colonna said very little as they went on; he was concentrating on supporting Ragoczy over the ruts. He noticed that Ragoczy's compact body was very strong, far more so than it appeared to be. As they neared Ragoczy's coach they saw the physician come bustling forward from the smaller carriage. "He says you're to help Rothofen—the fellow on top of that coach." He pointed.

"But I should attend to the Conte first," the physician protested. "I will offer my services to—"

Ragoczy interrupted him. "Go to his aid. My wound is not mortal." He waved the physician away, secretly relieved that he would not have to endure an examination or answer any of a number of questions that might arise. "Help me into my coach, if you would, Colonna," he said.

Ettore Colonna did as he was asked, lifting and shoving until Ragoczy was leaning back in the rear-facing seat. "I'll fetch your manservant."

"Thank you," said Ragoczy just above a whisper; the hurt was growing, burning like poison but he strove to preserve his self-possession. Only when the door was closed did he catch his lower lip between his teeth, holding back a groan.

"My master?" Rugerius asked, letting down the stairs and climbing into the coach. "Are you badly hurt?"

"Not really. Nothing like Baghdad, or Mexico." He did his best to offer a brief smile. "It will be sore for a while."

"Shall I take your boot off so your breeches can be removed?" He kept his emotions in check, maintaining the pragmatism that he had learned before Ragoczy had restored him to life over sixteen hundred years ago.

"Not yet: when the coach is on a decent road." He pressed his lips together, a thin vertical line forming between his brows.

There was a knock on the door of the coach. "Do you mind if I borrow your other coach, Conte?" Ettore Colonna asked. "I want to be sure that Rothofen gets home alive, and that Calaveria y Vacamonte does not take it into his head to try something petty."

"Do, please," said Ragoczy. "And be good enough to see the physician back to his house when his work is over, if you would."

"Eccellenza, you are too gracious," said Ettore Colonna. "I will call upon you tomorrow afternoon, to return your carriage and your coachman."

"I anticipate your visit—" Ragoczy began.

"—with happy enthusiasm. Yes, I know," said Ettore Colonna before calling out to Matyas, relaying Ragoczy's instructions, and then giving sharp orders to Ursellos.

Beyond the coach there was a bustle of activity; inside the coach, Ragoczy reclined on the seat, saying, "Tell Amerigo to take us back to Villa Vecchia."

Text of the testimony of Gennaro Colonna given to the Holy Office.

In the Name of the Father, the Son, and the Holy Ghost, Amen. As a faithful Christian and a dedicated Catholic, I swear by all I hold sacred that this account will be accurate, without guile or flaw, as if it were to stand before God's Judgment, and I will answer for what I state here as true with my body in this life and my soul in the life that is to come.

You good Fathers have reviewed the reports of the Dominicans and Franciscans regarding the Conde de San Germanno whom I had the honor to know many years ago in South America, and for whom I came to have the highest esteem. He was a man of strong principles and great learning, and it was through his skills as a physician that my life was saved as it was through his kindness that I came to my vocation. This good man was accused of many nefarious things by powerful men within the Church who sought to use their offices to maintain earthly power among the people, and who found San Germanno a staunch opponent to all their efforts to hamper and denigrate the people they had conquered. In spite of his long imprisonment, I never saw any trace of the crimes of which he was suspected, and at no time in his long ordeal did he behave in any way that suggested he had deserved his incarceration. I never heard any heresy spoken by him, nor did I ever see any sign of diabolism in anything he did, unless healing those our physicians could not heal could be thought diabolistic.

It is true I counted him my friend, and it is true I am not inclined to speak ill of him, but as I am sworn to speak to you as I would before God, I say that I have no doubt now, as I had none then, that this man had integrity that we would all do well to emulate: he has been my high example for many, many years, and I shall continue to hold his memory first in my heart. Because he was so much a part of my salvation, my recollection of him remains much more clearly defined than many another I have from that time in my life.

Your table of inquiry asks about Ferenc Ragoczy, currently residing at Villa Vecchia just beyond Roma. You want to know how closely this Ragoczy, who is Conte da San-Germain, might be related to the man I knew in the Viceroyalty of Peru: this man in Roma admits to being related to San Germanno, and, though my eyes are not keen anymore, I see a resemblance. But this man in Roma is not so tall as San Germanno, and is thicker of body. Also, there is a similarity of voice, as one often encounters in families, but this man's is more flexible than San Germanno's, which I assume is the result of his years as a musician; my friend had some ability to play the guitar, but he had nowhere near the accomplishments of his relative, whose talents are very great.

Regarding scars, I must tell you that I did not have many occasions to see San Germanno unclothed; on the two occasions I remember, I did not notice such scars as you say San-Germain has. I would have noticed anything so severe. Of course, being a man of wide experience, he had a few marks on his body, including a knot of bone on his clavicle, the remnant of an old break. You make no mention of such an injury on this man, so they cannot possibly be the same man, for I take it you are entertaining so astonishing a possibility.

Had San Germanno been alive now, he would be at least a decade older than I am, possibly two decades, not a hale fellow of forty years or so. Why should you come to so preposterous a conclusion as this: that the San Germanno I knew and San-Germain are one in the same? Surely you are being swayed by credulous or devious persons who seek to abuse the Holy Office by bending it to their purposes. I do not single any person out for criticism, for that is not my place, but I tell you that if you allow yourselves to be swayed by such fallacious testimony, you will be doing San-Germain a grave injustice as well as compromising the legacy of the truly great man who saved me so long ago.

I pray you will scrutinize all that you have gathered on these two men, keeping in mind that neither one has ever been proven to be inimical to the Church, not even after you, good Fathers, have conducted all but the most stringent inquiries into their lives. I believe it would serve the Church poorly to continue this long investigation into allegations that are so ludicrous as to be laughable if they did not impinge on the honor and reputation of two men of excellent lineage and character.

As one who counted San Germanno my most essential friend, I speak on behalf of his kinsman, both out of my obligation as a Christian to bear witness to the truth, and as the only person who can tell you beyond any question that Ferenc Ragoczy is not San Germanno. I will maintain this no matter what tales ambitious and jealous persons tell you, and I will challenge anyone to prove I am in error.

In true devotion and humility, and without recourse to my title, either familial or religious, I am

> *Your most obedient,*
> *Gennaro Colonna*

On the 15th day of September, 1690. By my own hand.

> *Deo Gratias*

Although he no longer needed it, Ragoczy walked with a cane because it was expected after such a wound, and not to use one would attract attention that would be awkward to have just now; he was supervising the placement of furniture in his new villa, Bonaldo Fiumara at his side. He was simply dressed in a plain waistcoat over a linen camisa and simple breeches; his shoes were thick-soled and practical, without ornamentation and he wore neither hat nor wig. It was almost mid-day, when the workers would eat and then rest for two hours.

"The rafters will be carved, of course." Fiumara could not conceal his pride in the superior craftsmanship his men had produced. "But that will be done when the weather turns colder, which it will do in four or five weeks. I don't want the workers to waste the last of the sun and the warmth." He pointed to where three young men were struggling to get a marble tabletop into place. "They will be finishing the shutters on the second-story windows when they have completed this."

"Very good," Ragoczy said, looking around the handsome entry the builders had made, and thinking it would be sad to have to leave it so soon after completion. He studied the pattern on the floor, an old Roman design of grapevines and fruit done in inlaid mosaic tiles. "This turned out well."

"So I think," Fiumara said with a rush of pride. "After so many difficulties, it is a good thing to have it all turn out so well."

Ragoczy did not say anything for a short while; he could not convince himself that all the adversities of the last year were finally behind him, or that the outcome had been a good one for everyone involved. He looked about the room and said, "Your efforts here have truly been exceptional."

Fiumara smiled broadly. "So I think, too. The men worked very hard."

"And were well-paid for their efforts," said Ragoczy at his most cordial. "It was worth every Emperor."

Fiumara coughed. "As to that, Eccellenza, it is the policy of the Artei to—"

"Yes, I know," said Ragoczy. "Have I protested the cost?" He did not wait for an answer; he went into the reception room on the north side of the new building. "The drapers should come in a week or two, should they not?"

"They will be here as soon as the Florentine velvet you ordered arrives. If you will permit me to say it, Signor' Conte, so much velvet might be seen as excessive. If you were part of the Papal Court, that would be another matter, but as you are a foreigner, living outside the walls of Roma, some could see so much luxury as ostentation, and could use it to discredit you again."

"They may be right: so much velvet would be ostentatious if I could not afford it," said Ragoczy. "I ordered four bolts of it be sent to the Laterano, as a gesture of appreciation." A smile tweaked the corners of his lips.

"How clever you are," Fiumara exclaimed, chuckling. "I should have known you wouldn't be caught out." He paced the length of the room. "It would be grander if you had mirrors along this wall."

"So it would, but it would also be very French; the Pope—Alessandro VIII or his successor—might decide to lock horns with Louis again, and then where would I be." He shook his head. "No. Mirrors are more problematic than velvet."

Fiumara pursed his lips. "When the next Pope reigns—and Alessandro is old, so it will be sooner than later—we may have more cordial doings with France."

"Or they might be worse," Ragoczy said. "Have the kitchens been finished yet?" It was a deliberate change of subject, and both men recognized it.

"Yes. Your cooks may begin their labors at any time." He paused at the window, looking out at the old villa. "That must have been very grand, a long time ago."

"It was," said Ragoczy, without a trace of nostalgia despite the centuries of memories the old villa housed. He crossed the room toward the withdrawing room behind the reception room. "The Velasquezes are to hang in here. The *Death of Socrates* should go on this wall." He indicated the eastern one. "There are some smaller works that can flank it; the Chinese chest should go under it."

"I will see that it's done," said Fiumara. "Do you want the old building taken down?" His voice was tentative and he almost held his breath waiting for the answer.

"I suppose it would be wisest," said Ragoczy distantly. He paused, then said, "Could you salvage enough of it to make a guest-house?"

"Of course," said Fiumara quickly enough, then added more cautiously, "It would be an expensive business: first the old building would have to be carefully taken down, and the stones examined and prepared before any construction could begin on a new—"

Ragoczy gestured impatiently. "I will pay for it. Have your Arte inform me how much is required in deposit." He smiled briefly. "It may seem an extravagance to you, but that villa has stood since the Caesars ruled in Roma. It seems a shame to lose it completely after so long." He knew he was being whimsical, but it did not trouble him. "Regard it as another of my eccentricities."

Bonaldo Fiumara bowed from the waist. "As you wish, Signor' Conte." He cocked his head in the direction of the study. "Do you want to inspect there next? The men are working on the shelving today."

"That will not trouble me," said Ragoczy, starting in that direction.

"My master!" Rugerius called from the reception room. "My master!"

Ragoczy stopped, turning awkwardly to face his manservant who hastened toward him; long experience with Rugerius told Ragoczy that although nothing in his demeanor expressed it, he brought bad news. "What is it?"

"Alfredo Cervetti has just ridden over from Senza Pari at a canter; his horse is all but spent. There is a fire—" He did not go on.

"A fire?" Ragoczy repeated, intent on the answer.

"Cervetti says the stables and the storehouses are burning." He met Ragoczy's eyes. "With Niklos Aulirios in France, Cervetti thought it wisest to come to you."

"Very prudent. Tell Matyas to saddle the Andalusian gelding for me," Ragoczy said briskly; as Rugerius hurried off, Ragoczy said to Fiumara, "I regret that I cannot finish this tour just now. Tell your men that what I have seen thus far pleases me very much: there will be bonuses for all of them."

Fiumara bowed again. "Of course, Eccellenza."

Had he been alone, Ragoczy would have tossed away the cane and strode to the old building; as it was, he pushed his speed as much as he dared, pegging down the front stairs with increasing frustration: delay could mean destruction at Senza Pari. By the time he had crossed the courtyard and entered the old villa, he was eager to put his cane aside. He rushed to his apartment, changed his shoes for boots, dragged a black-wool riding cloak from its peg behind the door, took up his sword, and was out of the room as quickly as he could be. Leaving by the side-door, he went directly to the stable where he found Matyas and Rugerius. "Where's Cervetti?"

"In the kitchen. He was worn out," said Rugerius.

"So was his horse." Matyas was securing the girths on the Andalusian. "I'll do what I can for the gelding, but he may be done for."

"I'll try to spare this one," said Ragoczy as he swung his cloak around his shoulders and reached for the bridle. "Tell me everything you can, Rugerius."

"Cervetti reports that the fire broke out in the stables about dawn, and he summoned the staff to help put it out. No sooner had they brought it under control, than another one burst out by the storehouses; he put the servants to fighting it and came to ask for your help. Cervetti says that the only household member he could not find is Bonifaccio." Rugerius remained calm through his report.

"Ah," said Ragoczy as he buckled the noseband into position, and lifted the reins over the snowy Andalusian's head.

"You are not surprised," said Rugerius.

"No; not surprised. Niklos said something about the man, oh, more than a year ago; I know he was concerned about him." He buckled on his sword and vaulted into the saddle. "Be sure Cervetti is given a chance to rest."

"And what of men to help? Should we dispatch any?" Matyas asked.

"Yes. Half a dozen of the strongest who can be spared." Ragoczy was ready to go. "Send them along in the smaller coach as soon as you can round them up. Put my red-lacquer chest of medicaments on the roof of the coach."

Rugerius inclined his head. "I know what is to be done."

Ragoczy shot him an understanding look. "Your pardon, old friend. I was maladroit." Gathering up the reins, he swung the Andalusian about with the pressure of his leg and said, "I will send word when you are to expect me if I am delayed until morning."

"Very good," said Rugerius, standing back to let Ragoczy ride out of the stables; he and Matyas watched Ragoczy put the Andalusian to a fast trot before they went about their duties.

The Andalusian was strong, with excellent stamina; the day was warm and just windy enough that it took the weight from the heat but the road was dusty, which the wind made worse. With distressing thoughts for companions, Ragoczy rode toward Senza Pari, certain that the two fires were not accidental, if for no other reason than that they were too convenient, what with Niklos Aulirios gone. He did not like to consider who might have wanted the fires set: those were the most bothersome notions of all. The irony of the situation provided him grim amusement: Olivia had died the True Death in an explosion at his Villa Vecchia, and now he was riding to a calamity at Senza Pari; had Niklos Aulirios not prevailed in his claim, this would not be happening. The possibility that the decision of the Magistrates' Court made in Niklos' favor might have something to do with the fire did not escape Ragoczy's attention; it added to his anxiety as he rode. After two leagues he pulled the gelding into a walk so as not to wear him out; at half a league farther on, he put the horse into the trot again.

There was a coil of dark smoke rising over the brow of the hill, marking the place of the fire. Ragoczy saw it as he came over the rise between Roma and the turn to Senza Pari. It was not large enough to suggest the fire had spread far, nor was it so faint that it would mean the fire was dying.

"Been like that all morning," remarked an elderly man on a donkey coming the other way; he looked unconcerned for the fate of those fighting the fire. "The monks are moving their treasures out of the monastery, in case the wind should blow it their way."

Ragoczy did not slow his horse, calling out, "Thank you for telling me."

The old man laughed, waving his hat as if for a grand occasion. "Too bad old Nerone is long gone: he would enjoy this."

At the turn, Ragoczy came upon the monks, all bustling to load up ox-carts to bear their chapel-goods away from danger. They worked in silence, still maintaining their vow; only one looked up as Ragoczy rode past. Then the monks were behind him and he was bound for Senza Pari, the smoke beckoning him on, undulating on the increasing heat of early afternoon. Finally he reached the approached to the villa itself, and finally let his gelding canter; the horse was tired and the smoke made him nervous, but he answered the nudging of Ragoczy's heels. Nearing the villa itself, Ragoczy pulled his horse around to the south-east side of the house, away from the stables. By now the air stank of burning, and the shouts of those fighting the fire added their own confusion.

Demetrio, the under-coachman, was the first to notice Ragoczy's arrival. His face and arms were smirched and sooty and his hair was singed, but he bowed to Ragoczy and grinned. "You are bringing help," he shouted. "Cervetti said you would." He ended this with a hacking cough and wheezing inhalation.

"In a while," Ragoczy responded. "They are coming by coach."

"We need them as soon as may be." He stopped still, gasping. "We've put out two, but now there is a third going, in the coach-house."

"A third fire?" Ragoczy frowned as he found a tree-branch to which he could tie his Andalusian's reins. "When did it begin?" he asked as he dismounted and secured his horse.

"More than an hour ago." Demetrio sighed, suddenly exhausted. "We had the second fire half-out, and the new one began. We can't spare anyone to search, but someone must—" He looked over his shoulder warily. "Ottorino and Felice have been sent into the house with barrels of water, in case anything more should happen."

"Do you expect anything more?" Ragoczy peered into the smoke feeling uneasy; fire was as deadly to him as to any man, and he had a keen understanding of what it could do.

"We did not expect any of this," said Demetrio. He pointed to the twenty or so men who were busy with buckets, drawing water from the troughs and the stream that cut through the nearest paddock. A few of the women-servants tended to those who had been hurt, and another pair of women were helping to fill buckets at the old well. "And when Cervetti left, we were in disarray until old Montecchi—the one who runs the winepress—assumed command."

"And where may I find Montecchi?" He knew the vintner by sight, but did not want to try to search without direction through the chaos for him.

"He was over on the far side of the coach-house, the last time I saw him, on the west side of the villa," said Demetrio. "I have to sit down a moment; I'm getting dizzy."

"Better lie down," Ragoczy recommended, hoping his men would arrive shortly, for he could see Demetrio would need something to help clear his lungs; the medicament that would do it was in his red-lacquer chest. "Let the others deal with the fire."

"But I should try to save the coach-house. It is my responsibility," he protested weakly.

"It may be, but if you collapse while fighting the fire, no one will benefit." He saw the chagrin in Demetrio's eyes. "Make sure my horse doesn't panic. That will help me."

Demetrio nodded. "I will," he said, and lay back, pasty under the smuts.

Satisfied that Demetrio would not overexert himself now, Ragoczy hurried toward the flames, looking about for Montecchi amidst the confusion of servants. Servants were rushing about through the thickening smoke, a few of them clearly suffering; ordinarily he would have stopped to help them: he would do that later, when his men arrived. He saw the stable was partially destroyed, the tack-room nothing but charred beams. There was no sign of burned horses, which was some consolation; he hoped they had been got out of their stalls in time.

"Who are you?" one of the servants exclaimed as he grabbed hold of Ragoczy from behind. "I have him!" he shouted before receiving an answer.

Some of the servants stopped what they were doing and gave their attention to Ragoczy and his captor. Questions and accusations jumbled with the snap and clamor of the fire; a few of the servants hurled pebbles and singed wood at Ragoczy.

"Do not!" Ragoczy said sharply as a number of the servants converged upon him. "I am not your enemy. I am Ragoczy. Alfredo Cervetti asked me to come!" He ducked as a wet rag flew by his shoulder; a few of the servants looked angry or troubled but most of them were disbelieving until the chief cook, the massive Nobile Cofano, trundled forward, squinting with blood-shot eyes.

"He is our master's friend. The foreign Conte." He motioned to the man holding Ragoczy. "Release him, Ebbo."

An elderly man with gnarled features and a cloud of white hair now tarnished by the smoke arrived. He took one look at Ragoczy and burst out, "You came very quickly, Signor' Conte," he said as he bowed and attempted to kiss Ragoczy's hand.

"Never mind this," said Ragoczy, trying not to snap. "We can worry about form when the fires are out." He regarded Montecchi. "Where do you need help the most?"

Montecchi pointed toward the coach-house. "It is still wild, as you can see." He made a helpless gesture. "Whoever is doing it—" To finish his thought, he shook his head.

"Then you are certain the fires are set," said Ragoczy, who had no doubts.

"One might have been an accident," said Montecchi. "But three? And starting suddenly? We haven't time or men enough to find the bastard."

"Then let us keep pouring water on the flames; the sooner the fires are out, the sooner we may discover who has set them," said Ragoczy, pulling up his sleeves and throwing his cloak toward the hitching-post where he usually tied his horse. "I have more men coming in a short while."

As if his presence encouraged them, the servants redoubled their efforts; for the better part of an hour they labored ceaselessly to quench the flames. Ragoczy carried water from the troughs to the men, showing no signs of fatigue, although he was bothered by the nearness of the fire. Finally the fire began to fade; most of the coach-house was in ruins, but the blaze had not spread. Ragoczy made sure most of the men who had been fighting the blaze were accounted for, and then carefully walked around the smoldering coach-house, doing his best to assess the damage.

"The house! *The house!*" came the horrified cry, and Ragoczy saw a curl of smoke rise from the north-eastern corner of Olivia's villa. There were howls of dismay and deep-felt curses, and the servants tried to muster the strength to stop another conflagration, and that in the part of the villa farthest from the well-fed troughs and the stream.

Ragoczy ran toward the smoke, not bothering to hide his extraordinary speed; running, he asked himself where his coach was, and why had no other help arrived.

The fire had started from a bundle of straw and rags that gave off the odor of burning pitch. There were dark streaks on the walls, as if they had been smeared with the flammable material in order to spread the fire more quickly, and the smoke it gave off was oilily black.

"Eustazio is inside!" The cry was from a woman, high and terrified. "He's sick! He can't get out!"

Others shouted, and Nobile Cofano made a ponderous rush at the kitchen door, only to be ordered back by Montecchi. "There is fire inside already."

A window on the second floor burst, and fire raged out. The servants drew back, a number of them weeping in futility and frustration. The woman who had shouted began to scream for her brother.

"Look!" shouted Ebbo. "Another fire. There, on the stairs!"

"What about Ottorino!" shrieked one of the stable-hands. "He's in the house!"

"And so is Felice!" Ebbo yelled, trying to make himself get closer to the fire.

From his place on the flank of the house, Ragoczy could see smoke filling the rooms, and knew that anyone inside would have to get out quickly or be stifled. Hating fire as he did, he hesitated only for a moment, and then ran toward the narrow windows of the old withdrawing room that looked out on the grapevines of the estate. He hit the glass with his arms folded over his head; it shattered around him, and the fire boomed on the floor above him. Looking up, he saw little flames running along the ceiling in waves; he had very little time to find anyone, let alone get him out. Over the pandemonium of the fire, he could hear a man coughing and trying to pray. Using this sound as a guide, Ragoczy went through the withdrawing room toward the corridor, his hands still raised to shelter his head. The heat was enormous, and the smoke made it worse.

In the corridor the smoke was thicker, concealing any flames that might be burning there; Ragoczy crouched low to avoid the heat, for he did not need to breathe, and now he was glad of it. He followed the sound of the voice, hoping that the man would not be overcome before Ragoczy could find him. The raging of the fire grew louder, and Ragoczy could feel it fan his face, crisping his eyebrows and singeing his hair. "Anyone!" he shouted, and coughed as smoke filled his lungs.

There was a faint cry ahead of him near the door leading down into the cellars; this was followed at once by a sound of choking.

Ragoczy made a quick rush toward the voice, nearly tripping over the prone figure. Blinking furiously, he reached down and grabbed the fallen man's arm, then started dragging him along the corridor toward the kitchen, where there had been the least fire when Ragoczy went into the house. Lacking tears, Ragoczy's eyes felt like cracked glass in his head, and he knew it would be many days before they would stop hurting, assuming he averted greater harm in this burning building. The weight of the man he was dragging seemed to be heavier; the fire was sapping Ragoczy's tremendous strength, making every step more arduous than the last; he could not bring himself to abandon the man.

Something struck him a glancing blow: a beam had fallen, black and hot. Ragoczy had to crawl under it, tugging the man behind him. The fire was much closer, fuming like a maddened animal, almost alive in its malignity. With a last, grueling effort, Ragoczy dragged himself and his burden onto the flagstones of the kitchen; they were hot to the touch, but by contrast to the corridor, they seemed cool. It was tempting to lie there for a time, to recoup his energy before trying to go on. Deep within himself, Ragoczy knew this was deadly folly. He pulled himself forward, using his forearm; he had not yet let go of the unconscious man. Each hand's-breadth of progress felt like leagues, but he kept on.

Then suddenly he was soaking wet, and there were shouts all around him. Ragoczy sputtered as a second bucket of water splashed over him, and he looked up to see Matyas bending over him, horror in his eyes. "The house?" he croaked.

"Most of it is gone," said Matyas, hauling Ragoczy to his feet. "Your clothes were burning."

"Small wonder," Ragoczy muttered, letting himself sag on Matyas' shoulder; they made their way out through the old stone arch of the kitchen, now bedecked with broken and charred sections of walls, beams, and flooring. "Did anyone else—?"

"No," said Matyas, and paused to cross himself. "May God welcome them as martyrs." There was furious activity around them as four of the servants rushed forward to take the man Ragoczy had dragged out of the house in hand. Their urgent shouts made it hard for Ragoczy to think.

Montecchi rushed up to Ragoczy. "Oh, Saints and La Virgine be thanked," he shouted, patting Ragoczy with a familiarity he would not dream of in ordinary circumstances. "You are alive."

"As much as I was before," said Ragoczy, clearing his throat.

"That was too near a thing," said Montecchi. "Much too near." He glanced back at the ruin behind him. "What will Signor' Aulirios think? How can I tell him?"

"I will do that," said Ragoczy. They were a dozen strides away from the villa now, and there was less activity. Ragoczy could see his coach standing a short distance away, Amerigo on the box, holding the restive team in order. Fatigue had him in its grip, and it would not be alleviated until he was revived with blood and intimacy or by his native earth. "Take me to my coach," he murmured. "I need to lie down." The floor of the coach was lined with his native earth.

"Just a while. An hour at most." He staggered as he attempted to climb into the coach, but he refused Matyas' help. "Go. You are needed elsewhere. Amerigo can guard me."

"That I can," said Amerigo at once. "I will see no one disturbs you," he assured Ragoczy as Matyas reluctantly went to assist the servants.

As he lay on the floor of his coach, Ragoczy let the annealing presence of his native earth envelop him; as he lapsed into what for him passed for sleep, he thought, I have spent too much time recovering in carriages; two times in as many months is too often. He did not know how much time had passed when he was jarred awake by persistent pounding on the coach door and Amerigo calling to him to waken.

"Conte! Signor' Conte! Eccellenza! *Wake up!*" Amerigo sounded worried.

"Another fire?" Ragoczy asked, his voice hoarse, his eyes feeling brittle and sore. He knew where every burn, scrape, and bruise was on his flesh; it was an effort to ignore them.

"No." Amerigo flung the door open. "You must come at once. Montecchi is beside himself."

"Why?" Ragoczy made himself sit up. "Give me a moment," he said without waiting for an explanation. He could see the light was beginning to fade, turning the hills a deep golden color and giving the sky a depth of color greater than the sea. The scorched stench hung on the air, but it was no longer new; now it carried dust with it, and the smell of water-logged wood. It was not easy to climb out of the coach, to leave the comfort of his native earth behind. Getting out of the coach with great care, he stood for a long moment hanging on to the grip on the side of the coach. Then he straightened up. "All right. What does Montecchi want?"

"He is with those who were hurt. He says there is something you have to see." Amerigo went to the head of his team. "I can't leave them—not with that milling herd out in the field." He jutted his chin in the direction of the pasture beyond the gutted stable where most of the horses of Senza Pari fretted.

"Just so," said Ragoczy, starting across the yard, feeling every hour of his age; he paid no heed to the stares the servants gave him as he passed. He caught sight of Matyas, and called to him. "Where is Montecchi?"

Matyas left off clearing away the fallen walls of the stable and came up to Ragoczy. "He's with the injured." He pointed to the makeshift table where wounds were being dressed.

"Thank you." Ragoczy saw his red-lacquer chest at the far end of the table and made his way toward it. Nearing Montecchi who stood guard over the chest, he raised his voice. "You wished to see me?"

Montecchi turned around, consternation on his seamed features. "Signor' Conte," he said, and faltered. "I . . . I don't know . . . how to—" He stopped himself by pointing. "That is the man you pulled out of the house, whose life you saved. He is still unconscious."

"Who is he?" Ragoczy asked.

"I do not know him," said Montecchi. "I pray you do."

This announcement served to perplex Ragoczy. "He is not part of this household?" He saw Montecchi gesture in the negative; suddenly he felt cold to the marrow. "Do you think he set the fires?"

"Who else could have done it?" Montecchi said, stepping out of the way so that Ragoczy could approach the supine figure lying on the ground under a horse-blanket. "If you know him, tell me."

Ragoczy looked down, his frown deepening; at first all he could make out was the soot and scrapes, then the countenance beneath became visible. "I know him," he said distantly as he stared into the face of Ursellos Calaveria y Vacamonte.

Text of a letter from Conte Balletti in Salzburg to Ettore Colonna, delivered by courier.

To the most excellent of good friends, Ettore Colonna, the greetings from one who had not been in Roma for almost a year.

Your kind letter of March 10th finally reached me through my holdings in Amsterdam, and I apologize that it has taken me so long to respond. For an explanation of this conduct I can only plead the exigencies of my new circumstances that have compelled me to place many obstacles between me and my life in Roma.

In that regard, as you see, I have taken your advice and used a name that is in no way connected to Ragoczy or Saint-Germain; as Conte Balletti I have a most worthy disguise. Rugerius is calling himself Rudiger, which is nearer his name than my alias is to mine, but different enough that it should not attract more than passing notice; he has used a walnut stain to make his hair a dark-brown and he has affixed a mole to his cheek.

So Ursellos Calaveria y Vacamonte and Ahrent Rothofen have become residents in the Pope's Little House; Rothofen's shoulder wound is still troubling him, I suppose, and to have the Holy Office added to his woes—appalling. As despicable as their acts were, I can find it in my heart to pity them, for no one deserves the hospitality the Holy Office offers its guests. Their condemnation by Magistrates' Court and the judgment of fines and prison against them seemed sufficient to me, but over the years I have become less inclined to exact vengeance masquerading as justice; not that these two have not earned the abhorrence of Roma for their crimes. Still, I would not wish the dungeons of the Holy Office on any offender, no matter how grievous their offenses might be. I have some experience of them myself and I know whereof I speak. You tell me that Leocadia has returned to Spain and entered a convent; may she find some peace there, for surely it has eluded her in this world.

I am indebted to you for all you have done on my behalf; your report on Bonaldo Fiumara's custodianship of Villa Vecchia is reassuring, although not surprising. I am also cheered to know that the rebuilding at Senza Pari is under way. When Niklos Aulirios finally returns he will have a home to inhabit, and a working estate that will once again be flourishing. Know that I am obliged to you for all you have done, and if there is anything I may do to show my appreciation, you have only to name it and it will be arranged.

Extend my thanks to your cousin, Gennaro, for I understand that his heroic account of San Germanno in South America has relieved Ferenc Ragoczy of any stain of connection beyond the accident of family. I have no way to acknowledge the great service he did me without compromising its good, so if you will convey my indebtedness to him, I would count it among your many kindnesses. Sadly, I must decline to answer the question you put to me regarding my age: suffice it to say that it is much greater than you have speculated; be content with that answer, I ask you for both our sakes.

If you would have more of my gratitude, tell me: have you any notion who will be elected Pope now that Alessandro VIII is dead? You hear all the whispers and know what will happen before the rest of the world. I ask only because the policies of the next Pope may take a toll on my homeland; the Carpathians are troubled enough without another shift in Roman procedures.

How good to know that Maurizio is such a sensation in London, although I am not surprised to hear it. One day I may travel there again and attend one of his concerts.

A letter to Count Balletti will find me here, and in the autumn in Praha. I will let you know where I will go from there when I have decided.

Know that this brings the most profound appreciation of one who signs himself only with his sigil:

(the eclipse)

On the 24th day of April, 1691, at Salzburg and by my own hand

EPILOGUE

*T*ext of a letter from Giorgianna Ferrugia to Ferenc Ragoczy, Conte da San-Germain, entrusted to Ettore Colonna for delivery.

To Su Eccellenza, Ferenc Ragoczy, Conte da San-Germain, the affectionate regards of Giorgianna Ferrugia:

Caro Conte, I have taken advantage of Ettore Colonna, who assures me he can get a letter to you within two months, and am entrusting this to his good offices. I am giving it into his care just before we—my husband and children and I—depart for Lago di Como where we are to spend August and most of September; with four children now—three sons and a daughter—it is a relief to get out of Roma in the worst of the heat and the mal aria.

Although it is more than seven years since you left Roma, I have been thinking of you of late, and I wanted to tell you at last how ashamed I am of how I tricked you for the Holy Office. I did not want our last time together to be so sullied, but the good Fathers insisted, and so I did as they bade me, and I have been sick in my soul ever since. You may not be able to write to me now, but I beg you to forgive me for what I did. It was a most unworthy act and I can only account for it because I was so frightened. My husband may be a Marchese, but to the Church, this is nothing. Had I protested, my twins might have been in danger, which was intolerable to me.

There. I have said it, and now I will pray that you will read and understand. I had no choice but to do their bidding, as many have before me. You were always understanding, always compassionate, which leads me to hope that my petition is not in vain.

Also, I hope you can now comprehend why I did not want to know any of your secrets, for a generous a lover as you were to me, I could not endanger my children: anything you told me I would have revealed to the Holy Office. It is just as well I would not let you tell me much. And yet, I am sorry I did not have the opportunity to know those things you tried to impart to me. I believe I have missed some ineffable part of you that I will regret missing; that is not your fault, it is mine. I fear it may be a much greater one than I assumed it was at first. Since you have been gone, I have become acutely aware that you did not ever treat me capriciously, or as an ornament; therefore anything you wished to impart was not of a trivial or cajoling nature, but intrinsic to the man (I nearly said creature) you are. I cannot ask you to remedy that now, for it would mean putting things on paper that are better left unrecorded. But if, sometime, you might send a message to me through Ettore Colonna that would tell me what I would not let you say, I would thank you in my prayers every night. I do that anyway, but I would thank you doubly.

Innocenzo XII is restricting travel to France yet again; he and Louis are as locked in disputes as much as Innocenzo XI was. I have had to refuse an engagement to sing in Parigi because of the Pope's ruling. Maestro Scarlatti has offered to try to find a way to arrange matters for me, but I do not hold out much hope. I tell you this in case you might be in France. I have understood you may be, or could be. I would like the opportunity to see you once more, not as lovers, but to talk, as friends do. If this would be welcome to you, as well, inform Ettore Colonna and I will strive to find a way to reach you. It will be more easily accomplished in a Catholic country than a Protestant one, of course, but even that is not impossible.

I have sung the Nerone four times since you left, and always to enthusiastic reception. I cannot begin to tell you what satisfaction that give me. It is as if the link between us remains unbroken. I have felt *that about you for some time; I thought at first it was nostalgia, but now it seems to be something more, and it has occasionally seemed to me that you must sense it, too. I wonder if this is female silliness, or the bond you spoke of? Then, I did not appreciate what you offered me; now, I have intimations of your intent, and I know I have been the poorer for declining the gift you were prepared to give me. It is probably beyond us now, but I want you to know that I have come to recognize that I have deprived myself of more than the rapture of the body—I have also lost the touching of souls. I did not perceive at the time what you and I achieved. Now that it is lost I apprehend what it was.*

Saints forgive me! how I have carried on! You must think me a flibberty-jibbet. Perhaps I am, but I am a wiser one than when you and I were in Roma together. And I have remembered the warning you gave me, that when I died I would be in danger. So I have arranged to have my head struck from my body before I am buried. Ilirio thinks I am being overly dramatic, but he has agreed that it will be done. I would not let you tell me why, but I have not forgotten what you said.

I must end this. The coaches are being loaded and Ettore Colonna will call to bid us farewell in a short while. May this find you wherever you are, and may you read it with clemency in your heart. If God wills it, you and I will meet again, and so I will sign this as friends do,

Arrivederlo,
Giorgianna

By my own hand, at Roma, August 1st, 1698